THE WATER HOUSE

THE WATER HOUSE

ANTONIO OLINTO

Translated by Dorothy Heapy

Carroll & Graf Publishers, Inc.
New York

First published in Portuguese in Brazil in 1969 under the title
A CASA DE AGUA.

First Carroll & Graf edition 1985

Carroll & Graf Publishers, Inc.
260 Fifth Avenue
New York, NY 10001

Library of Congress Cataloging in Publication Data

Olinto, Antônio.
  The water house.

  Translation of: A Casa da Agua.
  Reprint. Originally published: London : Rex
Collings, 1970.
  I. Title.
PQ9697.O49C313 1985   869'.3   85-419
ISBN 0-88184-137-4

Manufactured in the United States of America

CONTENTS

This book is for Zora

*To the memory of my mother, Aurea Loures Rocha
born in Pan, where Mariana's long story begins
and where it is always returning.*

Part I

THE JOURNEY

I do not know how to come upon her at the beginning of my story—of her story—but I can see her, on that morning of the flood, being dragged out of her bed and her sleep, hearing words the full sense of which she could not understand, knowing that there was danger and that they wanted to protect her—this is how I see Mariana beginning her adventure, being carried by some-one, it was still not completely light, a little of the night still clung to everything like water, and the idea that the river was overflowing its banks frightened her, but at the same time the feeling that the shoulder her head was resting on was a safe shelter made her think of the flood more as an exciting event which could be enjoyed, at any rate now that the daylight which had come at last showed up the house, the stone side entrance, the steps surrounded by bushes, the little stream the children bathed in which ran down to the bigger stream below, the bamboo planta-tion rustling when the wind blew, the piau-fish jumping on the flooded river bank, the miraculously agile body of the fish sud-denly immobilized by the blow of a stick. I place this awaken-ing with the flood at the beginning of Mariana's memories, and I have given much thought to how best I can tell what happened to her. I could have chosen the device of a separate narrator, removed from the events, but Mariana's story is so much a part of me that it seems I can only pass it on by putting myself inside it and telling it as if I myself were, at every move, taking part in the scenes, hearing the words spoken and experiencing the emotions of the girl's long journey. Because it is the story of a journey, and I am going to tell it starting from the morning when Mariana was pulled from her bed and taken out into the street, which was on a higher level than the house.

Suddenly she found herself on the ground. A man shouted:

'Fetch Dona Lelé! Fetch Dona Lelé! the water is in her room already.'

Mariana looked at the church, it was dedicated to the Holy Ghost, she had been told so many times about the Holy Ghost, she thought that the picture on the high altar of the dove with its open wings was so pretty, once she had been almost certain that the bird had moved, when she talked about it to the others they had laughed, but as time went by she became even more certain that it had.

'Who does the little girl belong to?'

'Epifânia.'

When she heard her mother's name spoken she began to look around for her, but the confusion had increased and she got up, went as far as the store on the corner, the store wasn't there, it had collapsed during the night and some people were poking around in the ruins.

'Anyone dead?'

'No. By the time the house went, everyone had left.'

A cupboard which had fallen over was covered in bricks, pieces of cloth showed through holes in it, an iron bedstead was leaning up against a tree, everything seemed out of place. Her mother ran to her, picked her up, looked at her hard, there was a lot of talk, the River Piau had never risen so high, the old people could remember 1864, but this time it was worse, the bridge beside Dona Julia's house had disappeared, the orchards alongside the river had been ruined, hens and pigs drowned, it was possible some people had died, Father Exuperio wanted to make a novena to avert disaster from the village, Amelinha's wedding would have to be put off, Seu Sao's wife had lost her baby, they said it was to have been born in a few days' time, and Mariana wondered how anyone could lose a baby even before it had been born, and it was night again, the wide kitchen in Uncle Inhaim's

2

house was full of people, everyone was talking about the flood and the journey.

'What an idea—you aren't really going?'

The old woman looked down at the logs in the stove, saw her daughter who already had so many children of her own, put her hands together, said again what she had said so many times before, and Mariana, the elder of the two granddaughters, was to remember years later what Granny Catarina had said that night, the black skin wrinkled round her lips, her eyes shining in the firelight as the coffee heated on the stove.

'I must go back and I want to take my daughter and my grandchildren. I left there more than fifty years ago, my uncle sold me. I lived in Abeokuta, I went on a visit to Lagos, my uncle had already sold me to some men, he took me to them, I was eighteen, I wanted to go to Lagos so much, but why did I go? As soon as I arrived my uncle gave me to the men, they put me in a ship, after a long time I arrived in Bahia, I was sold and since then I have never left Piau.'

There was a pause. It seems there was a pause.

'Now I want to go back. There are no more slaves here, Uncle Inhaim will help me, I have saved a bit of money and I have got a bit more from all the blacks on the plantations round here. Now I want to go back and take my daughter, who was born here, and my grandchildren.'

'But how can a few women and children go by themselves all that way?'

Mariana had gone to sleep in her mother's arms, a comfortable warmth came from the stove, her grandmother talked for a while about the journey, then stopped and thought, she saw the Piau brimming and remembered the River Ogun, the canoe had gone downstream and she had felt her face burning, drops of sweat had fallen on to the wood of the boat and she did not turn round to look at her home for the last time but how was she to know that

3

that was goodbye and who knows when the last time comes? She saw the green again, the green came back but it was green half awash, green with green water, she felt as if she had seen nothing but green on that voyage down to Lagos, the boatman caught hold of leafy branches in his hand, there was green in the bottom of the boat in the water that washed over her feet, it had been a delight to move her feet in the water and at each bend in the river the green which her granddaughter Mariana was to know one day rose up like a great wall in front of her and shut out all but a glimpse of the sun so that she could see nothing beyond the banks of the river.

The next morning some of the children caught fish with sticks, the girl went too, the water came up to her knees, she had a piece of stick in her hand, you just had to watch for the fish jumping and hit it and it floated, her brother and sister couldn't come, Emilia was five and Antônio was three, how could they have managed in all that mud, clumps of grass and reeds rose up out of the water in long green lines which the wind shook leaving ripples in the stream. The flood and the journey would always be linked in Mariana's memory, one happened just after the other, and I feel that all her earlier memories had been lost, perhaps because the flood and the journey did not allow anything beyond themselves to have any power, and however much I call on her memories she cannot push aside the curtain made by the two realities of the flood and the journey.

The time of the flood was full of images, one after the other, all clear-cut, Mariana had been to see the bridge which had fallen down, the river had swept away the brick support in the middle where the wooden crossbeams rested, the waters broke violently against what was left of the bricks, a dead ox had been carried down the stream and had caught on a stone, they said the body of the ox would have to be freed otherwise there would be

4

the most terrible smell, children played with bits of the wrecked bridge, they made toy bridges over the rivulets of flood-water that were running into the torrent, there was a feeling of holiday, like in May, little stalls in front of the church, the young girls crowning Our Lady, fighting was also part of the flood because it was just by the bridge that Mariana saw the two men going for each other like madmen, their feet raising up clouds of dust, people shouting, they moved them away because they had knives and there could have been a killing, another picture of the flood was a herd of animals swimming across the river, there were lots of donkeys and horses, the man who went ahead of them lost his hat and it fell into the river, the horses made a great noise swimming and came out streaming with water, some people laughed, they thought the hat disappearing was funny, delicious corn cakes were given out at night, and gossip about the flood lulled the children to sleep.

'Claudio lost ten head of cattle.'

'He can afford it, he has about three hundred.'

'Amelinha lost the most: all her trousseau went, dress, shoes, veil, everything.'

'Hasn't the wedding happened yet, then?'

'Not unless they're one jump ahead of the priest.'

They laughed a lot, grown-ups liked to laugh, the rebuilding of the corner store was part of the flood as well, the snakes that the children killed, there was one big one, it liked to sunbathe in the yard in front of the church, the little boys chased it right up to the church door, her mother told her that Our Lady had killed a snake with her feet, and suddenly there was a festival in church, very beautiful and gay, between the flood and the journey, Mariana went in a white veil, her grandmother Catarina was more and more restless, swallows flew about inside the church with that lovely noise that birds make inside buildings, the Holy Ghost didn't move even though the child encouraged it with imploring

5

glances, and now I find in Mariana an ineffaceable memory, her grandmother holding her and saying:

'You are ten years old. It is time to go back.'

It was in the room where they all slept, she, her mother, her grandmother and her brother and sister, there was a funny smell of smoke, the old woman smoked a clay pipe, but there were other smells which the child couldn't sort out, and she felt herself held tight in the arms of the old woman, she shut her eyes and thought about the river down there, the good taste of the fish she had eaten that day, and the day before, everyone was eating fish these days, her mother's voice reached her ears:

'What's wrong with her?'

Her grandmother replied:

'Nothing. I was talking to her.'

After the Mass where the swallows came in, there was a bullfight beside the drugstore. The men had made a sort of grandstand with bits of wood tied together with liana, between the people and the place where the bulls were going to appear they made a rough wooden barrier, Mariana looked at everything full of wonder, everyone was dressed in bright colours, and they were shouting, they said the bulls belonged to Claudio, the first one that came into the middle was yellow and white, the men teased it and it attacked, there was a man all padded with cushions waiting for the bull, the horns hit him and he didn't seem to mind, everyone laughed, another man sat in a big chair, the bull came at it from behind and the laughter grew, a boy was selling caramels and Mariana had a great longing for one, the sun beat on the grass in the middle where the men and the bulls were running about, until a bull appeared that only wanted to stick its horns through the wood of the safety barrier, people began to climb down from the seats, the child felt herself being lifted up in somebody's arms, and the bull in the end managed to escape and got as far as the

6

old bridge and there it broke a leg, it lay unable to get up, bellowing. They killed it that night and Mariana knew that the next day there would be beef for everybody.

The little village, only one street, lay between the hill and the river, the street bending round, houses on both sides, but in some places only on one side, Dona Generosa's primary school at the top of the hill and, halfway up the slope where the ground flattened out, the church and the square in front of it where the children used to play. The steps leading up to the square, the high tower right in the middle, the mango-trees along the side of the church, Mariana never forgot any of it, and in all her journeys which carried her so far this group of clear images seemed so real to her way that sometimes she felt that the truth was this, what had been, not this other, which was now happening.

I do not know how she spent the last days, I cannot find anything in her memories which sets aside these days from others, each the same as the next, going down to the river, milk and salt corn-cake in the morning, black beans and cabbage at midday, now and then dried salt meat and black beans, conversations about things that hid themselves in cellars, the mula-sem-cabeça, the priest's mistress who, when she was dead, turned into a mule without a head and came out of the cemetery in the middle of the night, dead people who came back to tell you what heaven was like, or hell or purgatory, the little girls playing ring games, here comes Margarida, Olé Olé Olà, I am poor, poor, poor, the night fell suddenly and the stars twinkled with happiness, when everything was dark the talking in the kitchen went on until very late, the stove crackling, the lamp lighting the way along the passage full of mystery. But yes, she does remember the last day, or rather not the whole day, but the moment of departure, four horses, her mother, her grandmother, her brother and sister, herself and a man who was going to look after them, from early morning

ses clattered their hooves against the stones, wak-
she heard them, bac, bac, bac, sometimes the
hooves slipped, she knows that her grandmother took a
wooden statue of Santa Ana which was there in the
room, then there is a gap of time which she does not
remember, did she have some milk, did she eat something? did they leave before the midday meal or afterwards? but her memory captured everything from the
moment when the horses began to move down the
street, even Uncle Inhaim came to see them off, he
asked them to give his greetings to his sister who lived in
Juiz de Fora, and to tell her that the worst effects of the
flood were over now, they were to stay with her as long
as they wanted to, and in Rio they were to go to his
brother's house, not to forget the address, it was in Senate
Street, at the moment of departure the sun was burning
hot, children were stretching their necks to see, Mariana
went along looking into the windows of the houses, mirrors inside, or beds, or benches against the wall, holy
pictures hanging up, a life-size Sacred Heart of Jesus,
photographs of people, the road went up behind the
church, up on the top they all stopped, her mother insisted on looking at everything for the last time, the roof
of the church was dark tiles, the cross in the square had a
cock on top, on the river a canoe was going straight downstream.

The children were enjoying the adventure, Epifânia
felt as if she was breaking up inside. She had never been
out of Piau except for short visits to plantations where
she knew people, now she had to follow her mother, who
insisted, would not yield. Years afterwards I was to see
through Mariana's eyes looking back all that Epifânia
had told her of her suffering at leaving everything behind. Her man had disappeared, she had had those three
children without much difficulty, she had never been a
slave but she had worked hard, all her things were there,
her pictures, her church, her Masses. She had stayed

8

there on the hilltop looking down at it all with a feeling that perhaps this journey which had scarcely begun was not inevitable. Perhaps everything that was going to happen would not happen and she would go back with her children to the house where she had always lived. But the man, who was ahead of them, loosened the reins, made a noise with his tongue and the horse went forward.

The same landscape repeated itself all day long. Mariana thought at one time that they had gone back. The horses went up hills, went down hills, crossed streams, stopped to drink water, they saw houses, and churches. She was tired when the time came to sleep. It was in a smaller house than Uncle Inhaim's, they ate in the yard, the man started to talk to some people:

'How are things up Piau way?'

'Everything's all right since the flood. The bridge fell down, you know. Claudio bought the Loures's plantation. Dona Lelé died. Everything else, same as before.'

'When do you go back?'

'I'm taking these people as far as Juiz de Fora, I'll stay there a day or two and I'll be through here again in a week's time.'

He drank some cachaça, said 'That's good' and began to tell them all about the flood, and Mariana fell asleep.

They started very early the next day. It was still quite dark, and cold, the child was chewing a piece of bread, it was hard, hard, in the houses people had just woken up, the dogs ran after the horses, behind the fences they were milking the cows, everything just as it was at home, however this wasn't her home, her mother said they were going a long way, to the place where her grandmother had been born. The little bone at the bottom of her back had started to hurt the day before, because of so much riding, now it was hurting even more, Mariana took a handful of cloth, pushed it between the bruised place and the saddle, it was the only way she could make it

9

easier, when the horses stopped to drink water she took the chance of raising her body in the saddle and the pain went.

When the horse raised its head and trotted off the bone hurt even more and the child stopped noticing things, she didn't complain because her grandmother didn't like children crying, and a reddish light, orange, yellow, it changed its colour every moment, grew at the bottom of the sky, clouds took the shapes of people, houses, giants, horses, angels, with the red gradually giving way to darkness and she felt such a great weariness that she didn't even notice that there were more houses and a big town was coming into sight until the man shouted:

'It's Juiz de Fora.'

Then she looked and saw tall double-storied houses like she had never seen before, and people strolling along, beautifully dressed, girls at the windows, handsome horses going up and down the cobbled street. The house where Uncle Inhaim's sister lived was small, it had a stream at the bottom of the yard, the new arrivals stayed in a cramped little hut separated from the main house and surrounded by mango-trees, the trees in rows looked like schoolchildren in ranks one behind the other. For a few days she wandered all over, escaping from her mother and grandmother, ran alongside coaches, stopped and looked into shop doorways, she didn't know when the man from Piau left, he was her last link with the place where she had been born, but she didn't realize, different scenes took shape each morning as if they wanted to surprise her, later she was to think often about that man from Piau, what had he been called? was he a relative? had he been paid to bring them that far? She remembered his long face and his flat nose, his easy smile.

Her grandmother organized everything they did with great vigour. She didn't want to linger here. She had known Juiz de Fora many years earlier, when she was

still a young girl, just arrived from Bahia, not under-
standing the language these people spoke, finding the
words harsh, remembering the resonance of the words she
had used at home, ekaró, odabó, mo fé jé, everything
so clear, open, simple. She had hated learning her first
few words of Portuguese, at first she refused to speak the
language, and it had been here in Juiz de Fora that she
had realized that the sounds were going into her mind
against her will and had begun to have meaning for her,
one day she was thirsty and asked for water, she was
hungry and said she was hungry. The town seemed to
her much bigger after all these years. She went to the
railway station because they said that that was the best
way of getting to Rio de Janeiro, she didn't show the
fear which struck at her eyes when she saw a locomotive
passing in the distance, she bought second class tickets,
cooked food in Uncle Inhaim's sister's house where they
had stayed, the train was due to leave at eight in the
morning, at five o'clock they were all there, the grandmother, the mother, the three children, huddling up to
each other because it was cold like they had never known
it in Piau, the station gradually became crowded, and
when the train came in Mariana went to look at it from
close to, her mother had to run after her. They had difficulty finding the entrance to the carriage, a man in
uniform with a peaked cap sent the two women and the
three children to two empty benches. The women were
frightened to look outside and kept their eyes on the
floor, not Mariana, Mariana ate up the delight of each
image, she leaned out of the window and gazed at the
things running past, houses, fences, oxen, trees, the river,
this one was full as well, in some places you could see the
banks covered by water, here and there a canoe motionless or moving along. It made her happy to see the train
running along, and it was good when it stopped in the
stations, by the time they had reached the third station
the child knew what to expect, it was as if she were

11

coming on people of her own world. They ate when they reached an enormous river that took up the whole of the view outside, Mariana stopped for a moment with some rice in her hand, she paused before lifting it to her mouth. The water and the iron bridge between the water and the train were a new fact that blotted out everything she had known before. On the other side of the bridge the train ran through unfamiliar country, but the child still wanted to see the water back there that was bigger than the flood.

In the afternoon, even more houses than there had been in Juiz de Fora and, without any one of the five being able to see how it happened, the train had stopped and it was time to get out. Catarina took charge once more, she went this way and that with a piece of paper in her hand, found out that they could walk to Senate Street. It was raining heavily, the water coursed over the cobbles in the street, the women took hold of the two younger children, Mariana could go by herself, they crossed a street, the carriages and the horses made a clatter on the paving stones, it was hard to find the address, when they arrived the old woman pushed her daughter and her grandchildren into the shelter of the entrance hall, waited until the water ran off her dress, she was soaked, it was only after a few minutes that she clapped her hands, from the window up above there came a voice:

'Who was it?'

'People from Piau.'

A tall man came down with an oil lamp, looked carefully at Catarina, asked:

'Are you from Joaquim's house?'

'Yes, senhor, he sent you a letter.'

The man read the letter there and then, he called inside:

'Sebastiana, take these people to your room and give them something to eat.'

A fat Negress appeared in the hall, led Catarina's

12

family into a room that was almost without light, told them to wait there while she went to see what there was to eat, but there was hardly anything, the travellers went to sleep without food, the mat on which they all lay stank of urine, the grandmother stayed awake smoking her pipe until late, thinking odd things, the day when the Negro Julião had run after her, he had stuck his thing right up her, a cock had started up in the bushes just beside them, a warmth had gone through her body, the morning Epifânia was born, they all came to see her, thought she was a funny little thing, the night when the planter's son had come to find her, they had done it together a lot, just as well there had been no more children. Where was Julião now? He had been sold to a planter in Rio Nôvo, nobody had heard of him since, the planter's son had come back often, it had got into a habit, it was she who held the keys to the store-room, a trustworthy person, who made good food and knew how to please men.

In the morning it was still raining, Mariana stood looking out at the street, from time to time a horse passed, its hooves splashing in the wet, around midday the sun appeared, the child went out, she stopped in front of a fountain where a crowd of people were drawing water, they were all laughing, saying funny things to each other, she took Emilia's hand, the two of them sat on a stone for hours just looking at everything. Above and all around them the city sprawled out, in Square No. 15, where Catarina went straight away on the first day, to find out from people who knew about travelling what was the best way to get to Bahia, the crowd was even greater and the children went there often on the days which followed, on Sundays they went to the New City, there was almost always a dance, a pianist called Motinha used to play lovely ballads, it reminded them of Amelinha in Piau, she had had the only piano in the place. I look briefly at the Rio of those days, see it as Mariana saw it

13

and felt it, as her grandmother tolerated it, simply an episode, a transitory resting-place which they had to leave as soon as possible in case they made roots there, and I see Epifânia coming to love it, everything seemed so fast-moving, strong men on the street corners, looking at the women with a boldness and an ardour which seemed natural here, but which in Piau would have been offensive. Catarina could not calm herself. She was possessed by a fear, which grew greater all the time, that her surroundings would take hold of her, that difficulties would arise, that her plan would come to nothing, and it disturbed her sleep, one day she realised that she had been in Rio for a long time and still hadn't seen the sea, she remembered how it had seemed never to end during that first voyage, she went to look at it. Mariana had already got into the way of sitting on the wall near Castle Hill and spending hours looking at the boats and the water, there was no current flowing here, only a to-and-fro movement, sometimes a procession caught her eye and she prayed thinking about the Holy Ghost which she had never seen again, she had seen real doves, but in the churches there were only holy people, no holy birds, and the one in the church at Piau took on a greater importance in her eyes. Italians in strange clothes went singing in the streets, and the three children often followed behind the singing for a kilometre or more, one day an Italian led them right up to Santana Square and they came upon a party, people dancing, drums beating, and on a certain Sunday night Mariana heard a voice which made her forget everything. The voice sang:

> Don't play me false love
> Just like the other
> Sweetly deceiving
> My heart was broken
> By someone like you
> Loving and leaving.

She was never to forget these words and this tune. In the years that were to come, they were to be for her the atmosphere of Rio, of her childhood, of a vague feeling, at once happy and sad, that things can change, can be deceptive, and still be good. She had heard the song on the night of São João, or had it been Santo Antônio? She had lived them both in Rio, the streets were full of bonfires, crowds came from all over to Santana Square, each group had their fire, boys with guitars sang in low voices. Mariana, Emilia and Antônio jumped over bonfires, ate sweet potato, and towards midnight the older girl came across a couple embracing on the grass, she stayed looking at them for a long time, she thought it was beautiful, and would have gone on looking if the boy hadn't seen her and shouted:

'Get away from here!'

On that same night Epifânia was in a strange room, underneath a staircase, with a bald Negro, the first she had ever seen, he undressed her, it was so long since she had had a man that she found it strange, she couldn't wait for his penis to go in, it was enormous, seemed to go through her until she felt she had to shout out. The man said:

'No shouting, honey, there are people right next door.'

Afterwards they went dancing, the sweat ran down from his head, she gave herself over to the movement with a delight and an ease which she had never known before. The candle flames flickered and the shadows swayed to and fro, there were splashes of light in the street, the dance went out into the street as well, balloons were floating upwards, an accordion was playing at another dance and got mixed up with the music of the dance where Epifânia was, it seemed to make everyone even happier.

Mariana remembers a festival in honour of Our Lady of Glory, her grandmother had said that Our Lady of

15

Glory was Yemoja, goddess of the sea, they went up the hillside, the church was surrounded with people, candles everywhere, the child lost her mother and grandmother for a few minutes, stood still in the middle of the crowd not knowing what to do, looked this way and that, suddenly she found herself being caught hold of by her mother who was saying:

'Come and see Our Lady.'

They went into the church, people were pushing and squeezing together, she doesn't know if she saw the statue, but she remembers the smell of flowers mixed with the smell of candles, and a feeling of happiness seeping in through her skin.

Catarina saw the time going by, Epifânia taking up with a man, Mariana getting to know the streets and the squares, the two younger children starting to go about freely by themselves, and she tried all sorts of people in her desperation to find some means of getting them away from that city. One day she found a captain who was willing to take the whole family for very little money.

'It isn't an easy journey, mother. It's only a small steamboat.'

'Never mind, we'll go.'

Catarina, Epifânia, Mariana, Emilia and Antônio left Rio de Janeiro at the beginning of a sunny morning, waves shook everything to and fro, the hills seemed to belong to another world, fragments of mist clung to the tops of the trees, the air smelt of sea, of fish and salt.

Sea, fish, salt and sun, all the time. Old Catarina chose a place for herself inside the ship, made herself a comfortable nest padded with cloth, propped herself up and stayed there for the whole of the voyage, her body rose and fell, in the rising and falling her young body came back to her, a menstrual flow had stained the wooden floor with blood, the man who looked after the slaves had come to see what had happened, he had moved her on to another deck, that night he had taken her on the ground, left her lying there naked, sea, fish, salt and sun, Abeokuta was always in her head during the crossing, at first she didn't even want to know where they were taking her, if they were going to use her body then let them, perhaps that was what her uncle had sold her for, she missed the beads she used to wear round her neck, dancing, the taste of yam which she loved, but especially she missed people. Strange, in Abeokuta she had not thought much of Ebun and Ojé, today she missed them bitterly, even if only to hear them speak familiar words to her, she imagined she was being born again, her body was squeezed in her mother's vagina as she tried to get out, but her head wouldn't go through and she was afraid, but more afraid when her uncle caught her by the legs and pulled her. The hot blood rose to her head, and the tightness grew worse, she couldn't get out, she would never get out, suddenly it relaxed and her uncle went on pulling her, the ground rose and fell, the smell of the sea penetrated everything, at night the oil lamp only lit one corner, her tongue had the taste of salt. One morning she saw the man whipping a tall thin boy, with light, swift movements, the sound beat on the air and hung there, with the noise that came from outside and the creak of things swaying. Catarina was in the past and in the present, she was here and she was in that other ship, the difference in time dissolved, it seemed to have grown less and less until suddenly she saw that she had not even boarded the ship but was still in Abeokuta, underneath a huge tree, near the tall rocks the mouth of a cave opened up, she had hidden there often, the drums were calling, someone had died and the festivities were beginning, but the sea, the salt and the sun invaded her again and Catarina found herself once more with her spent body, her withered genitals, the hair almost gone, her motionless hands, her unpassionate fear. In Piau she had refashioned her gift for living, she had relearnt steps, walking, looking, voice, words, she had

17

once more become a person, the language was different, but that had not mattered, the task of reorganizing herself had taken time, months, years, until she was once more whole, and it was only the visits of the planter's son which endangered for a moment this newly-won wholeness. I see her huddled up in her corner, I wonder about her return to the past and I see from her movement of adjustment that she is once more being forced to make a sort of departure, it was as if in adapting herself to Piau a new person had been born who had died now, on this journey to Bahia, or as if another person were being born at this moment, different from the Abeokuta person and from the one who had lived in Piau, but able perhaps to keep alive a bond of memory with the one dead long ago and the one newly-dead. These two dead people would never loose their hold on Catarina, she was to carry them towards an impossible reunion, towards the discovery of that young girl who had been sold in Lagos, and she needed to remake herself, restore herself, knowing that the dead are light and heavy to bear, that the assurance they give is continuity and fear, that what they offer is wholeness and disruption.

For Mariana, the flood and the journey went on together, the sea, the salt and the sun, the water that stretched away to where there was only more water. The sickness of the first few days stopped her from walking around much, she vomited for the whole of one afternoon, was so exhausted that she had no desire to leave her corner. Emilia and Antônio were crying, no-one was taking any notice of them, on the third day Mariana went out on to the deck, stood looking at the whiteness of the waves. In the distance there seemed to be land but it disappeared straightway, the air had a milky texture, the land came back and the entire curve of a hill showed itself clearly before disappearing again into a kind of cloud. There was a man she liked who wore a grey peaked cap, she talked to him.

'When are we going to arrive?'
'In a day or two.'
'Is Bahia big?'
'It's beautiful.'

It was twilight when she suddenly remembered Piau, the river, the yard in front of the church, the little girls playing, when would she play like that again? It seemed as if they were running away, her grandmother hadn't spoken since she came on to the boat, whenever her mother spoke she seemed angry, the whole world went up and down, the noise of the engine came from below, at night an accordion played in the dark, the next day she asked:

'Was it you playing the accordion yesterday?'

The man in the grey cap said no. He only liked the guitar, but he didn't have a guitar. The next night the child went to see who it was playing the accordion, just like she had heard it in Piau, it was a young man with a big beard, striped shirt, he didn't look at anyone, he hardly spoke, when he wasn't working all he wanted to do was play his accordion, she found out that his name was Nico.

'Why is your name Nico?'

'Because it is Antônio and they called me Tônico, now it's just Nico.'

Then he told her what Bahia was like, roads going up the hills, churches everywhere, sobrados and big houses on the tops of the hills looking out over the sea, happy people in the streets, and the next morning Mariana began to see exactly what Nico had described to her, houses down below, houses up above, the sunlight falling on everything, trees and bushes growing taller as the boat drew nearer to the land, little boats motionless in the middle of the sea, a smell of fish and of sea, salt and sun.

Catarina saw the city, it was the same one she had seen when she had arrived many years before, on the quayside then miracles had happened, almost everyone in the ship was from Abeokuta but they said that there was also a queen from Queto, made prisoner after a war, just when she was being sold in Bahia a handsome man appeared, whether he was white or black no-one could say, he wore light-coloured clothes, his shirt and neckerchief were bright, they said he was the god Oshumare who had come in person to free the queen, as soon as the slaves were put up for sale Oshumare bought the queen of Queto and set her free, Catarina was sold just afterwards to a red-faced Portuguese, Seu Manuel gave her as a present to his daughter, Gloria, who was going to be married in Piau and took the slave with her, a long journey on horseback, Catarina went days, weeks, without saying a word, it was only when they got to Juiz de Fora that she had felt like using her voice again, now she was going to look for Seu Manuel, he lived on a steeply-sloping street that Mariana thought was very pretty. The paving-stones in the street were irregular, groups of children ran across from one side to the other, from time to time a carriage went down, you could see the sea in the distance, everyone smiled a lot. It was a sobrado, a two-storied house, they stayed at the end of a passage-way, a make-shift curtain strung across the passage made a sort of room, the two women and the three children slept on mats, they went to eat in the market down below, where Seu Manuel had his shop. On the second day Catarina said to her daughter:

'We had better send Mariana to school.'

'Are we going to stay here for long?'

'It's difficult to find a ship. They told me not until next year.'

The two women were silent, considering their problems. Epifânia said:

'We will have to earn some money.'

'Seu Manuel will help. We two will have to find something to sell in the market.'

But it wasn't easy. They began by buying up flour a long way inland at a low price, and selling it near the sea. A few weeks later Seu Manuel arranged for some fishermen to give them fish to sell. Mariana had already started at school, she went out in the morning wearing a clean dress, her exercise book in her hand, she was going to study arithmetic and read pages of a big book which only the teacher had, she remembered Dona Generosa, who had taught her to read in Piau, now Mariana was one of the few in the class who read with enthusiasm in her voice, even though she didn't understand everything in the book, one day she was praised for reading—very well, the teacher said—this passage:

'The fado has many forms, each one of them very curious. Now one person, a man or a woman, dances alone in the middle of the room for some time, executing the most complex steps, taking up the most graceful positions, to the accompaniment of snappings of the fingers, and then gradually draws nearer and nearer to someone who pleases him, performs some inviting gestures and swift turns, and finally claps his hands, which means that he has chosen this person to take his place.'

Another day she won a prize from the teacher for reading:

'In the towns and even in the small villages youths gathered together for the revelry; it was said that before the night had run its course the oldest woman in the township would be sawn in two, and so simple and credulous were the folk in those days that there were old women who, trembling with fear, used to hide themselves all through the dreadful day, lest they be caught by the sawers.'

Mariana wanted to tell her grandmother that there was a place where old women were sawn up, but she remembered having seen women even older than Catarina in the market-place, she made friends with other children, they came out of school together, ran down the hill, played tag, singing games, the boys tried to lift their dresses up, there were shrieks and fights.

In the market, the women took it in turns to sell, the smell of fish became a part of their life, they carried it home with them, slept with it, Epifânia dreamt about fish, about a man stealing fish from her stall, she ran after him, caught hold of the fish and tried to pull it out of his hands, the fish was slippery, slippery, it seemed to be coming and going in her hands. She missed going to church, visited one down in the Low City. That was how she met Father José. When she saw him for the first time she noticed something strange about him. The priest's eyes looked right inside you, his brown skin was sallow, he looked ill. She got into the way of going to see him nearly every day, she went to the sacristy, knelt in front of a crucifix near where he used to pray after Mass. One afternoon she found him with his arms spread out on the table, a bottle of cachaça at his side. She was afraid to look at what she saw, wanted to go away, he asked:

'Have you never seen a priest drunk before, daughter?'

Epifânia looked at the ground, the priest put more cachaça into his glass, made as if he was going to drink, stopped and said:

'Priests drink wine in the Mass, don't they? Wine.'

A long time went by without either of them saying a word. She didn't know what to do next, then he told her:

'Sit there.'

She obeyed and the priest went calmly on pouring cachaça into the glass, drinking it in small mouthfuls, his eyes fixed on the window. A vast silence came from the church, entered the sacristy, an Our Lady in a white cloak looked on from the corner where she stood in a niche above the holy water font. At one point Father José laid his head down on his arms, the quiet was even greater, so that Epifânia stopped herself making the

22

least movement. After a long time, he raised his head and said:

'Take me inside.'

This was something Epifânia understood, she was used to helping people, getting on with things. She raised him up carefully, supporting him with an arm round his waist, the parish house had a parlour, a dining room with two doors leading in to bedrooms. The woman went with the priest into one of them, there was a big bed, a São José with his lily in his hand stood on a small altar, the sheets were rumpled, she sat the priest down on the bed, tried to take off his cassock, only managed it after some difficulty, he had a cream shirt on underneath and long combinations fitting closely round his shins, she laid him down, covered him with a blue blanket and felt pity for him, so thin and wasted was his body.

The next morning she went to his Mass. She noticed that he stumbled a few times, had he been drinking already? Epifânia went to communion, and in the moment when his hand came down to her with the host she felt a sort of tremor, an extraordinary happiness went all through her body and made her see colours suddenly clearer, the golden chalice, the red vestment, the greens, the whites and the blues on the altar. She didn't go to see the priest for some time. It was the good time of the year for selling fish, there were drums playing outside the city, Mariana was always asking questions. When she went back to visit him, she found him stretched out along the step of the altar in the sacristy. He was propped up on his elbow, his head on his left hand, and by his side there were drawn up a glass, a bottle, a crucifix and a little figure of Our Lady of the Rosary. When she came in, Father José filled the glass and said, his voice louder than usual:

'Your health!'

He banged the glass down on the ground and intoned the beginning of a litany. Then he stopped and asked:

23

'Well then, how is my helper?'

He picked up the glass again and, turning to the crucifix, said:

'To his very good health!'

And to the statue of Our Lady:

'To her health!'

She had to take him to bed again. She got his cassock off fairly easily and lit an oil-lamp. The light made shadows on the wall and Epifânia stayed there while he slept, sometimes she looked a long time at the São José, then she closed her eyes, thought about nothing. It must have been dawn when he woke up and, seeing her there, said nothing for a few minutes, then:

'Thank you very much.'

It was the third time she helped him to his room that the priest, when he woke, asked her to lie down as well. She got into the bed without embarrassment, lay motionless, a cricket was singing in the window, the first daylight was coming through a crack in the door and she could see her own body, black, on the sheet, when Father José opened her legs, played a little with the hairs on her sex and entered her calmly. She had never felt it like this. A serene enjoyment, the priest's penis went in and came out, the morning light grew stronger, and she felt herself utterly suffused by it as the church bell began to sound.

She left the room, went to Mass, heard it from beginning to end, then ran back to the house where Catarina was waiting for her, they went down together to the market, you could smell the fish from a long way off.

I do not know if it was that night, or some other night, that Mariana noticed her mother was different, she didn't listen to what Catarina was saying, just sat there on the doorstep, it was then that the girl began to understand things more clearly, she had begun to feel at home in this place where they had come to live, everyone knew her, on the street and in the market. She liked to go down the hill and stay there close to the fish-stall, she used to see men and women going by, drunks asleep in the sun, women murmuring prayers to themselves, she heard people talking about Ogun, Oloshoshi, Shango, Oshun, Nana, her mother said that her grandmother prayed to all of them, they were saints she remembered from her childhood, from that country over the sea which was pulling her again and all of them, Epifânia and all the children, had to go with her on her journey. Mariana noticed things, Piau seemed a long way away, there were times when she felt so overflowing with joy that she shouted out loud in the middle of the street, looking out to the sea far away there in the distance, and sometimes all the children tried to shout louder than each other as the night was falling and the stars burst out shining over Bahia, the churches down there below outlined against the gathering darkness, lanterns moving across the countryside, lights winking out at sea.

Epifânia didn't go to Father José's house for several days. One day she chose a fine fish and took it to him as a present, he seemed happy to see her, asked her to go in, he was sober, he didn't seem to have been drinking that afternoon, he started to talk to her, wanted to know where she came from, asked her all about Piau, who was the parish priest there, then he said:

'I would like to meet your children. What are they like?'

'There's Mariana, the oldest, she's at school. She's very clever. And the little ones, Emilia and Antônio.'

'Bring Mariana to see me.'

She spent the night with him, he didn't take his combinations off, the lamp stayed lit all night long, after he got off her she started thinking about all sorts of things, there was enough money now, earlier things had been difficult, but now she and her mother had got them-selves some good customers, Seu Amaro always came, and that lady in white, very serious looking, who came in

25

a big carriage, she always bought more than one fish, the stall had come to be a meeting-place for all sorts of people, from time to time someone would run his fingers over a guitar, it was usually just as night was falling, they were all quiet for a while, listening.

Epifânia took Mariana but, as they came to the church, they heard the bell ringing, some women who were standing there told her:

'It's the Father. He's up in the tower ringing the bell and he won't come down.'

The woman left her daughter in the house and ran back, went up the stairs behind the choir, found Father José lying on the floor, the mouth of the bell right above him, a bottle on the ground, his hands tight round the rope that was attached to the clapper. Epifânia tried to lift him up but he resisted, looked at her in a sort of fury, recognized her and said:

'No. Leave me alone, I know what I'm doing.'

He started pulling the rope again, the woman stopped her ears the sound was so loud. She stopped trying to fight him, sat in a corner, still with her hands over her ears. The priest drank a mouthful of cachaça, turned his head towards her, then fixed his eyes on the houses outside, from time to time he rang the bell until finally he let himself slump down on to the ground. His cassock had risen up, his combinations showed, they were dirty, Epifânia thought about looking after him, but where would she find the time? Darkness was coming into the tower when he woke. After a few minutes he said calmy:

'Shall we go?'

She helped him, they began the descent, there were a lot of women in the church. She put him to bed and came back to pray. She heard an old woman saying to the one kneeling beside her:

'She's the priest's mistress.'

'Who?'

'That black girl there: she's living with the Father.'

26

'Lord bless us!'

'They say someone is going to complain to the bishop.'

That night Mariana saw her mother cry, she thought about it but sleep came quickly and the next morning, eating her bread and drinking her coffee, she no longer believed in those tears. Epifânia collected her after school, they went down to the lower city, the child saw that they were going to the same church as yesterday, when the bell had been ringing, in the sacristy a priest looked at her for a long time, she only noticed him after she had looked at everything all around her, the Our Lady, the holy water font, the long cupboard, the vestments, the big crucifix.

'What is your name?'

She noticed that his cassock was torn, she liked being there, with the priest's hands on her face:

'Mariana.'

They left there late, went to the market, the fish was all finished, the child picked up a handful of scales from the ground, she tried to see through them, they said there was an Our Lady in every one, suddenly a procession passed in front of her, men in capes, the statue of a saint on a litter, candles alight, women singing.

She got into the habit of spending the night at the stall, with her grandmother. That was when the good things happened. Emilia and Antônio used to go to sleep in a corner, Catarina talked to people, she spoke an African language, Mariana could understand the greetings already, she learned to say 'Adupé' for 'Thank you', the open syllables sounded clearly in the dark, lanterns were lit here and there, the sea broke on the stones not far away, boats swung up and down, she ate fried fish with flour, sometimes she missed the dried salt meat they used to have in Piau. Her grandmother was happier, she laughed out loud, wore a cloth tied round her head like nearly all the women in the market, she had always worn skirts like they wore in Bahia, very full and pretty. Her mother wore the same sort of dresses as she had in Piau, closely-fitting, she never saw her at night now, the child liked to stay and listen to the men talking, telling stories about fishing, funny stories, mentioning the names of women she knew, the smell of salt came mingling with sleep.

Epifânia knew that they were gossiping about her and the priest, but she realized that they envied her as well. A lot of women who went to that church came to talk to her about him, they gave her advice.

'He can't go on drinking like he has been lately. If he does, he's finished. Listen, I once knew a man . . .'

Epifânia was too embarrassed to give any opinion, she didn't want to judge Father José, one morning he stumbled during Mass, the sacristan had a job getting him on his feet again, afterwards she went into the sacristy, he looked sad, he seemed to have lost his voice, he got worse as the day went on, drank the whole afternoon, went up the tower with her, threw pieces of stick down from the top, people came and stood in groups down below looking up at the bell, odd phrases stood out above the general noise:

'Poor soul! he had too much today.'

Two strong men helped her to get him down.

'Give him a good strong black coffee.'

She made the coffee carefully, took it to Father José, propped him up with her hand behind his neck, he spilled coffee on the sheet, afterwards the coldness of his body began to frighten her, she wanted to call someone, it was mainly his feet, they were as cold as stones, she rubbed them with a towel until she felt a bit of warmth in them, he began to breathe heavily, she didn't even realize when the dawn came, horses' hooves sounded on the cobbles outside, shouts cut across the morning, the bell rang, she shook the priest:

'It's time for Mass.'

He opened his eyes, still sad, his face worn, it took him

28

a long time to get up, he put his cassock on and went into the church.

Mariana learnt that there was a Republic, a president, her mother and her grandmother had only told her about the Emperor with his long beard, and about Princess Isabel, the president was something different, less important, the teacher said that the Republic had helped Brazil, she recited poems by Castro Alves about slave ships and slaves, she learned that José do Patrocinio had fought against slavery, she remembers having heard rhymes about President Deodoro, apparently they had changed the president, the president was called something else now, one of the rhymes was:

> Deodoro's lovely lady
> In business was rather shady
> She got herself a nice new dress
> Forgot to pay the tailoress.

She knew other rhymes, everybody sang them on feast-days, between the meals, when people they didn't know arrived they changed the words:

> Green beans, green beans,
> Salt meat and chilli pepper
> And may the devil come and catch
> Old Deodoro da Fonseca.

Bahia had once been the capital of Brazil, her teacher talked about this very proudly, the fort of São Marcelo, with the sea all round it, which Mariana was always catching sight of from a distance, must have been where the fighting was when Bahia was the capital. At night, the young girls used to gather by the little flight of stone steps that went down into the sea and tell stories, Mariana liked the ones about the priests' mistresses that changed into mules with no heads, there was one about a girl whose brothers turned into swans, the ones about the days when animals could talk, the windows of the houses

29

lit up one by one. Her grandmother liked to stay in the stall all night, she spread a cloth out on the ground and slept there, the noise of talk went on until dawn, Mariana heard the waves breaking on the steps all night long, she always used to go and count how many steps were under water, sometimes nearly all of them were, some nights were full of shouting, steps hurried through the dark, once she woke up and saw a soldier running after a man. Before the sun rose the fishermen began to arrive, the smell of fish got stronger, customers began to appear, women were selling fruit, cashews, mammee fruit, cajás, umbus, jack-fruit, oranges, the whole place was gay, full of colour and life.

I think it was about the time when she began to sleep in the market that Mariana began to laugh. She laughed all the time. For any reason. By herself or with other people, everything seemed funny to her, people, things, animals. One afternoon she was coming down the hill after school with about ten other girls, fat Susana was beside her, suddenly Susana slipped and sat heavily down on her bottom, Mariana burst out laughing, she laughed for a long time, she and another girl, they couldn't stop, she was afraid of this thing that came from inside her that she had no power over, she wanted to stop but couldn't, ran to a house, leaned her head against the door, waited till it passed. The next day her mother took her to the church again, she laughed at Father José, he was unshaven, and he was getting uglier and uglier, Epifânia caught hold of her roughly, almost shouted:

'Have you gone crazy?'

In the middle of Mass she wanted to laugh, she had to stuff her hands in her mouth, bite her lips, look away from the thing that was making her laugh, but then she saw something else to laugh at. In the market she could laugh at what she liked, at school the teacher couldn't understand what was wrong with her, Mariana laughed the whole time, she was given punishment week after

30

week, standing against the wall, even then her shoulders still shook with laughter. After one whole afternoon of punishment the teacher asked her:

'What has happened to you, girl?'

She couldn't bring herself to say that she found everything funny, even the smallest thing, no-one would understand, she looked sideways at the teacher, thought it best to say nothing. Her mother said:

'The child has the devil in her.'

Her grandmother seemed to know what was going on, at least she didn't ask her questions, she just looked at her over her pipe, let smoke come out of her lips. The desire to laugh went on for months, Mariana noticed that she was growing, her head came halfway up the blackboard now, and she could reach up and touch the top of the stall. During the holidays the priest fell ill, her mother went to look after him, she insisted on taking Mariana, who slept in the church house for several weeks, she would always remember when they went to live with the priest, she had the impression afterwards that she had lived in his house for many years. Every afternoon she climbed up the tower, and stayed up there looking at things. She guessed what was happening in all the houses, a lady went in by a door, came out into a back yard, a little boy was always playing on the ground in a garden, sometimes she saw people taking their clothes off, men pulled their thing out and peed at streetcorners. The priest talked to her a lot. He wanted to know how she was getting on at school, asked her questions about Tiradentes, said things like:

'Did you know that when the Dutch invaded Bahia they were in this very church?'

She wanted to know who the Dutch were, and why the Dutch were Dutch.

Suddenly it was Christmas, Mariana helped Father José to put up a little crib, the child in the manger, Our Lady and São José, the shepherds in a row, lambs, the

31

ox and the ass, the three kings. She brought sand and
pebbles in from the street to make the floor of the stable.
Mother and daughter went to see Catarina, Epifânia
said:

'You must come to Midnight Mass in Father José's
church.'

'Yes, I'll come. I will be there at midnight.'

When the two of them had left Catarina sat with her
pipe alight, watching the comings and goings in the
market, it was quite usual to see people with marks on
their faces, like people had in her home, three cuts on
each side, from top to bottom, she didn't know how she
herself came to be without the marks, she remembered
that her uncle had them, at first, just after he had sold
her, she had hated anyone she saw with them, today they
were like a rediscovery, or like a pause on the road to rediscovery down which she was travelling, laboriously
and slowly it was true, but she was going back, and in the
presence of her daughter and her granddaughter she
felt that she had a duty to get back on to the path from
which she had been turned aside, this return seemed to
her more and more essential, as if she were winning back
a life which had been lost, while she had been waiting
she had taken advantage of what good things the days
could offer, she had danced, been with men, sung, she
had ridden on horseback, that was the first exciting thing
that had happened to her after the voyage, she had slept
between white sheets. Since landing in Bahia she had
been at peace with herself. The people in the market
place were her people. The marks on their faces were a
natural sight. The flour she sold, the yam, the fish, were
all part of a world near at hand, the fried bean cakes with
pepper had the same taste as the ones of her childhood.
She sensed in everything a closeness to something which
had ceased to exist but which now, by some miracle,
was returning. She was no longer in a hurry. They told
her that a ship would be leaving soon, but no-one gave

any precise information. She had seen letters which had come from Africa, from people who had sailed from Bahia and now lived happily in Lagos, Abeokuta or Badagri. She had talked for long hours with men who were getting ready to leave in the next ship. There was one, called Suliman, who treated her with great civility. He was a Muslim, a different religion from hers, but he had a cheerful smile. He had been born beyond the River Oya, in the region of Tapa, had been in Bahia for a long time.

'I can't remember. I came here when I was five, my father showed me the direction of Mecca and told me I always had to pray facing that way.'

She, her daughter and her grandchildren would have to go on this next ship, I see Catarina thinking of this constantly, her eyes quiet now, the way she took up a fish and gave it to the customer getting more natural every day, squatting on her haunches helped to rest her legs and her arms, her eyelids were often lowered but her thoughts were active and her pipe alight.

She knew that she would be helped in the journey, Shango would protect the boat so that nothing bad would happen, his double-headed axe was all-powerful, Our Lady of the Rosary, the saint of the Negroes, would help as well, she had visited the sisterhood in Bahia, had met the people who organized the processions, the one of Our Lady of Joy was very big, she remembered the congadas in Piau, the king and queen in the front, the coloured ribbons, the pieces of mirror sewn on to their clothes, it had all been very different from the festivals with drums in Abeokuta. The next part of the journey was going to be more difficult, more clothes to take, they had hardly brought anything with them from Piau to Bahia. Now Catarina had five lace-trimmed skirts. The children had more clothes as well. Often her thoughts took the form of pictures, the river curving endlessly away, the green of the lagoon in Lagos, the rise and fall

33

of the sea during the crossing, rain in Rio de Janeiro, the first bamboo she had ever seen, yam leaves, big, with drops of water flowing over the green, cattle penned together, very white clothes, sheets and skirts, which she used to iron and iron all the time, the store-room full of rice and beans, salt and bananas, brown sugar and candles, the church in Piau, only one tower, Epifânia a little girl, playing. The pictures which came most often were of the old times, the older they were the clearer she saw them, lizards with green heads that stayed without moving for whole minutes at a time then suddenly shook their heads at you, wooden huts, pretty and cheer-ful-looking, colourful markets, women bathing in the river, children, everything always at peace. The neck-laces of those days filled her memory. She had started to wear them again in Bahia. Necklaces with scarlet beads, big beads and little ones, which she put round her neck happily and naturally, as if she had never stopped wear-ing them. She had given a necklace to Mariana, with yellow beads, she thought that was the child's colour. Epifânia didn't want one, she had said:

'No, mother. I'm a Catholic.'

'Look, stupid—Catholics wear necklaces as well.'

Just before Midnight Mass began Catarina was in the church, Father José entered on time, Mariana looked all around her, everywhere people in pretty clothes, the choir sang with energy and enthusiasm, Epifânia knew that the priest had had a little to drink in the afternoon, but he was steady and his face was grave, from the street there came the sound of music, and a drum play-ing further away, it all mingled with the joy of the Mass, lots of people went to communion, by that time Mariana was asleep, not even a drop of hot wax falling on her from one of the candles woke her up, Epifânia picked her up, said goodbye to the priest and went back with the old woman, the three of them walked without speak-ing through the streets, back to the market.

What was left of the night was full of voices, a drunk sang until dawn when the morning shone on the mangoes, red, yellow, golden, green, covering the ground, Mariana walked amongst them, they smelt very strongly, men and women were shouting, selling umbus. Canoes and fishing-boats were crowded together beside the wharf, the sea seemed to have disappeared, half-naked men jumped from canoe to canoe, from boat to boat, you knew the sea was still there because the ground went up and down, near one of the men Catarina stopped, the conversation went up and down, the smell of fish came in the sunlight. He said:

'There's no ship just now, Yaya.'

'When will there be one?'

'Nobody knows, but suddenly one will come.'

Mariana was sucking a mango, the juice was running over her hands, Catarina shouted to her:

'Don't dirty your dress, child.'

She went on:

'They told me that they were getting a ship.'

'A lot of people are wanting to go.'

'A ship that was going to leave next month.'

'That one isn't going now.'

The two of them were silent for a moment. The man looked up at the buildings of the high city, bright green showed between the houses, he turned his eyes back to the woman, he said:

'In the middle of the year there might possibly be a ship. It's not very big, but it does the voyage all right.'

'How much will it cost?'

'Five thousand milreis each.'

'Do children count?'

'Yes.'

'Very dear.'

For five people that would be twenty-five thousand. Unless children could go free or for less than the full amount. Catarina went back to the stall, smoked her

35

pipe all morning, she would have to buy a chest, the gathered skirts, the sheets, all the clothes, only a chest would be big enough, bundles were no good any more. A few days later she took Mariana with her, they went to look at a wooden chest, a beautiful one, big, the man said:

'It has just arrived from Portugal. It's a good one.'

The woman opened the lid, she felt the lining with her hands, the leather outside was pleasantly rough, it was like the one that belonged to Dona Aurea in Piau, everyone had admired that one, what a lot she must have been able to get in it. Catarina stood back and looked at it, a journey like that needed a chest like that, she decided straight away:

'We'll get it sent later.'

The chest was put at the back of the stall, Mariana sat on top of it, from there she could see the people who came to talk to her grandmother, Emilia and Antônio liked being on the ground, they played with earth, one day a Negro with no teeth told a story about a man who laughed all the time, she remembered when she hadn't been able to stop laughing, this was about a man who had laughed at another man, this other man had powers that he had brought with him from Africa, he was a friend of the orishas, the saints of the African lands did what he asked them to, the result was that the first man went on and on laughing, he got thin, he went on laughing, he shitted laughing, he peed laughing, he cried laughing, he was almost dead, people came from all over the city to see the man who couldn't stop laughing, lots of them went to speak to the other man, to ask him to take the curse off the man, but he said no, it wasn't him, it must be an illness, he was very sorry for him, he went to visit the man who was laughing, put his hands on his head, the man stopped laughing straight away, his eyes wide open with terror, the other, very serious, said:

'Never laugh at anyone again.'

Mariana would never forget the stories that were told around the stall. The Africans who came and brought news brought cowries with them as well, her grandmother made her a necklace out of the shells, she wore it proudly, she had got used to chewing cola-nuts, the obis and the orobos, the orobos were bitter at first, then they were pleasant, your mouth missed the taste and asked for it, it was Seu Miguel who brought all these things from Africa, Catarina wanted to know when he had come, in which ship, there would be another one some time, but nobody knew when, Seu Miguel told her what Ibadan was like, he told her about the night he had spent in Abeokuta, he had talked to the king there, he said that Lagos was growing, getting more and more beautiful. Catarina always wanted to know more, the man said:

'It's the English who rule there now, but in Lagos everybody speaks Portuguese, it's as if you were in Bahia. There's a part of the town that is full of sobrados, two-storied houses like we have here, and the names are the same as here. Around Abeokuta the region is called Oke. The king there is called the Alake.'

Seu Miguel got into the habit of spending hours with Catarina, sometimes they talked in low voices, one word in Portuguese, the next in Yoruba, he would burst out laughing, she would smile.

Catarina used to picture Lagos to herself, she saw the water that surrounded it on all sides, the River Ogun ended there, the houses beside the sea, the good taste of yam which always made her see images of green, Mariana noticed the men who came, there was one who had vertical marks on his face, three each side, he came nearly every day to the market, stopped at the stall, turned things over and looked at them, someone always asked him:

'How many children have you?'

He laughed:

37

'Sixty-one.'

'With how many women?'

'I can't remember. About forty, nearly all of them belong to Oya. Even the Swedish girl was Oya's.'

'Swedish?'

'I have a Swedish son. The woman was here and she was blonder than anyone I've ever seen. She liked me, we stayed together a few months, afterwards she wrote to me saying that the boy was very good-looking, mulatto, but afterwards she married a Swedish man and he adopted the boy.'

The man paused for a moment, then said:

'Very nice of him.'

'Then your son doesn't speak our language?'

'No, he speaks their language, Swedish, sometimes the girl used to talk to me in Swedish for hours, I was getting used to the sound of it, lovely sounds like songs to the gods.'

They used to say he had sons in Lagos, in Angola, in Trinidad and in nearly all the towns around Salvador. Women gathered at the stall near him, they loved to hear stories of how he had been in Trinidad, the things he had done, sometimes he said odd words in Yoruba, Iansã kobé oké, may Iansã be with you, without trying Mariana found she could understand short sentences, one night she was by herself on the seashore, a big wave had splashed up over her dress, an old Negro picked her up from the ground, he used the word beru, she replied no, she hadn't been frightened, it was funny the way she had understood him.

She remembered another man who spent hours sitting quietly in a corner, he wished her grandmother good health using the word aláfia, he greeted you by saying eku-jokô, whenever he said anything else it was always remembering the old days, the time of slavery, he had been a slave in a sugar plantation in the interior, now he liked living in a big city, with lots of people about, one

38

night he raised his voice and said something which Mariana heard and remembered. What he said was:

'Stones grow.'

And he explained that he had received a stone from the hands of Shango himself and that it had grown:

'Shango danced and gave me a thing, I thought it was an orobo, when I put it in my mouth I realized it was a stone, I put it in a clay bowl, the stone grew, today it is more than twice the size it was.'

Mariana saw the stones in the street growing as well, she imagined a day when a house might be balanced on a stone, but perhaps stones would only grow in clay bowls, or would stones on the ground and in the sea grow as well? Years later she was to pick up stones in Lagos and see again the face of the man who said that stones grew, she remembered his eyes, very wide open in his dark face, his body almost invisible, sitting in a dark corner of the stall. The child loved to eat yam with molasses, sometimes the stones man used to take her by the hand, he went to the corner and bought her yam with molasses, nothing better.

Catarina took Mariana with her when she went to talk to the man who knew about ships, he said that things were difficult, there wouldn't be a ship for a long time, perhaps a sailing ship, that would be quite cheap, but it wouldn't be for a year or two. It was about then that her grandmother got the girl ready, said that they were going to a festival, the two of them went on a little boat, at first Mariana was frightened, she thought of the word beru, the sail carried the boat along, fast and fresh, drops of water sprang up in the luminous morning. They landed in a place full of people, she heard them saying it was the feast of Bonfim, women in white were carrying huge vases on their heads, some of them were dancing, men were singing beautiful songs, the two of them went forward slowly, there were stalls everywhere crowded with gay people, her grandmother danced as well, at one time the woman and the child stopped beside some people, Catarina knew most of them, someone said:

'This year they are going to let us wash inside the church.'

The vases stood out against the sky and Mariana, looking at them, followed the movement of each one, her grandmother's was very big, it seemed the king of them all, flowers fell on to the ground, suddenly she noticed the church, it was the first time she had seen it, two high towers, five windows in the front, three in the centre and one on each side, the steps were crowded, the air was filled with a strong scent of flowers, getting up the steps was difficult, there were people everywhere, the dancing became more lively, a white skirt, full, lace-trimmed, spun out over the flagstones, the child followed the movement with her eyes, she nearly lost her grandmother, who caught hold of her with one hand and steadied the vase with the other. Inside the church she took a piece of coconut shell from her skirts, threw water on the ground and began to scrub the floor energetically, Mariana imitated her and noticed that other women were doing the same thing, each in her own way, one was talking or praying in a low voice, another one was singing, a subdued murmuring rose and fell in the church, there up above she could see the saint clearly, it was a cross, Mariana fixed her eyes on the high altar but kept watching the women in white and the flowers which were everywhere. They had to go out by a side door because there were other people wanting to come in at the front, they crowded together and pushed in an unending movement, skirts and flowers, the sun beat on the wall of a house opposite, it was blue and clashed with the white of the house next door, they stayed there until night, the old woman and the girl walked around among the stalls, the stones man was in one of them, as usual he was sitting in a corner, he greeted them with a nod of his head, Mariana ate some white coconut sweet, some peanut

40

toffee, it was dark when her grandmother gave her a plate of rice and fish, the girl took some and lifted it to her mouth, she had learnt to eat with her fingers without ever dirtying the palm of her hand, only the very tips of her fingers, that was the right way to eat, there was the fork and the spoon and the knife as well, but eating with her hands she seemed to taste the food better, she dipped her fingers into the plate and ate neatly and with pleasure. Afterwards she washed her fingers in a basin of water at the back of the stall, walked around for a while, her grandmother had sat down on a stool, a man began to play the guitar, people were still going in and out of the church, an old woman was singing in Yoruba in the next stall, the girl came back, curled up near her grandmother, suddenly she was asleep. Catarina looked up at the church and asked Our Lord of Bonfim to help them with their journey, make things a bit easier, from time to time the towers were lit up by a flash of light from a lantern passing, a man fell down drunk in the middle of the street.

Early the next morning the Mass seemed to be a continuation of the gaiety of the night before, everyone was happy, Mariana looked for a Holy Ghost on the altars but couldn't see one, it was the cross that was in the most important place. It was raining when they left, they had trouble finding a boat, this time it was a rowing boat, the rain soaked them during the crossing, they arrived back late. Mariana remembers Holy Week, her mother insisting that she should go with her to Father José's house, he was paler, his fair hair untidy, the statues and the holy pictures were covered in purple cloth. It was a beautiful Holy Week, Epifânia looked after the priest, she wouldn't let him drink, on the night of the Washing of the Feet Mariana saw feet being put into a basin, Father José washed them slowly, dried them, the lights in the church shone on the people, her mother wasn't far away. Epifânia sometimes went for days without

41

going to bed with the priest, during most of Lent she
abstained, sometimes she was longing to go into his room
and spend the night there, but she chose to sleep in the
dining room, with her mat in a corner near the water-
pitcher, the priest inside used to move things around,
Epifânia could identify everything by the sound it
made.

He was a man who hardly spoke. Only when he was
drinking did he say anything much, usually he just looked
at things, he was always rather sad, but he was good, the
women of the parish spoke well of him, they liked to go to
confession to him. One day the priest's sister came to
visit him. She didn't seem to notice that there was anything between him and Epifânia, or perhaps she did know,
someone could have gone and told her, the priest insisted that the two of them sit side by side at table, Epifânia forced herself to hold out until the end, another day
it was the priest's mother who arrived, she had come
from Cachoeira, she talked to Epifânia:

'Where is it you come from?'

'From Piau.'

'Where is that?'

'In Minas Gerais.'

'How is it you have come so far from there?'

'We are only here for a short while, my mother wants
to go back to her country, in Africa, my children and I
are going with her.'

Ah she said, as if she understood, then wanted to know
if Epifânia had been a slave.

'Never, Sinhá, my mother was, but I was born free.'

At dinner she praised the fish, she asked Epifânia:

'Did you cook it?'

'Yes.'

She went back to Cachoeira the next day, after giving
a coin to Mariana, who had got used to the priest now,
she would sit beside him for hours, playing with a rag
doll or a cork, or pouring water on to the ground,

42

pretending it was a river and there was a flood, the bridges were going to be swept away, and the houses. Father José had a habit of going out in the early evening, he went into the store at the corner, talked to the men, sometimes drank a cachaça with them, but he didn't get drunk, he just seemed quite normal and cheerful, when he came back he went into the confessional, there was always someone wanting to go to confession as night was falling. The month of May delighted the child, she went straight from school to the church, joined in the prayers, Father José was looking paler and paler, he seemed to Epifânia to be far away from her, untouchable, a holy man, at night she slept with him and felt a tranquil happiness, she had forgotten Piau, when she went to the market she stroked Mariana's head, laughed with the customers, Catarina looked hard at her, then turned her face away and looked at the people passing by. She felt that her daughter had stopped noticing things, and she was anxious to get on board ship, but she couldn't do anything while there was no ship, the man had been talking again about a sailing ship, in June she heard there was a festival of Shango, the killing of a ram, she needed protection if she was to get what she wanted, she talked to Epifânia, wanted to take Mariana to the festival, the younger woman said:

'I don't mind.'

The old woman and the child slept outside the city. There was a damp coldness in the air. From time to time noises came from outside the house, the rain falling on the earth, the wind in the leaves. It was still night when Mariana was awakened, she got up off her mat with sleep still in her eyes, stayed sitting on the doorstep looking out at the dark with the rain in it, women were carrying lanterns protecting the flame with their hands, dashes of light lit up the falling rain, Mariana was to remember this picture, and almost all those that were to follow, for the rest of her life, it was getting colder, the walls of the

43

house became taller and shorter as the lamps were moved from place to place, the wood in the stove crackled, a dog ran past, on the earthen floor of the kitchen some cocks and hens with their feet tied together lay turning their heads from side to side, watching the people moving around the room, there was a fat Negress sitting on a bench set against the wall, with her white skirts spread out around her feet, hands on her hips, waiting. The morning came in through the door of the kitchen and was beginning to show up more clearly the group of cocks and hens when the fat woman rose to her feet, at that same moment a lot of other women, some men as well, followed her, Catarina took Mariana by the hand, pulled her quickly after them. The room inside was lighter, red cloths hung down from the wall, wooden statues with big breasts, it was daylight when the women began to dance and sing in the tiny space in front of the red cloths, three men were playing drums in the room at the side. As they were dancing, the women and some other men who had just come into the room lifted up the red cloths and took from under them enormous wooden bowls, they took them singing and dancing and placed them on the ground. In the bowls there were long stones, black, pieces of objects, necklaces, but mostly it was stones, some were lighter in colour, they had strange shapes, all the bowls were put on the ground and the cloths were left with nothing under them. There were pauses in the chants, but they always started up again, until a man opened a door at the front, went out and came back with a ram. He pulled it by a cord tied round its horns, the animal dug its hooves into the ground trying to stop them pulling it along, but the man's hands were firm on the rope, some of the women went and caught hold of it as well, the fat woman said some words in Yoruba and in Portuguese, offered the ram to Shango, then the man got hold of a bunch of leaves and twigs, stuffed them forcibly into its mouth and began to tie up

44

its muzzle with the rope, twisting it between the horns. The animal, with its eyes wide open, shook its head from one side to the other, up and down, but could not free itself, the fat woman caught it by the ears, leaned her brow against the head of the ram, pulled it towards her breast, first one side, then the other, and one by one all the women did the same thing, the men as well, Catarina held the ram's head in her hands for a long time, then it was Mariana's turn, the girl looked straight into its staring eyes. The drums began to beat more quickly, the man was in the middle of the room again, he was saying something into the ear of the ram, he took up a knife from the ground, raised it in the air, began to cut the animal's throat at the same moment as the chant took on a higher tone, the blood dripped into a white bowl, a young woman, slim and dressed all in white, wearing lots of coloured necklaces, fell backwards shuddering, everyone shouted Kauô-kabieci, the blood filled the bowl, the fat woman placed another one under the throat of the ram, took the first and began to pour blood on the stones and the objects on the ground, she turned round and, dipping her fingers in the blood, smeared some on the forehead, the breast and the back of the woman who was lying shivering, the second bowl was full now, the rhythm of the chant had quickened, there were happy shouts of Kauô, the woman took the new bowl, poured the blood on to other stones, but two young girls began to tremble, their lips pushed forward, their eyes shut, the woman anointed the forehead, the breast and the shoulders of each of them with blood, some of the blood trickled on to the ground, Mariana saw that her skirt was wet with red drops, she looked for her grandmother, saw her at the front, kneeling, singing, then bending and putting her forehead to the ground, the sun shone full on the wall at the back of the room and wind was shaking the trees outside. The feet of the ram were twitching, they brushed against Mariana's feet and she was frightened,

45

beru, the stones were dripping with blood, the darkness of their surface darkened the blood, the girl tried not to look at the ram, but the man had finished cutting off its head, he lifted it up high and Mariana saw that the eyes of the animal were like two pieces of glass. The head was put on the stones, the chant changed and the cocks and hens were carried into the room, the man took the first one, slowly cut off its head, the body of the hen shook its legs, Mariana counted sixteen cocks and hens, killed one by one, the blade of the knife was still bright, he wiped it on the feather of a conquêm hen, the little bloodstain there had been on the metal disappeared, people were going in and out of the room, the general air of happiness was increasing. Mariana went with them when they carried the body of the sheep into the kitchen, straightway a group of women began to skin it, a dog arrived on the scene and began sniffing around the stove. Catarina called the girl back and touched her forehead with a little blood, Mariana went to play under the rustling leaves, there was a piece of cloth tied round the wide trunk of the tree.

The hearth blazed all day long, wood was brought in from outside and put to dry in the kitchen, enormous plates of mutton and chicken were ranged on the table, the room of Shango was washed, you couldn't see that the ground had been covered in blood, green leaves were scattered around, Mariana saw them putting plates full of meat on top of the stones, in front of the red cloths which hung down from the wall.

In the afternoon it began to rain again, Catarina called the child, they both went into a big room, the drums were beating and the women were singing, each of them bent over a mat, her hands on the ground, in the middle a pitcher of water beside a thin young girl, dressed in long skirts, full of bright colours, another girl, fatter and dressed simply, was dancing round the pitcher, slow steps, her feet moved along the ground in a leisurely

46

rhythm, suddenly she took up the jar, went dancing to the door and threw some of the water outside, she danced back, put the vase down in the same place, the chant went on in the evening which became night, the drums were not excited as they had been in the morning, now they gave you a feeling of peace, of contentment just to be there, when everything seemed to be finished the women didn't leave the room, they sat on benches and stayed talking until the drums began to beat once more, this time the beat was excited, everyone went into the centre of the room, they were in a circle, each step of the dance fitted with a movement of the arms, Mariana saw her grandmother go into the circle and dance like the others. The sound of the drums and the chants became gentle, but the dance was more vigorous, suddenly one of the women gave a cry and stood in a corner of the room, arms stiffened, eyes shut, her lower lip pushed forward, then she flung herself into a rapid dance, her body spinning and turning, everyone around shouted Kauô, and another woman did the same as the first, soon there were several who were dancing in wild abandon, the circle broke up in general exhilaration, Mariana watched the women as they spun round, sometimes it seemed as if they were going to bump into each other, but they always stopped in time. The child was tired, perhaps she slept a little, she remembers that the drums never stopped, the chants came and went, from time to time she opened her eyes, she saw the women dancing still and felt herself part of their movement, once she saw a man eating fire, dancing and eating fire, she closed her eyes again, the sound of the drums went through her whole body, the thud of feet on the ground went on and on, she was half asleep and half awake, she felt her grandmother lifting her up, now everything was quiet, a lantern burned in the dark, a little rain fell on her face, Catarina sheltered the child with a cloth until she fell into a deep sleep, deep and tranquil.

47

School was not so exciting as it had been, Mariana preferred the market, the conversations that sprang up every minute, the people who stopped near the stall. Emilia stayed with her, she was bigger now, the two girls used to lose themselves for whole afternoons among the other stalls, they used to go and see the men who drank cachaça, they were marvellous, all very gay, and nice to the children, they spent their whole lives telling stories, the one about Rubém who was married to an Indian girl from Maranhão and who had fired a shot at her was the one that amazed the girls most. Rubém explained:

'She had turned into a wild beast. Just because of a five-cent piece that I took out of her drawer the woman came for me with a knife, it hit me in the shoulder, touched the bone, I had to use my revolver and shoot at her. But she didn't die, not her, the bullet only took a bit out of her stomach.'

And he thought that was tremendously funny, the children laughed as well. There were stalls where the men sat to eat, the palm oil bubbled in the pans, golden fish lay on the plates, the flour and the pepper were worked together and mixed with the fish. One day a boy took hold of Mariana's hands, pulled her into a corner of the market, wanted to lift up her skirts, the girl fought him fiercely, her teeth clenched, she didn't shout or speak until she pushed him down a dip in the ground and ran to where her own people were. Her mother went for walks with her, they went down to the sea shore, the little boats moved slowly far away out there, Epifânia pointed out the Island of Itaparica, the child asked the names of fishes, of fruits, she liked the name jambo, pomegranate, mammee, murici, pitanga, she thought that jackfruit was a very small name for such a big fruit.

Her mother was very happy during the next months, she went to the market and to Father José's house on alternate days, chatted gaily with the customers, one day she heard the stories of the man who had had sixty-one children, she asked him:

'And it doesn't worry you?'

The man looked at her as if the question surprised him, he said:

'Yes, I do have one worry: stopping brothers and sisters marrying each other. With so many children of mine scattered about, it could happen. One night I saw that one of my daughters was looking very interested in a boy who was passing, I had to say to her: "You see that big strong fellow? He's your brother".'

Mother and daughter climbed up the steep streets, there were brightly-coloured houses on all sides, red walls and blue, Mariana sometimes hung back to look at a thrush in a cage or a tray of cashew fruits, Epifânia waited for her untroubled and the girl soon caught up with her, they knew all the streets in the centre of the city, in Seu Davi's shop, where they always went, there was a tiny monkey tied up by its foot, it made faces, gave little high shouts, ran away from you and then came close again, in the priest's house there was a turtle in the yard, it walked slowly, slowly, the child used to go and look at it, it was a time of fruit and animals, she remembered the dead ram, these other animals were alive and full of movement, the cashews, the oranges, big bananas and little ones, all were part of the world of here and now, and so was the smell of fish which reached out from her life in the open into her dreams. She got used to going to the cupboard to get cachaça for the priest, she thought it was funny when he toasted her and said 'Your health!', stayed near in case he should need anything else, she went back up the hill again and into the house with red cloths hanging from the wall, this time the wooden statues seemed like people she knew, the priest smelled of cachaça and sweat, took hold of her hair, wound it round his fingers, suddenly it was Christmas again. At New Year she went in a little fishing-boat

49

with her grandmother, they went with other boats, scattered upon the sea, the waves had white fringes, they went to the Island of Itaparica, she heard them say it was a festival of eguns, in homage to the spirits of ancestors which were called egunguns in Africa and eguns in Bahia, the eguns appeared late at night, in bright coloured clothes, they seemed flat like planks, was there anyone underneath the cloth? they had no faces, everyone knelt down, said agó, rubbed one hand against the other, asked questions, gave thanks for the reply, the adupés and modupés echoed through the room, Mariana slept at dawn, she saw eguns going in and out until morning, on the way back her grandmother talked to the man who knew about ships and he said:

'For ten thousand I'll take the lot of you: two women and three children.'

Catarina counted her money and saw that she had nearly nine thousand milreis, she would easily get another thousand before the boat left, it would be in March, in February Mariana went for a week to a sugar plantation, what she liked best was being beside a well where everyone came to draw water, she thought about the voyage they were going to make, from Bahia to Africa, she sucked mangoes, saw corrals where there were a lot of cattle, went to see them milking the cows, Piau came back to her memory, it was a long time since she had thought about the flood or about the house down on the bank of the river.

Epifânia talked to the priest about their departure, she told him:

'The time is getting near, Father. I am going to take the ship with my mother and my children.'

'It's the right thing to do, Yaya. Others have gone already, I will pray that you will be happy there.'

'Yes, pray, Father.'

Mariana went to see him as well. Father José went out with her into the street, bought her coconut sweets, laughed about happy things, in the market the only topic was the voyage, how many would go this time? a family from Cachoeira, Catarina's group, Suliman's, the Ribeiros, the Sousas, the Borges sisters, Mariana knew nights that were full of people, the chest was ready, petticoats, skirts, cloths, sheets, everything ironed and carefully folded, one day her grandmother closed the chest and locked it with a key, said goodbye to Seu Manuel, no-one went to sleep until very late except Emilia and Antônio, in the morning Father José came to the stall, it was the first time he had been there, he gave medals to the women and the children, and a procession formed, two mulattos carried the chest, a little ahead of them three men with white beards walked calmly along, from time to time they stopped and embraced friends, some people were crying, others were laughing, finding it all very amusing, the morning moved on clear and bright, Mariana saw that the people who were going on the ship were the ones in the middle, there was the most handsome boy she had ever seen, holding a small drum under his right arm, she kept losing sight of her grandmother in all the bustle, Epifânia kept hold of the children, her close-fitting, smooth dress stood out from all the others, the first ones to arrive got into boats, it was Catarina's turn next with her people, they stood waiting. The sea broke against the jetty, a boat came close to them, it had two oarsmen, one of them helped the old woman to get in, then Epifânia, Mariana, Emilia, Antônio and a few more, they felt the canoe rising up on a wave, a little farther off the sun shone on the side of a bigger boat, the child heard them saying that that was their ship, she was lifted up on to the deck, Catarina led the whole family down into the hold, she chose a corner, unrolled the mats, Mariana went out, the deck of the ship was cheerful, men were shouting things, the words olorúm, aláfia and Alá were the ones she heard repeated most, a fat man naked to the waist sat on a

51

barrel laughing, the city lay there with its confusion of
doors and windows, hills and steep streets, rows of banana
trees and coconut palms showed between the houses,
she amused herself looking at all the ropes on the ship
and at the masts which rose upwards towards the
sun.

The captain took her by the arm:

'Come with me.'

They went down into the hold, as he went he looked
at the people, he stopped beside Catarina and said:

'It's not here you sleep, Yaya. Tell the men to bring
your chest and I'll show you the place.'

They went up ladders and down ladders, arrived in a
long room, there were enormous shelves up against the
walls of the ship, they were the beds, the captain pointed
to three of them next to each other:

'You sleep here, you and your daughter. The children
will all have to manage in one bed.'

Mariana tried to reach the bed, it was very high up, her
mother helped her, there was a mat and some cloths on
the boards, they put Antônio at the back where the
boards met the wall, Mariana jumped down to the
ground again as Seu Miguel, the man who seemed to like
her grandmother so much, came in and said:

'How could I possibly forget to come and take my
leave of you and your family, Yaya?'

He made an elegant bow, with his hat in his hand and
a big smile on his face:

'May the sun, when it rises each day, find your family
happy and contented, well-fed, fire in the hearth, food
in your store-cupboard, joy in your life.'

Her grandmother murmured an adupé. The man went
on:

'May the moon when it appears shine upon a happy
and united family, with the day well spent, ready for
peaceful sleep.'

This time Epifânia joined her mother in thanking

52

him, and her adupé was the first word in Yoruba that Mariana heard her say. The man was still talking:

'May you always have in your house, Yaya, much palm-oil, much fish, much flour, much yam, fruit in great quantities . . . .'

He gave a wicked smile and added:

'. . . and, if it is your desire, may you never be without cachaça.'

Around them everyone laughed, the man himself more than anyone. When he stopped he put his hand on Mariana's head and ended:

'May the children of the family grow up strong and healthy, and give much joy to you, Yaya.'

He had finished, he smiled, gave a little bottle of perfume to Catarina, a group of people gathered near her, everyone was talking at once, there was a general air of nervousness, by now almost all the beds were occupied, children were crying, Mariana ran out, went up the ladder and back on to the deck, where the confusion was even greater, men were climbing back into the boats, bundles and baskets were being passed from hand to hand, suddenly the ship raised anchor, the canoes had drawn off and were waiting a short distance away, orders were shouted, men in dark-coloured trousers were climbing the masts, the sails began to unfurl, straightway they swelled out, a joyful shout of farewell broke out from the deck and from all the little boats, Mariana sat down in a corner and looked at the city which was already far away, the houses were getting smaller, you couldn't see the windows and doors now, only little dark dots in the surrounding brightness, the hills lay scattered along the horizon. Soon not even the boats could be seen, Epifânia came and stood beside Mariana, now there was silence on deck, hardly anyone spoke, only the men at their work, the sea was calm and the ship went forward smoothly.

The first day went very fast, Mariana ate fish with

flour, a little piece of dried salt meat, went to sleep afterwards. An enormous weariness seemed to weigh on everyone and this strange feeling of walking on unstable ground created sudden silences, as if they were all waiting for something to happen. In the afternoon the sea had little white edges to its waves, the ship pitched from side to side, the sun set in the sea a long way off, there was no more land. It was night when Mariana noticed a very fat lady sitting near her grandmother's bed, sewing a shirt, she found that the lady was called Fat Maria. The wooden structure of the ship creaked, everything shook, her mother and her grandmother didn't say a word, they hid themselves at the back of their beds, an oil-lamp had been hung from the ceiling, it swung from side to side, the shadows were never still, Mariana watched the shadow of a wooden beam growing bigger and smaller on the wall in front of her, sometimes it looked like an animal, other times it was just a beam, you could hear the noise the sea was making outside. Fat Maria took her on her knee and began to talk, she had a good fat voice, she told stories, wanted to know where the girl came from, where she was going to. Mariana forgot about the beam, answered the questions and asked in her turn:

'How long will the voyage last?'

'On a patacho, it will take us more than a month.'

'What's a patacho?'

'It's a sailing-ship, like this one we are in.'

The girl looked around her, saw what a sailing ship was like, Fat Maria went on:

'The sails are those cloths on the masts outside, the wind blows against them and makes the ship go along.'

Fat Maria's face was even blacker than the faces of the people Mariana had known in Bahia or the rest of the people on the ship. The next morning she went to see the sails, the wind filled them, the sail at the back was flapping, ropes of all sizes and lengths hung down and swung to and fro, men were talking in loud voices, they were looking at the sea, pointing at things, she wandered around everywhere, Emilia and Antônio did too, they played with the other children on the ship, once Mariana saw a group of Negroes wearing long skirts bow down to the ground and pray in the direction of one of the sides of the ship.

'They are Muslims,' said Fat Maria. 'They pray turned towards Mecca, it's their holy city.'

The Muslims were quiet people, Mariana walked around amongst them, Suliman, her grandmother's friend, had a blue shirt, later she found out that not all the men who wore skirts were Muslims, there were the Yorubas who had a different sort of skirt. In the middle of the big room where almost everyone slept the women made little hearths like stones, lit fires and began to cook their meals, the children played around on the ground, the fires heated water and boiled things. The captain came and said they were not to cook there, on the deck it was all right, they could light fires outside, but in this airless place it would bother everybody. One of the women, who was always smiling and making jokes, said:

'We're all used to smoke, captain—children as well.'

In the afternoon the sea was rough again, Mariana sat for a long while on Fat Maria's knee looking at the high waves. She spent days inspecting every part of the ship, realized that the captain was white, but only him and one or two of the men who worked, brought the sails down and hoisted them, climbed up the masts and pulled on ropes, all the other people in the ship were black, like in Bahia, but the captain was white and pale like Uncle Inhaim and Father José.

Catarina got out of her bed to go and cook, she spent hours squatting in the middle of the room, smoking her pipe, talked in a low voice, lived as quietly as she could, she didn't want to disturb the pattern of things which was allowing her to fulfill the promise she had made to

55

herself, the promise that she would go back. She was in the ship which was carrying her, with her daughter and grandchildren, towards Africa, all around her she saw her own people, even the Muslims, whom she had been afraid of when she was young, were her own people, she began to speak only Yoruba, as if she had forgotten Portuguese, even when one of the children came and asked her something in Portuguese she replied in Yoruba, and soon Mariana and the other two children were using what Yoruba they knew when they spoke to her, Epifânia looked annoyed, tried not to talk to her, when she had to she spoke Yoruba, the language came easily to her already. The fear she had had on the first few days became a part of her life, it was that the ship would turn over and sink, but there was nothing she could do, Epifânia prayed that it wouldn't happen, she remembered Father José, but there was no point in thinking about him either, she had cut all her ties, things were going to be different from now on. The women of all the families talked together about the new kind of life they were going to have, one night Epifânia realized that she was afraid of this life, she had been doing everything without thinking, without preparing herself for any of the newness, and here she was on her way to changes she couldn't even imagine. She always dreamt about Piau. She saw green and more green, in the ship there were no plants and she felt the need to see green leaves, after a few days she found that she also felt the need of a man. In Bahia she had only slept with Father José, a good man, undemanding, she was going to have to accept any man, like she had before, this also made her more afraid. For Catarina fear did not exist. The waves could be high and the ship could roll as much as it liked, she didn't even want to know what was happening. Shango would be nearby to help her, and she took in her hands a stone in the shape of a double-headed axe which she had brought with her from Bahia, she held the stone to her breast, kept it inside her clothes. Mariana liked to eat with the other families, sometimes she spent the whole day away from her mother and grandmother, once Catarina said to her:

'Eating is a thing you should do with your own people, with your mother and your brother and sister, you must not eat with strangers. You can play as much as you like outside, but when it's time to eat come here to the family.'

It was the first big speech in Yoruba that Mariana understood. She promised she would, when she was hungry she went up to her grandmother, stood there ashamed to say that she was hungry, at night Epifânia took her hands, joined them, made her pray to Our Lord and ask him to make everything go well, Mariana saw the holy bird again, the dove from the altar in Piau, sea-gulls had followed the ship for a few days, at first she thought that they were like the Holy Ghost, but no, their beaks were different, she learnt the Our Father in Yoruba, but when she asked the blessing from the older people she spoke in Portuguese. The medal of Our Lord of Bonfim, which Father José had given her that morning when he said goodbye, was round her neck, with the yellow beads of the necklace that her grandmother had made for her, Mariana ran about the ship, sometimes the necklace and the medal showed in the open neck of her dress, she hid them, that was another thing that her grandmother always said:

'What you wear round your neck you don't show to anybody.'

Some nights there was great gaiety on board, guitars and drums were brought out, the deck-hands sang, the passengers danced, Fat Maria told Mariana about Yemoja, the mistress of the sea, worshipped in Lagos and in Bahia, it was said she lived at the mouth of the River Ogun, in Bahia the women used to throw gifts for Yemoja into the sea off the sea-wall, Mariana remembered seeing a canoe full of flowers and white bundles drawing away from the land. As time went by the place where they all slept began to smell of food and of bodies, Fat Maria smelt very strong, sometimes the child fell asleep with her consciousness full of this smell, as the woman rocked her and sang, her mother used to sing her to sleep, but that had been in Piau, there was one song that went:

> Sleep little girl
> All the night through
> Or the bogeyman will eat you
> In his peas and pepper stew.

One night instead of peas and pepper it was beans and pepper, Mariana wanted to know why, she heard her mother saying to her grandmother:

'This girl isn't frightened of anything. Instead of being frightened of the bogeyman she wants to know why he's going to eat her with beans instead of peas.'

She wanted to sing, but she only knew songs that went with games, she began to play hopscotch with the other girls, they marked it out on the deck of the ship and jumped around, they made a ring and sang:

> Poor little Teresa, she sits all forlorn,
> She fell on the ground and her dress has been torn
> But here come three riders from faraway lands
> They bow very low with their hats in their hands.

A lot of people never left the big room below decks, her grandmother agreed to come up one morning, she stayed for a while looking at all that remoteness of water, then went back to her place, lit her fire, fried her dried fish, mixed it with flour, gave a plateful to each child, and stayed in her corner chewing at a hard piece, seeing in her mind's eye the end of her journey. Would she still have any family in Lagos or Abeokuta? The uncle who had sold her must be dead by now, or else he would be about a hundred. These days she talked a lot to Epifânia.

58

While they had lived in Bahia the two of them had not had much to say to each other, but on the ship they spent hours together sitting on their beds, Epifânia spoke in Portuguese and Yoruba, she remembered things that had happened in Piau, praised Father José, such a quiet and good man, there was no-one like him, she spoke of her fears about the future, what was going to happen to Mariana and Emilia and Antônio? Catarina replied in few words, she often said 'I want', the Yoruba words mô fé resounded in her daughter's ears, she dreamt about them, her mother had never been very strong-willed, she had always been rather self-effacing, now she announced that she wanted this and wanted that, in Lagos she was always going to be wanting something, and I see Epifânia walking aimlessly on the deck holding on to Mariana's hand, when the ship pitched violently everyone had to stay in the cabins, it was usually in the afternoons, the masts were shaken from side to side, the sails whipped the air, one day a sailor got in the way of one of them, he fell and broke an arm, the captain tied a piece of wood to his arm, the man went for weeks with it tied up in a cloth that went round the back of his neck. Epifânia and Mariana felt very close to each other, the ship was full of mothers and daughters, from time to time the men got into a fight, the captain called their attention to the abuse of cachaça, they could drink, but within reasonable limits, Epifânia felt a pain in her head when she thought of Father José and his cachaça, one afternoon there was a bad fight, a créole drew a knife on a mulatto from Pernambuco, they were rolling around on the ground, the deck-hands had to separate them, they said it was on account of a woman, the daughter of Dona Julia, a tall, demure Negress, she was only fifteen, her name was Abigail, she had a little sideways laugh, danced beautifully at all the parties, the mulatto used to whisper to her in corners, the créole, who had been friendly with the family since they lived in Bahia, didn't like it.

They had been at sea a long time now, Suliman, who was marking the days off with a knife on a piece of wood, said that it had been twenty-eight days, four weeks, one morning when dawn broke the ship was still, Mariana went out on to the deck, the sea was like a cloth stretching far away into the distance, nothing moved, the sails hung limp, there was no wind, no waves, the men leaned on the rail, Dona Julia's daughter laughed in her funny way and said:

'About time, I couldn't have stood any more of that shaking about.'

Suliman looked gravely at her:

'Don't talk about things you know nothing about, girl. The worst thing that could happen to a sailing ship is for the wind to fail.'

Nevertheless there was a general air of happiness in those first few days, Mariana played more freely, the mulatto from Pernambuco played on his drum until late, Fat Maria threw something into the sea, was it a gift for Yemoja?, Catarina had a sudden clear memory of something she had seen long ago, it was the moment when the man who had brought her by canoe down from Abeokuta had pointed into the distance and said: Look. The lagoon was as still as this sea now, and what she saw was a cluster of houses, the town where her uncle was going to sell her. For day after day the wind did not come, the ship did not move, after a week of stillness the captain asked them all to gather on the deck, he came and said:

'We are becalmed. Our water will last for more than eight months and there's no worry about food, you have all brought what you could and the ship itself has provisions for a long time.'

The men were saying that the Southern Cross couldn't be seen now, during the day a lot of people fished, rods and hooks were brought out, a big créole called Rodrigo caught enormous fish and one day he discovered that

60

mussels had attached themselves to the motionless hull of the ship, he climbed down a rope, prised them off, asked Epifania to cook them and got his friends together to share the meal. Mariana looked at the sky, she had never seen so many stars, some of them left scratches on the night, the captain talked to her and told her about the other planets. about falling stars, other worlds, suns, comets.

Happiness dominated the ship for another week, but slowly it disintegrated into bigger and bigger pools of silence. Mariana began to feel a weakness in her body, the women and children didn't come up on deck any more, it was only the men who walked to and fro, stood looking at the motionless sea, some of them chewed tobacco, at night they nearly all drank cachaça, then a little happiness came back. The first to fall ill was the mulatto from Pernambuco, one day he didn't get up, the captain went to see him, Mariana heard the word dysentery, and soon there were three more sick, one of the Borges sisters passed blood, they took the jar for the captain to see, all sorts of remedies began to appear, Epifânia looked after Luzia Borges with great gentleness, Catarina did not stir from her place, immobile in a corner of her bed, drawn in upon herself, it was Epifânia who cooked all the meals now, the water came round at a fixed time each day, a sailor brought it in a big tub and gave some to each of them, Mariana went back on deck, she found all the Muslims bowed down to the ground, praying towards Mecca, every now and then they got up, then knelt down again, Suliman had got thinner, it looked as if his clothes had grown bigger, Mariana got into the way of spending hours looking at the sea, Mariana and the sea, she lost herself in it, forgot everything, saw again the flood in Piau, the face of Father José, the glassy eyes of the dead sheep, sometimes she felt light-headed and then once more the sea was before her, Mariana and the sea, it seemed as if the ship was moving, but no, everything was still, the next day she took an old blanket to a higher place, near the helm, spread it out on the deck, lay down and stayed like that looking at the sea, her two eyes looking at the level horizon, she never felt hungry, Epifânia had to go and look for her and make her eat, Emilia and Antônio didn't play so much, the smell down there below began to be very strong, it was sour, putrid, after a few minutes you got used to it, you didn't think about it any more, the flour and the rice stuck in Mariana's throat, made her cough, there was no water for washing your hands after you had eaten, Mariana went back to her place and waited for darkness to fall, many people spent the night on the deck, in the morning hardly anyone moved, the captain gave out water and hard bread, Mariana went to see her mother and her grandmother, more people fell sick. Epifânia wiped the faces of the bedridden, cleaned out Luzia Borges's mouth, one night the drums beat more strongly, people danced down in the hold, sailors with knives in their belts stopped to watch the passengers dancing, one day Mariana felt dizzy, her mother gave her water and biscuits, later she boiled a piece of dried meat, the child chewed it carefully, she doesn't know how long she was away from life on the ship, she remembers one moonlit night, she was better by then, the sea seemed a continuation of the deck, the water was utterly still, flooded with light.

The first death took place when they had been becalmed for more than a month, it was a Negro from Alagoas, he had been one of the quietest, he had stopped eating, he was travelling alone, without a family, and no-one had paid any attention to him, one morning he was dead, the captain told them to take the body up on deck wrapped in a sheet, Mariana went with the others, outside all the faces were looking at the face of the dead man, a sailor said an Our Father and a Hail Mary out loud, the men who were holding the sheet carried it to the rail of the ship, let the corpse slip overboard, but it didn't sink, it stayed there floating, after a while fishes came and attacked the body, the captain said they should have tied a weight to it, but that there weren't many heavy things on board that they could spare, the men stayed looking at the corpse with the fish dragging at it, then one by one went back to their beds, only a few stayed at the rail, their eyes on the struggle in the sea. The second to die was the mulatto from Pernambuco, they found him on the deck with some pieces of biscuit in his hands, his mouth seemed to have stopped in the act of chewing, when his body fell into the water a piece of cloth floated up on to the smooth surface. Then little Joana died, Abigail's sister, she had cried for days on end, one afternoon she was quiet. After three months without wind six people had died, now Catarina insisted on coming up on to the deck each morning, she took the sun supported by her daughter and her grandchildren, deep in her thoughts all she saw was the arrival in Lagos, nothing else existed, death did not touch her, what was important was sun, and food, she ate with determination, she chewed the rice and the flour carefully, sometimes she had a cola nut, she asked them to take her back to bed the moment she felt the sun too strong, closed her eyes and concentrated on waiting. They were saying that the ship had gone off course, one afternoon one of the Muslims died, the others prayed for the dead man, tied his feet to pieces of stone they had found in the hold, his body plunged into the sea without a sound, Mariana was often writhing in misery, her mother took her face between her hands one day, looked at her in amazement, said:

'Daughter, you are thirteen years old.'

She was. She felt older, she only wanted to talk to Abigail, who was already a young woman, but sometimes she ran to her little brother and sister longing to play games again, or she spent hours without saying anything, looking at things and people, the sea looked like an enormous shining floor, as if you could walk along it. She noticed that the food had got less, the captain went around with a revolver showing, then the day came when two people died. Mariana was half asleep when she heard the news. Fat Maria's voice sounded frightened:

'Last night two went: Sebastião and the Ribeiros' son.'

Mariana went to look at the place where the Ribeiro family slept, the little boy who had always been there had gone, she looked for Sebastião, a thin Negro with a straggly beard, but she couldn't find him. She found out that both the bodies had been thrown into the sea during the night.

The wind, when it first came, did not seem enough to carry the ship along. The air moved gently for many days, the sailors hurried around in ceaseless activity, hardly anyone on board felt like eating, in certain places the smell of faeces beca·ie more marked, the captain ordered three men to clean everything, they threw water into the hold, over the decks, scrubbed the floors with brooms, even so three people died in one afternoon, just as waves were forming on the sea and the ship was beginning to rock. Two old women and an old man, whom Mariana had never even noticed, were wrapped up in sheets and carried up on deck, the captain prayed for them, this time the noise the bodies made sounded clearly in the beginning of the night. And then the drums beat violently, her grandmother recognized the beat of the eguns, the axexê, the ritual death ceremonial, but it was a beat of joy too, afterwards the drummers went on to beat for Iansã, Abigail jumped into the middle of the hold, danced wildly and stamped her feet on the old floor, waved her arms, sang in Yoruba. The next morning the ship was moving, the sails shook in the air, the ropes swung from side to side, the deck was crowded, black faces drank in sunlight, no-one said much, at midday everyone ate with a will, Epifânia put palm-oil on the dried fish, gathered her children around her, Mariana,

64

Emilia and Antônio ate in silence, they took up fish with their hands, put flour into the oil, worked it all into a little cake, put it into their mouths, Emilia was the most fastidious, she didn't wipe her hands on her dress, Mariana leaned up against her grandmother after the meal, they all stayed there in a stupor, feeling the wind blowing across the deck.

The ship ran before the wind for many days, sometimes the wind was strong, not many people could cross the deck in safety, Fat Maria fell down, Mariana remembered the time when Susana fell down on the hill in Bahia, she hadn't been able to stop laughing, these days she didn't find things so funny, quite the opposite, in spite of the wind and the liveliness of everyone on board she still felt a weakness in her body, didn't want to do anything, eating became an effort. The wind had been blowing for two weeks when a sailor died, it was the last death of the voyage, they said that the man had lain for days unconscious of everything around him, the people who gathered to drop the body into the sea were possessed by a sort of rage, they looked angrily at the sheeted figure, all they wanted was to throw him overboard as quickly as possible, as they picked up the body it was as if they knew that there would be no more deaths and it had become essential to have done quickly with this one, get rid of the corpse and concentrate their attention on the wind which was carrying the ship up and down over the waves, the storm that broke that night didn't give rise to many fears, wind and rain didn't stop the ship moving, it was the calm weather next morning that frightened them, but the wind still filled the sails.

One night Mariana heard Suliman saying to her grandmother:

'We'll arrive tomorrow or the day after, Yaya.'

'Is it true?'

'It was a sailor who told me. You can see the coast of Africa already with binoculars.'

Catarina wanted to go up on deck, they helped her up the steps, she clung on to the rail, the world was wrapped in darkness, the stars were hidden by the canvas moving in the air, they shone for a moment then disappeared, Catarina stood looking at the motion of the masts, after she had gone down Mariana stayed trying to see something in the blackness, down below they began to beat drums and dance, Epifânia joined in and danced with the young girls, red skirts, blue ones, white ones, flaring out and floating in the room, the oil-lamp threw its light on sweating faces, the women seemed to have more energy than the men, Mariana was going down the ladder, she stopped on one step, sat down and the weakness flooded her body, her head was nodding with sleep and she fell asleep sitting there, waking now and then when a drum beat more loudly, at dawn she found herself leaning against the cold damp wood of the door, a confusion of voices rose up near her, land was in sight.

Catarina, Epifânia, Mariana, Emilia and Antônio gathered together to look at it, there were coconut palms and a beach, a rock jutting out into the sea looked like a place in Salvador, at midday everyone was talking, the food went down easily, Catarina opened the trunk, took out the folded clothes, looked at the whiteness of the sheets and petticoats, they were within sight of land all that day, in the evening the sun set into the horizon opposite the coconut palms, pinks and reds tinged the coast for a long time, in the gathering darkness the curve of the shore in the distance could still be seen.

Not many people managed to sleep that night, they stayed on deck chatting, pointing up at the sky, Mariana remembered that in Piau she had heard the saying: 'He who points at a star will have a wart on the tip of his finger', nobody mentioned the dead people, in the morning they saw that the land was nearer. It was about five o'clock in the afternoon when the ship sailed into the bay of Lagos, there were houses reflected in the water, a tree with red blossoms stood isolated, then a boat came up to them and the men who climbed up out of it wore white uniforms, they were a kind of people that few on the ship had ever seen before, fair hair, a thin man with twisted mustachios came round with the captain to inspect the whole ship, he went where the passengers slept, lifted up all the bedding, looked into the corners, then he made some rather high sounds, Mariana heard people saying that he was English, when he spoke again she paid even more attention but still couldn't understand anything, whoever could understand that? The man went down the rope ladder and got back into the boat.

They were told that they could not go on shore, the Englishman had said that they had to stay there—in quarantine, the captain said—because of all the illness and the people who had died on board. For Catarina the voyage was at an end, a few more days looking at the houses on land didn't trouble her, she saw fluttering robes going to and fro in the town, recognized the sky of her childhood, but some women became frantic, one of them, from Sergipe, threatened to swim ashore, they had to tie her up. The next days passed quietly, a doctor came on board from the land to examine the passengers, Mariana had lost her appetite, one afternoon when Epifânia got a tub of water and was giving her a bath she saw that the girl's pubic hair was beginning to grow, Mariana saw it as well, passed her hand over it, the hairs prickled, from then on whenever she made water she touched the hairs, there was one big one, right inside, afterwards a few drops of urine always trickled down it.

Mariana cannot remember how many days they spent there, there were some days when there were parties, everyone danced except her, she seemed to be losing interest in everything, when the men in white came back it was to announce—the captain told everybody on deck —that they could disembark, but without their clothes, it was essential that the clothes should stay there for

67

longer, they might be able to have them back later, it was worth it if it meant they could go on shore, they had to show the papers they had got in Brazil, early the next day some boats would come to take the passengers off. Catarina at first would not consider the idea of going ashore without the trunk, she opened it again, dresses and petticoats all so beautifully packed, Epifânia explained to her that everything would be kept safely in a warehouse in the town, I see them standing there arguing about the trunk, the white clothes spread out on the bed, the three children around them, Mariana not paying too much attention to the matter, at dawn mother and daughter were still talking, a warm wind blew from the land, there was rain in the air a long way off, it was the rainy season, Suliman, who had marked off the days on his piece of wood, said that it was the beginning of September, Mariana slept badly, in the morning the English boats brought sheets for them, every passenger had to take off his clothes and leave the ship wrapped in a sheet, Abigail was indignant, she didn't want to take off her red dress, she had dreamt of wearing it as she arrived in Lagos.

Catarina took off her skirt and the cloth that was wrapped round her chest. Her breasts fell down to her navel, Mariana stood looking at her grandmother, she thought how thin she was, near her navel the skin was even blacker, Epifânia took off her dress and thought of Father José, her black body on the priest's bed, the children were naked, Emilia and Antônio enjoyed the game, they ran around the deck, Catarina covered herself with a sheet, tying it over her breasts and under her arms, Epifânia put hers round her shoulders, Mariana did the same, they went down the rope ladder, the boat wouldn't stay still, it was difficult to get Catarina into it, the oarsmen were two black men, with marks on their faces, naked to the waist, Mariana felt bad, could she be ill again?, the distance between the ship and the coast was not long, but how slow it was, suddenly she felt a pain going down her stomach, a pain and a feeling of heat, it was as if something has burst inside her, the heat was strongest in her sex, she put her hand there and felt that it was wet, she lifted the sheet, there was blood on the bottom of the boat and on the white of the sheet, Epifânia held her close, the boat was coming up to the land, the woman and one of the oarsmen helped Mariana to a patch of grass underneath a tree, her mother took the sheet, opened her daughter's legs, cleaned the insides of her thighs, Mariana covered herself with the sheet again, a strong acrid smell hung in the air, the sun beat down on the yellow earth that lay beyond the grass.

Part II

THE HUSBAND

A group of Brazilians who lived in Lagos came towards
Catarina with clothes in their hands, she accepted a blue
cloth with lighter coloured patterns, wrapped it round
her body, knotted it above her breasts, Mariana tried
to hide the red stains on the sheet, a tree-lined street
stretched out away from them, houses on one side and
the sea on the other, more boats were coming in to land,
Fat Maria was in one of them, a confusion of words in
Portuguese and Yoruba rose up all around. Abigail embraced a smiling Negress, told everybody:
'She's my sister.'
An old woman, one of those from Lagos, came towards
Epifânia:
'My name is Teresa. Take this for the child.'
And she gave her a dress and some cloths, Epifânia
put the dress over her daughter's head, the old woman
made one of the cloths into a sort of napkin which she
fixed between Mariana's legs, the sheet lay where it
had been thrown in a corner, the dress was too long, it
nearly reached the ground, Fat Maria thought it was very
funny, now everyone seemed happy, they were all talking and laughing at the same time, an English soldier
standing at a doorway was laughing as well, Catarina
headed the family towards a street that ran off from the
sea, a man said:
'The Brazilian quarter is a little farther on, in Bangboshe Street there are lots of houses where you could
stay.'
Mariana felt heavy, the heat made breathing difficult,
the sun beat down on the houses, there was a lot of

humidity in the air, on the horizon black clouds promised rain, Epifânia went on through the town, it was different from everything she had imagined, clothes in clashing colours, people carrying sunshades, she had thought it was going to be like Piau, or Bahia, or Rio de Janeiro, but here there were no mountains, everything was flat, suddenly old Teresa said to them:

'Here is Bangboshe Street.'

Catarina was taken into one of the houses, in the centre a sort of patio with several rooms opening on to it, she thought the whole family would fit into one of them, one man was telling another:

'The patacho *Esperança* has come again, she brought a lot of people, more than twenty of them died at sea.'

They were making it up, thought Epifânia, only twelve had died, and Mariana knew then that the ship's name was *Esperança*, nobody had told her that before. On the first day, Emilia and Antonio had gone out to play in the street, Mariana preferred to stay in the room, in the afternoon it rained heavily on the town, the two children came running back, Catarina and Epifânia, who had been to visit Brazilians living round about, came in with a piece of fresh meat in their hands, they roasted it slowly, it had been months since they had had that taste in their mouths, Mariana fell asleep early, and heard her mother and grandmother talking all night long.

In the morning they went to see Dona Zezé, one of the rich women in the street, she lived in a sobrado with windows painted green, over the main doorway there was an inscription: *Bahia House*. A rocking chair in a corner, a sofa, armchairs, Catarina and Epifânia stood waiting, Mariana held on to the other two children, Dona Zezé came in, walking slowly, said 'God be with you', sat down on the rocking chair, began to speak in Yoruba, then changed to Portuguese, she asked:

'Have you come from Bahia?'

'Yes.'

'Have you any relatives here?'

Epifânia told her they had no-one, or rather, her mother perhaps had, but in Abeokuta, she had left there when she was a young girl, eighteen years old, had heard nothing more of her family since then. Dona Zezé clapped her hands, a servant arrived with a tray full of corn cakes, Mariana ate one, the mistress of the house said:

'Many Brazilians have come here recently, but none of them have the slightest idea of what it is like in Lagos. They think they are going to find one thing and they find another. What people say over there about this place is wrong, life isn't easy here.'

'I never thought it would be, Dona Zezé, but this is my home.'

'It is and it isn't, Yaya. For the most part it was our grandparents who left here and went as slaves to Brazil, they got used to it there but they always thought of this place as paradise. Well it is paradise and it isn't, Yaya.'

There was a silence, the noise of children shouting came in from the street, she went on:

'What can I do to help you?'

'You are the one who holds most authority here. All I want is that you be kind enough to give us introductions to people. You can see how we arrived, with nothing, not even our clothes, we came from the ship just with the sheets that the English gave us.'

'It's not the first time. And it's as well they do it because sickness like you had on the ship could spread right through Lagos.'

She seemed tired, but asked:

'What is your full name?'

Catarina waited for a moment before replying:

'I am Catarina dos Santos, my daughter is Epifânia dos Santos, and the grandchildren are Mariana, Emilia and Antônio, all dos Santos.'

'Where does your surname come from?'

'From my master, Joaquim dos Santos, we called

73

him Uncle Inhaim. When I was freed I took his name and I gave it to my daughter and her children.'

Dona Zezé rocked to and fro, thinking, there was an Our Lady on the wall, a paper flower in front of the statue had stains on its petals, she said:

'I can let you have cola nuts and tobacco for you to sell in the streets. You can sell here in Bangboshe or in Campos Square. Do you speak English?'

'No.'

'You'll have to learn. Everything here belongs to the English.'

She turned suddenly to Mariana and said:

'Is this the girl who arrived saluting the land?'

'Yes.'

'God bless her.'

When they went down the stairs there was a group of naked children waiting down below, Mariana stopped beside a young girl, just a little older than herself, bare-breasted, the heat was greater every minute.

They spent the rest of that day seeing passengers from the *Esperança*, Fat Maria arrived wearing a print dress, took Mariana on her knee, said:

'So my little girl has become a woman.'

Mariana laughed, hid her face in Fat Maria's arms, her body felt light today, she went out into the street with her friend, they went right along Bangboshe Street, ended up beside an enormous lake, fisherman's canoes quite still out there in the distance, they spent hours going right round the island, stopped for a long time in front of a huge bridge that was being built between Lagos and the mainland, water everywhere, they went back to the place where they had landed from the boat, Mariana saw the patch of grass where her mother had cleaned the blood off her thighs, they went on walking, a canal separated that island from another, where there were no houses, they found out that it was called Ikoyi, they ate bean-cakes, by the time they got back to Bangboshe

Street it was almost dark, Epifânia had been worried about her. She was on her way to sell tobacco and obis and orobos, the sweet and the bitter cola nuts, on the corner of Campos Square, she said:

'Your grandmother is there already.'

Mariana went to see, her grandmother had got hold of three packing-cases and had made a sort of counter with them, she had arranged the goods on top and was sitting on another box, smoking her pipe, Emilia and Antônio were playing on the ground, dirty water flowed down a gutter beside them. Catarina taught Mariana how to put ori on her body, Mariana wanted to know why she should do it, her grandmother told her that it was coconut oil, it was good for you, protected your skin against the humidity and against sickness.

The sounds of Yoruba fitted in with things around her, Mariana found herself speaking Yoruba to two young girls, it was night, little lamps lit up the places where women were selling things, it felt as if it was going to rain again, Mariana noticed another sort of weakness in her body, a laziness, a desire to sleep well, to rest, she went to her mat early, the door had left open, when it rained the drops made a noise in the patio, a few days afterwards Abigail came to call for her:

'Shall we go and see the *Esperança* leaving?'

They went. The ship seemed more beautiful to them now, far away from them, her sails swollen in the wind, they had all come in her belly, people had died, and there she was, setting off again for Bahia, rising and falling on the waves, her tallest mast shining in the sunlight.

They moved a month later, Catarina had found a house at the other end of Bangboshe Street, nearer to Campos Square, it had a living-room, a bedroom, space for a kitchen and some trees out at the back, Epifânia preferred to cook in the open air, the kitchen was turned into a bedroom for the children, Mariana would always remember it, the floor was made of red bricks. Emilia

75

and Antônio slept away from the door, which opened on to an alley, on Sundays they all went to Mass, the priests spoke English, only one of them had learnt Portuguese so that he could get on with the Brazilians, there were some Irish and French Sisters of Charity, Epifânia tried to talk to one of them who could speak a little Yoruba. Mariana wandered through the whole city, went to see the sobrados that were like the ones in Brazil, Seu Alexandre da Costa's, Seu João de Sousa's, Seu Gaspar Antônio Sales's, Seu Alexandre was at his window one day, he called to her, Mariana ran up the stairs and went up to the man who was sitting on a sofa, he asked who she was, he spoke Portuguese slowly, in a soft voice:

'What is your mother's name?'

'Epifânia dos Santos.'

'And your father's?'

She stood looking at him without replying, the man waited for a moment and then asked:

'How is Bahia?'

She didn't know what to say, smiled and answered:

'The day we left it was very sunny.'

He laughed and said:

'Bright girl, eh?'

He came towards her, but slowly, and with his lips still open, this terrified her and she ran down the stairs. She only went back to Seu Alexandre's house with her mother and her grandmother, it was some Brazilian festival, everyone was whispering, it must have been a secret, it was almost night when she discovered what it was all about, a man said:

'The calungas are coming out.'

The calungas were the huge figures of the woman, the ox, the ass, the ostrich, that made up the bumba-meu-boi, Mariana found out straight away that in Lagos they called it burrinha, she saw a man getting inside the framework of the woman, they were playing musical instruments and singing, the ox was pretending to attack the people nearby, they all screamed and ran away, the man who was inside the ox danced well, he did pirouettes in the centre, everyone shouted é boi é boi. Suddenly a fight started in a corner, men with bits of packing-case in their hands started to beat up the ones who were dancing, people rushed from the house to protect their friends, the ox ran inside, above the door of Seu Alexandre's house there was an inscription which read: *Viva Deus*, it was at the very moment the ox went through the doorway that Mariana made out the words, in the light of a burning torch a boy was holding, Epifânia came to get her, pulled her away from the fight, this was different from the one in Piau where there had only been two men, here everybody was fighting, the noise of the sticks and the shouts made you wonder if they were having fun or really fighting, Seu Alexandre ordered the door to be closed, the bumba-meu-boi went on inside, even more lively than before, Epifânia was talking to old Teresa who was saying that it was always like this, it only needed the Brazilians to show themselves in the streets with their festivals for the Africans to interfere and start a fight. Epifânia asked:

'Why do you call them Africans?'

'Because they are Africans.'

'Then what are we?'

'We are Brazilians. You have just arrived and you don't know what things are like here. We are civilized people, different from these others. It was us who taught the people here joinery, we taught them how to build big houses, and churches, we brought cassava, cashews, cocoa, dried meat, coconuts. They stare at you with big round eyes and don't know how to enjoy themselves. The only thing they do know is how to cause trouble at our parties. It only needs a good bumba-meu-boi to come out and there's a fight.'

Epifânia had gone back to speaking Portuguese, these days she didn't see much difference between life in Lagos

77

and life in Bahia, lots of things were the same, the heat, the language, Mass, the fruits, she only spoke Yoruba to her mother, Catarina seemed as if she had forgotten Portuguese, she began to spend a lot of time with people born in the land, the Africans, they stopped in front of her packing-cases, bought obis and stayed talking, when someone from Abeokuta appeared the questions and the replies went on even longer, all the water for Lagos came from there, the water in the canal was brackish, no-one could drink it, it came in pitchers and tubs, by canoe, down the River Ogun, and everybody went to fetch it from one end of the island, Mariana learnt to balance jars on her head, you had to pay for the water, people who had been in the city a long time said that in the old times there hadn't been any money, everyone had used cowries, one penny was equal to twelve cowries, Mariana had learnt that there were twelve pence in a shilling, it was English money, so a shilling in cowries was twelve times twelve, she did the sum, a hundred and forty-four cowries, to buy something big you would have to go with a cart full of cowries, because a pound was twenty shillings, you would have to multiply a hundred and forty-four by twenty to get a pound in cowries, she pronounced shilling with the stress at the end of the word, one day an African corrected her, told her it was *shi*lling not shill*ing*, cowries were a pretty shape, Epifânia made two bracelets out of them, one for herself and one for Mariana, one Sunday Catarina got the family together and said they were all going by canoe to Abeokuta, she had made arrangements with a man she had known when she was young, first she insisted that they should all put on Brazilian dress, she chose clothes with brightly-coloured prints, when it was time she collected Epifânia, Mariana, Emilia and Antônio, they got the boat at one end of the island, crossed the lagoon, it seemed never to end, they entered the mouth of the river, so this was the River Ogun that Catarina had talked so much about, two men

78

rowed them upstream, on the banks naked women and children laughed, said things in Yoruba, waved, some of the women were in the river, their breasts dripping, Catarina saw the green of the land, each bend in the river opened up like a rediscovery, the noise the oars made in the water was peaceful. They landed in Abeokuta, the old woman went through the streets and stopped in front of the palace of the obá. She said:

'This is the palace of the Alake.'

After all this time she spoke in Portuguese, Epifânia and the children looked at her amazed, and Catarina went all around, showed them the tall rocks, went along streets full of people, at one point she stopped and stood in silence, looking for a long time at a group of African huts, then she said:

'I used to live there.'

She fell silent again, there were some children playing in the street, Epifânia wanted to go in, her mother said roughly, in Portuguese:

'It's no good. None of the family live here now.'

Later on they sat down under an enormous tree, Epifânia looked all around her and liked it, mountains rose up, there were groups of tall rocks beyond the houses, she had been born amongst mountains, she loved landscape that rose and fell, in Lagos everything was flat, the rocks of Abeokuta were like a rediscovery for her, they ate in the market-place, saw piles of adirés, the cloth with dark blue patterns, Catarina bought a piece, wrapped it round herself, the return journey was quicker, Mariana slept, it was dawn when they arrived back in Lagos, they walked through the dark streets, one or two lamps were burning where they were selling things, a few weeks afterwards Catarina and Epifânia decided that it was time for Mariana to go back to school, the one run by the nuns was a long way away, on the island of Topo, in Badagri, and Mariana found herself, on the day that

79

had been fixed, wearing a new print dress, with a bundle in her hand, waiting for another canoe, Epifânia was with her, they went through the strait, they had come that way when they arrived in Lagos, then through a series of lagoons, the boatman told them:

'You can go all the way to Porto Novo through the lagoons.'

And he told them that Porto Novo was French territory, it was a long way beyond Badagri, and I see Mariana arriving in Topo, the beach stretched out white and endless, the coconut palms bending over the convent school, the wind whipping up sand, the sunlight fell through the foliage and made a lacy pattern on her face.

Her first difficulties were with language, the nuns only spoke English, but at recreation all the Brazilian girls got together in a group, talked as much as they could, Abigail was at the school as well, out of forty-five girls about thirty were Brazilian, Mariana used to walk slowly along the long corridor that led to the dormitory, before going to sleep she would stop by the window, and stand looking at the stars, a feeling that there was something missing rose up in her, the coconut palms were rustling on the beach, she cupped her hands round her breasts which were full now, thought about the town crowded with people, the gaiety of the market-place, all the brightly coloured clothes and herself far away from everything, praying and studying, for how long? The girls went for walks along the beach, sat down beside the sea, on the lagoon side fishing canoes sometimes went by, the nuns had to forbid walks on that side because the men on these boats were naked, in the chapel an Our Lady with a gentle face looked at each one of them, the smell of incense mingled with their prayers, Mariana remembered the Holy Ghost, the bird with its two wings spread wide, hovering in the air, Our Lady had her arms open wide and her white cloak was welcoming.

At Christmas she went back home, she saw the crib in the church, Lagos rose up before her eyes full of activity once she was walking along the seashore with Fat Maria when a pleasant wind began to blow along the street and on to her face, at the same moment she felt good, as if she had just shaken off some worry or sickness, and her body felt liberated, she could breathe, and smell, and walk more freely. A little farther on, one of Seu Alexandre's sons told them:

'It's the harmattan, it comes this time every year.'

Mariana and Fat Maria walked on contentedly, everyone seemed happy, her grandmother, in Campos Square, smiled at the rediscovery, she had forgotten about the harmattan, now she remembered.

Before bathing herself in the basin the girl looked at her transformed body, rubbed ori into her skin, her breasts hard, thick hair between her thighs, her hips becoming more rounded every day, her mother had started to take in sewing, she made dresses for Dona Zezé, for Seu Alexandre's wife, for Seu Costa's wife, everyone praised the things she made, she put trimmings on like they did in Brazil, used lace on smocks and petticoats, the money helped with the expenses, Emilia and Antônio were studying with a Brazilian teacher who lived nearby, they were beginning to read and write.

There was a party at New Year, Mariana noticed how happy her mother was, she danced to the music of the guitars, her grandmother's face was unsmiling, she didn't seem to hear the music and suddenly it was time to go back to school, Topo gathered its young girls together once more. I am with Mariana as she travels there by boat, wearing a new dress made by Epifânia, the girl put her hand into the water and left a track in the lagoon, I see her beginning to understand and speak English, sometimes the sounds stayed in her head all night long, she dreamt about words in the different languages she knew.

The sisters were preparing groups of girls for their first communion, Sister Mary said to Mariana:

'How is it you haven't made your first communion yet, at your age?'

'It's because we have all spent so many years travelling, my grandmother, my mother, my sister and brother and me, there was no time for communion.'

They learnt the catechism, a priest from Lagos, fair with blue eyes, came to hear their confession, Mariana thought she would like to be a saint, she saw herself dedicating her life to the good of others, carrying out noble works, she thought about Father José, his kind face when he looked at her, the morning of the communion was beautiful, she was up at dawn, she dressed all in white, stood at the window watching the sun rise, at Mass she prayed with her eyes downcast, her hands together, the communion made happiness run through her body, for the rest of the day she walked slowly, thinking all the time that she was carrying God inside her and that a sudden movement might hurt him. The nuns noticed that her piety was increasing, she went more often to the chapel, one afternoon Sister Victoria, the Superior, asked to see her:

'You should pay more attention to your schoolfriends, go out with them at recreation, spend your time with them.'

Mariana replied:

'Very well, Sister.'

English was coming more easily to her now, she still spoke Portuguese and Yoruba, she had become friendly with an Ibo girl called Mabel, they could only talk to each other in English, by the time her mother came to collect her for a festival the wave of sanctity had passed and Mariana was once more gazing out to the other side of the lagoon where men, women and children sometimes gathered waiting for canoes, they shouted remarks, their laughter came over the surface of the water.

It was the feast of Our Lady of Joy, as soon as she went into the house Mariana saw the chest, her mother told her about all the trouble they had had getting it back, Mariana went up to it, ran her hand over the rough leather that covered it, opened it and rummaged around among the clothes inside, on the feast-day the women all wore dresses made of the same material, the Mass was full of long hymns, afterwards Fat Maria carried a banner, two men played wind instruments, a drum began to beat, the women went out into the streets of the Brazilian quarter, singing and dancing, Epifânia was one of the gayest, Mariana danced as well and noticed that there were people crowding at every window, today there were no fights because it was the morning, even so the faces at the doorways looked as if they didn't find all this quite proper, they went up the stairs in Dona Zezé's house, on the first floor cakes and sweets on the table, coffee, milk, and Mariana laughed with the girls who were dancing beside her, some of them she knew from the *Esperança*. There was a pause, the music stopped so that everyone could eat the sweets, from time to time someone shouted *Viva Nossa Senhora*, Catarina had walked in the procession but didn't dance, she sat quietly drinking her coffee, at one point Mariana sat down beside her, her grandmother put her arm round her waist. When they had finished, Dona Zezé got up, went up to the statue of Our Lady of Joy that stood at the back of the room, the music started again and the mistress of the house danced for the saint, with steps that drew near to the statue and then went away again, everyone clapped their hands and danced joyfully, Mariana thought it was quite right to dance for Our Lady of Joy, she had never thought of it before, at the feast of Bonfim, in Bahia, there had been a lot of dancing, but that had been different, today it was specially for Our Lady.

Fat Maria spent the afternoon with her, they talked and laughed, then the older woman said:

'You'll be married soon.'

'Oh goodness, Dona Maria, it's early yet.'

'Don't you know the story of what happened in that school you go to?'

'What story?'

'About the man who went to look for a bride. The sisters made all the girls stand in a row, he came in, looked at them all and when he had decided he stopped in front of one of them and said: "I want this one!"'

'How horrible!'

'Why horrible?'

'To get married like that, to someone you didn't know, without any preparation.'

'Perhaps it's quite a good way. They said that the one he chose was delighted, she was crazy to get away from school.'

Back in Topo, Mariana imagined the scene, all of them lined up, who would be the chosen one, the one he liked best? Abigail, Mabel? Seu Alexandre's daughter? perhaps Abigail, she was the prettiest, that is if the man were a Brazilian, because if he weren't he might well choose Mabel, she had these very pleasing marks on her face, on the days when she had to serve at table Mariana had to be careful not to break anything, she seemed to be always in a dream, images of the sea, the sand, the coconut palms, the stars at night, the water-plants that grew on the surface of the lagoon became confused in her mind with communion, Mass, sewing lessons. On the feasts of St Antônio, St João and St Pedro she went back home, her mother made a huge bonfire in Bangboshe Street, suddenly there were a lot of fires, one in front of each sobrado, the taste of the roasted sweet-potatoes brought back memories, Emilia and Antônio jumped over the bonfire, Mariana was a bit shamefaced, she was rather big to be hopping over bonfires, she knew quite a lot of people in Bangboshe Street now, a solidly-built youth called Jorge, with a black, open-looking face,

asked her to go for a walk with him, they went across
Carter Bridge which had just been opened, went to the
market, the boy gave her a red necklace, Mariana thought
of Emilia and bought her a painted wooden doll, her
sister played with it for years.

Her grandmother wasn't earning much, the money
from the sewing was falling off as well, Mariana noticed
one day that she hadn't been sent back to school, she
had to go and fetch water from the usual place, stay in
Campos Square and sell obis and orobos, there wasn't
much tobacco about, and cachaça, which her grandmother had sold at one time, was forbidden, at any rate
for a street-seller, her mother had started to make corn-
meal biscuits like the ones they used to have in Piau,
and Mariana went selling them from house to house,
Seu Alexandre always asked her to come up to the first
floor for him to buy some, she wasn't frightened of him
now, one day he asked her:

'How do you like the Protectorate and Colony of
Lagos?'

'Like what?'

'What do they teach you at school? Protectorate and
Colony of Lagos is the name of the place you are living
in now. Do you like it?'

'Yes, I do.'

'Not homesick for Bahia?'

'Yes, when I remember.'

One night Emilia cried, Mariana didn't know what
to do, Epifânia brought a banana, gave it to the child
and silence fell once more, Mariana went to talk to
Fat Maria, who put her on her knee, she protested 'I'm
too big', Fat Maria looked at the house opposite and
said:

'Things are difficult for all of us just now.'

There followed a few months when a lot of people
died, Mariana remembers that the death of a young person was sad, but not the death of an old one, then there

was a party called a 'serenata', one afternoon she met a group of egunguns in the street and went running back home, an egungun with a huge mask came after her, came into the room, Catarina was there, she sat down, rubbed her hands together in greeting before the masked figure, bowed her head, soon Mariana got used to them, she used to go and watch them in Campos Square, followed them from a distance, there were boys with sticks who stopped you getting very near them, her grandmother thought that she and her sister and brother should see African festivals, make sacrifices to the orishas, at first Epifânia was against it, then she agreed:

'All right, but you will have to go with them. I'm not going.'

'Why not?'

'Because it's different from Bahia. Here if you're a Catholic, you stay a Catholic.'

Catarina took Mariana to Seu Gaspar's house, he was the Brazilian who organized the cult of the orishas in Bangboshe Street, he looked after the egunguns as well, the festivals in honour of the ancestral spirits, sometimes Emilia and Antônio went along with their grandmother and Mariana, they used to play with a statue of Shango, there were long conversations, the man had eyes which stayed fixed on you, he spoke calmly, one day Mariana asked Epifânia:

'Mother, are we Brazilians or Africans?'

'We are both, my child.'

These days she spent many hours in the market-place. There was a certain air of contentment in the people who were buying and selling, Mariana wandered all around, saw the pretty cloth, the one with dark blue patterns, and the brightly-coloured dresses, the hats, the animals, there was one place where you could buy monkeys' heads, she thought of the dead ram in the festival of Shango, one day she saw them killing sheep in all the streets of Lagos, they made a hollow in the ground, cut

86

the animal's throat, let the blood drip into the hole, it was a Muslim festival, the men bowed down to the ground like her friends on the *Esperança*, Mariana went to see the Brazilian mosque, she couldn't go in but she saw Suliman who hugged her:

'How is your grandmother?'

'Very well, thanks.'

'A good strong woman.'

In the market there were ornaments to wear in your hair, necklaces of all colours, children on the ground, the women used to take off their skirts and go around without clothes, there was a strong smell of bodies in the air, Mariana stayed in one place quite still for a whole day, just looking at the coming and going around her, she forgot to eat, other times she went to watch the fishermen at work, the lagoon was like the windless sea of the voyage, the water utterly still, great piles of wood were stacked near the berths, men arrived loaded down with nets, the canoes with the drinking water, which had come down from Abeokuta, jostled in among the fishing boats, the men talked together in Yoruba, sometimes one of them spoke in a different language, Mariana used to stand around to see if she could understand.

Her grandmother went about silently, she hardly spoke, Epifânia tried to cheer her up, wanted her to visit Abeokuta again, the old woman didn't leave her bedroom for a whole week, one night Mariana was talking to her mother, the lamp light fell on a roll of tobacco which had just arrived from Brazil that morning, there was some cachaça as well, but it was hidden underneath the packing-case, Epifânia began to talk about the sadness of Catarina, who could ever know what she had expected to find in Africa?, all she remembered was a happy childhood, a beautiful town, now she found nothing like that, in Abeokuta no-one had known anything about her family, perhaps they had all died, for the first few months she had still felt some pleasure and happiness in

87

her return, but now everything was losing its novelty. Epifânia looked out into the dark street, with now and then someone going past, she said:

'She is beginning to realize that nothing has changed, there isn't much difference between this place and Bahia, the only difference there is here is for the worse, there we belonged, here we are foreigners to the English and foreigners to the Africans, not many of us care much about the festivals of Shango and the saints she prays to, what our people here like is feast-days like we had in Brazil, the Blessed Sacrament, St José, Bonfim, Our Lady of Joy.'

Epifânia untied the kerchief from her head, stood up for a minute, shook the cloth in the night, then sat down again and said:

'Nothing has changed.'

Mariana thought that things had changed, but she couldn't explain how, everything seemed different to her, the school in Topo, the way people looked at things, the way they thought, the look of the people in the street, but perhaps her mother was right and everything really was the same, Mariana went into her grandmother's room, lay down on the mat beside her, the silence lasted for many minutes until the old woman said:

'What was your mother talking about?'

The words in Yoruba didn't seem to mean that, had she understood properly? She leaned against the wall, replied:

'She was talking about the feast of St João next year. She wants to order sweet potato a long time in advance so that we won't be short when the time comes.'

Catarina looked towards the window, a branch of a tree was outlined against the stars, a few days later she was weaker, Epifânia dismantled the stall and carried the packing cases back to the house, they all went into her room, the light was coming in through the

88

window, Catarina told them to sit on the ground, near her mat, she spoke in her calm Yoruba, there was a pleading note in her voice:

'I don't want you to call me Catarina any more. That is not my name. I want you all to call me by my name.'

'Of course, mother. We will all do as you wish.'

The old woman had a cushion, she was holding the edge of the sheet in her hands, she looked at each of them around her and said:

'My name is Ainá.'

'What, mother?'

'Ainá. I was always called Ainá. It was in Brazil that they changed my name, and I ended up Catarina, but I have a name: my name is Ainá.'

She caught the hand of Mariana, who was nearest to her, and went on:

'They shouldn't be allowed to change people's names. My name is Ainá.'

She closed her eyes, rested a little, when she opened them again she seemed to have forgotten what she had been talking about, but no, she went on as if there had been no interruption:

'A name is a sacred thing, it shouldn't be spoken too much, it shouldn't be used carelessly, and only the family should know your name. For people outside the family a nickname will do.'

At night Fat Maria came to see her, and Dona Julia, and Suliman, there were long conversations in Yoruba, Mariana looked down at the brick floor of the kitchen, she went out for a while, a strong smell of the sea came from the direction of the harbour, Emilia was playing with the wooden doll, Antônio had got into the way of going about naked, he was rolling about on the ground in the street, he was going to get all dirty, a noise of little girls shouting came through the night, Mariana thought about her grandmother's name, Ainá was a pretty name, nicer than Catarina, how could she have hidden that name for all those years?, she examined her own name, Mariana, it wasn't at all bad, at the end of the street she met Abigail, asked her how school was, the girl replied:

'I've left as well. My mother thinks it's time I got married.'

'How is Sister Mary?'

'She's fine, at first she was always going on about you not going back. She says you need to study.'

Abigail told her about the boy she was going to marry, he was from Alagoas, he had arrived in Lagos a year before her, had a shop on the sea-front, then she said that Mabel was married already, to a rich Ibo, but it seemed his penis was very big, at the beginning Mabel had had a bad time, then she went on to tell the story about the man who had a small penis, he went to the doctor, who gave him some medicine for it, the man took the whole bottle, his penis wouldn't stop growing, he had to wrap it round his waist to get to the doctor's again, Mariana was in the middle of laughing at this when they called her, her grandmother was worse, candles and lanterns filled the room, the girl spent the whole night sitting on a corner of the mat, Ainá, who had been known until then as Catarina, died at ten o'clock in the morning, the sunlight was blazing on the front of Dona Zezé's house, she came out with a long dress on, tiny steps, she looked for Epifânia:

'We must wash the body and prepare the serenata. You are going to need drink, lots of biscuits, pastries, bean-cakes, carurú, cakes, two drummers, a guitarist, a flute-player, a clarinetist, tables and chairs. And you will have to kill a goat. Anything you don't have, I'll lend you.'

Epifânia agreed, the other went on:

'She is the first one to die of those who arrived on the *Esperança*. A lot of people have died already from the other ships. You must have a fine serenata. I'll get a lot of cowries for you to give out as people arrive; that way they'll all think well of her.'

Fat Maria, Dona Julia, Old Teresa, Seu Alexandre's wife, Seu Costa's wife and Abigail's sister took Ainá's body, Dona Zezé gave instructions, they carried it out into the yard, put it on top of three packing cases, told stories about other deaths. Ainá's body was wasted, the women brought tubs and more tubs full of water, poured it on to the body, scrubbed it hard, soaped the hair, the ears, Mariana watched the washing with a sort of fear, old Teresa shouted at her:

'Come and help to wash your grandmother's body. Rub hard so that she can go into your belly and be born from you, be your daughter, come back to the world through you, and if that does happen it will be a good thing if she's born nice and clean.'

Mariana took a brush, went up to the body, old Teresa guided her hand in what she had to do, the soapy water made a channel that ran into the big drain in the street, Ainá's body when they had finished was clean and sweet-smelling, it was afternoon when some servants of Dona Zezé came with chairs and tables, which they put down in front of the dead woman's house, there was a general air of happiness as the time for the party drew near, Dona Zezé changed her clothes and sat down with Epifânia:

'We'll bury your mother in the square over there where the English still allow us to have burials. The best thing is to bury your dead in the room where they lived or in the front of the house, but unfortunately they don't allow us to do that here in the town. Early tomorrow morning, straight after the serenata, we'll have the burial.'

Epifânia went to the kitchen in Dona Zezé's house and helped with the pastries and the cakes, Mariana went with her grandmother's body which they took to her room and placed on top of the boxes, Seu Gaspar came

91

in, said he had permission from Epifânia, he had a knife in his right hand, he began to shave off her grandmother's hair, Teresa explained:

'She was consecrated to a saint, she must have *ossu* in her head.'

When all the hair had gone a little lump stood out on the hairy scalp, Seu Gaspar made a cut in it and took something out, while this was happening the women were singing lovely songs which Mariana was hearing for the first time and which seemed to come from long ago, straight afterwards Teresa, Dona Julia and Fat Maria came up to the body, tied a coloured kerchief round Ainá's head, Mariana thought it made her grandmother look more handsome, almost imposing, dressed in blue cloth, her hands crossed, a neighbour came up to the body, said some words in Yoruba and danced a few steps in front of the dead woman.

Night was falling when Epifânia came back, she dressed Emilia and Antônio, told Mariana to put on the dress she had worn for her first communion, the four of them went to where the party was to be held, there were a lot of chairs in the street, Dona Zezé arrived and Epifânia gave her a cowrie, Suliman came with his family, each of them was given a cowrie, when Mariana counted there were more than a hundred people, the drummers played by themselves for a while, then the man with the guitar arrived, later on the flute-player and the clarinetist, they started to play gay music, at one point Dona Zezé filled a plate with pieces of roast kid, bean-cakes and caruru, and covered it all with a lace cloth that was very white and stiff with starch, she called Epifânia and her family, and said:

'It's the food for the spirits.'

She took the plate out to the back of the house, left it in a dark corner of the yard, now the music was getting more lively, Dona Julia was walking around between the tables and singing, a boy danced to Mariana, the bottle of cachaça went from hand to hand, Suliman laughed but didn't drink anything, a youth arrived with a tambourine, at one time the man with the guitar was playing by himself, he sang:

> If Ainá knew
> That today was her day
> She'd come down from heaven
> And be gay.

Fat Maria said:
'Perhaps she does know and she's here, with us all.'
Everyone laughed, Mariana looked all around her, tried the cachaça, it had a disgusting taste, it burned her tongue and throat, the guitarist went on improvising:

> Ainá was good and gentle
> By night and by day
> She always smiled, she always laughed
> Cheerful and gay.

It was late when Mariana realized that a lot of people were drunk, Seu Alexandre had closed his eyes and fallen asleep sitting in his chair, lanterns and oil-lamps lit up the street, there was still some roast meat left, the bean-cakes and the pastries had all gone, she went in and out, bringing more plates, boys and girls were flirting in the corners, once when she went into the house she went into her grandmother's room, the body was wrapped in a brightly-coloured cloth, four candles alight, the rest of the room empty, the noise of the dancing came in from outside, the clarinetist could be heard over everything else now, when he stopped the two drums beat on alone, Mariana went back outside, the boy who had danced for her wanted to talk, she refused, said she was busy, she had to look after the guests, Seu Alexandre had laid his head on the table, Fat Maria looked very happy, she burst out laughing when the improviser sang:

If Ainá comes back to this world
Let her come rich and come wealthy
Let her come cheerful and gay
Let her come fat and come healthy.

Fat Maria looked as if she had had quite a lot to drink, she slapped Mariana on the back:

'It's much better to be fat, girl. Try to put on weight.'

The musicians stayed until the end, they played fados, polkas, a lot of people were asleep in their chairs and there was one lively group, Abigail and Fat Maria and four men. The coffin, which had been ordered from a carpenter called João, arrived just before dawn, Dona Zezé protested:

'Where have you been?'

'I had no wood today, Dona Zezé. I had to send for it by canoe.'

They picked up Ainá, placed her in the coffin, by the time the sun shone on the dead woman they had already taken the tables and chairs away fron the front of the house, at seven o'clock Father O'Malley arrived, prayed over the body, and left again. It wasn't far to go, Epifânia started to cry, but Dona Zezé wouldn't let her:

'A dead person who has lived a good life should not be wept for. Be happy.'

Then she knelt down and kissed Ainá's hand, said:

'The dead are gods. They know more than we do.'

The clarinetist held his instrument carefully, he looked exhausted, he went along at the head of the procession and improvised some tunes that were half happy, half sad. There weren't many graves in the square, some flowers were growing in the middle, children were playing in the distance, the coffin went down slowly, Mariana watched, each of them took a handful of earth, threw it into the grave, four men with shovels began to fill it in, Epifânia saw herself leaving Piau, Uncle Inhaim's house down there below, now she was far away from everyone

94

she had grown up with, surrounded by new friends, Mariana was a woman, she would be getting married soon, the little ones were growing, she had to face up to life, but who knows whether it might not have been better to have stayed in Piau, with her own people, or in Bahia, with Father José? Mariana saw that her first communion dress was dirty, she must have been careless during the night when she was carrying plates of food about, the children who were playing came up to the grave, Fat Maria embraced Epifânia and Mariana and the two children, at the end they were left alone, her mother pulled Mariana, they walked back to Bangboshe Street, went into the house, Epifânia got hold of the three packing cases and said to the girl:

'Do you want to help me? Bring the box with the obis and the orobos.'

They went out into the street again, at the corner of Campos Square Epifânia arranged the packing cases like a counter, piled the obis and the orobos up into little heaps, unrolled a piece of tobacco, told Mariana to sit beside her and shouted to the children:

'Play here beside us.'

A few days later the teacher Seu João Batista, who gave classes for the Brazilian children, asked Mariana if she would go and work for him.

'What would I do?'

'Teach the youngest ones.'

'But I have never taught before.'

'That doesn't matter. You went to school with the Sisters, you must have learnt a lot.'

Seu João Batista lived in Tokunboh Street, the classes were held in the front room of his house, Mariana spent the whole of Sunday unable to think of anything else, how could she face it?, she didn't sleep all night, on Monday she put on a print dress, in the teacher's house the pupils sat on the ground, Mariana stopped being frightened as soon as she began giving the class, the children were working from Brazilian primers, afterwards she went to talk to the teacher:

'They are talking in Yoruba and learning to read in Portuguese. It's all going to get mixed up inside their heads.'

'There aren't any Yoruba primers. And in any case, they are all Brazilians or children of Brazilians. They must learn their own language.'

Their own language, which language belonged to whom? She had learnt Yoruba and English, she was forgetting the English she had learnt at school now, she would have to go and see Mabel and her Ibo friends who spoke English if she wasn't to lose it. Seu Batista didn't pay her much, but it helped, and Epifânia was proud to be able to say that her daughter was a teacher, the children began to call for her at the house, when Mariana went to sell obis and orobos some of them stood there talking to her, Emilia and Antônio began to study with her, Emilia was a quick learner, but Antônio was careless, he couldn't draw the letters properly, and when she asked him to read 'Ivo viu a uva' he mixed up the vowels, maybe on purpose, he would say 'Uva vio o Ivo' or 'Vivo vuva viu', afterwards Mariana thought that they were wrong to force him, he didn't want to read, he liked making things, playing about with pieces of wood, making little tables, perhaps it would be best if he were to go and work with João the Carpenter, she talked to her mother, who said:

'He can go and work with João the Carpenter afterwards, but first he must learn to read.'

Emilia was attractive, she had a sweet smile, she was getting prettier every day, every so often Mariana asked herself: Am I pretty?, here in Africa she found that people weren't very interested in whether you were pretty or not, in Brazil they had been, she stood naked in her grandmother's room, which was hers now, saw that her sex was thickly covered with hair, her breasts were big, during classes, while the pupils were writing out exercises she forgot all about them and looked out of the window, life outside there, the warm winds of Lagos coming in carrying the smells of life.

Epifânia spent most of the day and the night on her corner. During the long rainless months she slept out there, beside the boxes, Mariana was big now and could look after the house, on one of these nights Jerónimo turned up, he was a fisherman, he sat down beside Epifânia, they started to talk, soon they were in each other's arms, the street was deserted, a dog was barking in the distance, she put out the lantern, the mat scratched against the ground, this man was heavier than any she had known, he smelt of fish, she remembered Bahia, the stall in the market-place, Father José, this was the first time she had had a man since she arrived in Lagos, the gutter of water which ran alongside shone when she lit the lantern again, clouds were moving through the air against the stars. Jerónimo came to see her from time to time, they didn't have much to say to each other, he only talked about fish, what both of them wanted was to enjoy each other, afterwards Epifânia would lie naked on the mat for a long time, thinking about life, going over the things she had done or was going to do, planning her expenses, until one day what they earned was more than what they had to spend, Mariana had started giving lessons to the children of rich Brazilians, one night Jerónimo asked:

'Wouldn't it be better if I came to your house?'

'No. The house is not the place for this.'

'What is the place then? Here in the middle of the street?'

'That's right: the middle of the street.'

Another night he told her:

'There's a Brazilian ship anchored in the harbour.'

'Is it the *Esperança*?'

'No. It's a different one.'

The next morning Epifânia and Mariana went to see

97

it. It was the *Biáfora*, a medium sized steamship, had it brought many people?, apparently it hadn't, only one family, but it was unloading tobacco, and cachaça and dried salt meat. One Sunday, Father O'Malley came to speak to her after Mass.

'Would it be possible for Mariana to teach the catechism at church?'

'Of course, Father, she will be very happy to do it.'

Epifânia's English was dreadful, the Brazilians didn't make much effort to speak it well, but there was the church, all the priests were Irish, only one of them had managed to learn Yoruba, he was the one who had made all the other priests agree to let men and women come to communion wearing brightly coloured hats, sometimes paper hats, they looked like fantasies out of a Brazilian carnival or ornaments on egungun masks. Mariana started to teach catechism, it was good for her because the catechism was written in English, it stopped her from forgetting the language.

Epifânia talked a lot to women who belonged to the country, the ones who spoke only Yoruba and not Portuguese, she didn't agree with polygamy, she knew that a lot of Brazilians had taken it up, there were some men who, a year after they were married, took a second wife, then a third, one of her new friends said:

'It's quite right for a man to have more than one wife. And we can have more than one man.'

'But not in the same house.'

None of them were jealous, it was true that Epifânia herself didn't know what it was to be jealous, the man she had liked best had been Father José and there had been no cause for jealousy with him, at night when Jerónimo came she asked herself if she could ever be jealous of him. No, never. In Piau, when she was a girl, there hadn't been time to think about things like that, there was plenty of work to be done, but no real worries, it was in Bahia and here in Lagos that she had to calculate exactly how much she was going to earn, everything cost money, the smallest profit was important.

They were laying tracks all round the island, one day Bangboshe Street had a celebration, they were going to start a suburban train, there was a little engine, with a tall thin chimney, behind it there were wagons for people and goods, it ran to most parts of the island, along the sea front, whenever it appeared the children would scream happily. On Sundays, after Mariana had given her catechism class, the family used to go out for the day, Epifânia liked Ikoyi, that was where the Brazilians had planted cashew trees and had their picnics on the feast of Bonfim, or else they went to visit friends, especially the ones who had come in the same ship, it seemed that the *Esperança* had been the last ship to bring a large group of people, each of their companions on that voyage had his own life now, Suliman had opened a shop, Alberto was a carpenter, Ambrósio, Ciriaco and Silvanus were masons, Rosinha, Abigail's sister, was going to marry the son of a Brazilian in Warri, Fat Maria took in washing and starching, Dona Julia made sweets and cakes and biscuits, when Epifânia went to see her with the family they all had delicious things to eat, all of them visited each other regularly, they formed a sort of society in Lagos, alongside all the other groups, the fraternity of St José, of Our Lady of Joy, of Our Lord of Bonfim. Other Sundays they would cross the bridge and visit Apapa or Yaba, or they would take a canoe and go through the lagoons and canals which stretched across Badagri as far as Dahomey, Togo and Zorei. On the other side lay the peaceful expanse of Tarqua Bay, once they went to Victoria beach, huge and deserted. They had been in Lagos for two years before they went on foot to Ibadan, the train was too dear. Up and down hill they went, Mariana found the town enchanting, she wandered through the market, creatures she had never seen before, an enormous snail, with a shell that looked like a sea-shell, they stayed with the Borges sisters, their friends from the ship, Luisa was married to an important Yoruba, she took Mariana and Epifânia into a temple of Shango, it was dark inside, the girl looked at the wooden statue, once again she saw the killing of the ram in Bahia, the statues had been the same, her mother put her hand on the ground and then on her forehead, she did the same, in the afternoon Luisa gave a party to welcome the visitors, two drummers sat outside the house beating their drums and singing, while the guests arrived, only women, it was the first time Mariana had been to a party without men, after they had eaten bean-cakes and drunk something that tasted rather bitter the mistress of the house began to dance, she stopped in front of the guests, Epifânia got up and danced as well, the others were clapping their hands, one of them made a sign to Mariana to join in, she obeyed, afterwards they chatted, Luisa sat next to her, they talked of this and that until the subject that Mariana had been wondering about came up:

'Do you often have parties without men?'

'A few times every week.'

Mariana wanted to know why, her friend told her that she had thought about it a lot but hadn't been able to discover the reason, she had heard that in some villages in the interior they cut off a woman's clitoris so that she didn't feel such a need for men, her head was clearer, she took control in business, ruled the village, it was a sort of matriarchy, but this didn't happen in Ibadan, at least not as far as she knew, none of her acquaintances had had their clitoris removed, but they still had a sort of liberty in their relations with men which amazed the Brazilians. She added:

'But I agree that it's better to have parties without men. I've got used to it now. You don't need to be so self-conscious, you feel freer.'

'What about your husband?'

'He's never at home in the afternoons.'

That night Mariana thought of the paths she had travelled, from Piau to this place, for the first time she remembered the face of the man who had taken the family from Piau to Juiz de Fora, what had he been called?, he had been pleasant, nice to have at a party, in Lagos too there were nice boys with smiling faces, who loved dancing, she saw again her grandmother's serenata, the boy who had tried to talk to her. She would have to get married one day, go to bed with a man, have children, look after them, cook, she had done it all already except sleeping with a man, she looked after her brother and sister, worked in the kitchen, a sudden wind came in through the window, Mariana got up and went to look out, Ibadan had lights everywhere, tiny points of light going up the hills, life didn't stop at night, it seemed to get more intense, people were going by in the street, voices that were excited, or calm, or raucous, laughter, the market beside Luisa's house was full of activity, Mariana leaned her cheek against the side of the window, the brick was cold, she watched the ceaseless life of Ibadan until dawn, the next day they all said that she and Epifânia ought to go to Ife, the sacred city of the Yorubas, it wasn't far, they set out with a group of women who were carrying bales of cloth on their heads, they stopped halfway there to eat, all spread their mats out on the ground, untied the children from their backs, told stories, the sound of the Yoruba in that region was a bit different from the Yoruba of Lagos, Ife was a quiet, calm place, it made you want to close your eyes and let things take their course, they slept in the market-place, a good smell of meat roasting on an open fire filled the place where they slept the whole night long, then they started back, they were on the road for several days, it was full of life, like a city street, they never went many minutes without meeting groups of people, usually women, huge roots of yam on their heads, or calabashes of palm wine, or fruit, or bales of cloth. Epifânia thought of Emilia and Antônio, who had stayed behind with Fat Maria, the Yoruba women travelled with their small children tied to their back, it was easier, when they arrived back in Lagos the heat was unbearable, she got out the boxes and set them up on the corner of Campos Square, as well as obis, orobos, tobacco and cachaça she now sold bean-cakes made by Fat Maria, at night Jerónimo came to see her:

'I thought you were never coming back.'

She didn't like this:

'And I think you're getting too much like a husband. Husbands are too demanding.'

They talked for a while, soon they were clinging to each other, the rainy season came, the sky dark, water falling unceasingly for days at a time, it was impossible to sell in the street, the only money they had was what Mariana earned, one day she got the idea of making the front room into a sort of eating-house, providing meals for men who were living away from their families, who were working for the English and didn't know where to go to eat, within a few weeks they had four steady customers, one Yoruba, one Ibo and two Hausas, the Hausas were like Suliman, they prayed facing Mecca, wore gaily-coloured cloths round their heads, the Yoruba tried to get hold of her one afternoon, she pushed him away, she used to set the table twice a day, at night she stayed at the window watching the rain falling and listening to the neighbours talking, there was a Brazilian book called *The Guarani* that Seu João Batista had given her, it entertained her for a long time, it was the story of a Brazilian Indian and a young white girl, the Indian did everything he could to make the girl happy, at the end the two of them were left clinging to a palm tree which was being swept away by the river, she imagined the flood in Piau and the Indian and the girl being carried past Uncle Inhaim's house on the rushing torrent.

She saw herself in the place of the girl and the Indian had the face of the young Negro with the drum whom she had caught sight of just when they were leaving Bahia, he hadn't come on the ship, Mariana wanted more books to read, she found another, *The Little Dark-haired Girl*, in Fat Maria's house, asked:

'How did this book get here?'

'I can't think. Probably someone left it behind.'

Then Mariana got tired of reading, it was better just looking at things, even when it was raining, the little train went backwards and forwards, sometimes she felt a kind of remoteness, as if she had stopped being who she was, or being anybody, and had become an object, almost immobile, one day Fat Maria protested:

'You never laugh these days. What's wrong?'

It was true. She didn't laugh any more. She felt sorry for her mother when she noticed her dejected air as she served at table, carried the plates to the customers, or the way she stopped Jerónimo visiting her, Mariana found him repellent, his enormous hands, they seemed like the hands of a giant, but his body was small, his eyes seemed oddly tame. Mariana stayed awake at nights wondering what life was going to be like for all of them, her mother had got used to Lagos, she went to parties, talked, worked, but she wasn't the same. The last time she had seen her really happy had been in Bahia, when they were at Father José's house, Mariana remembers how Epifânia used to smile, and sing, even when she was silent her eyes had a light of enthusiasm, she recalled scenes of that time in her life, when she too had felt free and happy. It hurt when her mother told her:

'I'm here in Lagos, daughter, but I only need to close my eyes and I feel as if I'm back in Piau, the yard in front of the church just across from our house, the window that opened on to the river. Other times, it's as if it were Bahia, Father José's house is there in front of me, the church on one side, the tower he used to throw things off, it was very high and grand.'

She paused for a minute, as if she were searching for details, then went on:

'He used to drink a lot, do you remember?'

The noise of Bangboshe Street, where a group of women were talking, came into the room for a moment. She put an end to the subject:

'He drank a lot, but he was a good man.'

Thinking about all this, Mariana tried hard to adapt herself to Lagos, to see the good side of everything, when she went out into the streets she walked quickly, every time the rain stopped she was there walking along the sea-shore, she always stopped at the place where the blood had flowed from her for the first time, she went to see the fishermen casting their nets out into the lagoon, went to friends' houses, talked for hours to Dona Zezé, to old Teresa, to the Sisters of Charity, to Father O'Malley, she didn't want to be like her mother, living here but with her thoughts somewhere else, she noticed the fights between the Brazilians and the people of the land, said that she thought they ought to stop, there was one aristocracy of people who had come to Lagos in this or that ship, and another of people who had lived there for a long time, Seu Alexandre had not let his daughter marry a Yoruba from Oshogbo, Mariana began to visit African houses more often, she became friendly with several Ibo families, the Ibos were Catholics as well, she had to speak English to them, she got into the way of discussing the problems of life in Lagos with Yorubas, it was better with them, she spoke in Yoruba, one day, when she went into the parlour of one of their houses, it was Ogundip's, she saw him painting a set of wooden masks, it was just before the geledé festival, men wearing the masks would go out into the street and dance to the sound of drums to placate the evil spirits, Mariana took up the first mask that was to be used in the festival, put her fingers through the eyes of the carved face, at night she told her mother what she had seen. When classes began again she was glad to see her pupils, many of them had forgotten their Portuguese because of talking Yoruba so much in the streets, now the classes, the street-selling and the meals they sold brought in good money.

One night Mariana had gone out to see some friends, her mother had decided to stay at home, the children were playing in the street, when a man came in and tried to get Epifânia down on the mat, she picked up a piece of brick and hit him on the head with it, the blood dripped from his forehead, when Mariana got back she found her mother sitting on the ground, a lamp alight beside her and a man lying wounded and unconscious. She went and called Fat Maria who lived very close, the three of them dragged the man out into the street, Mariana stayed awake for most of the night at the window, watching to see what would happen, at daybreak the man got up, looked around, brushed down his clothes and walked off towards Campos Square. The women decided to lock the door at night, until then they had never used a lock, a bar or even a latch had seemed enough, suddenly Mariana realized that she was sixteen years old, Emilia must be nearly a woman, it would be a good thing to send her to Topo, Antônio went on playing in the streets, sometimes he disappeared for the whole day, ate in the house of someone they knew. When Seu Alexandre told Epifânia that there was a young man interested in marrying Mariana the family were astonished. Who was he? No-one had noticed any young man showing particular interest. Seu Alexandre explained:

'He is Sebastian Silva. His father came in the *Santa Isabel*.'

Mariana saw the boy at Mass the next Sunday. The bench the Silva family sat in was at the front, Epifânia asked:

'What does he do?'

'He works for the English.'

Seu Justino Silva, the father, came to visit Epifânia and informed her that his son wanted to get to know Mariana better, with a view to marriage. Sebastian spent one evening with her, they walked along Bangboshe, sat down beside the sea. Her mother was worrying about the African custom of polygamy, she asked everyone if there were any men in the Silva family who had more than one wife, they said that there was one, he lived in Ogbomosho, who had four wives, the first had been Brazilian, she had refused to accept the situation, had left him to the other three, each of them had her own room. While Sebastian and Mariana were out walking, Epifânia knocked on the door of Seu Justino Silva's house, after they had talked for a while she said:

'You know that a Brazilian woman won't have anything to do with a man who has more than one woman.'

The man laughed, he asked:

'Where is there a man who has not had more than one woman? He hasn't been born yet.'

She was confused, but managed to explain herself:

'It does no harm to have more than one woman in the street. The bad thing is to marry two or three and have them all as legitimate wives.'

Seu Justino assured her that that would not happen, his son had been well brought up, he had studied for a long time, he worked for an English firm, was a Catholic.

On the bench, with the sea in front of them, Sebastian was saying:

'I've noticed you ever since your grandmother's serenata. Did you know?'

No, she hadn't known, the first time she remembered seeing him was at Mass the previous Sunday, he had a good face, his lips, thick and strong, had a slow smile, it came slowly and went slowly, he wore light-coloured clothes, not in the African style, but a jacket and trousers like the Brazilians. The next day, Fat Maria sat out with

Mariana on chairs in the street, told her about the Silva family, they weren't rich, but everyone thought well of them, they all liked Seu Justino, the boy hadn't done anything much yet, but they said the English praised his work.

A few days later Seu Justino came looking for Epifânia, asked if Mariana was a virgin. Her mother replied:

'Of course she is, but if she hadn't been, what would have been wrong in it?'

The girl saw very little of Sebastian, every week or ten days they met, sometimes they sat in the parlour or, like in Brazil, put chairs out in the street and talked there, with Epifânia and Fat Maria, Antônio would sit on Sebastian's knee, pull his watch out from his pocket, listen to its tick, Emilia looked at the boy from a distance, when the date of the betrothal party was fixed Epifânia counted up her money, she would have to buy presents for the boy's parents, order Mariana's dress, and pay for the drink, make food for the day, she decided to ask all the passengers of the *Esperança*, the voyage came back not only to her memory but to her body as well, again she felt herself living through the long weeks of calm, the ship motionless, the sea as smooth as the floor in a house, from time to time she remembered people she had seen when she had been in a strange state of detachment herself, or she remembered the hunger, when she didn't want to eat in the ship, not because there was not enough flour or dried meat, but because she had no desire to eat or to make any other effort, at each moment then Epifânia had felt that the past was returning, and this return to the past continued in Lagos, she even went to ask the priests at the church about it in her clumsy English, the oldest of them, Father O'Neill, tried to tell her what he felt, for him the past and the present were all one, they were not separated, that afternoon Epifânia wished she was dead, she truly desired it, just to rest, it seemed to her that Father José was waiting for her just a little way beyond Bangboshe Street, perhaps in Campos Square, or at the end of the island, or in Abeokuta, it was the memory of her mother, the woman called Ainá, that gave her strength to resist the temptation to go up to the priest from Bahia, lie down with him, open her legs for him, smell the drink on his breath as he entered her, in that calm way that Father José had of doing everything, today it was different, she had to get her daughter married, Mariana was grown up now, her breasts pushed at her dress, she didn't laugh any more, spent whole days looking out into the street, or going out, talking to all sorts of people, the best thing would be for her to have a man as soon as possible, no matter who, Seu Justino Silva's son would do as well as any, she felt herself bound to the world in which her children were growing up, but it was as if these bonds were always on the point of breaking, she forgot that she was in Africa, heard the voice of Uncle Inhaim, it had been the first sound she had respected, she saw the River Piau running at her feet, now the waters rushed by, mud-coloured, now they were calm, almost green, the grass dragging in the flow of the gleaming water which ran away from you and disappeared at the bend where the old house was, Epifânia had never seen anyone living there, it was there that she had first been with a man, Mariana's father had taken her there one hot afternoon, nothing seemed to move in Piau, just as the man made her cry out with pleasure a dog came in, it barked a bit, neither of them paid any attention to it, now Mariana would soon be penetrated by another man, the marriage wasn't far off, when Epifânia saw Sebastian she tried to decide what sort of a man he was, what he would be like in sex, what he would do with her daughter, or perhaps here in Africa they weren't in such a hurry as they had been in Piau, there as soon as a girl began to grow hairs they grabbed her, the black girls anyway, one used to tell the others what had happened, then the ones who hadn't been with a man yet were wild for it to happen to them, one night Epifânia saw Sebastian holding Mariana close, the street was dark, only one lantern shone far away, she turned away and looked at Emilia who was asleep on the floor, went to her and pulled a blanket up around her shoulders, sat down and closed her eyes.

Mariana had got used to Sebastian, she didn't miss him during the week, but she liked it when he came, on a day they had fixed, or after Mass, and they talked about all sorts of things, she found that he didn't try to dominate her, she had heard it said that in Lagos the men liked to have several wives, she had thought about it a lot, perhaps it wasn't such a bad idea, although her mother said that no Brazilian woman could stand it, she remembered the party without men in Ibadan and decided that, even if the men did have more than one woman, at least they left them free to enjoy themselves in their own way, nevertheless one day she was furious for hours simply because Sebastian, as he was coming out of Mass, had given a long look at one of the Ribeiro girls, she was only thirteen, but she seemed older, Mariana was amazed at her own reaction, how was it that she could think it didn't matter if a man had more than one woman, or a woman more than one man, and yet at the same time be wretched because she saw Sebastian looking at someone who was still just a child? The next time he came he pretended she wasn't interested in him, looked around her all the time and wouldn't meet his eyes, she ended up even more furious because he didn't seem to notice that anything was wrong, the next Sunday she missed Mass, told her mother she was ill, Sebastian wanted to come and see her, she wouldn't let him come for week after week, Epifânia wanted to know:

'What has he done?'

Mariana made a show of being busy, putting something away in the parlour, or in her bedroom, she answered:

'Nothing. I don't want to talk to anybody.'

By the time they finally did meet again, Mariana was sure that it wasn't right for a man to have a lot of wives, she had thought about it a lot, in Piau all the men only had one wife, in Bahia as well, of course there was the man with sixty-one children, but everything seemed different to her now, the things that had been funny in the market-place talk now seemed wrong, Seu Justino Silva came to see her mother to fix the day of the betrothal, they decided on the month of January just after the feast of Bonfim, on the feast-day that year the Mass was even more crowded than usual, there was no room at all in the church, her mother said it was because some Brazilians had arrived from Dahomey, at the picnic afterwards on Ikoyi Island Mariana found some cashew trees, Sebastian pulled down some of the fruits for her, now whenever he touched her hands Mariana felt a liquid forming in her sex, she was afraid to move from where she was because she knew she was all wet and the fear that everyone would look at her and notice this held her still, unable to move.

On the day of the engagement party, very early, Fat Maria, Seu Alexandre's daughter-in-law, Abigail, old Teresa, Suliman's wife, Luisa Borges, who had come from Ibadan, and two more Brazilian girls who had arrived in Lagos since the *Esperança* all gathered in the back yard of the house, they began to make sweets, Epifânia had bought trays, Mariana tried on some beautiful pieces of cloth that Luisa had brought her, she tried them on her head and round her body, as darkness was falling people began to arrive, there wasn't enough room inside, chairs were put in the yard and out in the street for the guests, the girl stayed until late in the room that had belonged to her grandmother, she heard the voices of the people arriving, sometimes it was an old passenger of the *Esperança*, all the jokes about men and women seemed to her in bad taste, she put dresses on, took them off again, looked at her face in a little mirror that Sebastian had given her, she couldn't remember who it was who had told her that mirrors brought bad luck, lots of Brazilian women in Lagos wouldn't look in one, Dona Zezé declared that the mirror took away your soul, or at least it could take it away little by little, until, after looking in a mirror for a few years, you felt yourself empty, no soul, no anything. It was dark when her mother brought her a glass of cachaça. She said:

'Drink it.'

She drank it. Again she felt the strong taste of the drink, concentrated on fighting against it, then she saw Fat Maria, who was coming in with a coloured cloth in her hands:

'It's time.'

Epifânia and Fat Maria called some other women into the bedroom, the noise of their voices was gay, Mariana smiled at all this happiness, Fat Maria put a cloth over her own head and shouted:

'Now I'm going out.'

In the living-room, Seu Justino Silva and his wife, with their relatives all around them, were laughing at everything, a jug of palm wine was going the rounds, others were drinking cachaça, when the woman came in with the cloth over her head, with women crowding around her and Luisa and Abigail at her side, the Yoruba words cut through the noise, they said:

'Is this her?'

The father and the mother of the boy shouted:

'No!'

And everyone in the room shouted No. Luisa and Abigail lifted the cloth and Fat Maria's head appeared, her smiling mouth, she pulled a face, danced a few steps and went back into the bedroom. The next one to put on the cloth was Abigail, she was taken out into the other room, the shouts were louder still:

'Is this her?'

The father and the mother and everyone else shouted No even louder.

It was time for Mariana to cover her head and go out into the room, for a moment she didn't know what to do, pushed away the cloth that Fat Maria, laughing, had thrown at her face, went to the door and looked out, Seu Justino was refilling his glass, the whiteish colour of the wine rose up it, they put the cloth over her by force, pulled her out of the bedroom, Fat Maria made her kneel down, she was on the ground when she heard the question, now a deafening shout:

'Is this her?'

Everyone joined in a *Yes* that made the whole place echo, Mariana felt them pulling the cloth off her head, the smiling face of Seu Justino was in front of her, the girl did as she had been taught, got to her feet and took up a tray on which there was fruit and several bottles of drink, gave it to Sebastian's parents, everyone shrieked their approval, Seu Justino took the tray, put his hand on the fruit, looked at the bottles, and, with a ritual laugh, nodded his head as a sign that he accepted the gifts. Then the girl smoothed down her dress, put the cloth that had been on her head around her shoulders, knelt down with her hands together as if she were catching water from a fountain and put her forehead to the ground in front of her bridegroom's parents. Seu Justino Silva and his wife touched her head with their hands, raised her up, kissed her on the cheeks and embraced her. Mariana greeted the old people who were there, there was one Brazilian woman of ninety-five, they said she had been in Lagos for more than sixty years, she had been a friend of the Brazilian Papai Bangboshe, who had been opposed to the English in those days, she came up to the girl, took her in her arms, touched her cheek to Mariana's first one side, then the other, Mariana went out of the room into the kitchen and brought in a tray of bean-cakes, pastries and other things to eat, Epifânia, Fat Maria, Abigail, all did the same, even little Emilia came in with a plate in her hands, they were the presents from the bride's family to the bridegroom's, now the drummers speeded up their beat, the flute-player was waiting with his flute ready in his hand, when a silence fell he played alone, night was around them with the sound of the flute.

Then a big noise came from outside, happy cries, shouts in Yoruba that seemed to mark the rhythm of a dance, and Sebastian came into the room with lots of friends, he was wearing a suit of fine English wool, his waistcoat adding a final touch of elegance, his friends were dressed in African style, coloured cloths draped round their bodies, embroidered caps on their heads, there were blue robes, red ones, everyone was smiling, the flute broke into a series of variations, everyone clapped their hands, Sebastian knelt in front of Epifânia, put his forehead to the ground, then sat for the interrogation, all around him everyone was laughing, Seu Alexandre asked:

'Have you enough money to support a wife?'

The laughter grew even louder, old Teresa wanted to know:

'Do you know how to treat a woman, in bed and out of it?'

After almost everyone present had asked a question, and the bridegroom had replied respectfully or wittily, Sebastian sat waiting, broadly smiling and looking as if life could not be more delightful, when Mariana came back into the room she put her hand in his, the two of them stayed seated, replying to all the questions they were asked, one wanted to know when they were getting married, another how many children they would have, all the drink began to have its effect, Mariana remembered the betrothal of Amelia in Piau, they had played the piano, the child she had been then had felt cold that night, her grandmother had stayed in the kitchen the whole time, when they left there was poor Amelia with her wedding put off because of the flood, now over the candles and the lamps she saw the faces of her friends in Lagos, black faces shining in the light, men smoking corn-husk cigars, Fat Maria quaking all over as she danced alone in the middle of the room, making everyone shout with laughter.

Mariana spent the months of her betrothal getting to know Sebastian, each meeting took them further into their knowledge of each other, men react to things in a different way from women, from childhood she had learnt how to deal with women, her grandmother, her mother, Emilia, her girlfriends, Antônio didn't count, he was still a child, she thought of Father José, he had been good to her, but she had never paid enough attention to him, during those months Mariana looked more carefully at all men, examined their behaviour, Seu João Batista used to go for days without speaking to her, a lot of men came to the stall where she and her mother sold things, sometimes they would take up an obi, bite into it slowly, look at the girls going by, a lot of them had their breasts uncovered, they were from the interior, some men only seemed to want to drink cachaça, they didn't take any notice of women, and then there were men who had a lot of children like the man in Bahia, and men like the one who had come on board to say goodbye to Ainá and had saluted her so beautifully, Mariana could still remember his orikis, she heard orikis sometimes in Lagos, especially in the houses of people who had been born in Africa, they always received her with a special greeting, O you who come clothed in a red skirt and are mistress of all rich things, may your family be strong and happy, O you who sell obis in the street, may your riches grow and multiply, O generous one, queen of the yam and the fish, may your abundance feed a whole city, the orikis, they stayed in Mariana's memory for weeks, she thought in orikis, O bridegroom, you who come to give me sons, may you be chief of the land and master of horses, O mother who brought me to the light and taught me to walk, to see and to judge, may your serenata be celebrated after a hundred years, she imagined orikis all the time, said them inside her head to Seu João Batista, to her friends, to Father O'Malley, to people who were still in Bahia, O Father José who drank peacefully with your arms outstretched on the table, may your faithful love you always and surround you with affection and respect, she thought up orikis for the children who came to her classes, invented them for streets, for trees, there was a flamboyant on the road to Ikoyi, from far away Mariana sent it orikis, O tree with scarlet blossoms may your roots be always firm within the earth, she composed orikis for animals she came across in the street, O sheep browsing in the garden may you never guess how you are to die, at night she made orikis for everything around her, the table, the chairs, the boxes from which she sold obis, in her mind she sent orikis to the lizards that appeared in every corner, some had green bodies, some had bodies the colour of ash and scarlet heads, they nodded their heads as if they were greeting you, on Sundays she prayed in orikis, O Lady of Joy may you always be my guardian, O Blessed Holy Ghost of Piau, holy bird, sacred bird, may your wings be for ever beautiful and may you light up my mind so that I can understand everything that should be understood, orikis came to her for Shango, O lord of the fire and the thunder may we always receive justice from your two-headed axe, for the soul of the dead, for Ainá, O you who are gone, O dead one, O washed, O clothed, O praised, O buried, may you be happy wherever you are, and if you return to this life may you come as a beautiful woman or a wealthy man, she made the orikis in Yoruba and in Portuguese, felt herself at one with things around her each time she made one.

The wedding was to be in May, for weeks beforehand Mariana imagined to herself how it would all be, I see her standing at the window, her mind a confusion of thoughts about the wedding and orikis, Seu Justino was insisting that after the wedding his son and daughter-in-law should go and live with him, Mariana refused, she preferred to stay where she was, with her mother and brother and sister, Seu Justino's house was crowded, he had a lot of children, six people slept in one small room, Fat Maria helped to make her dress, all in white, O bridal gown may you bring only happiness, no affliction, may you be kept long into the future and remembered as a good thing and not a thing of sorrow, Mariana tried it on one hot afternoon, there was dust hanging in the air, she was afraid of dirtying it, the lace was stiff, the cloth shone.

The morning of the wedding began with Epifânia giving Mariana a bath, they had got the water in tubs the day before, she heated some out in the yard, two big stones, wood underneath, she poured it into the basin, mixed it with cold water, Mariana took off her clothes, stood in the basin, her mother took mugs full of water and poured them over the girl, water flowed down her body, her arms, her black skin shone through the soapy lather, afterwards Epifânia began to do Mariana's hair, she divided it into bunches, tied each one and plaited it, at midday Emilia boiled rice in the yard, roasted pieces of meat, made food for all the family, Antônio didn't know how to eat properly with his fingers yet without dirtying his whole hand, Mariana moved her hands slowly as she ate, she couldn't stomach the taste of the meat, only wanted rice and flour, groups of women began to arrive, in blue robes, almost all the same, the dress was on the table in the parlour, Mariana touched it before she put it on, the feel of the cloth was pleasant, she began to put it over her head, Abigail held the little mirror up so that she could see herself, Fat Maria adjusted the dress at the waist, when everything was ready they all stood around waiting for the bridegroom's family, Seu Justino appeared in the doorway with a hat in his hand, he was saying:

'This is the style of hat that's in fashion in Brazil just now.'

Suliman, who was just behind him, asked:

'How do you know?'

'The sailor who sold it to me arrived from there only last week, he told me that this is what they are all wearing.'

Sebastian came in, he was wearing dark-coloured clothes, didn't seem very happy in his new jacket, Epifânia called her daughter, organized the procession in front of the house, Sebastian and Mariana in front, arm in arm, then the parents of the bride and bridegroom, then their families, and their friends, in twos and threes, they set off along Bangboshe Street, went into Oke-Suna, the church tower appeared away in the distance, they stopped for a while at the entrance, Seu Justino went in to see that everything was ready, came back smiling, the bride and bridegroom walked through the church, went up the altar steps, Seu Alexandre and Fat Maria were Mariana's sponsors, a friend of Seu Justino's stood for the bridegroom, four Englishmen in light-coloured clothes, from the firm where Sebastian worked, were waiting near the altar, Father O'Malley appeared in a white surplice and a coloured stole, Mariana remembered Father José, so many times she had smoothed out his surplice, put her hands on the lace round the hem, she could see her fingers through the pattern of the embroidery, she looked up to the altar, prayed an oriki to the Holy Ghost, they both knelt down, she stretched out her hand for the ring which Sebastian was holding, the marriage ceremony didn't take long, by the time she

117

stood up again she was married, Epifânia hugged her close, everyone else did the same, they stood around for a while in the street then started back, Mariana and Sebastian in front, Suliman's long robe stood out in the procession.

The party didn't seem to last long, everybody ate and drank, Fat Maria and Dona Zezé had helped with the expenses, when everyone had gone home Epifânia got the mat ready for the couple, they were to have the room that had been Ainá's, Epifânia would sleep in the living-room, the children would stay where they were in the kitchen, Mariana put her wedding-dress away in the chest, she was wearing an ordinary dress, Sebastian only had his trousers on, they went together into the bedroom, neither of them spoke a word, he took her clothes off and passed his right hand roughly over the whole of her body, his hand was cold and Mariana shivered, then both his hands took hold of hers and pressed them on to his penis, it was warm and limp, she felt it growing and escaping from her hands, and Sebastian was separating her thighs and opening her sex, it was difficult for him to enter her, Mariana lay there waiting forever it seemed, she was all wet between her legs and that helped, when she felt him again his penis was going in slowly and then, with a thrust, it was inside, a pain came and went away again, Mariana opened her arms wide on the mat, her hands touched the cold ground, it went in and out, at one moment she was thinking that Sebastian was heavy but it was good to feel his weight on her, a feeling of pleasure came from a long way off, it seemed as though it would explode inside her, but it went away, went far away again then began to come back, not very quickly, not quickly enough, until it burst in a great rush that left her free, a strong smell came from the woman and the man, O husband with the warm and soft penis that gave my body such pleasure.

Mariana thought about this for many months, in the

nights that followed one after the other, the rainy season kept her in the house, she talked to Emilia, knew when her sister had her first flow of blood, she looked after the house as if she were its mistress, Epifânia went out in the morning and didn't come back until late at night, or else she didn't come back at all, she slept beside the packing-cases in Campos Square, it was only during the rains that Mariana had her mother near her for any time, Sebastian spoke English at home, he had got into the habit at work, Mariana thought it would be good for her brother and sister, their English wasn't anything special, now that they didn't sell meals any more the money was not always enough, Sebastian didn't earn much and he didn't seem inclined to start up anything by himself, he was quite happy working for others, one day Mariana realized that she was expecting a child, she was overcome by a feeling of sickness like she had had on the ship, she wanted to eat unripe, acid fruit. Her belly grew big, at Christmas the harmattan brought a feeling of relief, she walked through the town feeling the wind on her face, sat on the patch of grass on the sea-front, saw ships coming into the harbour and leaving, it seemed as if it was someone else who had arrived on the *Esperança*, but the smell of the sea brought back to her things that had happened on board, she got used to Sebastian coming in from work, he would get bits of packing-case and make tables, sometimes he went to visit his parents, Seu Justino had married off one of his daughters, he was always complaining that hardly any ships came from Brazil now, for many weeks there had been no dried salt meat, one day Sebastian told Mariana that Emilia would have to be married soon. He explained:

'There are a lot of men after her.'

Mariana called her sister, they talked about it, perhaps it was rather early for her to be married, Epifânia wouldn't say what she thought, Emilia was different, very pretty, proud of being pretty, she enjoyed teasing men in the street, once when a man was bothering her she lifted up her skirt and stuck her bottom out at him, Fat Maria roared with laughter as she told this story, Mariana said to her sister:

'The danger is that a pretty girl like you will end up losing her virginity before she is married.'

'Is there anything wrong in that?'

Mariana thought for a moment, then said:

'No, nothing. But if you can avoid it, you should.'

She saw that Emilia wanted to do things her own way, it was good that she should, her belly seemed to have grown impossibly big, Fat Maria advised her to go and visit an old Yoruba woman who lived in Odunlami Street, the woman put her hand on Mariana's stomach, told her all was well.

'Don't worry. The thought of the wolf is enough to kill the sheep.'

The woman used a lot of Yoruba proverbs, Mariana went away with some of them in her head:

'Fair words don't fill the basket.'

At another time during her visit the woman had said:

'It's good to have a son so that he can bury you. Only the man who has been buried by his son has truly had a son.'

She told Mariana to think about Oshun, mistress of beauty and riches.

'Oshun is patient and strong. She cures the sick with cold water, she is the mother and queen who cures her own children and helps us to bear our children. She is rich and her words are sweet, she is mistress of wealth and mistress of the parrot's plumage, she is the mother who feeds her sons with honey.'

Mariana remembered the woman's words, she thought orikis for Oshun, O mistress of beauty, O you whose skin is smooth and soft, O you whose eyes shine like metal, protect the child who will soon leave this body, may he never lack food, may he live without fear, may he have a song in him for ever.

Epifânia engaged the best-known midwife in the Brazilian quarter, Dona Filomena, when Mariana was lying on her mat and felt that her time had come the woman arrived, told them to fill a basin with water, all the women from round about gathered in the parlour, Mariana heard them talking, the straw of the mat was coming to pieces, it was an easy birth, the midwife cut the umbilical cord with a knife, Emilia refilled the basin, the baby was a boy, Mariana fell asleep as soon as the pains stopped, she did not see her son until later, when Sebastian got back from work, he laughed more openly, he didn't seem to know what to do with himself, went in and out of the bedroom, out into the street to talk to his friends, Mariana called Epifânia and said:

'My next child will not be born on a mat. It will be born in a bed.'

She became pregnant again shortly afterwards, she was still teaching a few private pupils, there were some children in the neighbourhood whom she hadn't even known about, she got hold of some English books and began to teach the children to read in English and Portuguese at the same time, one day she went to see João the Carpenter, asked him to make a bed for her, when the bed was ready Fat Maria, Epifânia, Emilia and Antônio carried it through the streets of Lagos, Mariana filled a mattress with jute, that night Sebastian tried it out, they didn't get to sleep until dawn, he told her about the difficulties they were having in his office, the English head office wasn't happy about the business they were doing in Lagos, he might have to find himself a new job, that didn't seem a problem to Mariana, one could always find work, every now and then she passed her hand along the edge of the bed and wondered what name to give her child, he was going to be baptized in a few days' time, she thought of José, after Father José, Epifânia was very happy that she had remembered, Sebastian said:

'Then call him Joseph. One day he will have to live in an English world, it's best he should start off with an English name.'

Abigail was Joseph's godmother, he cried when the water was poured on his head, Father O'Malley didn't charge for baptisms, afterwards they came back home and ate sweets, Emilia had disappeared, she spent a lot of time away from home now, Mariana suspected that she was no longer a virgin, she was almost fourteen and had got a little fatter, but she became more beautiful every day, her hair was smooth and soft and easy to do, sometimes she spent a whole day doing it in this style or that, Antônio was twelve, he had learnt to read, but he didn't want to study any more, he was happier gathering cashews on Ikoyi, Mariana took him along to João the Carpenter:

'My brother seems to be quite good at joinery. We'd be glad if you would teach him.'

The man agreed, he was busy making a vast number of pews for the church and trying to finish a pulpit he had started a year earlier, another pair of hands would be a great help, but he warned her:

'At first he won't earn anything. Only a tip now and then.'

The birth of her second child was as easy as the birth of the first, the midwife had a new knife, Mariana was delighted when she heard Fat Maria saying:

'It's a girl.'

She chose the name for the baby straight away. Before Epifânia could say a word she said:

'She's going to have my grandmother's name.'

'Catarina?'

'No, Ainá.'

'Catarina is better, it's more Brazilian.'

'No, mother, she's going to have an African name.'

Epifânia looked at the baby, its eyes were still shut, its mouth seemed to be searching for something, she repeated the name:

'Ainá.'

'Grandmother would have preferred Ainá to Catarina.'

Epifânia picked the baby up, walked up and down with it saying Ainá in a soft voice, Sebastian agreed with whatever Mariana decided, two months after the birth of Ainá he lost his job, the Englishmen gave all their employees a month's salary and closed down the Lagos office, Sebastian stayed at home for a few weeks, meanwhile Mariana was teaching her classes, giving private lessons in the living-room or selling obis in Campos Square. There hadn't been a consignment of tobacco or cachaça for months, ships had stopped plying between Bahia and Lagos, the thought occurred to Mariana: what if she should want to go back to Brazil? the idea had never come to her before, even now she found it impossible to take seriously, she belonged to Lagos now, but anything could happen.

When Sebastian came and told her that he was going to leave for the Island of Fernando Poo, he had been offered a job in an office there, she didn't know what to say. She went to sleep that night without speaking a word to him, these days Joseph and Ainá slept sometimes with them, other times with Epifânia, that night Mariana took both of them in with her and lay wondering where Fernando Poo was. The next day her husband answered her question:

'It's an island that belongs to the Spanish, not far from here.'

'If it's Spanish it must be a long way away. Here everything is English.'

It was difficult to persuade a man not to do something he had decided to do. She said to Sebastian that it would be better if he found a job in Lagos, no matter what it was, he thought that he should try out the life

123

in Fernando Poo by himself, he would send money for her and the children, when he came back he might be rich, but the way things were here, with no work, with nothing to do, he just couldn't go on.

Sebastian left on a steamship that would call first at Calabar, Mariana, the children and Epifânia went to see him off, Seu Justino wouldn't go, the island of Lagos, with all the houses along the sea-front, looked different when she saw it from the ship, Sebastian had collected his things together in a small bundle, when Mariana climbed down into the canoe that was to carry the family back to land it was as if she were disembarking once more, when the men rowed and the water leapt up on both sides of the boat she looked at the ship and wondered when she would see Sebastian again, they said that all men like adventure, it must be true, the ship disappeared behind the rocks far away, Ainá was crying, Mariana got out of the canoe, sat down on the grass, took out her left breast, gave suck to the child, suddenly heavy rain fell on the mother and her baby.

Epifânia brought the boxes in from Campos Square that afternoon, Mariana sat down on the bed and reckoned up how long their money would last, perhaps they should start selling meals again, but now that the bed was in her room it would be difficult, before they had put tables in the parlour and in the bedroom, the rains seemed to last even longer that year, Mariana put basins and tubs in the yard, to catch the rainwater, a gutter along the roof collected more rainwater which ran down into a tank, she felt as if she were cut off from the world, she had left Piau, left Bahia, today she lived on this island which had no link with any other place, they said that Dahomey was a good place to live in, the Brazilians who lived there spoke another language besides Portuguese, it wasn't far away, only a few hours in a boat, Emilia spent her time in Abigail's house, or in Fat Maria's, Antônio was working with João the Carpenter, he tried to be like a man now, she felt sad to see the boy going out every day to struggle with the wood, the rain went on and on, O rain may you bring much water to the town and make the yam grow, Antônio came back home with some bits of wood, began to make a drum, he said they needed sixteen drums for Obatala, father of all, father of laughter, the boy could still speak Portuguese, but he was happier with Yoruba, his English was getting better, he had been to the house of some white people from England taking measurements for chairs and tables, Mariana realized that she had never talked to an Englishman, only on the day of her wedding, when they congratulated her she must have said a few words of thanks, she had talked to the sisters and the priests, but that was different, the Ibo girl who was married to the man with the big penis came to see her, the sky was almost black that day, the rain seemed to be endless, you would think the houses would dissolve in all that water, the two of them remembered Topo, the nuns, Joseph was crawling about in the street, playing in the puddles of water, he went out naked and came back filthy, Mariana had got used to tying him on her back, like the African women did, one seventh of September Seu Alexandre came to find her, said it was a holiday, what holiday? the independence of Brazil, there was a meeting at his house, Mariana went, heard them arguing about ships not calling at Lagos any more, there was a shortage of dried salt meat, tobacco, cachaça, one old man of ninety laughed:

'I've got used to palm wine by now. The only thing I miss is chewing tobacco.'

At one point Seu João Batista got up and asked for silence: 'The number of children learning Portuguese is going down. All parents should see to it that their children come to the classes, otherwise it won't be long before no-one speaks Portuguese any more, and we will forget the country we came from.'

Mariana decided to say something:

'When my son is older he's going to learn Portuguese, but I think the children should learn English as well. They will need it if they are going to find good jobs and get on with the English.'

Dona Zezé thought differently:

'They will learn English talking to the English and doing business with them. There's no need to study it.'

'Conversation isn't enough.'

Fat Maria said that there weren't many priests at the church, they needed more priests, and none of the ones there now spoke Portuguese or Yoruba. Old Teresa said:

'In the old days they used to speak Portuguese. No priest would have dared to come here if he hadn't learnt Portuguese before he came.'

Almost without knowing what she said, Mariana spoke:

'The best thing would be to have a black priest, someone like us.'

There was a silence and her father-in-law, Seu Justino, was the first to break it:

'But who would want to be a priest here? I've never come across any of our boys who wanted to be priests. Priests can't marry and none of our boys can wait to get a woman.'

Abigail's mother replied that she had heard of two boys who had wanted to enter the seminary, but their families hadn't had enough money, apparently in the Ibo region there were black priests, Mariana looked around the room, saw the blue robes the women were wearing, cloths round their heads, Seu Alexandre presided over the meeting, Joseph was playing in a corner, Ainá was tied to her grandmother's back, Epifânia looked at them all without saying a word, she saw all those men and women arguing, what she would like to do would be to go back to Piau or Bahia, let life take its course without worries, here there was always something that had to be sorted out, each day brought its trouble, O God, what sort of a place was it that old Ainá had brought her family to?, all they needed was food when they were hungry, work to do, money, not too much, just enough, Epifânia looked around the room and counted up the people who had come in the *Esperança*, everybody had a certain pride in the ship they had come in, now she knew who had arrived in Lagos in the *Biáfora*, or in the *Carlota*, or in the *Vila Isabel*, the *Esperança* had been the slowest, no other ship had taken six months to get here, and the fact that she had been a sailing ship added something to the prestige of the people who had come in her, she saw Seu Alexandre's wife, a little woman with a shrill voice, lifting her hand for permission to speak:

'We need a Brazilian hospital here. And we need medicines as well.'

Someone replied:

'We don't need a hospital. Seu Gaspar knows all the healing leaves.'

Seu Gaspar was from Pernambuco, he lived in Bangboshe, and as well as looking after the orishas and the festivals of Shango, Obatala, Oshun, Ogun, Nana, Oya, he knew the mysteries of the herbs and could cure the sick, Antônio had learnt a lot from him, Seu Gaspar had a society of egunguns as well, he led the cult of the ancestral spirits, sometimes he went out into the streets with the enormous masks and the coloured robes, they were beautiful, strips of bright cloth falling to the ground, when a family wanted to do homage to one of its dead they asked the society of egunguns to take the dead person out walking, the masked figure represented the dead person, it went along the streets he had walked along when he was alive, went into the houses he had gone into, through the market he had gone through, the family followed it at a distance, they saw their dead relative alive again, one day someone came and told Mariana that Antônio was going out with the egunguns, Seu Gaspar had given him the job, she didn't say anything to

127

him about it, she felt like asking them to do homage to old Ainá, she wondered whether egunguns of women went out into the streets as well as egunguns of men?, whenever anyone was ill Séu Gaspar gave them some leaves which were boiled, then the sick person ate the leaves or drank the water, they almost always got better, Mariana remembered that she had eaten some herbs that Seu Gaspar had given her when she was pregnant, she bowed her head because Sebastian wasn't there,where in heaven's name had her husband gone?, she had had no letter from him, no-one could tell her anything about Fernando Poo, she had looked at the island on a map that Seu João Batista had, the place he must be in was called Santa Isabel, and here was she, a married woman, alone, speaking at a meeting, looking after his children, working, as if she were a widow or an unmarried mother.

'Our biggest problem is water and hygiene. The Brazilian quarter is getting dirtier and dirtier.'

It was Marcelina who was speaking, she lived in Oke-Suna, everybody agreed with her, Mariana stopped listening because Joseph had disappeared from the corner where he had been playing, she looked around for him, went out and found him on the stairs, he could have fallen down them, the noise of the rain spread a sort of sadness over everything, she picked up the child and stood looking out of the window for a while, that night she put the lamp down by the side of the bed that João the Carpenter had made for her, began to think of all the time that had passed, she was almost twenty, it was six years since she had left Brazil, she undid the adiré that she wore now and looked at her body, her breasts hadn't fallen yet, the hair on her sex was thicker, she lay naked on the bed, opened her legs and imagined Sebastian coming into the room and into her, fell asleep she didn't know when, she was awakened by Ainá making a noise, it was time to eat, the rain was still falling, O rain when will you end, she noticed that her mother didn't seem to feel like working, she preferred to talk to her friends, pay visits to the people from the *Esperança*, Mariana wondered whether it would be a good thing to get Emilia to sell the obis, but it wouldn't work because you can't sell anything without a bit of enthusiasm and Emilia hated looking after the stall. The best thing would be to send her to school in Topo, but the money was getting low, how could she feed six mouths by herself?, she couldn't expect any more from Antônio, he made no work in the house, ate with João the Carpenter, sometimes turned up with some money that the carpenter or Seu Gaspar had given him.

Mariana was beginning to sense an answer to her problem when the rainy season came to an end. One day she heard that they had started bringing water from Abeokuta again, the first idea she had was at the back of her mind, she tried to catch it, but it slipped away, for days she was sure that the idea was there, it only needed an effort for her to be able to get hold of it, she went back to giving classes at Seu João Batista's house, one day she saw a group of Fulani men driving cattle along the street, she remembered the week she had spent on the sugar plantation, the oxen and the cows she had seen there. And she saw the well in front of her. That was it: the well. She had loved sitting beside it, watching all the girls who came to it, carrying jars on their heads or on their shoulders, when there was no-one else there Mariana drew water up herself, it spilled over her dress, she tried to see what was down there at the bottom. That was it: Lagos needed a well, Mariana would make one in the yard of the house, she would sell water instead of selling obis.

In silence, without saying a word to the others, she went about her daily life with her thoughts fixed on the well, in the morning, in the afternoon, at night, she thought of nothing but the well, she dreamt about it, could see it springing from deep down under the house, O

well that brings water and opens up the earth, she heard
of a man who had come in the *Vila Isabel* and had worked
in the building trade, she looked for books on the subject but couldn't find any, one afternoon she went to the
main office of the English government in Lagos, she
asked the white man, he had blue eyes, wore a uniform,
looked like a ship's captain, where she could get books.

'On what subject?'

Mariana's English wasn't as bad as she had thought,
she replied that she wanted to teach her pupils English,
any book would do, but it would be best if it were about
something useful. The man let her look for a book, it
was only hours afterwards that she found what she
wanted when she was leafing through a dictionary and
looked for the word 'well' in English, she copied it down,
it occurred to her that perhaps a Brazilian had written
a book in Portuguese, Seu João Batista had a dictionary
but it was only little, in the end she found a bigger one at
Dona Julia's, it had been her father's, nobody had ever
noticed it was there, Mariana took it home and studied
the subject, the sides of the well would have to be faced
with stone or wood, perhaps wood was the simplest, with
Antônio working for João the Carpenter she could get
whatever she needed and Antônio would help her, she
got a pencil and some paper, drew a well, drills would be
necessary, said the book, now what was a drill?, she saw
in the dictionary that it was an instrument for boring,
asked her brother:

'Do you know what a drill is?'

Antônio looked at her doubtfully:

'What's this? an exam?'

'No, it's just that I need to know what it is.'

'I'll bring one home for you tomorrow.'

Mariana looked at it, asked:

'Is this what they use for making holes in the ground?'

'This is for wood, but there are bigger ones that make
big holes.'

It was December, the harmattan was blowing cheerfully, Mariana got everyone in the house together, she
had asked João the Carpenter to come too, and Antônio,
and Ricardo, the man who knew how to make holes in
the ground. The three of them looked at her in bewilder-
ment when Mariana told them what she wanted. João
the Carpenter exclaimed:
'A well?'
'A well.'
'What for?'
'To get water out of, of course.'
She went on to explain that the yard was a good size,
it was more or less in the centre of the island, a long way
from the sea and from the salt water canal, so that
the water would probably be drinkable, the important
thing was to get it all planned in advance, the walls of
the well would have to be protected with planks of wood
as the digging went on, it was impossible to know
at what depth they would find water, but she hoped
it wouldn't be too far below the surface. It was difficult
for the others to get used to the idea. Mariana asked
them:
'Please, don't mention this to anyone. A thing like
this had to be got on with quietly, otherwise we'll have
everyone in giving their opinion.'
The next week she went out of the house often, going
with the three men to fetch planks of wood into the yard,
they had got spades, hoes, picks, big drills, just before
the New Year they set to work, Epifânia and Emilia
came to see, Epifânia said:
'Have you gone mad, daughter? the yard will be full
of holes.'
'Don't worry, mother. I know what I'm doing.'
Emilia didn't say a word, she watched the work for a
while then got bored with it, Fat Maria and Seu Justino
came to find out what was happening, Seu Justino said:
'So you're going to sink a well?'

'Yes, I am.'

The news ran through the Brazilian quarter, Mariana had to stand at the door waiting to catch people and stop them from going in, she explained what she was going to do, some Africans came to look, one of them said, in the heavy Yoruba of the interior:

'What she is doing is right. Water comes from the earth.'

Mariana stopped giving her classes, it was holiday-time and no-one would mind, but Seu João Batista's pupils were paying for their lessons, she made excuses to him for her absences, it would take another month to finish the well, when the Feast of Bonfim came she helped with all the preparations, went to Mass, sent Epifânia and Emilia into the kitchen, they made a delicious dish of beans, she bought new material for clothes for the whole family, all with the same pattern, you could recognize any of them from a long way off, Epifânia, Mariana, Emilia, Antônio, Joseph or little Ainá, all the robes were made the same, at the picnic on Ikoyi they put chairs out, drums were beating on the clear January afternoon, a guitar and a flute made the party more lively, Dolores, Abigail's youngest sister, danced and sang:

O father I want to marry
O mother I cannot stay
O mother I want to marry
Today, today, today
O the feast of Bonfim mother
Will be my wedding day
O mother I want to marry
Today, today, today.
But who's the man, my daughter
O daughter tell me who.
O he is a cobbler mother
O he's no match for you.

132

Everyone laughed, they took the flour, sprinkled it on the beans, ate happily, Papai Agudá washed his hands in a bowl and sang:

> Now what's a cart without a horse
> And what's an eye without a blink
> And what's a mouth without a voice
> And what's a song without a drink.

There was some good cachaça, just arrived from Brazil, Papai Agudá took a mouthful, rolled his eyes up, Joseph and Ainá were giggling at everything, once the little boy did a little dance, everyone applauded him. Seu Machado, whose hair was completely white, picked up a guitar, strummed it for a minute or two, his voice was tired, but sweet:

> The créole girls of Bahia
> Come to the dance from afar
> Ai guitar, guitar, guitar
> Ai guitar, guitar, guitar.

He paused for a minute, everyone was silent, they all felt pleasantly tired after the meal, Mariana tied Ainá to her back, she saw Emilia whispering to one of Dona Zezé's sons, and laughing helplessly, perhaps she had been drinking a bit, Seu Machado's voice made them all fall quiet again:

> O mother mine who bore me
> Give me your blessing
> For I'm going to the black man's land
> I'll die without confessing
> Run, run, my little horse
> And gallop to the jewelled sea
> And tell them this in my Brazil—
> Remember me, remember me.

The party was still full of life as darkness began to gather, Emilia was dancing by herself, boys began to put coins on her forehead as she danced, they stuck there in the sweat, Emilia was smiling happily, Mariana thought she was looking prettier than ever, her white teeth, her lips weren't as thick as those of the rest of the family, the black of her skin seemed to have light and shade, her enormous eyes spoke more clearly than words.

They were having trouble sinking the well, there was no sign of water. One night Mariana was thinking how slowly it was going when she realized that she would have to buy that house before they found water, it belonged to an old Brazilian, called Adebulu, who lived on the mainland in Yaba, Mariana crossed the bridge, went to see him, as soon as she had inquired after his health she brought up the subject of the house. He looked at her with his reddened eyes, he seemed to have no lashes:

'So you want to buy my house, young woman?'

'Yes, Seu Adebulu, I know you own several houses in Lagos, my family and I have lived in this one ever since we arrived, we've got used to it.'

The old man liked tea, he ordered a servant to make some, insisted that Mariana have some as well, promised:

'I'll think about it, perhaps I will sell.'

When she got back home she went to look at the hole in the ground, João the carpenter and Antônio had shored up the walls of the excavation which was almost two metres deep now, soil was working its way between the planks, Ricardo complained that the ground was hard, it was dry and full of stones, it was getting more and more difficult to dig it out, for a fortnight Mariana couldn't think of anything else except the house, she didn't forget the well which was there at the back of all her worries, but Seu Adebulu's reply was the most important thing just then, when she got a message from him she was delighted, again she crossed Carter Bridge, he must have found his eyelashes but his eyes were damp and old, he chatted to her without mentioning the business of the house, only at the end, as he was saying goodbye, did he say:

'Do you know how much the house costs?'

'Yes.'

'I want cash. Have you enough money?'

'I haven't got that much now, but I can get it.'

'Get it then.'

Mariana went to see Dona Zezé that night, to borrow some money.

'But how much do you want, child?'

'Three hundred pounds.'

'That's a great deal. How are you going to pay it back?'

'With my well, Dona Zezé. When I have water in that well no-one will buy any more water from the boats, they will all come and buy my water'.

'So you're going to sell water?'

'Yes, I am.'

The next day Dona Zezé gave her reply:

'I'll lend you two hundred pounds. You'd better get the rest from Seu Alexandre or Seu Machado.'

Once she had got the three hundred pounds and had paid for the house she put the documents safely in the bottom of the chest, then ran to the hole, it was more than three metres deep, the earth was damp now, they had to get longer planks to shore up the walls, it was March, very near the feast of St José, the men of the Brazilian quarter were getting ready for the festival, there was an argument about whether they should have the name of the society in English, Saint Joseph Society, João the Carpenter, who was called João but who had a great devotion to St José, told Mariana all about it, she was thinking of taking little Joseph to the Mass, her mother often talked about Father José, one day just about then Antônio shouted for Mariana, she ran and saw the water welling up down there in the bottom, Ricardo put some of the mud into a tin and Antônio pulled it up on a rope, Mariana plunged her hand into the clay, it felt cold and pleasant, she asked when there would be clear water in the well. Later Ricardo explained:

'It will be like this at first, more mud than water because I'm still digging in there, but soon the water will accumulate and the mud will settle.'

João the Carpenter took a while to shore up the sides of the well. On Palm Sunday, the family walked in the procession, they all carried palms, Epifânia clutched hers fiercely, O lord of the palms may your powerful arm protect our steps, Ricardo had started to line the walls of the well with bricks the afternoon before, on Monday of Holy Week Mariana decided to have a low wall with a rounded edge like the one she had seen in Bahia, for people to lean over as they were drawing up water, and she asked Antônio to make a wooden cover to stop things falling into the well. On Easter Sunday everything was ready, Mariana made a special lunch, invited Seu Alexandre, Dona Zezé, Fat Maria, Abigail, Ricardo, João the Carpenter, the flute-player, before they sat down to eat everyone took a glass of water from the well and drank it, O water which has sprung up for all of us may you always flow abundantly and bring happiness to the mistress of the well, Ricardo said:

'It's very nice, but I prefer cachaça.'

The next day, Mariana sent for Seu Neco the painter and ordered a big notice with three words on it: water in Yoruba, water in Portuguese and water in English. She wanted the words to be spaced out like this:

omi

agua

water

The man spent all Monday and Tuesday painting the lettering on a big piece of wood, on Wednesday, Shango's day, Mariana got them to fix the notice board over the door of the house, O Shango may your day bring us good fortune in this undertaking, may your fire light up our water, she bought a ram, took it to Seu Gaspar:

'The ram is for Shango, Seu Gaspar. I'm asking him for something.'

'I didn't know the Sinhá liked Shango.'

It was the first time anyone had called her Sinhá, Sinhá was someone important, in Brazil all the women were Yaya, only grand ladies were called Sinhá, mistresses of big houses, rich and well-dressed, Uncle Inhaim's wife, the woman her grandmother had belonged to when she was a slave, had been Sinhá, Mariana smiled, then she explained:

'I went to a festival of Shango in Bahia and my grandmother always used to tell me stories about the orisha of the thunder. Pray to him for me, Seu Gaspar.'

She could see the notice-board over the door from a long way off as she was going back to the house. When she got back she called Epifânia and Emilia, told them:

'A pitcher of water this big costs twopence. That means that six pitchers full will cost a shilling. Everybody needs at least six a day.'

The first woman who came for water was called Nanã, she was a Yoruba who lived in Campos Square. Mariana told her how much the water cost, the woman thought for a minute then said:

'It's quite cheap.'

Now there always had to be someone in the house to sell the water, in the mornings there was a queue in front of the door, Mariana used to give water secretly to the ones who couldn't pay, but for the most part it all got paid for, there were some days when they made more then ten pounds, on the eves of the big religious festivals, Catholic, Muslim or Protestant, they took almost thirty. Mariana decided to engage someone to sell the water, she sent Emilia to Topo, the girl complained:

'How can I go to a school run by nuns? I'm not a virgin.'

'In my time there were lots of girls who weren't virgins. The sisters don't ask you any questions.'

Emilia was wearing a lovely cloth wrapped round her body, her big eyes were dismayed, Mariana's voice softened as she said:

'It's the best thing for you, this way you'll learn all sorts of things, when you leave you can do what you want, get married or not, but it's always good to study for a while.'

Emilia went, Mariana left Joseph with her mother, asked her to keep an eye on the man she had found to sell the water, tied Ainá to her back and went with her sister, the boat went through patches of lagoon covered in water-plants, the green leaves floated apart, then there was deep shadow where they went along under the trees, the canoe slid almost without effort along the peaceful canals, when she saw Topo in the distance she had a feeling of rediscovery, O house where I learnt so many new things may the memory of you help me in my efforts today. Emilia seemed quite happy, when Mariana left her with Sister Mary and went back to get the canoe she felt sorry for her, Emilia was so full of life, she loved dancing, singing, flirting, men, and she had to stay there, far away from it all, but it was the best thing for her.

Towards the end of the year, Mariana decided she would like to make the house bigger, make it into a proper sobrado, build an extra storey on top with at least four more rooms. Ricardo thought it wouldn't be difficult, he would have to get some Brazilian carpenters from Ibadan to come and help, it might cost a lot, but it would be worth it, Epifânia asked:

'Will we be able to afford it?'

'Yes, mother, we will. I've already paid back Dona Zezé and Seu Alexandre, all the money that's coming in now is ours.'

Ricardo started the work in January, Mariana walked around the streets of the town and looked carefully at all the Brazilian sobrados, some of them had carved shutters on the windows like the ones in Bahia, others had ornamental gates of wrought iron, one afternoon she went out with Ricardo and took him to the other side of the island where there was a house she liked, it occupied about the same amount of ground, he said:

'If you like I'll make you a façade just like this one.'

'I don't mind if it's not the same, as long as it's something like it.'

Mariana liked walking, now she sometimes took the little train that ran along the sea-front and Bangboshe Street, she went to other parts of the town where there were no Brazilians, crossed Carter Bridge, when Emilia came back home on holiday she sent her on the train to Ibadan, gave her money for her expenses, the girl found such generosity very strange, the upper storey was beginning to take shape, but she still had no news of Sebastian, Mariana asked everyone she could think of, went to the English Governor's office, a young man with fair hair said he would try to find out what had happened, when she was summoned to an office in another building she thought it was because she had news of her husband, but it wasn't. The Englishman asked her to sit down and said:

'Your name is Mariana da Silva?'

'Yes.'

'We have received a report which says that you are selling water illegally.'

'Is it forbidden to sell water?'

'It's not exactly like that—you must have a licence if you are going to sell anything, and this report says that your prices are very high.'

Mariana kept calm, and when she spoke it was in a gentle voice:

'You see, I have a well at the back of my house, it cost me a lot of time and money to sink it. It's my well, and I give water to whoever I like, but if I don't want to give water to someone, then I don't. If the people I give water give me presents in return, that's their problem.'

The Englishman laughed, told her that the Governor had plans to sink a large number of wells, and had ordered a lot of quinine to combat malaria, he wanted to know if there were many people suffering from malaria in the Brazilian quarter.

'No, hardly anybody.'

The news that the Government was going to build wells wasn't very pleasant, Mariana went along the seafront the next day, saw a house that had been handsome once, it had four doors at the front, it would make a good shop, she made enquiries about the owner, at home she talked to Antônio:

'We're going to open a furniture shop on the Marina. You and João the Carpenter will make the furniture, I'll sell it. We could sell other things besides furniture, and we could import stuff from Brazil.'

She paused for a moment, then added:

'Or from England.'

She concluded the purchase of the house on the seafront on the same day that the sobrado on Bangboshe Street was finished, Emilia arrived back from Ibadan, of the four rooms on the top floor one was to be for Mariana, the second for Emilia and Epifânia, the third for Joseph and Ainá and the fourth for Antônio. Downstairs there was the kitchen, and the other rooms would be used for receiving visitors. Before the party Mariana was standing beside the well, the queue in front of the house was getting longer and longer, especially for people living in the Brazilian quarter it was much easier to come and get water here than to go across Carter Bridge for it to Ebute Metta, the first one to arrive at the party was Fat Maria:

'So today's the inauguration of the sobrado?'

Mariana had a new dress on, Joseph was starting to talk, he could say a few phrases in English with a perfect

English accent, everyone thought it was very funny, João the Carpenter had a white suit on, and a Panama hat, he thought the idea of a shop was marvellous, Mariana was planning to import cachaça from Brazil, there were lots of things she could sell in the shop, a great many Africans came to the party, soon the only language you could hear in the parlour was Yoruba, Epifânia watched all the gaiety and felt happy and sad at the same time, she wanted all this, but in Brazil, if only she could transport the new sobrado, the well, all their friends, the whole Brazilian quarter from Lagos to Piau or to Bahia, it would be heaven, but then life was never perfect, Ainá was starting to walk, Fat Maria had a bit to drink, got Mariana into a corner, kissed her:

'Look, child, you're rich today, don't ever let yourself slip back, go forward all the time.'

She took another mouthful of palm wine, then looked around her and said:

'Everybody is born naked, but we have had two births. First when we were born, again when we arrived in Lagos. We landed naked on that beach, nothing but an English sheet to cover ourselves up with. You, with the blood running down your thighs.'

Mariana kept her money in the bottom of the chest, when she went out to pay for the shop she wrapped the notes in a handkerchief, she spent a whole day organizing the place, Antônio had brought chair and tables to sell, as they didn't have anything else yet Mariana put up a little brown counter at one of the doors with obis, orobos and tobacco, Emilia had arrived back from Ibadan with some news, she wanted to get married to an African called Ebenezer Okinoyi, Epifânia was against it, any daughter of hers would have to marry a Brazilian, Mariana didn't say anything, it wouldn't have helped if she had interfered. Emilia would marry whom she liked, she let her mother go on for a day or two, sent her sister back to Topo, when they told her one afternoon that

Ebenezer Okinoyi had arrived to ask for Emilia's hand, she said to Epifânia:

'Don't worry yourself, mother, I'll sort it out.'

The young man was tall, his Yoruba sounded strange to her, he seemed very polite, his voice sang as he spoke, he did his best to explain himself, Mariana replied that she didn't see anything to prevent him marrying her sister, only her family wouldn't have anything to do with polygamy, so he had been warned, also her sister would have to stay at Topo for a little while longer. Ebenezer was wearing a pink robe in the Yoruba style, he had a certain elegance in the way he moved, she got a good impression of him, when he left she said to Epifânia:

'He's a good man, mother.'

Antônio took over the shop on the sea-front, João the Carpenter made cupboards in a style that was fashionable just then, beds, rocking-chairs, Mariana used to go there every afternoon, she began to write letters, the first one was to Father José in Bahia, she asked him to put her in touch with firms who wanted to import orobos from Africa and would export dried salt meat, tobacco, cachaça, sugar, Seu Alexandre and Seu Machado got hold of some addresses for her, she wrote more letters, sitting at the back of the shop, sometimes she looked out to the sea, the ships coming into port were outlined against the trees on the other side of the bay, she wrote letters to the Island of Fernando Poo, one to the Government there, there must be a Governor, someone who was in charge of the place, she sent another one to a Catholic church, she didn't say which, the Spanish were Catholics and Sebastian must go to a church, a third one she sent to the English Consul in Santa Isabel, surely she would get some reply to one of them.

It wasn't long before Mariana had replies to all three letters, but nobody seemed to know Sebastian Silva in Fernando Poo, Father José's letter was long, he gave her the names and addresses of a lot of firms, asked after Epifânia, who took the envelope, looked at the priest's writing, sat thinking.

When Emilia refused to go back to school the problem of marrying her began to worry Mariana again, and one day she invited her mother to go out with her on the little train, they went for a trip through the town, afterwards they sat in a garden beside the sea, everything was peaceful, Mariana began:

'Mother, it would be best to let Emilia marry this Yoruba from Ibadan. We aren't in Brazil now, this is Africa, I think it's foolish the way people try to hang on to the old ways.'

Her mother was about to speak, Mariana wouldn't let her:

'I respect the ideas of the Brazilians as well, I married one, I speak Portuguese, I eat our food, I'm a Catholic, but that doesn't stop me seeing that the younger ones are going to have a very different life from us. They will all be African. Look at Joseph, he was born here, he speaks English fluently, he's going to be a completely different sort of person from us.'

Her mother didn't say a word, it was a little cooler now that night was approaching, Mariana went on:

'We must let Emilia marry who she likes. If it's Ebenezer from Ibadan, then she'd better have him.'

'But they'll have to be married in a Catholic church.'

'We'll tell him that that's a condition: it must be in a Catholic church.'

That same night Mariana wrote to Ibadan, a few days later Ebenezer arrived, took Emilia out in the evening, said that his father would be coming to Lagos in a month's time, his father turned out to be a short man, very fat, his mouth spread wide like a frog's, he had a huge laugh that went on and on, it was settled that they would be married in October, Mariana realized that Emilia was a beautiful woman now, tall, but not too tall, like one of those Fulani women she had seen in Ibadan, the line of her nose was very clear in profile, her eyes looked at you with such tranquillity and silence that you felt uncomfortable and turned away. Emilia was very gay during the time they were making her dress, she looked at herself in the mirror, walked unhurriedly through the streets, went to the shop and looked at the furniture, she was going to live in Ibadan, she wouldn't need any furniture from Lagos, Mariana had the whole house decorated, coloured streamers over the doors, like they had for parties in Brazil, a week beforehand they began to make sweets and prepare food, they got small tables and chairs for the guests to sit out in the open, the thought occurred to Mariana that João the Carpenter and Antônio could set up a business hiring out tables and chairs to be used at parties, the population of Lagos was getting bigger, soon there would be lots of parties, how could people get hold of enough tables and chairs?

All Ebenezer's family stayed in the sobrado, the father had three wives, only two of them had come with him, Mariana wouldn't let herself think of the possibility of her sister's husband ending up polygamous, on the morning of the wedding day she was touched, she remembered Emilia in Piau, so small that she couldn't fish with them in the river, then the train journey to Rio de Janeiro, the steamer to Bahia, the months they had spent in Bahia, the whole family sleeping in the market-place, the smell of fish, Father José, the sacrifice of the ram, the white skirts on the feast of Bonfim, the conversations around the stall, the voyage in the *Esperança*, the calm, the hard time they had had when they first arrived in Lagos, the party went on all night, Ebenezer's father found the Brazilian customs entertaining, tried the cachaça, danced fat as he was, at one time Fat Maria and he were dancing opposite each other, it was so funny, the flute-player played sad tunes, Mariana heard herself singing:

Don't play me false love
Just like the other
Sweetly deceiving
My heart was broken
By someone like you
Loving and leaving.

The song came to her naturally, she had heard it in
Rio de Janeiro, the tune the flute had played was the
tune of the song, she smiled when everyone clapped,
Emilia and Ebenezer left by train for Ibadan, Abigail
was pregnant, Mariana remembered Sebastian, what
else could she do to find him? The next day she heard
that the Government was sinking wells at several places
in the town, but there wasn't going to be one beside her
house, her well would still be of use and bring in money,
but in any case she could do without the well now, the
shop on the sea-front was doing good business, selling
obis and orobos at the door had brought some regular
customers, it was sad that Sebastian couldn't see it all,
he had left in search of money and the money was here
in Lagos, one day she asked her mother:
'Do you think that Jerónimo would be able to work
for me in the shop?'
Epifânia lifted her head and looked at her daughter:
'I thought you didn't like him.'
'If you like him, that's all that matters.'
They were standing talking beside the well, Mariana
pulled on the rope and went on:
'And in any case it's always better to have someone you
know than a stranger.'
Epifânia used to meet Jerónimo at night, beside the
garden where Ainá had been buried, sometimes they
used to sit on her mother's grave, the next week Jerónimo
was helping Antônio in the shop, little Ainá played at the
door, waved her arms when the train passed the corner,
a sign nailed up in front of the shop announced that

tables and chairs, small and easy to carry, could be hired there for parties and meetings, the other signboard, with omi, agua and water on it, was part of the scenery now in Bangboshe Street, when Mariana was thirsty she thought about that need to drink omi, drink agua, drink water, which had helped her to earn so much money, sometimes she amused herself by turning Portuguese sentences into Yoruba or English, the *mu* in the Yoruba verb to drink sounded to her like the noise an ox makes, one afternoon she had to go to a Government office for something, they wanted to know what language she spoke, she told them:

'Portuguese.'

'No, what we want to know is your African language, it's for the statistics.'

'Yoruba.'

She would soon be twenty-two, she had been in Lagos for nearly nine years, and Mariana felt weary, she thought of getting on a ship and going to Fernando Poo, in search of that husband who had disappeared, she agreed to visit Emilia in Ibadan, Ebenezer lived in a big house, her sister seemed happy, but you never knew with her, when she came back Mariana came face to face with a new machine running through the streets of the town, it was a motor-car, she watched it until it disappeared at the other side of Campos Square, now that was something she would like, to have a car of her own, the little train only went at certain times and couldn't escape from its track, the next day she stopped in front of the Central Government Offices and looked carefully at the car, she had heard all about it, and she was standing there, intent as if she were trying to disentangle some mystery, when she heard a voice calling to her, she knew straight away that it was Sebastian, he was thinner, wearing dark-coloured clothes, a little older but his eyes were shining, they clasped each other's hands, he said in a voice full of happiness:

'I've just arrived. I was going home and I saw you here.'

They didn't talk much, went back together to Bangboshe Street, he was carrying a bag, Mariana let go of his hand and ran ahead of him:

'Mother, here's Sebastian back.'

Epifânia came out, he was standing still in the middle of the street looking up at the house, Mariana took him by the arm, they went inside, she said:

'I've earned a lot of money, Sebastian, I had a well made in the yard, started to sell water, I've bought the house, that's to say I bought the house first, Dona Zezé and Seu Alexandre lent me the money, then I made the well and started to earn money. I've bought a shop on the sea-front as well.'

He went to look around the upper storey, came back and sat down beside her:

'Well I didn't earn much. It was terrible in Fernando Poo, everything you managed to earn you had to spend. I was lucky to get away. Some people will be there for the rest of their lives, hoping times will get better.'

Sebastian put Joseph on his knee, Ainá looked at him wonderingly, the neighbours heard and came in to see him, the first one in was Fat Maria, she joked with him, said he looked better now than he had when he went away, Seu Justino arrived with his whole family, held his son close, said he thought they should have a party, first they went to church to give thanks, at night the flute-player and two guitarists were called in, the drummers played for a while to get the party going, Mariana sent out for English beer and biscuits, Epifânia made beancakes, it was like their wedding-party all over again, only when everyone had left and the two of them went to the room upstairs did she realize she had been longing for the moment when Sebastian would take her again, she opened her legs in a great hunger to have him inside her, much later she still felt the delight of his return, the joy of discovering him again. The next day he went to see the shop, sat down on the chairs that João the Carpenter had made, asked her:

'What would you like me to do?'

'I think you'd better manage the shop. There are a lot of letters waiting to be answered, next month we have to ship seventy-five barrels of palm-oil to Bahia. And Domingos Antônio Sousa & Co in Bahia will send us forty cases of dried salt meat.'

Sebastian fell back easily into the rhythm of life in Lagos, one night he went to the well, drew some water and stood there thinking, it was good to be back, who would have said that that quiet girl would have had the energy to do all this?, in Fernando Poo he had thought about going to Brazil and sending for his wife and children to join him there, but there hadn't been any ships. And meanwhile all this was going on, his father had told him that she was the most respected person in Bangboshe Street, everyone's eyes were on her as she went by, someone said:

'She arrived here without a stitch of clothing, today she's rich.'

The peacefulness of those first weeks after Sebastian's return meant that Mariana could give more time to her children and her mother, Epifânia seemed sad, one day they both went to the serenata of one of the women who had been with them on the *Esperança*, weep for a young death, but not for an old death, the worst is violent death, you can't have a serenata for someone who has died violently, Fat Maria used to say:

'Death by dying means a party. Death by killing means tears.'

Mariana danced at the party, asked Epifânia if she would like to go for a holiday, go to Ibadan or Abeokuta, her mother said quietly:

'What would I do there?'

Seu Alexandre danced in front of them, sang:

> Corpus Christi comes again
> Tomorrow is the holy day
> If you've got clothes, then go to Mass,
> If not, then stay away.

Sebastian spent the night sitting in a corner, at one time he took hold of Mariana's hand, smiled at her, he was quieter than he had been before, he worked very hard in the shop, but it seemed as if he had lost all his enthusiasm in Fernando Poo, when Mariana asked him if anything was wrong he shook his head. He stayed watching the party for a long while, it seemed he was going to say nothing, but then he said:

'Don't take any notice of me. I got so tired of living in a foreign country that all I want to do now is stay here, listening to familiar words, seeing familiar people, just rest with things I know and people who know me.'

João the Carpenter came up to them. He had started to sing now that he was earning more money making furniture for Mariana, he had always been very withdrawn before, his voice was stronger now:

> O light the lamp Maria
> I want a light to see
> I want some starch for starching
> So light the lamp for me.

Over on the other side of the room, standing beside one of the dead woman's sons, Ricardo took it up:

> Samba I want to dance
> O cashew, cashew tree
> I want to samba, samba
> My Sinhá is calling me.

Mariana remembers this time with happiness, it was the best time of her life, the best?, perhaps the most peaceful, so peaceful that in her memory the images

mingle in a series of untroubled scenes, Joseph growing,
Ainá saying funny little things, Epifânia enjoying parties,
going to serenatas, Mariana went to talk to Seu Gaspar,
picked up the orishas, Shango with the double axe on his
head, Oshun naked, she brought honey to offer to Oshun,
O black skin like black velvet, O beautiful among the
beautiful, O gentle among the gentle, O loving among
the loving, O rich among the rich. Oshun was guardian
of beauty and riches, the Yoruba orisha that Mariana
thought about most often, when she went into the silence
of Seu Gaspar's temple she felt rested from the work of
the day, Sebastian lying in bed at night by her side made
the darkness so peaceful, all the nights in the world were
hushed waiting for sex and the sweat that ran down their
bodies.

What happened afterwards could not have been fore-
seen, after all what is a happening?, the orishas must have
been jealous of them, the oldest Brazilian woman in
Bangboshe Street, Yaya Joana, who was a hundred and
two, said to Mariana once:

'Hide the good things, girl. Always hide them. Don't
let anyone know that you are happy, or rich, or healthy.
There is so much envy, envy is all around you, and soon
along comes illness, unhappiness, poverty.'

She liked to go and see Yaya Joana on feast days, Our
Lady of Joy, Bonfim, when Sebastian wanted them all
to have a photograph taken together, himself, her and
the children, Mariana changed the subject, didn't take
up the idea, because of something Yaya Joana had said
to her the week before:

'Photographs destroy your soul. Every photo you have
taken is a little bit of your spirit wasted away.'

Afterwards she was to be glad she had given in to
Sebastian and let the photograph be taken, even though
she had been afraid because of what Yaya Joana had
said, because otherwise how would she have had anything to remember that time by, that peaceful happy

time? Perhaps the orishas were jealous of people, or rather not the orishas but the evil spirits, perhaps there were such things, but for the first few months after Sebastian came back everything seemed good to Mariana, the Government still hadn't got far with the construction of its wells, the shop on the sea-front was always busy, there seemed to be plenty of time for everything, so much so that Mariana decided to have her own bumba-meu-boi. She had some wooden frames made for the painted canvas, the pasteboard, the ribbons, the figures of the ox, the donkey, the ostrich, the giant woman.

Seu Gaspar, who painted the masks, taught her how to mix the paint with egg, Mariana spent weeks drawing the face of the ox, lingering over this or that detail, patiently she drew in one eye, stood back to look at it, asked Sebastian:

'Is it all right?'

He laughed:

'Everything you do is all right.'

Antônio found all sorts of things wrong with it, said the head was too big, she said:

'But it needn't be exactly like an ox. It's just to give you the idea of one.'

Joseph got hold of the canvas, helped with the painting, made it all dirty, Mariana laughed and got some new canvas. The queue for water in front of the house was still long, while they were waiting a lot of people came to see what she was painting, passed remarks, Mariana began to put on weight, one day Antônio said:

'If you go on like this you'll be fatter than Fat Maria.'

That night she looked at herself, she really felt wonderfully well, a gush of health seemed to come from her, she felt a new strength in her body and she walked around, did things, noticed things happening, later she had strange thoughts which, if she had put them into words, might have been: who has any power over what happens? She had control over herself, she seemed to have control

151

over what was happening to her family, but she came to realize that this sort of power is tiring. Sometimes she felt a need to be controlled, directed, she wanted someone else to tell her what to do, what to want, what to think. The figures were beginning to take shape, the ox was beginning to look like an ox, the big woman really was big, all the Brazilians in Bangboshe Street came to see them as they grew, Fat Maria was ecstatic as each new character appeared. Abigail's son played with Joseph beside the ox, Sebastian came home from the shop in the afternoons when it was very hot, ran his hands over the huge dolls, Mariana went into Seu Gaspar's house to visit Oshun, it was Seu Gaspar who told her that Emilia was expecting a child in Ibadan and that she had a temple of Shango in her house how. Mariana went to visit her again, her sister seemed frightened, Mariana saw the statues of Shango in a special room that Emilia had had built at the bottom of the yard, she was silent for a while, then said:

'You've done the right thing, sister. It was our grandmother's religion.'

Ebenezer wasn't very happy with all this:

'I don't know what's happened to her. I'm Anglican and I don't want anything to do with this, but something has changed her.'

Emilia had changed, she was still gay, but her face with its great wide eyes seemed to have a purpose, a strength, which she had never shown before, back in Lagos Mariana asked Seu Gaspar:

'Will you make an Oshun for me?'

It took him weeks, Mariana went to watch him working, with a tiny knife he cut here and there, it was a beautiful piece of wood, at first nothing seemed to come out of all this cutting, one day Mariana could see the head of a woman, would it be like anyone? Seu Gaspar held the wood in one hand and told her:

'If it comes out right, it will look like you, Sinhá.'

'Like me?'

The presence of a person in the sculpture became clearer as the weeks went by, the breasts took shape, the sex was a deep gash, Seu Gaspar made necklaces of cowries and yellow beads for the statue, one afternoon Mariana took it back to the house, put it in a room, from time to time she placed some water in front of Oshun, O water from the well may Oshun receive you gladly, may the goddess of sweet water and gold be content with you, Sebastian asked what it meant, when he heard that it was Oshun he stood looking at the statue for a long time, said:

'My mother had one in Brazil.'

Epifânia had something to say about it as well:

'It seems to me you are turning out to be very like your grandmother.'

At Christmas the whole family went to Midnight Mass, Ainá slept on Mariana's knee, the choir sang, Joseph loved all the colours, afterwards groups of friends stood chatting in the street, from time to time someone went by carrying a lantern, one of the neighbours started playing a guitar, the sobrado stood outlined in the first light of day, Mariana went to look at the calungas before she went to bed, the bumba-meu-boi would be out in January, a few days before the party two of Sebastian's brothers, a son of Seu Alexandre's and Seu Machado's nephew practised with the dolls, they got inside them and went out into the street, Mariana thought they looked good.

The whole of Bangboshe Street, and Oke-Suna, and Campos Square, and Tokunboh Street, and Odunlami all came to the party, Mariana wore a dress made of English material, she combed her hair flat and tied a Yoruba cloth round her head, Sebastian wore white, Fat Maria turned up very early, Abigail brought her whole family, so did Seu Alexandre, Mariana remembered the

bumba-meu-boi she had gone to in his house, Seu
Machado shouted:

> I was sad when they came and told me
> That the donkey would never come out
> But the donkey is there in the street now
> And the people all give a great shout.

The party began with the ox running out and scatter-
ing people on all sides, children shrieked with joy, the
men sang and the music sounded new as if it had just
been composed, the street's flute-player blew on his
flute and made a funny face, he seemed proud of the
sounds he was producing, people came from every direction, wearing all sorts of clothes, Yorubas from Ibadan,
Itsekiris from Warri, Ibos from Onitsha, they all came
and stood watching the party, men in long skirts, blue,
yellow, pink, a lot of them had stopped in front of the
sobrado to buy water, the ox did big dance steps, the
donkey, with the man who worked it peeping out from
underneath, did smaller, more delicate steps, the big
woman dominated them all, soon the Brazilians were
going from the ox to the big woman and back, running
so as not to be caught, torches and lamps burned cheerfully, there was an interval when the people who made
the calungas work got out, the lifeless figures were propped up in the yard, the musicians played happy tunes,
Mariana looked around, saw the sobrado, with its
imposing façade, the ox, still now, Sebastian laughing
with a group of friends, Fat Maria got her into a corner
to talk:
'It's the best burrinha I've seen in Lagos.'
Mariana agreed, anyhow she doubted if any of the
others had been made with such care, Fat Maria went on:
'Do you think any of us will ever go back?'
'Where?'
'To Brazil.'
Mariana looked at her in amazement:

'How can you even think about it? When you leave a place like we left Brazil, you never go back. When we got on to that ship none of us thought about going back, it was for good. Brazil is on the other side of the sea, remember how far it is, the ship took months coming. Our life is here, none of us will ever go back, never.'

Fat Maria shook her head, as if she had only just realized what Mariana was saying:

'It would make me very happy to see Brazil again.'

'Lagos is a beautiful place, I like it here.'

'So do I, but I'm always dreaming about the markets in Bahia. Did you know I used to sell bean-cakes in the middle of the city?'

'My mother and grandmother had a fish-stall. How was it we never met each other there?'

'You were very young, we might have met but you wouldn't remember it now. When I first saw you on the ship you were a skinny little girl, whoever would have thought you would end up mistress of a sobrado in Lagos?'

'Everyone who owns sobrados here was poor when they arrived.'

'You weren't just poor, you were a child as well.'

Mariana laughed, and said:

'Or rather I stopped being a child the minute I set foot in Lagos.'

The men were laughing noisily over something, someone beat a drum and the sound hung echoing in the suddenly still air. Fat Maria asked:

'How are things with him?'

'Sebastian? Fine. He's the best man in the world.'

'I wondered how he would feel in the sobrado with you in charge.'

'But you're wrong, I'm not in charge.'

The little train went by over the way, it must have been the last journey of the night, Mariana watched it going, the flute-player began a Brazilian polka, the silence held the sound clearly, afterwards Seu Alexandre sang, the men who worked the dolls got into them again, the drums beat as the ox went around, Mariana sat there seeing the night slip away full of everyone's happiness, Joseph and Ainá running along beside the ox, afterwards she was to remember whole scenes of that party, people's gestures, one moment when Sebastian lifted his arms up trying to imitate someone or something, the people around him intent on what he was saying, another moment when Ainá appeared beside the big woman and Joseph tried to catch her, the little girl ran away to one side, the taste of the bean-cake the Fat Maria had made was different, stronger, afterwards Mariana thought she must have smiled a lot that night, perhaps that had increased the envy that surrounded her, and I see her with her hands resting in her lap, her dress spread out over the chair, her black face shining in the light of the party.

A few days later there was a meeting of the Brazilian community, Seu Machado said that there was something important that had to be discussed, where would they meet?, in his house? in Dona Zezé's?, in the end three Brazilians came to visit Mariana, they wanted to hold the meeting in her house, more chairs were brought up from the shop, Sebastian sat at one side, there were children crawling around the floor, Seu Machado spoke first:

'Something very serious is happening here. The other day I was asked to go to the Government office and one of the officials, a captain, sent for an interpreter and told me that from now on all business here will have to be transacted in English.'

No-one said anything, he went on:

'You all know that in the forty years I have been in Lagos I have never managed to learn English. The captain told me he has received an official directive which says that everyone must learn English, and he says that I can only go on doing business with them if I speak English.'

In the silence that followed a child cried. Seu Alexandre asked:

'What did you say to him?'

'I told him that I can't speak English, but my sons can and they can do business in my name.'

'What did he say then?'

'He didn't say anything. I think he understood my point of view.'

'So what's the problem?'

'The problem is this directive that everyone has to speak English.'

A confusion of words broke out, everyone wanted to speak at once, one very old Yoruba managed to make himself heard:

'English is a foreign language. Portuguese is a foreign language. What we ought to speak is Yoruba.'

No-one said anything for a minute until Mariana spoke:

'We'll have to organize English classes for everyone. The ones who know most English can teach the others. They are right, really. They are in control, they impose their language on us. That's only right. The children don't need to learn, but the older ones, the ones who came from Brazil, will have to go to classes. You can use my house, we'll have to decide about days and times, we'll have timetables like at school.'

Dona Zezé put in:

'You can use my house as well.'

Mariana went on:

'We ought to have an association as well, with a president and everything, to deal with our affairs, a Brazilian association.'

Then voices rose on all sides, no, you couldn't have a Brazilian association, because the ones born in Lagos weren't Brazilian now, perhaps an association of descendents of Brazilians would be better, or, suggested Fat Maria, an association of Brazilians and descendents of Brazilians. It was founded on the spot, Mariana proposed Seu Alexandre as president, old Teresa was vice-president, the first job for the newly-formed society was to get English lessons going in different houses.

The next day Seu Machado appeared at the appointed time:

'Will I need a book and an exercise-book?'

Mariana looked at the old man, he smiled, he found the situation very amusing, she said no, he wouldn't need books, smiled back at him, they began the class, it was difficult for him to understand the sounds, on the same day there were classes in other houses, whenever people met in Bangboshe Street they asked:

'How's your English getting on?'

'So-so.'

They all laughed, for a while the need to learn English gathered them all together in a sort of collective funny story, a word or a gesture was enough to set people off laughing at parties or in processions, at one serenata, for the death of an old woman, Dona Marcia, who had come from Brazil before the English had taken over in Lagos, Seu Machado said:

'This one died without having to learn English.'

Then one of the guitarists sang:

> Dona Marcia, Dona Marcia
> A saintly life she led
> They told her to learn English
> But she went and died instead.

Then other people improvised verses, the dead woman's family joined in the game, around midnight the ones who were learning English started to practise with the ones who could speak already. English words flew about in the gaiety of the serenata.

Sebastian had a letter from a friend he had met in Fernando Poo who lived in Ouidah now, in Dahomey, where there were a lot of Brazilians, this man insisted that Sebastian should go there with Mariana, in Ouidah they needed people with money, they would be able to open shops, buy houses, the couple agreed to make the trip after the rains.

When Mariana heard that Emilia was about to have her child, she took the train to Ibadan to visit her. Sebastian went with her, he stood at the train window watching the houses go by outside, Mariana smiled, remembering her journey all those years before, from Juiz de Fora to Rio de Janeiro, the countryside rushing by as if it were the train that were still, again she began wondering about the name of the man who had taken them from Piau to Juiz de Fora, she could remember his features so clearly, his open smile, his easy way of talking, the way he could start up a conversation with strangers, when she arrived she saw her sister standing at the door, her stomach was enormous, she protested:

'You didn't let us know you were coming.'

'It's a surprise.'

Shango's room was better arranged now, there was a long stone that looked as if it had had blood on it, like the ram's blood that morning in Bahia, the floor was beaten earth, can stones grow?, from the window of the room Mariana looked out at the town and saw it as she had never seen it before, all the colours yellowish, the houses different from the houses in Lagos, that night one of Emilia's friends, in the middle of a conversation about places to live in, said:

'Ibadan is a holy city.'

Another one retorted:

'No it isn't. It's Ife that is holy.'

Ebenezer hardly spoke, Mariana found his silence odd, she asked her sister what was wrong, apparently he wanted to leave his father's cocoa trees and go off and be a preacher, he loved quoting the bible, for each little daily event he had an appropriate verse, Emilia said:

'Some days he takes me into the bedroom and prays

159

over me for hours. He gets hold of the Bible, reads a bit out and then talks about what he has read, explains the meaning of the words. He gets furious when I fall asleep. Once he wanted to do the same thing to the whole family, his father said he wasn't going to listen to any sermons from his own son.'

'What's happened to him?'

'I don't know. He says he's always wanted to be a parson, it was his father who wouldn't let him.'

'And what about his mother, what does she think?'

'She doesn't say anything.'

Ebenezer's mother was the oldest wife, who managed the house, the other two wives had to do as she said, Mariana asked:

'Has he ever said anything about having another wife?'

'No. He's not very interested in women any more. You don't know how difficult it was to persuade him to give me this child.'

Mariana tried to talk to Ebenezer, but her brother-in-law avoided her, she thought he seemed to be half out of his mind, Emilia was different as well, she was still pretty, but she had lost all her gaiety, the old women in the family said that as soon as her child was born she would go back to normal, one day Mariana spent some time with the three wives of Ebenezer's father, the second one was called Dagbá, she talked a lot, in the end she asked, full of curiosity:

'What is it like to be the only wife your husband has?'

Mariana laughed, she wanted to ask the opposite, what was it like being married to a man who has other wives besides you, Dagbá thought that was funny, she said:

'It's bad to be the only wife, you must get no rest. The most important thing is to have children and to look after them. How can a woman look after a husband and a small child at the same time? it's not right. When there are a few wives it's different, the work is shared out, when I'm expecting a child and looking after it, at least until it is four years old, another wife can satisfy my husband and free me from that duty.'

'And aren't you jealous?'

The question hung in the air, without a reply, because Ebenezer came in, picked up a Bible that was on the table and went out again. Dagbá said:

'Ebenezer isn't my son, but I think his father has tried to organize his life too much, now he has this craze to be a parson and he's driving us all mad.'

One day they took Mariana to see Seu Anthony Okinoyi's cocoa trees, the cocoa fruit was gold-coloured, it was Oshun's colour, underneath the trees the ground was damp, her feet sank into the wet soil, she thought of the well, she had heard that the Government wells would be ready that month, now it didn't matter, she had sent a lot of palm oil to Brazil, a boat called *Altiva* had brought a cargo of sugar and tobacco which Mariana had already sold, Sebastian loved writing letters and looking after the shipments, he went on board wearing a hat, spent whole days talking to the sailors, asked them about Bahia, he couldn't remember much about it, Mariana had been older when she came over, she had safe in her memory every part of the market place, Father José's church, the hills, the shops she had been in, the animals she had seen, sometimes she heard voices, the man telling about all his children, the other man telling how stones grew, Sebastian couldn't remember much about the voyage, but there were certain scenes he could remember very clearly, another ship, the *Audaz*, was the one he liked best, he always spent the night on board when it came in to Lagos, from the shop on the sea-front you had a clear view of the entrance to the harbour, he saw all the ships coming in and going out, the furniture was still selling very well, more and more people were coming to live in Lagos, they were coming from the interior, Ibos, Efiks, Ijos, Hausas, people from Tapa, Calabar, Zaria, Sokoto, the tables and chairs that João the Carpenter and Antônio hired out were always booked in advance, they never spent any time in the shop, one day Mariana began to tell Sebastian about things that had happened on the voyage:

'I didn't know the name of the ship, it was only in Lagos that I heard the name *Esperança*. I used to like watching the sea for days on end, sometimes I forgot to eat. That was where I met Fat Maria.'

He was silent for a moment, then he said:

'Our ship was the *Santa Isabel*, there were so many people on board that we didn't all fit below decks. I was very little but I can remember that there used to be people asleep in every corner. The *Santa Isabel* arrived in Lagos a long time before the *Esperança*.'

In Emilia's house they had plenty of time, they could talk as much as they liked, there was no well, no need to look after the shop or the children, Joseph and Ainá had stayed behind with Epifânia, Mariana found out a lot about Sebastian, she got to know the way he had of leaning his arms on the window-sill and the way he pulled his shirt off, later she was to remember all sorts of characteristic gestures, a certain way he had of opening his mouth slightly just before he said something, they went out into the streets of Ibadan, walked around the markets, Mariana went to another party without men in Luisa's house, Emilia laughed a lot that afternoon, the drummers gave rhythm to the conversation, a few days later when Emilia began to feel the pains Mariana was there beside the midwife, Emilia had asked her to be there at the birth and to help because she was afraid of two things, one was that the women in that region gave birth sitting on a mat, two people took hold of the hands of the one who was having the child, another two held her legs, when she groaned all the women in the room groaned together, han, han, as if they were helping, hands without number pulled on the child, afterwards they threw boiling water over the woman's parts, Emilia didn't want it to happen like that, she had arranged for a midwife from Bahia to come and had told her she didn't want any water thrown over her, her other fear was that the child would have a big umbilicus, like she had seen babies in Ibadan, she told Mariana to watch the midwife, when the time came Mariana couldn't pay much attention to what the midwife was doing because it was twins that were born, the midwife shouted:

'Ibejes. Twins.'

Emilia had fainted, Seu Okinoyi came into the room, delighted with the news, Ebenezer was grave, he hardly spoke, looked carefully at the babies, later Emilia was happy with her children, she decided to call them Cosme and Damião, and listened to what everyone was saying about her husband, Seu Okinoyi's third wife said:

'He didn't say much before, but when he saw the babies he lost his tongue completely. He stood staring at them as if they were animals.'

Mariana and Sebastian went back to Lagos, they felt as if they had been away for years, when the train drew into the station they thought more houses seemed to have sprung up, they crossed the bridge and arrived on the island, friends and acquaintances everywhere, you could see the sobrado on Bangboshe Street long before you got to it, Joseph was playing at the door. Epifânia was just drawing a pitcher of water from the well as Mariana came up and shouted the Yoruba greeting:

'Mother, may you never die as you carry water.'

Epifânia replied:

'Daughter, may you never die as you return from a journey.'

And then she said:

'Has it come?'

'It was twins, two boys, Emilia is so happy.'

Ainá came running out of the house, grabbed her mother round the neck, the air was hot and heavy, later Mariana went to see Seu Gaspar, she asked him:

163

'Will you make me two nice ibejes?'

'Who for, Sinhá?'

'For my sister, she's had twins.'

Seu Gaspar chose the wood and said he would start the carving that very minute, Mariana stayed there a while, his knife went into the wood, cut away slivers which fell to the ground, there were some brightly-coloured egungun masks in a corner, the memory of that afternoon remained with her, figures of Shango and Oshun looked at her, the noise of the little train in Bangboshe became clear for a moment, then it seemed as if silence fell on the whole island.

At night they put chairs out in the street, Sebastian had on an old pair of trousers and his pyjama jacket, Epifânia was talking to Fat Maria, Mariana caught hold of Ainá when they heard loud voices in the street, it seemed like a fight, she heard a man shouting:

'He's got a knife.'

They all got up, Sebastian went and stood in front of them, a stocky Negro, bare-breasted, was advancing on another, who was backing away, looking around as if he was trying to escape, Sebastian went between them and said to the one with the knife:

'Stop that. Give me the knife.'

The man looked at Sebastian, who smiled, he went on looking at him without blinking, Sebastian said again:

'Give me the knife.'

The man said:

'Here.'

And he threw himself forward with the knife, buried it in Sebastian's stomach and ran off along the street, Mariana ran up with Ainá on her back, her husband had fallen with his hands clasped to his stomach, Seu Alexandre was bent over him, suddenly she found herself cradling Sebastian's head, Fat Maria was shouting:

'Someone get Father O'Malley.'

An English soldier came, and then four more, they

kept back the crowd that was forming, in the middle
there was just Mariana with Sebastian, the one who
seemed to be in charge asked them to tell him what had
happened, another one made Mariana let go of her
husband, felt him, she heard him say:

'Dead.'

She looked down at Sebastian, but only minutes ago
he had been sitting on that chair, the night calm, nothing
could have happened, the images became confused, she
saw when they took him away, where to?, someone told
her they would bring him back later, it was for the
inquest, Epifânia put her arms round Mariana and took
her into the parlour, people everywhere, Ainá was
crying noisily, Joseph was wandering about with terrified
eyes, violent death and young people's death is sad, only
death by dying is happy, O young husband who stayed
so short a time, Abigail sat down beside her for a moment,
held her head, she remembers that a lot of people
embraced her that night, sometimes the lamp only lit
up half of somebody's face, O violent death how is it you
happen, at one time she realized that Dona Zezé was
talking to her, old Teresa, Suliman, Ciriaco, people
from the ship, so many people had died on the *Esperança*,
they wrapped the bodies up in sheets and threw them into
the sea, who has any power over what happens?, friends
came, passed in front of her like a procession, Father
O'Malley held her hands in his for a while, his lips moved,
English didn't mean anything, what was he saying?,
words in Portuguese ran inside her, and in Yoruba, the
greeting that always spoke of death, may you never die
in bed with your husband, may you never die as you walk,
may you never die as you work, may you never die when
you are sitting, or lying down, or eating, or looking at
things, or with a stone in your hand, stones grow, how is
it that things happen?, the sound of a flute came from far
away in the night, but she didn't want a serenata, it was
a young death, she realized that it wasn't a flute, it must

have been a whistle, she doesn't know how long it all went on, she saw them bringing Sebastian's body back, the men brought him into the parlour, Fat Maria and Seu Alexandre pulled the big table into the middle of the room, Dona Zezé said:

'First we must wash him.'

Mariana got to her feet, took hold of Sebastian's hand and said:

'All right.'

She took the head, Seu Alexandre the two legs, Fat Maria and Abigail the shoulders, they carried the body into the yard where there was another table, Mariana went to the well, drew up some water, the others took off Sebastian's trousers and pyjama jacket, when Mariana came back she saw him lying naked on the table, the wound in his stomach was open and ugly, she threw the first stream of water over him, then began to wash him carefully and slowly, his penis fell limp, she washed it with soap, the others were helping, Seu Justino came then, someone had put a lantern on the roof of the well, Mariana brought more water, took clean towels, wiped his body dry, Epifânia brought out a suit that was almost new, Sebastian had only worn it twice to go to church, they dressed him in it, when they put him on the table in the parlour he didn't look dead, he looked as if he were just resting, Mariana stayed standing beside him, she didn't cry, all night long people kept coming into the house, all their friends from the *Esperança*, Seu Machado came with a bottle of cachaça, the men needed something to drink, Epifânia tried to make Mariana have some but she refused, there were moments of utter silence, as if there were no-one in the room except herself and the body of Sebastian, it was almost morning when she noticed that one man was drunk, it was one of Dona Zezé's sons, he was leaning against the wall of the house opposite and had pulled out his penis, the spurt of liquid that came out wet the bottom of the wall, Mariana

166

noticed people coming in and going out, but kept her
eyes on her husband, it was as if he realized everything
that was going on, the man peeing, the quiet voices of
the people outside drinking, the words of his friends, the
English spoken by the Englishmen he had met over the
palm-oil shipments, João the Carpenter came with the
coffin, they picked up his body and placed it inside,
Epifânia came and said:
'We are going to bury Sebastian in the square.'
It would have been good to bury him in the bedroom,
after the old African custom, let him be buried in the
place where he had lived and where he could always be
seen and remembered, every day the family would put a
plate of food beside the grave, the dead man would be
present at the family's festivities, at the births, the
baptisms, the dances, he would hear the drums, know
everything that was going on, Father O'Malley arrived
wearing his white surplice, said prayers over the body,
Seu Alexandre and João the Carpenter closed the coffin,
Ebenezer and Seu Okinoyi had come from Ibadan, as
the retinue was leaving the house a car drove past down
Bangboshe, the grave was already open, Mariana followed
the coffin with her eyes as it went down, she helped to
throw earth on to it, Epifânia and Fat Maria came and
stood beside her, when it was all over Mariana walked
back slowly, along the street where she lived, went into
the parlour, up the stairs, she hadn't seen her own room
since yesterday, she sat down in a rocking-chair, she saw
that Epifânia had brought her something to eat, she felt
an enormous desire to sleep, closed her eyes and became
absorbed in herself, she could hear voices and odd words,
noises of people outside, O night that was so violent, O
day coming with smells and weariness, even with her
eyes closed she could still see things, she could not sleep
and it would have been so good to get away from it all,
at one time she heard Ainá's voice, now Sebastian was
with the other Ainá, the old one, she had scarcely noticed

Seu Justino, Sebastian's father, all night she had seen him, he and his wife had been standing at the other side of the coffin, as they came back along the street they were behind her, but it was only now she remembered them, O memory that comes so late, who has any power over what happens?, O dead man, gone and yet still here, suddenly Mariana realized she had been sleeping in the rocking chair, but sleeping and waking, waking and sleeping, she opened her eyes once and saw that it was dark, night had fallen, she closed her eyes again, the chair rocked gently in the darkness.

Part III

THE WATER HOUSE

Mariana stayed in her room for three days. Sometimes, but rarely, she ate from the plates that Epifânia and Antônio left by her side, she wasn't always certain where she was, once she thought she was in Bahia, sitting at the back of the fish stall, she raised her head and could even smell the fish, but what she saw in front of her was the wall of her bedroom, the very colour she had chosen, pale blue, and then she began to be aware of things once more, the bed she and Sebastian had slept in, the blanket, afterwards she lost herself again and saw herself sitting on the horse that had carried her from Piau to Juiz de Fora, the kind black face of the man constantly turning round towards her, she heard the shouts as the children caught the piau-fish, the fish was jumping, slowly she recaptured the reality of the moment she was living, the chair rocking, but again she let herself drift away and felt the deck rising and falling, the ship driving through the waves, alone in the bright sunlight, the scene of Sebastian's death came back to her from time to time, once she heard Ainá crying, she was like this for three days and three nights. When she went downstairs, on the fourth day, she saw her mother and her children and found them strange, as if she had become detached from the real world and her world, from now on, was to be different. The well, when she saw it again, asserted itself as something real and solid and indestructible, the same as before, unchanged, the water transparent, at the bottom of the yard the lifeless calungas lay waiting for another party, Mariana knows that Fat Maria, Abigail, Teresa, Seu Justino and

Jerónimo were all beside her, talking, saying things, she replied to them all, she doesn't think she smiled, but she was polite to them, at the back of her mind she was thinking of leaving Lagos, where would she go?, in her search for new ground, a different horizon, going back to Brazil would be difficult, perhaps it would be better to go somewhere where there were more Brazilians, Badagri, Porto Novo, Ouidah, she remembered the letter from Sebastian's friend who lived in Ouidah, she let several weeks go by, took up ordinary life once more, went to the shop, replied to letters, looked at the dried salt meat that had just arrived from Brazil, did the accounts for the sale of furniture, one day she told Epifânia:

'I'm going to Dahomey to see what it's like there.'

Her mother looked at her hard, asked:

'What for? It's the same as it is here.'

'I want to see from close to.'

She left very early, by canoe, she could have gone by land, but she liked travelling on the water, she sewed a fair amount of money into a cloth which she wrapped around her waist under her dress, she wouldn't let any of her relatives go with her, the man rowed all morning, they stopped beyond Badagri, pulled the boat ashore, she slept on the bank, covered up by a heavy piece of material, they started off again as the sun was rising, when Mariana saw Porto Novo in the distance she thought it looked an attractive town, she got out of the boat beside a bridge, looked for the house of a Brazilian called José de Almeida, they had a long conversation, he was in trade, he wanted to know how long she would be staying in Porto Novo:

'Are you going to set up in business here, Sinhá?'

'Perhaps.'

'It would be wise to get friendly with the French. They are in charge here, not the English.'

Mariana thought that nobody was in charge anywhere, she had never taken much notice of the English in Lagos, they had always been kind and considerate when she had met them, but life went along very well without them, grew without them, it even ended without them, she asked:

'Is Ouidah very far from here?'

'No. You can reach it in less than a day, Sinhá.'

She found a guide, the son of a Brazilian family, called Jean da Cruz, he was a cheerful boy who told stories, talked about his parents, said:

'Ouidah is the best place for you, Sinhá. It's full of Brazilians.'

They passed expanses of sand, beaches and more beaches, Mariana felt at ease in those wide stretches of country, in Ouidah she stayed in a sort of guest-house opposite the Portuguese fort, when she heard that there were still some Portuguese living there she decided to visit the main residence of the fort the next day, the men had an accent, a strong unfamiliar accent, like the one that used to make the children laugh in Brazil, the two flights of steps in front of the house reminded her of the grand sobrados in Bahia, Mariana spent the whole morning talking to two Portuguese men, one of them said:

'There are a lot of Brazilians here. Are you going to stay long?'

'I might come here to live.'

She walked along the streets of Ouidah, she saw the Brazilian doorways, visited the house that had belonged to Xaxa de Sousa I, the Brazilian who had grown rich in Ouidah and had founded a dynasty, the friend who had written to Sebastian was related to the Sousas, she stood on the beach where huge numbers of slaves had been put on ships for Brazil, everywhere she saw new things, and the possibility of a new life, the first difficulty she met with was when she stopped at a store and the man couldn't understand Portuguese or Yoruba or English, afterwards she found out that the languages he spoke were French and Ewe, she would have to learn them, but Ouidah seemed too big to her, what she liked was one day when she was going along the road and came across a stretch of land in front of a beach running down to the sea, you could smell the salt on the wind, she learned that the land belonged to a Brazilian, it would be a good place to build a house, a big sobrado like the ones in Bahia, facing the beach and the waves that you could see far off there. She spent weeks arranging to buy the land, went back to Lagos, found that old Teresa had died while she had been away, told Epifânia that she was going to have a house built on the other side of Ouidah, near the frontier between French territory and German territory, between Dahomey and its neighbour Zorei, she needed Ricardo and the bricklayers, her mother and Antônio were to go on looking after the shop and the well, Epifânia told her:

'The English wells are working now.'

'That doesn't matter, the important things now are the shop and the export of palm-oil to Brazil and the dried meat and sugar and cachaça and tobacco we get from there.'

She spent more than a month in Lagos, talking to the bricklayers, discussing the design of the new house with Ricardo, looking after Joseph and Ainá, would she be able to take them with her now?, it would be better to wait, her mother would look after everything while she was gone, there was a lot of money now, that wasn't a problem any more, when she sat down one night in front of the house everything came back to her, Sebastian there beside her, the damp darkness, the noise of the little train, she made herself look all around her, carefully, to see that Sebastian was no longer there, the night was different, Joseph was taller, Ainá cried less, more had changed than had stayed the same, God how things change.

This time she went overland, along an English road

that went to Porto Novo, she took Ricardo and six bricklayers, she was in a hurry to get to Ouidah, when Ricardo saw the piece of land he exclaimed:

'It's huge.'

He drew the different parts of the house on a piece of paper, Mariana told him:

'I don't want the staircase outside, I want it inside, there was one like that in Piau.'

One night Mariana felt ill, as if she were going to faint, she realized that her monthly period hadn't come, she was certain she was with child, went and found a Brazilian woman who knew about these things, who examined her closely, pushed a finger up her sex, said:

'Yes, of course. It will be a boy. And he's three months gone already.'

Mariana went back to her room without saying a word. She sat on the bed and looked out into the street, so everything was going to begin again, another child of Sebastian had been forced to live, O you who come so unexpected, may you be welcome and find happiness, may you be master of lands and horses, beloved of women if you are a man, of men if you are a woman, she spent the whole night thinking, perhaps she ought to go back to Lagos to have the child, but that would delay the house, she decided to stay, the next day she went and supervised the building, asked Ricardo:

'How long do you think it will take?'

'About ten months.'

The child would be born before then. She saw the walls going up, Ricardo didn't like the sawmill he visited in Ouidah, he went to Porto Novo to order the wood, it was a pity João the Carpenter wasn't there, Mariana wanted a well at the back of the house, a group of coco-palms at one side stood clear-cut every evening against the setting sun, O palm-oil tree that gives oil and makes the house beautiful, everyone told Mariana that she should go to Aduni to have her baby, it was the capital of Zorei, there were very good German doctors there, but what did she want with a doctor?, she had given birth to two children already without the help of doctors, she watched her stomach growing bigger, from the fifth month she began to feel very ill, this hadn't happened to her before, now she could say some sentences in French, she used to talk to an old Ewe woman, who when she wanted to say no said paditu, as if it were one word, Mariana saw in a book that it was three, pas du tout, the woman advised her again to go to Aduni, in the sixth month she scarcely left her bed, in the seventh she decided to go across the frontier to Zorei, she arrived in Aduni one rainy afternoon, looked for the hospital with the old Ewe woman who had come with her, they put her in a white ward, she had never seen so many beds together, the doctor was a huge German, brown hair, he smiled at her in a friendly way, talked to the old woman, Mariana closed her eyes and thought about this child who was going to be born in a foreign country, but she was from a foreign country too, she asked herself which was her country, Brazil where she had come from?, Lagos where she had married and had children?, Ouidah where she was building her house now or Aduni where her third child was to be born? The Ewe woman said:

'This hospital is very dear.'

'Never mind.'

A fortnight later she felt well again, looked out of the window and saw the town, a pleasant garden, houses on the other side of the square, she began to understand a few words of German, there were two doctors, both very serious, she was ill again at the end of the last month, the doctor insisted that she should eat more, round about the day when she was due she felt as if her veins were bursting, O Oshun of the clear and tranquil waters grant me your protection in this birth, she doesn't remember what happened for a long time, one day she saw herself awake, her legs apart, a stabbing pain drove through her body, sweat was running down her face, when the mass of stuff that was coming out of her sex came right out she closed her eyes and breathed deeply, in a great relief, the crying of the child filled the room and the doctor came up to her:

'It's a boy.'

She decided that moment. His name would be Sebastian, Sebastian Silva like his father, O son who came in pain and sweat, O new Sebastian born surrounded by foreign tongues. This time she would have a Yoruba festival for the ceremony of the naming, it would be in Lagos, with the rest of the family, instead of the child's father his grandfather would preside at that very private moment of the consecration of the new Silva.

When Ricardo came to fetch her from the hospital he asked:

'What is he going to be called?'

'Sebastian. He has been registered in Aduni already, I gave the name Sebastian. The ceremony of the naming and the baptism will be in Lagos.'

On the way back she could see the long road that stretched from Aduni to the frontier of Zorei, coco-palms, salt fish from Togo being sold at the roadside, houses scattered amongst the green, a Brazilian name here and there, she saw Sousa written up over one doorway, before they arrived she told them:

'No matter what state the house is in, I'm going to live there from today.'

'You can't. It's not ready yet.'

'That doesn't matter. Even if it hasn't got a roof, it's not raining, I can sleep without a roof.'

The house rose impressively, the walls were finished, Mariana fed Sebastian and lay down beside where the staircase would be, the child sucked strongly at her breast, from the sea there came a luminosity, like moonlight, a very gentle wind shook the palms.

The next day she decided it would be best to go

straight to Lagos, she gave instructions to Ricardo and the bricklayers, started the journey on foot, then took a canoe, went past Topo, where she had studied, you could see the nuns' school over on the other side of the island, arriving in Lagos she felt as if she were coming to an unknown land, people crowded into the sobrado, amazed to hear of the birth of her son, Epifânia smiled, Fat Maria arrived glowing with happiness, Seu Justino took the child from her, held it close to him, said:

'One more Silva.'

They had the naming ceremony that same day. A few guests in the parlour, Joseph and Ainá sitting on the ground, Epifânia moving chairs around and pulling out the table, Fat Maria, Abigail, Dona Zezé, Seu Machado, Seu Alexandre, João the Carpenter, Jerónimo, when Seu Justino and his wife arrived Mariana went inside and brought out a little bowl full of water, she put it on the table in the middle of the room, Epifânia came in with a tray on which there were three saucers, one with salt, the second with honey and the third with palm-oil. Seu Justino took the child, Mariana sat by his side, the old man dipped a finger into the water, moistened Sebastian's lips with it, said:

'Water is the basis of everything, it is the most important thing in the world, may the life of this child be calm and serene like water.'

He took a pinch of salt, put a little into the mouth of his grandson:

'Salt makes things clean, may this child be pure and just.'

He took a little honey, rubbed it on the lips that were open now:

'Honey sweetens life. May this child's life be full of sweetness and gaiety.'

He dipped his fingers into the palm-oil:

'The oil of the palm-tree is a symbol of what we eat. May this child always have enough to eat his whole life long and may he enjoy the pleasure that food can give.'

Seu Justino paused for a moment, then said:

'You are Sebastian.'

Then each person in the room, beginning with Seu Justino and Mariana, put in their mouths first water, then salt, honey and oil, while she was doing this Mariana looked at Sebastian who had his eyes fixed on his grandmother's dress, Epifânia brought Joseph and Ainá to the table, they took part in the ceremony as well, they stood looking at their little brother's face, Mariana asked if they could read yet, Epifânia told her:

'Joseph can, but he's lazy.'

'What language does he read in?'

'Portuguese and English.'

Fat Maria asked them to give a party with the burrinha, Mariana protested that it was less than a year since Sebastian had died, but Fat Maria insisted:

'It's to welcome the new Sebastian Silva and his return to Lagos.'

'But I'm not going to stay in Lagos.'

'What do you mean, not going to stay?'

'I'm building a house near the frontier with Zorei. I'm going to stay there for a while.'

'But that's only for a while. This is where you live.'

Was it? One afternoon Mariana leaned over the well, looked down into its depths, you couldn't see the water, but if you threw a stone down it would make a splash, she thought of the well as a salvation, O well that has made the prosperity of the whole family, the well was her home, her thirst, her centre, but the sobrado on the beach called to her as well, it wouldn't be difficult to spend a few months in one place and a few months in the other, it wasn't far, when the roads got better she might buy one of these new motor-cars, that night she talked to her mother:

'We'll give a baptism party with the burrinha and then I'll go back to Ouidah. I've still got a lot to do there.'

She looked at the shop accounts, there was a letter from England confirming that a shipment of beer had been sent off at her request, and there was an offer of sugar from Cuba, she realized that the prospects of this business were excellent now, from Ouidah she would be able to build up the trade, the first thing would be to increase the export of copra, there were large quantities of ground-nuts to be had in Ouidah as well, they could be shipped to Europe, one day Seu Alexandre, who kept up with the news, said to Mariana:

'Things don't look good in Europe. There might be a war there.'

War, war was something remote, no-one could work if they thought about war, it was best just to get on with things, she went about with Sebastian tied to her back, on the day of the party the house was more crowded than it had ever been before, Dona Zezé called her into a corner and said:

'Daughter, I think that we ought to have a serenata even when young people die. We are all going towards death, it is always a good thing. When Sebastian died you wouldn't have been able to accept this idea, so we want to have this party today as a homage to him because he led a good life, he left three children behind him and he was very happy.'

The ox charged against the crowd and é boi echoed through Bangboshe Street, Mariana looked at everybody, she was amazed that she knew so many people in this town, sometimes she didn't know their names, she had seen this face, and that one, and that girl challenging the ox must be a daughter of one of the Brazilians, perhaps one of the little girls who used to play on the *Esperança*, the beer arrived, Seu Machado drank a glassful and began to sing:

I'd sooner drink cachaça
Cachaça when I'm dry
While the donkey runs along
While the donkey passes by.

Little Sebastian slept peacefully, he didn't seem to be disturbed by the singing or the music, Ainá followed the movements of the ox, from time to time a louder burst of noise came from the thick of the party, it was when the dolls came together, each of them dancing in its own style, the head of the ostrich was outlined against the sudden light of a torch, when the last guest had gone Mariana took Joseph, put him to bed, held Ainá on her knee for a few minutes then took her to the room upstairs, she herself didn't feel sleepy, the house seemed full of heat, she took out her breast, gave suck to Sebastian and began to think about the journey back to Ouidah, she would set out the next morning, the noises of the night came faintly to her, a dog barking in the distance, people going by in the street, a child crying, the house she was building was far away from everything, there were no neighbours, as soon as the sun rose she woke up Epifânia and Antônio, told them:

'I must go back today. Ricardo and the bricklayers are expecting me and the house has got to be finished quickly. I'll come back to Lagos one day soon.'

She set off with Sebastian, took a canoe, as soon as she saw the walls of the house she knew that Ricardo had been pressing on well with the work while she had been away, in Ouidah Jean da Cruz's father and a young girl called Marie Vieira used to come and talk to her, Mariana was managing to speak French now and could understand everything they said to her, deep down there wasn't much difference between the Brazilians in Ouidah and the ones in Lagos, it was only the English and the French that were different, Marie had a pretty face, she laughed a lot, loved dancing, she confided to Mariana that she and

179

Jean da Cruz were hoping to get married as soon as they could, one day she asked:

'How did your husband die?'

'He was killed with a knife.'

'Who killed him?'

'I don't know. We never found out.'

She was amazed to realize that she didn't know the name of the man who had killed Sebastian, to her it was as if her husband had died by drowning, or by being struck by lightning, the man who had killed him had never been important, it was possible that no-one in Bangboshe Street had known who it was, otherwise Fat Maria would have told her, one day the house was ready, Mariana had been sleeping in different places, first beside the staircase, then on the upper storey, still without a roof, then in the big parlour, last of all in the room that was to be hers, it was a big room, eight metres by six, she remembered having seen one something like it in Piau, she had the bed put in the centre, bought cupboards, near the bed she had a big table where she wrote letters, the shipment of tobacco she had ordered was on its way, it had all been sold already to traders in Abomey, she had sacks of cola-nuts ready to be loaded on to the ship going back to Bahia, the house when it was finished attracted the attention of all the Brazilians in Ouidah and Porto Novo. Mariana spent whole days receiving visitors, it still wasn't properly furnished, but she could offer coffee and cakes to the people who came to see her, she became a well-known figure all along the French-speaking coast, in Ouidah and Porto Novo they called her Dona Mariana, a lot of them used Sinhá when they spoke to her, the Sousas came to look at the sobrado on the beach and Mariana saw that Sebastian was already starting to walk and to say little things, she made another journey to Lagos, stayed there a long while seeing to the business and to her children, when she came back she brought Epifânia, Joseph and Ainá with her, Antônio stayed behind to look after the business, she enjoyed the amazement on the children's faces when they saw all the new sights, Joseph tried to say things in French, everyone laughed at the way he pronounced the words, Ainá put her hand into the water of the lagoon, caught seaweed, put it into the bottom of the canoe, when they arrived at the sobrado Epifânia stood speechless, then went in, looked into every room on the ground floor, went up the stairs, saw Mariana's room, came down and went out to the back, said:

'It's bigger than Uncle Inhaim's house in Piau.'

'From what I can remember of Uncle Inhaim's house, it's a lot bigger.'

'And you live here by yourself?'

'Why should I need anyone else?'

'You could get married again.'

She could, but she had so much to do and there was the delight of dreaming up new things, of sharing with Sebastian his discovery of the world, Mariana had engaged two Calabari servants, one of them cooked the food, the other looked after the house and the yard, she would have to find more people to help with the copra production and the selling of it, eventually she would need to have about twenty people working for her, Joseph, Ainá and Sebastian played together, Epifânia got so used to it all that she forgot Lagos, it was almost a year later that a letter from Antônio saying that Emilia was ill forced her to go back there, she insisted on taking Joseph and Ainá with her, Mariana stood at the upper window watching her mother and her children as they went away, she had to go to Aduni the next day to see about the sale of cassava and palm-oil that she had bought in the interior, little Sebastian went with her, the town was serene and welcoming, Mariana felt good there, she wanted to find out where there was a good school for small children, she thought it might be a good idea to send Sebastian to school in Zorei, after all that was where he had been born, when she got back she asked Marie Vieira to come and live with her:

'When is Jean going to marry you?'

'He hasn't any money and he doesn't want to marry like that.'

'Tell him to come and work for me.'

Jean da Cruz came and talked to Mariana two days later, she needed someone to take charge of the copra production and to deal with shipping and unloading, the best thing would have been for Antônio to have come to Ouidah, but she couldn't persuade him to leave the business in Lagos, when she got another letter about her sister's illness she took Sebastian and set out along the road, Jean would look after her affairs, as the canoe crossed the lagoons that stretch between Porto Novo and Lagos she wondered what could be wrong with her sister, the letter didn't say, her mother couldn't explain:

'She's very thin and she scarcely ever sleeps.'

'And what about her husband?'

'He's disappeared.'

'What do you mean, disappeared?'

'Apparently he decided to be a preacher, now he goes about preaching in the towns and villages, goes on foot from one place to the other, no-one knows how he lives.'

'Where is Emilia living?'

'With her father-in-law, but his oldest wife, Ebenezer's mother, is dead.'

Mariana went by train to Ibadan, took Joseph, Ainá and Sebastian, looked for somewhere she could sleep with the children, Luisa told her about a house that let off rooms, then she went to see her sister, she found Dagbá, the second wife, sitting on the doorstep, the woman greeted her:

'May you never die as you walk towards me.'

'May you never die as you are sitting.'

'It's a good thing you have come, Emilia isn't well.'

Mariana went in, saw the twins playing naked in the

yard, they had been born just before Sebastian died, her sister was in another room, thin but still pretty, they smiled at each other, Mariana said:

'Well, how's my little sister?'

'Not very well, I feel so tired and no-one can understand why.'

They talked for a long time, Emilia talked to her sister more freely than she had ever done before, Ebenezer's father came in, greeted Mariana, complained about the cocoa prices, the merchants in Lagos were robbing the producers, Mariana asked:

'Where is Ebenezer, Seu Anthony?'

'I don't want to hear anything about that son of mine. He's abandoned his wife and gone off preaching. He wants to save other people's souls, he should have started with his own.'

Mariana thought it would be a good thing if Emilia went back with her to Ouidah, for a while at least, but her sister wouldn't agree, it was sad to see a pretty woman like her in bed, pale, in a dark hot room, the next day she brought her children to meet her sister's twins, the five of them played with earth, covered themselves with mud, Sebastian decided that he would go naked too, he took off his clothes, Mariana laughed, when she was saying goodbye she said:

'If you need anything at all, sister, let me know and I'll come straight away.'

She stayed in Lagos for two weeks, the shop was doing better and better business, there were several people employed there, what seemed unreal was the news of the war, this time she hired a car and took Antônio and the children to Ouidah, Epifânia stayed by herself looking after the house and the shop, Marie Vieira had fixed the day of her wedding, Jean da Cruz told Mariana;

'I've bought a piece of land not far from here and I've already started to build a house. It's only small, but it will do.'

183

Mariana went to have a look, thought it was just right for them, the wedding party brought together a lot of the Ouidah Brazilians, they opened bottles of French wine, Mariana tried it, the three children were all dressed in clothes of the same pattern, there was a clarinettist playing for the dancing, Seu José de Almeida sang:

> O Lagos is a good place
> And Bahia's good as well
> But the town called Porto Novo
> Is the poor man's dream of hell.

There were shouts of laughter, the night air was damp, everyone was sweating, Mariana thought of her first night, how she had sweated, tonight it was Marie Vieira's turn, the beating of the drums reverberated through the ground, the beach stretched out under the lights of the party, a kid tied up out there reminded her that it was a long time since she had offered a ram to Shango, she had left her Oshun in Lagos, she would have to have another made, Sebastian had got tired, he lay down in a corner and slept, Joseph and Ainá were sitting beside their brother and amusing themselves by throwing three stones up and catching them on the backs of their hands, the stones that the man had said could grow, Marie and Jean were determined to spend the night in their new house, even though it wasn't finished, Mariana tied Sebastian on her back, gave her right hand to Joseph, her left to Ainá, left Antônio dancing at the party, went up the stairs of her house, she wanted to go to Aduni the next morning, she was interested in a shop she had seen in the same square as the hospital where Sebastian had been born, she went with Antônio, he liked the town, he thought that the shop was in a good position, she said:
'I've found out that the man wants to sell, but we shouldn't show too much enthusiasm to buy just yet.'
'Is the owner Brazilian?'

184

'No, he's an Ewe.'

Mariana talked to the man for two hours, he didn't show too much interest and he didn't say how much he wanted for the house, in the end she took her leave without pressing the matter:

'I live just beyond the frontier, or rather, between the frontier and Ouidah. If you should decide to sell and no-one else shows any interest, you could always send word to me there. Just ask for Mariana Silva, everyone knows me.'

Antônio didn't think the man would try to find her or send any message, but one afternoon three weeks later Mariana saw someone coming up to the house, it was him, she ran to tell her brother:

'You were wrong. The man's here about the shop.'

This time the first thing he said was the price he wanted, in half an hour it was all settled, Mariana promised to go into Zorei in a day or two to pay the money and sign the papers. One day she crossed the other frontier, into Togo, the sea on one side and the lagoon on the other, she was thinking that now she had a house and a shop in Lagos, another house between Ouidah and Zorei and another shop in Aduni, Ricardo and Jean da Cruz would have to look after this one for the time being, later on Antônio could spend some time in Lagos and some in Aduni, she would have to travel back and forth as well, the demand for palm-oil in Brazil was getting bigger and bigger, here they needed sugar, her children would grow up and help her with the business, her sister's twins would help too, especially now that Ebenezer had disappeared, where had she been wrong with him?, he had seemed such a fine young man the day he had come to ask for Emilia's hand, she was usually sound in her judgement of people, that time she had been wrong, but perhaps he was a good man, only he was no good for a marriage, after all there are people who don't fit in to marriage.

When the papers had been signed, Mariana went to see a Sousa who she had been told lived near the shop, she talked to him, asked him to keep an eye on the shop, she was going to shut it up for a few days until she decided who was going to act for her in Aduni, then she ordered a board to be painted with these words:

The Water House

and when she got back to the sobrado in Ouidah she had it put up over the main door, Jean da Cruz asked her what the name meant:

'I only began to be myself after I had made a well.'

Ricardo agreed to go to Aduni, Mariana realized that she could already speak French and German fairly fluently, she understood a little Ewe and Fon, as she had already learnt Portuguese, Yoruba and English she was becoming quite a linguist, but she only felt at home in Portuguese and Yoruba, during the next few weeks she went to Aduni often, Sebastian always went with her, he was already beginning to speak some French, Joseph and Ainá liked the new shop, a ship with a huge cargo of dried meat, sugar and tobacco was about to dock in Lagos so Mariana had to go there and see Epifânia, who was getting old now, but she seemed strong enough, she took all the children, left Antônio in the Water House, Sebastian could tell one town from another now, he knew which was Porto Novo, when they arrived in Lagos he remembered that it was the town on the island, the news of Emilia wasn't very good, one Saturday, when it was getting dark, Mariana saw Ebenezer in Broad Street, preaching, about thirty people were grouped around him, she stopped and listened, he was saying:

'Only Jesus is the answer and Jesus says that by your acts you will be judged. Beware of those who teach you witchcraft, who deceive you with lies, beware of false prophets who come to you in sheep's clothing, but within they are ravening wolves. By their fruits ye shall know them. Can you gather grapes from thorns or figs from thistles? Only Jesus can give you the right answer and the answer is: save your soul. What doth it profit a man if he gain the whole world, but suffer the loss of his own soul? The tree which does not give good fruit is cut down and cast into the fire. Every one of you who loses his soul will be flung into the fire and it will not help if you cry "Lord! Lord!", for such a man will never enter into the kingdom of heaven, but only he who beats his breast and repents.'

Ebenezer knelt down and cried:

'Let us beat our breasts and beg God to forgive us our sins, the sin of lechery which brings us to sleep with women and sin with women, the sin of greed which makes us eat more than we need to keep us alive, the sin of envy which makes us hate the man who has more possessions than ourselves, let us beat our breasts and ask forgiveness for all our sins.'

Two women and a man had come with Ebenezer, they knelt with him and beat their breasts, some others seemed inclined to do the same, others again seemed indifferent, Ebenezer got to his feet and went on:

'Lagos is a sinful town. All sin and all crime have come together in this modern Babylon and woe betide you if you do not repent. Remember that you must not only abstain from sin, but speak out against sin, fight against it, and if, in one house or in one town, they will not receive you or will not listen to your words, when you leave that house or that town, shake its dust from your feet. Go alone, without wives, without children, carry neither gold nor silver nor copper in your belt, nor shoes for your feet, nor clothing, nor food because on the way you will receive what is your due.'

Ebenezer noticed Mariana, turned towards her:

'And woe unto you who hoard up wealth and do not follow the way of the Lord, woe unto those who give bad counsel and who kill the soul. Have no fear of those who kill the body, be afraid rather of men who speak idle words, live idle lives, and of the evil man who brings forth evil things from his ill-gotten wealth. I tell you that every idle word that men speak must be accounted for on the day of judgement. For by your words shall you be justified, by your words shall you be condemned. Let us use words to ask forgiveness for the sins of all the women and all the men in the world, let us beat our breasts and ask forgiveness.'

He knelt again and beat his breast, Mariana walked away towards Tinubu Square, back home she said to Epifânia:

'I've just seen Ebenezer.'

'Where?'

'He was preaching on Broad Street.'

Mariana thought for a moment then said:

'He seems sincere and at the same time he seems mad.'

'Do you think he might get better and come back to Emilia?'

'I doubt it.'

She saw him a few more times in Lagos, which he seemed to have chosen as a centre for his preaching, they said that many people followed him, listened to what he said, some of his followers wanted to stay on Ikoyi and found a religious centre there, Mariana talked to Seu Gaspar about it, he told her:

'Ebenezer is a very religious man, Sinhá. He deserves respect.'

He picked up a figure of Shango, then Oshun, added:

'The orishas love religious men, our way of religion is different, but your sister's husband has great power.'

Now Ebenezer went to and fro in front of the sobrado where he had married Emilia, one day he preached right in the middle of the street, Fat Maria went to listen, his voice carried inside the houses:

'He who listens to my words and puts them into practice will be like the wise man who built his house upon a

188

rock, for my words are not mine, but His who died for us, Jesus Christ who sends me to you as He has sent many others before me. When you pray do not be like the hypocrites who pray standing and need rich churches, go into your own room and pray in silence, without anyone to see you, and your Father, Who sees that which is hidden, will repay you. Do not think that the Lord can be deceived by the hypocrisy of the many, He sees within your thoughts and knows what you feel, and for this reason let your words be: yes, yes; no, no. The lamp of the body is in the eye, do not sin through your eyes for they are the greatest source of iniquity, through them sin enters into your soul, do not swear by Shango or by Oshun or by Ogun, for false gods will not prevail against the Lord and you must believe in the Lord alone, in Him only must you put your faith.'

Fat Maria came looking for Mariana after Ebenezer, followed by a crowd of people, had gone away down Bangboshe Street, she said:

'He doesn't seem the same man as the one who married Emilia.'

Mariana thought of her sister, wondered how she was. Ebenezer spoke imposing English which made his preaching sound very grave and serious, she had heard that in the interior he spoke Yoruba and had even greater success, when she had finished her business she went back to the Water House, this time with Fat Maria who had never been out of Lagos since the day she arrived, she thought the town of Porto Novo was beautiful:

'It's not so big as Lagos, but it's lovely.'

She liked the Water House, went into all the rooms, Joseph and Ainá ran down to the beach, Ricardo had come from Aduni, he said that the shop was doing good business, he was selling a lot of palm-oil and a lot of cachaça but the Germans were talking about war, nobody knew if it were true, she could imagine the confusion there would be if war did break out, here at the

Water House it was French territory, a little further along, in Zorei, the Germans were in charge, on the other side too, in Togo, but it was crazy to talk of war, nobody wanted war, the copra output was increasing under Jean's management, when Mariana got the news that Seu Anthony Okinoyi had died she went straight to Lagos, by herself, took a train to Ibadan, found her sister not knowing what to do, packed Emilia's things up, there wasn't much, wrapped up the figures of Shango and the Ibejes, took the twins and two days later they all arrived in Lagos, Emilia heard that Ebenezer was preaching on the other side of the bridge, in Ebute-Metta, she went there with the twins, Mariana insisted on going with her, Ebenezer was saying:

'A leper prostrated himself before the Lord saying: Lord, if thou wilt thou canst make me clean. And Jesus, stretching out his hand, said, I will, be thou clean. And immediately he was cleansed of his leprosy. And so it will be with you if you go in faith to the Lord and say: Lord, if thou wilt, thou canst cleanse me of my sins. And your faith will blot out all your sins. He who has ears to hear, let him hear: he who wishes to save himself must abandon all his own, father, mother, wife, children, wrap a cloth round his body and walk alone down the ways of truth, for only the man who is free of all the chains of this world can dedicate himself completely to Jesus Christ. The word of the Lord is being heard in Lagos, many are following it, but verily I say unto you: unless you leave off sin, unless you cast away sin, you will never find salvation, sin sticks to man like slime, like filth, and only by depriving himself of all bodily indulgence, of all the comforts of the flesh, will man created by God and for God find his true destiny which is to live for God and by God.'

Emilia didn't show herself, the twins began to cry, some of his helpers told her to keep them quiet, from a long way away she still kept turning round and looking back at the crowd that was listening to her husband, the next day she set off in silence for Ouidah, they went by canoe, passed by Topo, the two women looked at the convent school with the coco-palms growing round it.

Mariana was very happy to see so many children together, she could only remember it happening on board the *Esperança*, but here they were all related, the twins loved the sea, they spent their whole lives on the beach, Emilia went to Aduni, looked over the shop, decided to stay there for a few days with Ricardo, she could help with the selling and learn the way they did business in the town, she found German very strange, had great difficulty in learning the first few words, got friendly with a Lebanese who had a shop in the same street, Seu Haddad, he talked a lot about his own country, far away, he had come to Aduni to earn money, had got quite rich, but couldn't go back, he liked the place where he had earned his money, but all the same every now and then he had a great desire to go back, who can understand what goes on in a man's heart, when Emilia went back to the Water House she began to take some interest in her sons, talked a lot to Marie, who was pregnant, told her about when she had had the twins, the pain she had suffered, she had thought it would never end, Marie sat there staring out at the beach, Jean was working near a coco-palm, the children were playing in the sand.

Fat Maria got friendly with the Ewe woman who had helped Mariana:

'Her name is something like Adjá. I'm going to call her Jajá. She likes it and we get along very well.'

Emilia spent weeks at a time in Aduni, sometimes she took the twins with her, the shop was stocking cotton from Atani now, in Dahomey the production of copra was growing, Mariana thought it was time to send Joseph and Ainá to school, they could both read well, but they needed to learn other things, perhaps in Lagos, or in

Porto Novo, she visited a Nago family that lived near Pobé, she took Antônio and the children, they all slept in open huts, the ground was soft and pleasant to the touch of her hand, she wanted to ask Ifa what to do about her children, the whole of this family was skilled in divination and Ifa, the god who predicts the future, lived here, the chief was called Fatumbi, his brothers were Fatundé and Fagbemi, his sons were Fadoro, Falana, Fadebi and Fadayi, there were others she didn't see, they said that Fatumbi had sixteen wives, sixteen was the number of Ifa, and each wife must have sixteen children, which was sixteen times sixteen, a vast number of children, the settlement was quite small, Mariana counted the huts, sixteen, probably each wife had a hut, children everywhere, Fatumbi said that only Mariana and Antônio were to come into the main dwelling, he told them to sit down on the ground, he offered a drink to Eshu, without that offering nothing could be done, unfolded a cloth, took up a chain on which were threaded sixteen flat discs, it was the rosary of Ifa called Opele Ifa which the diviner threw on the ground or on to a special bowl, and from the position of each disc and the combination of their positions he drew his conclusions about the future and found the answers to questions he had asked, Mariana watched the man's hands, heard him saying words she could not understand, saw him throwing the chain to the ground, examining the position of each disc, again he said incomprehensible words and threw down the chain, once he lifted his head and said:

'You have three children?'

'Yes.'

After he had thrown the chain several more times, sometimes correcting the spacing between one disc and the next and looking with wide eyes to see how they lay, Fatumbi said, his voice clear, each syllable clearly pronounced:

'Your first two children must study in one place, the

last must study in another, they are the same but do not mingle.'

Mariana went on foot from Pobé to Porto Novo, with Sebastian straddling her right hip, Joseph and Ainá walked quickly, every now and then they stopped and picked something up off the ground, there were naked women going along the road, their bodies tattooed all over, purple marks started on their faces and went down their necks, over their breasts and stomachs, and down their thighs and legs, girls and young women with pointed breasts, men with their penises hanging, Joseph and Ainá looked with fascination at everyone they met on the road, in Porto Novo Mariana hired a canoe and they went on to Lagos.

She decided that Ainá would go to Topo, Joseph would have to go to the Grammar School first, she found that houses had sprung up all over Lagos, Tinubu Square looked much better, in Bangboshe there were two new sobrados, one belonging to the Pereiras, the other to one of Dona Zezé's sons, Epifânia and Antônio stayed in the shop in Lagos for a while, Mariana went to talk to the sisters in Topo, Ainá was eight years old, nearly nine, a good age to start, Joseph would study in Yaba, Mariana visited Sebastian's parents, talked to a lot of people in the street, found that Mabel, her Ibo schoolfriend, was living in Odunlami, spent a lot of time with her, asked Seu Gaspar to make her another Oshun, this time the goddess came in a light-coloured wood, the gash of her sex deep, three tribal marks on each side of her face, when war broke out between Germany on one side and England and France on the other Mariana hurried back to Dahomey, found the frontier closed, Emilia was still in Aduni, Jean da Cruz said:

'The frontier between Dahomey and Zorei is only closed here, on this road, further north it's easy to get across. The war is between whites, nothing to do with us.'

They found a man of the Adja tribe, tall and strong,

he wore nothing but a pair of brightly-coloured shorts, he would take Mariana across the frontier, they set out one morning and met a lot of people, Mariana realized that the Adja tongue had words in it that she knew, the man spoke some French as well, it was getting dark again when they turned towards Zorei, she asked:

'When are we going to cross the frontier?'

'We've passed it already. Here there's no-one to notice, no marks on the ground.'

The next day they arrived in Aduni, the man was called Pedoké, he went to sleep in the shop, Mariana thought it would be best if Emilia went back with her, they said the war would soon be over, the Germans would be attacked by the French on one side and the English on the other, the shop in Aduni could stay shut up until the fighting was done, sometimes you met Germans in the street, they seemed quite natural, they didn't give any sign that there was a war on, but there were more soldiers about, the women went to talk to the Lebanese man, Seu Haddad was sad at the news coming from Europe, he offered them meat rissoles, he had a kind of bread that seemed to them more like something to put on your head, Pedoké looked at the Germans and said:

'It's just like our wars in the old times, Abomey against Atakpamé, King Ghezo against the Mahi people.'

Mariana shut up the shop, left the keys with Seu Haddad, one morning very early she left Aduni with Emilia and Pedoké, this time they went by another route, Pedoké said:

'Never travel the same path twice.'

At the Water House there was talk of an imminent attack by the French, one day a group of white soldiers stopped in front of the sobrado, their commanding officer came to talk to Mariana, he was a sergeant called Duval, he asked if they could have some water, they spent a week there, bought meat and cassava, it was the last

inhabited place before the frontier with Zorei, the spot
that Mariana had chosen for her house was becoming the
centre of a little village, three Fon families were building
nearby, many of the people who worked in the copra
production were building huts for themselves, Jajâ had
come to live near the beach, Pedoké asked Mariana for a
piece of land so that he could bring his wives and
children and live near her, in the end everything happened very quickly, the French attacked in the north
the English came by sea, invaded first Togo and then
Zorei, within a month the Germans had surrendered, the
frontier was opened, Mariana crossed as soon as she could,
nothing had happened to the shop, there hadn't been any
fighting in the town, Pedoké said:

'It was a war without emotion.'

'Better that way.'

Sebastian would study in Aduni, at least that was how
she had understood Fatumbi's words, the first two
children must study in one place, that is, in Lagos, the
last will study in another place, that is, in Dahomey or in
Zorei, since Sebastian had been born and was registered
in Aduni it would be a good thing if he were educated
there, Mariana sat now in the top room of the sobrado,
she could see the front of the house, the beach, the sea
far away out there, started to think about everything,
forgot herself, thought in amazement of the tiny moments
that make up a person's life, if her husband had not gone
to take the knife from that man in the fight he would not
be dead, or if instead of sitting in front of the house in
Bangboshe he had been at the well drinking water, he
wouldn't have seen the beginning of the fight outside, but
no, he was in his place, he got up from his chair at that
exact moment, tried to come between other men fighting,
there must be a pattern behind it all, if a man died
without a child the people of Dahomey buried him in
silence, almost as if his family were ashamed, there was
no music or drum-beating, no-one was invited, other

people out of kindness pretended they hadn't heard of the death, Sebastian had had two children while he lived and had left a third in her womb, Dona Zezé had been right, his had been a useful life, a full one, a man of the Pila-Pila people had come to live beside Mariana not long ago, he had told her that even if he died old a man without children was not given a feast, he was buried naked, with only a cloth thrown over his sex, she remembered the dead bodies on the *Esperança*, thrown into the sea in a sheet and often without their clothes, Emilia's young beauty had all come back to her, she was fatter and laughed more, she danced at the parties, an old Nago in Ouidah died around about then, the serenata began at seven in the evening and didn't end until seven the next morning, Emilia was the only person who danced all night long, the twins were growing, Mariana thought they should have a burrinha at the Water House, already there were people who called the place Aguá, they pronounced the word in the French way, as she came back from the serenata she noticed that there were more than twenty houses and huts grouped round the sobrado, on church festivals she went to Porto Novo, went to confession, met a French priest who looked like Father José, the news from Europe about the war was confusing, the Germans had advanced, then they had retreated, the English and the French were fighting on the same side, she wondered if there was a war in Brazil as well, ever since the fighting had begun no Brazilian ships had arrived, the import of dried salt meat, cachaça and tobacco had come to a halt, Mariana thought that the English, the French and the Germans were all exactly the same as each other, why did they have to fight, but she supposed they had their reasons, when she went to Lagos she found out how Joseph was getting on, he was a serious boy, knew a lot, spoke beautiful English, they had never heard anything like it in Bangboshe, Epifânia had started to smoke a pipe, she had found a wooden one in the market, smoked it slowly, complained about the shortage of tobacco, she was well, liked the shop, Jerónimo slept there now, Antônio wanted to develop the furniture-making side, João the Carpenter didn't work so much these days, there were several apprentices, the sign **omi agua water** was getting a little worn now, you guessed at the words rather than saw them, she went to see Seu Gaspar, getting older, he asked her:

'How is little Sebastian?'

'Very well. I'm sending him to school in Zorei.'

'Why not Lagos?'

'Joseph and Ainá study here, Sebastian studies there.'

One day she counted up and realized that she was almost thirty, looked at Emilia and knew straight away that she had a new man, found out that he was a Nago from Cotonou, sometimes the two of them met and went out together, she said to her sister:

'Why don't you marry him?'

'I'm having nothing more to do with marriage. This is the best way. Anyhow, Ebenezer's still alive. Or perhaps he's dead now?'

'No. If he had been, somebody would have told us.'

'You're a widow, you could marry again.'

She could and the desire of a man caught at her from time to time, usually when she took off her clothes and felt the wind on her skin, a wind that came from the sea, salty and warm, came into her room eight metres by six and made her whole body shudder, when Fagbemi, Fatumbi's brother, came to live near the sobrado she began to look at him, he was tall and slim, walked calmly, didn't speak much, and when he did he didn't seem to have much he wanted to say, he only saw the immediate things, work to do, food that had to be eaten, the road he had come along, Mariana didn't want to look at him and she looked at him, she tried to escape from him and went always to the places where he was working, at night she thought about marrying again and once more having a man enter her, Emilia had solved the problem without any trouble, it wasn't so easy for her, she decided in the end that she needed to give all her attention to Sebastian and to the children in Lagos, she felt a burning run through her body, lay there naked, her legs apart, looking out at the night journeying there outside, the best thing would be to have a man straight away, no matter who, and forget it, get on with all her commitments, one day when she had just arrived back from Aduni, where there was a sugar shortage, she decided to go to Lagos, Epifânia or Antônio might be needing her, so might her children, but they didn't need her, she found everything calm, the English were getting ready for a new stage in the fighting in Europe, she found that the whole of the region was called Nigeria now, Lagos, and Abeokuta, Ibadan and many other regions to the north and east, the lands of the Hausas, the Ibos, the kanuris, the Fulanis, the Efiks, the Ibibios, the Itsekiris, the Ijos, Tapa, all of it now had only one name, she was back in Dahomey by the time news arrived that the war had ended, it was in November, the rainy season was over, Mariana had brought sacks of sugar back with her to Ouidah and Zorei, on the way she noticed that Cotonou was growing and becoming a big town, it was as lovely there as it was at the Water House, she took Sebastian to Zorei, she needed to find a school for him, tried to remember how many times she had made the journey from Ouidah to Aduni, from Ouidah to Lagos, all the time she saw before her roads going round bends or the calm lagoon stretching out, green weed floating on the surface of the water, Sebastian was a grave little boy, conscientious, he was at the stage of asking questions, but whereas Joseph had been happy with your first answer, this only made Sebastian ask a second question, and a third, and a fourth, as if he wanted to get to the end of everything, Seu Haddad advised Mariana to send him as a private pupil to a French teacher who lived in

Aduni, Sebastian could go on living at the shop, with whoever was there at the time, or with Haddad himself, perhaps that would be best, there was a Frenchman who needed money, he was a teacher, he didn't want to go back to France, had decided to stay in Zorei, perhaps that would be the best solution, Mariana went to see the teacher, I see her going into the house built by the Germans in a quiet street, the Frenchman was called Armand Casteller, she looked at him before she spoke, thought he had a sad face, he asked:

'Is this the boy?'

'Yes.'

The man smiled, went on:

'Where are you from, Senhora?'

'I'm Brazilian.'

'Do you live in Aduni?'

'I have a shop here, but no house. I live in Dahomey.'

There was a silence, she pulled Sebastian forward.

'I would like you to teach him to read and write and whatever else will be useful for him later on. Then when he knows enough, he'll go to school and get on with his studies.'

They decided how much she would pay, Mariana thought it would be quite enough for the Frenchman to live well in Aduni, unless he was a big spender, there were books in his room, the important thing now was for her to buy a house in the town, she needed to spend more time there, Sebastian was going to want someone near him, as soon as she left the teacher's house she talked to Seu Haddad, who said:

'There's a little house here, in that street that leads off the square.'

They went to look at it, Aduni was going through bad times, a lot of people were leaving, the owner told them how much he wanted, Mariana went back to Ouidah with Sebastian, O road between the beach and the lagoon may you always be trod in happiness, saw how things were, got money to pay for the house, Fagbemi was standing motionless under a palm-tree, O need for a man that strikes suddenly and leaves the body exhausted, she bought the house and the following day sent Sebastian along to the teacher, it was best for him to go by himself, in the evening she talked to him, put a chair out in the street, sat there watching the people going by, it was different from Lagos, you didn't hear Portuguese spoken, only French and German, Sebastian could still remember some German, if he didn't forget it that would be one more language for him, she would have to ask the French teacher to see that he didn't forget his German, she spent months in Aduni, went to visit the teacher very often, one day she invited him to go to Ouidah, he accepted, she realized that he was the first white man to set foot in the sobrado, the sergeant had only stood talking to her at the door, the teacher liked talking to the twins, he got on well with everybody, Mariana asked Emilia to stay in Aduni while she went to Lagos, first she went to Fatumbi's village, asked advice about the teacher, and about whether she should marry again, Ifa said that the teacher would be good for the boy, but that another marriage might be very bad, he said:

'Why not have a man without marrying him? or have one from time to time? If you want something to stop you having children, take these leaves, there won't be any danger.'

Back in Ouidah, Mariana went to bed with a Nago called Atondá, younger than herself, she felt much happier afterwards, for a week she let him visit her, then she decided to go to Lagos, bought a car, drove along Bangboshe, Abigail shouted out of her window:

'May you never die while you drive in a car.'

She went back to Ouidah by car, she had found a Calabari driver, a smiling youth who called her *Lady*, she seemed to have forgotten the heat in her body, when she saw Fagbemi she smiled at him, imagined the look

Fatumbi would have given her if he had realized that the man who had made her think of marrying again had been his own brother, it wasn't the sort of thing you could say to a priest of Ifa, best to let him interpret the message of the god without human influence, on certain nights the burning came back and grew fierce in her body, Sebastian was becoming more talkative, he spoke French easily, didn't pause to search for words, but went back to Portuguese when he saw his mother frowning as she tried to understand him, he spoke Yoruba to the twins, just before Christmas Mariana took him to Lagos, he was delighted with the Midnight Mass, picked up English straight away, he and Joseph went around the streets together, Ainá was very well-behaved, the perfect young lady from a convent school, she walked modestly, smoothed down her dress, didn't get herself dirty in the street, everyone wanted to go out in Mariana's car, the driver, who was called Sunday, took the children to Ebute Metta and Apapa, Mariana was wondering about where Joseph should carry on his studies, Sebastian could wait, but Joseph was big now, there wasn't much for him to do in Lagos, England was the only place and one day she said to herself:

'Why not London?'

She had spoken out loud, Epifânia asked:

'London what?'

'I'm thinking of sending Joseph to London.'

'What for?'

'To go on with his education.'

She went to talk to an English official, who sent her to another man, who directed her to a third, this one asked her about her financial situation, when he heard who she was he said:

'Are you the lady who used to sell water?'

He said that she would be able to get a place in a good school for her son, the boy would have to sit an examination, he would let her know the details in a day or two, the English government had organizations that gave help to African students, when she got back to the house she told everybody the news, Epifânia wanted to know if London was farther away than Brazil, Joseph asked who would be going with him, Mariana had already thought about that, she replied:

'Antônio. If he wants to, he can study as well. If not, he'll stay there for a while until you get used to it and then come back.'

There was a farewell party, Joseph was seventeen years old, Ainá sixteen, Sebastian twelve, Mariana visited her husband's grave, there was a new cemetery now, it was forbidden to bury people in the public garden, in the afternoon the whole family went to church for the blessing, the priest sprinkled holy water over each one of them, the party began with the drums beating out a greeting, Mariana noticed that the flute-player had got very old, she remembered him as a young man, it was just after they had arrived in the *Esperança*, he had been there at all the parties, there were always different clarinettists, and the guitarists weren't always the same, but the flute-player, what was his name?, he appeared without a word, took up his flute, played the whole night long, didn't eat much, went away without speaking, girls and boys that Mariana recognized happily, the son of this one, the daughter of that one, Joseph's friends arrived, Eze, Bayo, Adebayo, Onoura, Kunle, a young girl called Ami, a whole group of them dressed in green, there was plenty of beer, they hadn't been able to get cachaça since the end of the war, some people liked whisky, no more dried salt meat came from Brazil either, in the Lagos shop Mariana sold beer from England, in the Aduni shop she had French wine, Fat Maria and Emilia had come from Ouidah the day before the party, some young people were drinking toasts to Joseph, Antônio seemed the happiest of them all, Ainá was looking pretty, Mariana thought of sending her to London as well, perhaps in two years' time, when everybody gathered on board the ship to say goodbye to her son she looked around her, how different from the sailing ship that had brought her from Brazil and from the steam-boat that Sebastian had travelled in to Fernando Poo, she stood for several minutes forgetful of where she was, the deck rose and fell, I see her thinking about ships and voyages, people live their lives travelling, they set out and arrive, there is no end to the movement, perhaps it would be good to stop for a while, once she had asked the Frenchman who taught Sebastian if he would ever go back to France, he had told her:

'I'm tired of travelling from one place to another. I want to live in Zorei until the end of my life.'

She embraced Joseph as she left the ship:

'Take care, son.'

And she laughed because she thought it was a happy moment, on the way home she said to Ainá:

'Now you must go back to Topo. In two years' time you can go to London.'

She took her daughter to Badagri by car, crossed the lagoon by canoe, left her at the school, Sebastian was glad to get back to the Water House, the teacher had missed him, he thought the boy ought to start at a secondary school in Aduni, he would look after him still, he wanted to help him, it was on that day that Mariana slept with the teacher for the first time, it seemed strange to see a white body lying beside her in the bed, the teacher did things calmly and peacefully, when she got back to Ouidah, Mariana checked the copra production, it was bringing in a big profit, she found that the whole region was French now, Togo and Zorei as well as Dahomey, asked an official in Cotonou if she could export copra from Togo now as well as from Dahomey, was told:

'In theory you can, but the two regions are under different administrations.'

She ordered calungas to be made for a bumba-meu-boi, like the ones in Lagos, they never had them in Dahomey, on the feast of Bonfim she went to Porto Novo for Mass and organized a burrinha that gathered together all the old Brazilians, many of them she hadn't even met, old Vieiras, old Almeidas, some Sousas from Zorei, for the first time in her life she ate beans and drank wine at the same time, the ox charged people, the é boi sounded out just like it had in Lagos, O ox that brings everything back, you come from the earliest days of Africa, O grandmother who brought me to this activity which never ends, she felt that ever since she had left Piau she had never rested for a moment, even the time they spent in Bahia she had been learning, finding out new things, O curiosity that leads people on to try new things, the next party was a serenata for Seu José de Almeida, Mariana agreed with his family that he should be buried on the beach, she would have a cemetery there, her own, right in front of the house, she could bury her own dead in the sobrado, in the ground the house was built on, but the beach would be a huge cemetery, she saw them putting up the inscription for Seu Almeida, Born in Bahia 1847, Died in Aguá 1923, the time was coming when she would have to get Ainá ready to go to England to study, one day she had a letter from Antônio telling her how everything was going, London was a huge city, much bigger than Lagos, Porto Novo, Cotonou, Ouidah and Aduni put together, Joseph's letter was about his friends and his lessons, he was going to be a lawyer, this way he thought he would be able to help his mother in her business, the second letter, which came a month later, still didn't mention anything about Antônio coming back, there was something he was not saying, it was only from the fifth letter she got that she found out the truth, Antônio wanted to marry an English girl, a good girl, Elizabeth, she wanted to live in Africa, the two of them went for walks along the banks of the river, would Mariana write and say whether she agreed and would she talk to Epifânia, perhaps his mother would be against it and want him to marry a Brazilian girl, Mariana sat down and wrote her reply:

'Dear brother, you marry whoever you want to. You know I have always thought that way and I let Emilia marry outside our community. If she wasn't happy it wasn't our fault. But take care and explain properly to this English girl just what our life is like over here so that she won't be disappointed. If she doesn't mind then marry her and come back as soon as you can. Your sister —Mariana.'

In Lagos, two days later, she talked to her mother. Epifânia thought that the English girl would want an easy life, she wouldn't be willing to work, but if Mariana thought it was all right then she agreed.

'Where are they going to live?'

'Antônio has some money of his own and he's a partner in our business. He'll have to buy a house or build one himself.'

He wrote and asked Mariana to buy a house for him, she understood these things, the one she chose was Seu Alexandre's, he was moving to Ibadan because nearly all his children were living there, she remembered seeing her first burrinha in that sobrado, the inscription *Viva Deus* was still up, they would need a few weeks to move her brother's things in and have some good furniture made, Epifânia was insistent that the wedding should be in the Catholic church, even if the girl was a Protestant, it was for the man to choose and the bridegroom's religion should come first, Antônio replied that Elizabeth agreed, they were married in London and spent their honeymoon in Brighton, Elizabeth's choice, it was a town she loved, a month later they were on board ship on their way to Lagos.

Everyone came to meet the couple, Emilia, Fat Maria, friends from Dahomey and from the interior, João the carpenter, Epifânia, Mariana, Ainá, Sebastian and the twins, they were thirteen now, Elizabeth was blonde, pleasant, Mariana always thought that very white people must be ill, at any rate they couldn't be very strong, she put her arms round her sister-in-law and kissed her on both cheeks, saw that her mother couldn't think what to say to the girl, Ainá was more at ease, she said:

'My uncle chose well. You are very pretty.'

Elizabeth laughed, Emilia took her arm, they all went to church for the blessing of welcome, the English girl didn't seem worried by anything she saw or else she had been very well brought up, when she saw the house she was going to live in she thought it was very big, she asked with her ready laugh:

'How many children am I going to need to fill a house as big as this?'

Fat Maria said:

'Eight will be enough.'

'There's one on the way already.'

Mariana began to get ready for Ainá's journey, Elizabeth said that her niece could stay with her family in London, Ainá wanted to study medicine, Epifânia was against it, it wasn't suitable for a woman, Mariana said:

'Nothing is unsuitable for a woman.'

She went to see a white doctor in Lagos, talked to him about it, yes, there were a lot of women doctors, the care that Mariana lavished on Ainá's clothes, her trunks, her papers, O Ainá the old one buried out there in the garden may you always protect the young Ainá, before her daughter's voyage she decided to ask Seu Gaspar to pay homage to her husband's memory and send one of his egunguns, representing the dead man, out through the town, one Saturday a figure about Sebastian's height came out of Seu Gaspar's house, wearing the most beautiful mask Mariana had ever seen, the colours of its robe were scarlet and yellow, boys with sticks beat the way in front of the egungun and behind it, Mariana, Epifânia, Ainá and Sebastian followed the masked figure at a distance, it went all along Bangboshe, into Mariana's shop, she felt that her husband had come back, was walking in all his favourite places, seeing his own things, the flamboyant in the middle of the road, the church where they had been married, the market where he used to buy things, the bench in the garden where he used to sit, O husband who have come back and see your wife and children again, suddenly she thought what if he had really come back already, what if little Sebastian was really the other Sebastian returned, born again, come to be her son, first her husband then her son, O Oshun who understand men and understand what it is to be a mother may you watch over the footsteps of this son of mine and may his father, if he has not come back, rest peacefully wherever he is, the egungun's walk took a long time, the sun was disappearing into the sea and the mask went out of sight with the red and the yellow into Seu Gaspar's house.

Ainá's party was the gayest they had ever had in Bangboshe, and the most original, Mariana kept noticing new things all the time, people enjoyed themselves in a different way these days, and everyone spoke English, only the old people still talked to each other in Portuguese, for months she hadn't heard a word of Portuguese from Antônio, Emilia, Ainá, Sebastian or the twins, she noticed that her mother missed speaking Portuguese, so she used to talk to her in it about this and that, one night they were talking about Father José, Epifânia asked:

'Do you remember him, daughter?'

'Very well. He had a good face. I wonder if he's still alive?'

'Who knows?'

Young people danced at Ainá's party, whisky and beer were the fashionable drinks, people were wearing brighter colours now, Ainá had a calm, serious face, she seemed like a grown woman analysing the behaviour and the words of younger people, Mariana left her on the ship, went back to Bangboshe with Sebastian, that day she only spoke Portuguese, made her son reply to her in Portuguese, she felt the need of old things, sat down beside the well, the wall around it was crumbling, the bricks were showing, after all it was twenty years since it had been built, Ricardo had taken the trouble to paint it in gay colours, afterwards she climbed slowly up the stairs, went to the chest, opened it, began to take everything out, touched the white cotton sheets, skirts, petticoats, smocks, ran her hand over the surface of the chest, remembered clearly the day her grandmother had bought it and all the times she had sat on it at the back of the fish-stall in Bahia, for a long time the chest had smelt of the sea, because it had spent more than a year in that stall and then six months on the *Esperança,* or perhaps it didn't smell of the sea at all and Mariana could only smell it because she associated it with the market and the voyage, now the chest belonged in Lagos, it lived in the sobrado, she took up a lace-edged skirt that had been her grandmother's, came upon the red dress that she had worn when she first left the ship, her thighs still stained with her first flow of blood, old Teresa had given it to her and old Ainá had altered it, she hadn't had it off for weeks, had worn it for the burrinha at Seu Alexandre's, today she couldn't get it on, it was too small, a young girl's dress, the chest was empty and Mariana felt the inside with her fingers, the smell wasn't fish, it was of something that has been shut up, she decided to take the chest to Dahomey with her, she would need it, there weren't many sheets at the Water House, a few days later she thought that she could take it in the car with the hood open, that way it could go in the back seat, she and Sebastian and the chauffeur sat in front, they went back along the same old roads, Pedoké's saying that you should never travel the same path twice didn't apply to her, she spent her whole life going backwards and forwards over the same roads, in Ouidah the chest was carried up to the big room,

Mariana spent a whole day putting clothes into it, every time she looked out on to the beach she saw all the graves over on the right, five more people had died since Seu José de Almeida, the wooden crosses stood up against the wind, the language that was spoken most around the house now was Ewe, sometimes Yoruba, Fon and French, she had got into the way of visiting the people who lived round about, the Brazilians called her Sinhá or Dona Mariana, the Ewes were always saying funny things, teasing her, every now and then there was a fight and she had to decide who was in the right, one night a Yoruba killed another Yoruba with a knife, he ran away when the French soldiers came, Mariana was a witness, but there wasn't usually any killing, people fought over money or possessions, she had learnt to look at the face of each person and have a good idea which one was lying, sometimes the problem wasn't one of lying, both would be telling the truth, the difficult thing was deciding which of two truths would give justice, the men married more than once, the women thought it was a good system, they praised it, Mariana learned to tell the difference between the first wife, mistress of the house, and the others, Pedoké's first wife was a big woman, she had two children, shouted at her husband's other wives who did what she said without a word, they waited until she had gone away before they spoke to each other, the Nagos were gay people, they were always singing, Mariana saw the symbol of Eshu everywhere now, the god appeared as fertility, male phalluses rising up from the ground, made of earth or stone, she stopped in front of one of them, thought of the pleasure a woman has with a man, sometimes now she felt the lack of a man and couldn't bring herself to go out and look for one, now though she knew how to caress herself in bed and stimulate her clitoris with her finger, but the satisfaction it gave her was not complete, one day she saw a sculpture of a man entering a woman, it was carved out of wood, she saw it

209

in a village near Pobé. Emilia had put her Shango in a little room at the back of the sobrado, sometimes Mariana went in there, put her forehead to the ground like she had seen her grandmother doing in Bahia, when she needed to consult Fatumbi again she went on foot along the road with Sebastian and came to Ketu, it was the land of Oloshoshi, the hunter god, the Nagos who lived in Aguá were always talking about him, she liked that stretch of country, talked to a black Catholic priest, the first one she had ever seen, the priest put his hand on Sebastian's head, said:

'A handsome head. This boy could grow up to be somebody.'

Mariana laughed, she asked:

'Father, do you have a devotion to Ifa?'

Very serious, he replied:

'No, I don't, the Church accepts the idea of foreseeing the future, but not in the way you think. But all my family are very close to Ifa.'

When she got back she found that Ricardo wanted to get married to a young Ashanti girl who everyone said was very beautiful, she thought it was about time, he told her:

'I'll have to go to Accra, on the Gold Coast, to talk to her father.'

'Where did you meet the girl?'

'In Aduni. She came to stay with some relatives.'

The shop in Zorei was doing well, Sebastian was going to classes in a school, he slept in the house that Mariana had bought, ate with Seu Haddad, he loved reading, whenever he turned up at the Water House he brought books with him, one night he got hold of *The Guarani* which Mariana had found in the chest, and asked her what it was about.

'It's a Brazilian story about an Indian falling in love with a white girl.'

Sebastian read the whole book in one night, asked her

if she knew the place where the story had happened, the river, the big house, Mariana said:

'It could have happened in Piau, where I was born. The river there used to flood, but I can't remember any Indians living in the village.'

Monsieur Casteller thought that Sebastian was old enough now to go and study in France, he had finished secondary school, he could go on to a lycée, choose a career, Mariana had been hoping that this would happen, she wanted everything of the best for her son, Sebastian had grown into a youth with fine-drawn features, serious eyes, some days he didn't say a word, loved to walk by himself on the beach, he was like his father, except that he was taller and looked as if he would get taller still, it took a long time to get everything ready for the journey but the time went so quickly that Mariana was terrified when she realized that the day of departure was nearly upon them, Ricardo had married and come to live in Aguá, the Ewes gave a special feast for Sebastian, played drums until dawn, Atondá and Pedoké danced, Mariana went back along the road to Pobé, Fatumbi was looking older, he smiled when he saw the bottle of wine that Mariana had brought for him, talked with her for a long time, asked about her family affairs, how were her other children, what had happened to Fagbemi, he hadn't been to see his family for a long time, then he concentrated on the ritual, put his right hand on Sebastian's shoulder, threw the chain down on to a wooden bowl, seemed to have forgotten the woman and her son, threw the discs many times before he said anything, finally he spoke:

'Everything will go very well for him. He will be respected by his own people and by other men, he will have fame and money, but his life will be a hard one.'

On the way back Mariana stopped at a market on the roadside, saw a wooden sculpture that showed a bird with open wings resting on a man's head, it was probably some sort of geledé mask, Mariana bought it and said to Sebastian:

'Take it. The Holy Ghost is a bird and he protects your intelligence. In the place where I was born there was a big Holy Ghost on the main altar. It was like this bird. Let's think of this bird as the Holy Ghost. I'll pray to him to take care of your mind.'

There was another feast, in the Adja style, in homage to Sebastian, then a third, with a bumba-meu-boi, one Sunday Mariana, Emilia and Epifânia who had come from Lagos and brought Antônio, Elizabeth and the mulatto grandchild, a boy who had been called after his maternal grandfather, William, and reminded Mariana of the children she had seen in Bahia, all of them went together to the ship which had anchored a long way out at sea, there were boats to take the passengers on board, they had to say their goodbyes on shore, Mariana looked at the little boat rising and falling on the waves, tiny figures appeared on the ladder going up the ship's side, then they all went back to the shop, night fell calmly, there was some trouble between Antônio and Elizabeth, Mariana went straight to the point:

'What's wrong with you two?'

Antônio changed the subject, said that it was nothing, in the end he said:

'She wants to visit her relatives in England and insists on taking Bill with her.'

'Why don't you go as well?'

'I have some big shipments that will keep me busy for at least four months.'

'Then ask her to wait four months.'

'Elizabeth doesn't want to wait. She's in a bad way. If she could have she would have left on the same boat as Sebastian.'

The next morning, back at the Water House, Mariana talked to her sister-in-law, found her changed, she left sentences half-finished and forgot what she was talking about, she had grown very thin, perhaps it was the change of climate, she held tight to her son, wouldn't answer anyone's questions, Mariana told her brother:

'You'd better let her go and see her people otherwise she won't go on living with you.'

Antônio went back to Lagos, life in the Water House fell back into its old rhythm, Jean da Cruz took his sons to Porto Novo, where there were schools for children, Mariana gave them each a present, she visited Cotonou, it seemed bigger than Porto Novo now, she had lived in Dahomey all this time and had never yet thought of having a shop there, a place like Seu Haddad's, selling cloth and trimmings, soap and thread, pins and ribbons, when she went up the stairs in the sobrado her legs ached, she sat in the front window, looking out at the sea, and fell to thinking about herself: she was almost forty, how was it possible?, it seemed only the other day she had arrived in Lagos on a sailing ship, slept on a mat in a little house in Bangboshe Street, her husband had been dead more than fifteen years, the sand stretched away into the sea, the movement of the waters out there was like the rocking of the *Esperança*, Mariana took up her Oshun, the goddess showed the gash of her sex with pride, immutable, permanent, with the power of the orishas and the saints, to do a thing was better than to think, Mariana bought a piece of land in Cotonou, took Atondá with her, told Ricardo what she wanted:

'All we want is a small place, just big enough for the shop, Atondá will be in charge of it.'

While the little house was being built Mariana bought up textiles, European and African, she had ordered adirés from Abeokuta and kentes from Accra, Ricardo's wife wore kentes in very unusual colours, one of the Ewes was sent to the Gold Coast to find the cloth she used, Mariana heard that Elizabeth had left for London, one day she had a letter from Joseph:

'Mother. Your blessing. Here everything is going well. I've started my third year of law and I'm finding the work relatively easy. There is a big difference between English law and the traditional law of the tribes that make up present-day Nigeria. I think that an African lawyer should concentrate on this problem because it's going to be more and more important for us. For example, how are we going to reconcile the polygamous marriages which are still the custom in some parts of Nigeria with the monogomous system in England? Money doesn't go far, but I'm getting some help from an English organization. I see Ainá nearly every week. She is well. Greetings and love to Granny and all the family. Joseph.'

A letter came from Ainá:

'Mother. Can you imagine, today I saw snow for the first time. Last winter it was cold, but it didn't snow. Today I went out and everything was white. I stopped in a garden that had been all green and it was all white, it feels wonderful walking along in all that whiteness. It's sad you can't see the snow. I have to do entrance exams for Medical School quite soon. I've worked hard and think I'll be a good doctor. I've decided to rent a room in the centre of London rather than live with Elizabeth's family. Here there are lots of other African students, from Guinea, from the Gold Coast, Sierra Leone. Elizabeth has arrived and seems to be ill. I'll send more news of her later. When I walk along the banks of the Thames I miss our sea-front and your shop there. I saw Joseph today. He's very tall and strong. How is everybody? Write to me and send me your blessing. Ainá.'

Mariana read Sebastian's first letter one wet afternoon, the beach was invisible in the drifting rain:

'Dear Mother. I am missing you very much, but it has got to be like this and I will have to stay here a long time, far away from you, getting ready for the future. Paris is

214

a huge city. After the first few days when everything was confused, I am finding it all very beautiful, and beginning to understand how the city works. I think the best thing I can do is study to be a teacher. Then I can teach in Aduni or in Cotonou. We are going to need teachers in our country. Men like Monsieur Casteller who want to stay and teach in Africa are rare. I've found a good cheap room, I'm already getting used to doing a lot of things for myself, so as to save money. How is Aunt Emilia? and Granny? is she at the Water House or in Lagos? Please tell Pedoké that I haven't forgotten what he asked me to get. He wants a watch. The introductions that Monsieur Casteller gave me have been extremely useful. Without them I might have had a very difficult time here. Please tell him this. Bless your son who sends his love. Sebastian.'

The twins didn't spend much time at the Water House, they went to Cotonou, went to parties, Mariana thought that they ought to go to Europe and study but they didn't want to, and Emilia didn't think it was important, the next time Epifânia came to Ouidah she decided to take Cosme and Damião back with her, there was work they could do in Lagos, the Water House was lonely without them, Mariana went around looking at the copra production, talking to people, one night a labourer she had dismissed tried to attack her, Atondá chased him in the darkness, began to give him a beating, Mariana went to them:

'Don't do that, Atondá, let him go.'

He did as she said and the man went off, perhaps she ought to offer a ram to Shango, envy might come to surround her again, and sometimes envy kills, she went back to the house, put her hands on the statue of Shango, the next day she asked Atondá to kill a big ram, at the moment when he spilt its blood on the stones in front of Shango she went to watch, stayed there quiet for a few minutes, then took the car and went to Lagos, where there was some trouble over the import of beer, the best thing would be to send Cosme and Damião to London to see to it, Joseph hadn't any experience in the business and besides he was studying, the twins liked the idea, they sailed in a white steamer, when she got back from the boat Mariana heard that Dona Zezé had died, the serenata was to be that same night, she remembered that Dona Zezé's house had been the first house she had entered in Lagos, she had been there often, for meetings of Brazilian descendents, on feasts of Our Lady of Joy, Portuguese wasn't the only language spoken at the serenata, about fifty metres of Bangboshe Street were taken up to fit in the people who came to the party, there was plenty to eat and drink, soon the only Brazilians left alive would be a few who had come on the *Esperança,* all the older ones were dying, most of them felt sad to see how things had changed, everything was different now, Lagos was a different town, it wasn't Brazilian any more, everyone spoke English, a brother of Dona Zezé, who had been in Trinidad for fifteen years, had started to speak Portuguese when he came back and found that all the young people in his family, nephews and cousins, had never even learnt the language of Brazil, he had been so sad that he had decided to move to Ife, a string of fairy-lights had been hung along where the party was being held, she saw a clarinettist, where was the flute player? Mariana danced by herself that night, in homage to Dona Zezé, who had been good to her and her family, who had made it possible for her grandmother Ainá to start selling obis in Campos Square, who had lent money to her, Mariana, so that she could buy the house with the well, she closed her eyes as she danced and felt lifted out of herself, as if an orisha possessed her and controlled her, the sound of the drums and the music seemed to come from within her body, her breasts rose and fell, the sweat which did not come from striving with a man in bed began to run down her face and her arms, but it was good sweat, through it she sent Dona Zezé her thanks, when she finished she fell on to a chair, breathing heavily, a lot of people clapped.

When she got back to the Water House she found letters from her children. The one from Joseph said:

'Mother. I have been to spend a week in Scotland. I went to Glasgow and Edinburgh. In Edinburgh there is a beautiful castle. A friend of mine, who is Scottish, wants to be a lawyer in Nigeria, he says there is a shortage of lawyers in Lagos. I've met people here from all over the world. An American called Abraham has become my friend. He is a Negro from New York and he plays the piano in a band. He's very amusing. You would like him. I saw Ainá yesterday. She's looking good, dresses very well, and seems to be liking Medical School. Greetings to everyone and your blessing for me. Joseph.'

Ainá's:

'Mother. The Medical School isn't as difficult as I had thought it would be. The thing I'm most frightened of is having to deal with corpses, but I haven't had to do it yet. So far the classes are all theory. The other day I met Julia, Dona Abigail's daughter. She has come to do a course in accountancy. At the weekends I go with some of my friends from Medical School, we usually go out of London. We went to Brighton once. There is a boy from the Gold Coast who is courting me. I've told him that I'm busy with my studies and can't be bothered with that sort of thing just now, but I let him take me out because I don't think it does any harm. I haven't seen Elizabeth for a long time. Your blessing. Ainá.'

Sebastian's:

'Dear Mother. I hope that you and everyone at home are keeping well. I have been working hard, but am in good health. The situation here in Europe is looking very bad. There's great confusion in France. No political party seems to be able to hold office for long. No one knows what is happening. In Germany there is a lot of dissatisfaction over the Great War. By the way, I'm happy to find that I haven't quite forgotten my German. I met a boy from Berlin who is studying here and we talked for a while. I have met an Ewe girl, from Aduni, who is very intelligent and pretty. Imagine: we are both from Aduni and we had to come to Paris to meet. Please ask Granny to give me her blessing, love to Aunt Emilia and everyone and your blessing for me. Sebastian.'

The rainy season had come, Mariana spent days in the house, saw people from round about who came to ask about this and that, remembered an Italian street-singer that Antônio and she had followed through the streets of Rio de Janeiro, he had had rings in his ears, she had never seen anyone like him since, she felt peace surrounding her as if she were living in a church, not even at school in Topo had she felt anything like this, that had been a time of disturbance, the girls whispering to each other, talking about sex, gazing with longing at the other bank of the river, now one day merged peacefully into the next and suddenly she realized that several weeks had gone by without her having done anything at all, except eat, sit in front of the window, she began to read *The Guarani* again, there were descriptions of jungle, here all she could see was beach, coco-palms and a few other trees, the Portuguese words filled her thoughts, she dreamt about them, at meal-times she tried to get used to a knife and fork, Sebastian and her other children all used knives and forks, it wasn't difficult but it seemed artificial to put anything between your body and your food, she tried to imagine London and Paris, Joseph and Ainá speaking English in London, studying, having new friends and new interests, Sebastian in Paris, talking to people in French, Monsieur Casteller got letters from him as well, almost every night neighbours came looking for her, Ricardo's Ashanti wife was pretty and much younger than him, Atondá and Pedoké argued over prices of things, Atondá came to her saying orikis:

'O mistress of the land, O powerful mistress of the coconut palms, may Oshun bring you many riches and much happiness.'

The Nagos told stories, about orishas and people, about Ifa or Fa and foretelling the future, Ifa knew everything, he knew everything that was going to happen, there were priests of Ifa who foretold horrific things, woebetide anyone who decided anything without consulting Ifa, Eshu, Eshu-Legba was the friend of Ifa and always received offerings before any of the other orishas, the Yorubas divided the cola-nut into four pieces, rubbed the pieces in their hands and said: May Ifa protect me from all misfortune, but who can escape from that which is to be? Mariana heard stories about the railway engine that went to consult Ifa, the god told it to make sacrifices, offer hens, eggs, bananas, the train didn't want to, perhaps that was why before going anywhere by train you had to ask Ifa if anything was going to happen, there are ceremonies when the divinity, using the voice and the body of some person, sings:

Engine, the power of Ifa has defeated you,
I will outstrip you on your lines and on your tracks,
I will go further than you, engine.

Mariana imagined the engine consulting Ifa, a car would have been more humble, at least it could get nearer than the engine, the car would go into Ifa's room, join its two front tyres as if they were hands, rest on its two back wheels, its headlights were eyes, Ifa would listen attentively to the car, would talk to it, he would ask it about the roads, then he would say that children were going to like the motor-cars more and more, they would go for rides in it, fill it with laughter and happiness, the bicycle could consult Ifa as well, every single thing had its future, one day Atondá sang a song about Ifa:

Ifa wanted something to eat
Ifa wanted to eat the tortoise
Sadly the tortoise stuck out its head
And begged: Spare me! Spare me!
Let me survive your gracious desire.

A Muslim had come and built a house in Aguá, he was
from Abuja, his father had been in the war between
Abuja and Zaria, he had fought under the Emir Ibrahim
Iyalai, the man told stories about how Ibrahim had
beaten the Emir Yero, battles on horseback before the
city, three hundred prisoners who had been killed after
the battle, he had been a child and had followed his
father until he was very near the fighting, he had seen the
kwasau, the Emir Yero's son, surrounded by enemies and
trying to escape from the circle, today there weren't any
more wars like that, every now and then the Fulanis used
to sweep through the whole district, then ten or fifteen
years later the ones who had been conquered would rise
up again and attack the ones who had won, when it was
time for prayer Kauran put his forehead to the ground,
he was never without his green Muslim rosary, Mariana
had met people of his religion who took no notice of
women, she remembered Suliman, who had been a
friend of her family, he had always been different, so was
Kauran, he said that in Abuja the women fought in the
battles, once Zabiya, mistress of the professional beggars,
led a great band of women in among the men as they
were fighting, they sang to give heart to the combatants,
there were other stories about Dahomean women who
went to war and knew how to fight, the Yorubas used to
play drums all night long, the sound seemed to be coming
out of the sea, one Brazilian had a flute, you could hear
him playing on it during the hot evenings, Mariana used
to go to the well, draw up a bucket of water, pour it over
her head, the sound of the guitar gave her a strange feeling of sadness, she was happy when the Ewes played the

xylophone, it sounded so different to her from all the other instruments, she went to look at it, hit the pieces of wood with calabashes underneath them, asked Jajá to get her one, put it in the parlour, Emilia thought it was silly to have an instrument that was never used taking up space in the house, one day a telegram arrived, it was the first one she had ever had, it said:

'Elizabeth dead tell Antônio letter follows blessing Ainá.'

She had seen so little of her sister-in-law, Mariana felt she ought to have paid more attention to Elizabeth, but there hadn't been time, Ainá going away, then Sebastian, everyone led such a busy life that perhaps they could be forgiven for not having more consideration for others, Antônio didn't say anything when she told him, he sat down, stared at the ground, after a few minutes he managed to say:

'She hadn't written to me for months. What did she die of?'

'The telegram doesn't say.'

'Where is Bill?'

'With her parents, of course.'

Ainá's letter arrived at the Water House with more details, Ricardo took it straight to Lagos.

'Mother. Elizabeth's death was dreadful. She was so young, when it happened I just couldn't believe it. She caught a fever, and apparently couldn't get over it. Her father sent someone here to the hostel to tell me, I left straight away and went to see Joseph, we put on dark clothes and went to the funeral. Bill is big now and clever, I have a feeling that his grandparents want to keep him with them. I didn't talk to them about it because it wouldn't have been right just then. Perhaps it would be best for Antônio to write directly to his father-in-law and arrange with him what is best, send me word what you decide so that I'll know what to do. No more now, I'm getting on all right with my classes. Your blessing. Ainá.'

For a while Antônio had no reply to the letter he wrote, his friends began to advise him to lodge a complaint with the English authorities in Lagos, in the end a letter came from Elizabeth's father offering to educate his grandson, the boy would have everything he needed, Antônio didn't know what to reply, Mariana asked him:

'Do you want the boy here with you?'

'Of course.'

'Then write just that: that you want to keep him, but promise to let Bill spend some time in England, and when he gets old enough to go there and study he can live with his grandparents.'

The business dragged on for a few more months, one day Antônio had a telegram from his father-in-law:

'Come collect boy personally England.'

He went. Once more Mariana's feet were on the deck of a boat, as soon as he had gone she went to visit Abigail who was going to marry one of her daughters in a few days' time, they talked about Lagos, the town was growing, getting to be an important place, hardly anybody spoke Portuguese now, Abigail asked her what life was like in Dahomey, Seu Machado had died without her knowing, Dahomey was quite near, but a long way away, Epifânia was looking after the shop on the seafront, when Mariana went to look at the furniture in the warehouse she met Jerónimo, he was very old now, he smiled at her, didn't seem as unpleasant as he had before, in those days Mariana had thought he was the sort of person who wanted too much space to live in, some people needed a lot of space physically, their hands always on their hips, when they were sitting on a chair or in church they were never still, as if they were trying to show you that the space around them was theirs as well, but Jerónimo seemed to have calmed down now, João the Carpenter came to see Mariana, he had a big carpentry workshop now, lots of employees, Mariana began to notice that the old Brazilians were always seeking each

other out, wanting to talk to each other, prove to themselves that they still lived in their own world, a lot of the
ones who had made money had sent their children to
England, they would come back more English than
Nigerian, and not at all Brazilian, it was a good thing
really because everything had changed, the young people
needed to live in new surroundings, Ainá might end up
being the doctor for the whole Brazilian quarter, Joseph
hadn't said much about his studies in his last few letters,
Epifânia was managing the shop well, every morning her
friends came to visit her, Fat Maria spent part of the year
in Lagos and part of it in the Water House, when she was
in Nigeria she never left the shop, tried to help Epifânia
all the time, Mariana went back to Dahomey for a party
in the Portuguese fort, she felt she had to go, that little
plot of land, a hundred metres square, was all that was
left of the Portuguese presence in the region, all around it
was French territory, Mariana used to send cakes to the
Portuguese officers, usually the sort her mother had
learnt to make in Bahia, she liked the fort because it had
trees like the ones in Brazil, cashew-trees, mango-trees,
a garden full of cabbage, green onion, lettuce, one afternoon Ricardo was wearing a cream-coloured robe and
now he had a little scar underneath his lower lip, he came
to tell her:

'My father-in-law is coming next week. He's going to
bring one of his wives, but there isn't enough room in my
house. Could he stay here in the sobrado?'

'Of course. Where does he live?'

'In Kumasi, on the Gold Coast.'

The man was called Yao, he wore the most beautiful
robes, kentes in tones of gold and bronze, he arrived with
a young girl who could only have been thirteen at the
most, his daughter or his wife?, for the first few days
Mariana was longing to ask, Ricardo didn't know either,
Yao became friendly with her, told her stories about the
Gold Coast, said that the child's name was Abá, but

didn't explain who she was, as the days went by Mariana realized that the two of them spent all their time playing together, she would laugh, say a rush of words in what must have been Ashanti, he in his turn would laugh hugely, while he was talking he would put his hand fondly on the child's back, she would push him gently with her finger, it was as if the man himself were a child as well, they amused each other for hours on end, Mariana gave a party for her guests, all the drums were gathered together in front of the house, the Ewes and the Yorubas showed off their different beats, the xylophone sounded out gaily, later on a flute began to play, Yao clapped his hands, sometimes Abá shouted out loud like a child, it was the day after that the man explained to Mariana, his eyes looking far away out to sea:

'According to the custom of my family and my village, Abá is my companion and spends all her time with me.'

Then he told her that when a man was getting old, or even before then, but when he was perhaps fifty, he needed to have with him a very young woman, but without any shackle of authority or near relationship, so his family found this company for him in the person of a pretty young girl, who went everywhere with him, played with him, treated him familiarly, gave him friendly shoves, later it could happen that the girl would become his wife, the third or fourth, but that wasn't necessary and might not happen, the important thing was for them to live together and keep each other company, it rejuvenated the man and meant happiness and added experience for the girl, Mariana thought for a while about it then said:

'It's a very wise custom.'

The guests stayed in the sobrado for two weeks, Yao went to see Mariana's shop in Cotonou, visited Aduni, when they went back to the Gold Coast they had to go through Togo, the car took them both back to Accra, the rainy season was on its way, Sebastian's letters spoke of political troubles, one of them said:

'In the face of what is going on in Europe, Germany resenting her defeat in the war, France unable to keep a stable government for any length of time, England refusing to define any clear lines in her foreign policy, what is to become of us, in Africa, whose lives are subordinated to these powers? Will we be independent one day? Like Ethiopia and Liberia? I think a lot about these things, mother, and I want to write to you about them but I must talk of other things. The firm that gives me my money every month, the one that exports goods to you in Aduni, has been in difficulties because of some economic trouble locally, but the manager has apologized to me and everything has been put right now. I get more certain every day that I'm doing the right thing in studying to be a teacher. It's what we need in Aduni. I knew that there weren't many teachers in Zorei, but I've just seen some statistics published in Paris and there are even fewer than I had thought. Paris is so beautiful at this time of year. It's autumn here, all the leaves on the trees are golden. How is Pedoké? Is Granny keeping well? and Aunt Emilia? Did Cosme and Damião enjoy their trip to England? Bless your son who loves you – Sebastian.'

Yes, the twins had enjoyed the journey, now they were getting interested on the cocoa plantations that had belonged to their grandfather, they spent part of the time in Ibadan, when Antônio arrived from England with his son Mariana went to meet them, Bill had greenish eyes and his skin was light brown, he laughed a lot, seemed strong, Antônio told her:

'His grandfather wanted to change his surname, but I wouldn't let him. My son can call himself William Santos and be proud of it.'

She remembered that they had got Santos from Uncle Inhaim in Piau, she had heard her grandmother telling Dona Zezé about it, but there was no harm in that, it was a good surname and well thought of in Lagos, Silva was good too, there were three Silvas who would carry on her husband's name for a while yet, Joseph Silva, Ainá Silva and Sebastian Silva, she went to visit the first Sebastian's grave, the children had made the garden into a football pitch, one of the goals was between old Ainá's grave and her husband's, Mariana thought of objecting, but then thought that after all it was a good idea, it was life going on on top of the dead, they must have a feeling of fresh life hearing the noise of the children playing ball up there, dribbling, trying to score goals, back in Dahomey she went to look at her own cemetery, the wind blew along the sand, whipped it up, Emilia seemed sad, Mariana asked her why:

'Fagbemi has gone to Queto and he might stay there.'

So her sister had ended up loving Fagbemi, he was a handsome man, she remembered the time when he had had an effect on her, she had gone about for months with the image of him inside her head, Mariana had learnt a lot of sayings from Fagbemi, sometimes he would say, about something that had happened at the Water House:

'A child can't walk the day it's born.'

He had never talked much, a man very close to Ifa, he had known how to keep secrets, whenever Mariana heard him speak she tried to hear what he was saying, it was always some direct affirmation, this is this, that is that, or a phrase from the cult of Ifa, Mariana felt that something was missing, she went to Shango's room, sat down before the god as if she were waiting for something, I see her with her hands resting in her lap, no longer young, her body strong, thickened by work, her full dress, Mariana opened the chest, looked at the white sheets that had come from Bahia, some of them still hadn't been used, she spread them out on the table, took out the tablecloths with their edging of crochet, then put them away again, I see her in the tedium of the rain's endless presence, when she rubbed ori on her body she found she had got fatter,

226

the film of ori shone on the black skin, sometimes she was lost inside herself, she became a thing touched by the noise of the rain, she let her eyes rest on a pestle, on a pan, on a chair, on a coco-palm leaning down over the sand, her eyes registered the outline of each object, lingered as they examined each part of it, stayed fixed on one spot, after a few minutes the object seemed to disappear and her body experienced an utter peace in which the rain came to rest, the rain and everything beneath its limpid sure fall, another Christmas without children was coming up, as soon as the rain stopped Mariana took care to fill up that day, she invited everyone in Aguá, took the ones who wanted to go to Midnight Mass to Cotonou, then had them all to a party, there was rabanada like they used to have in Piau, the Ewe drums and the Yoruba sounded out together, Atondá jumped around by himself in the middle of the compound and danced until dawn, later when he came to Mariana's bed it was a body covered in sweat that joined with hers, morning was breaking over the beach, a ship went by out in the distance.

Between Christmas and New Year, Antônio came to Aguá. He had a reason for his visit:

'I want to go to Bahia. There's a ship that goes from Lagos to Luanda and then from Luanda to Bahia.'

Mariana heard the news and said nothing, she wanted to know what her brother was going to do there, but perhaps he didn't have any clear idea, it might just be a desire to travel, he had been very young when he left Bahia, couldn't remember much about the city, all she asked was:

'Are you going to take the boy?'

'No. Mother will look after him. What I do want to take is goods, palm-oil, cola-nuts. I'll stay there for a while, buy what I can and bring it back to Lagos.'

Mariana changed the subject:

'How is Bill?'

'He's growing big. Getting more and more like Elizabeth's father. It's as if the father had turned mulatto.'

She thought again about her brother's voyage, it wasn't a bad idea, there was nothing more being said about war, a letter from Sebastian brought news from Europe:

'Dear Mother. I'm going to spend Christmas in the south of France with a friend whose family has a house near Marseilles. There's a lot of talk here about a German leader, Adolf Hitler, who looks like taking the place of Hindenburg with the German people. The important thing is that he shouldn't come with any idea of vengeance, otherwise war will be inevitable. There's still a lot of trouble, quite often people I know who come from Senegal or Togo have had to go back home because their money has run out. I am still speaking German and can read it quite well now. This could be useful when I am teaching. How are you all? I haven't had many letters from you lately. Why not? Are you well yourself? And Granny? and Uncle and Aunt? Every day I look at the geledé mask of the bird you gave me and pray to the Holy Ghost to guide me. Write soon to your son who loves you and asks your blessing. Sebastian.'

Mariana didn't go to see Antônio off when he left for Bahia, she hardly left Aguá during the first months of that year, her body refused to obey her when she wanted to walk along the beach, I see her sitting beside the chest, a pen in her hand, the lined paper receiving her neatly-formed writing:

'Sebastian, my son. Your uncle left this week for Bahia. Who would have thought that any of the family would have gone back along that path? Only this time it was in a steamer that will stop at Luanda, and I think he'll reach Brazil in a much shorter time than it took us to get from there to Lagos. How are your classes? Has our agent in Paris given you the right amount of money each month? I haven't been out of the house much. Sometimes I get tired for no reason, and sit looking out of the window without the energy to get up and walk. They say a new French administrator has arrived in Cotonou, I'll have to go there one day and see what he's like. Study hard, my son, study hard so that you can be someone in this life. Your Aunt Emilia is here beside me and sends you a kiss. My blessing. Your mother.'

When she got the letter from Joseph saying he was coming home, she spent a whole day just sitting looking at the statue of Santa Ana, Seu Gaspar had told her that Santa Ana was Nana Brucu, the mother, the oldest one, the one who looked after people, who brought them up, the saint had come from Piau, wood didn't seem to age, but people got older all the time, Joseph said how happy he was to be qualified, to be coming back to practise law in Lagos, he said he had a very rich friend, an Englishman of very good family, this friend was coming to Nigeria as well, he had been appointed manager of an import business, this way he would have someone he had known in London living in the same town, the man's name was Adolph, Mariana thought of the other Adolph, the German who Sebastian said was leader of the German race, she began to get ready to receive her son, asked Emilia to stay in Aguá:

'I need you here. I'm going to Lagos for a while.'

'When will you be coming back?'

'I don't know. It depends on Joseph.'

I see her travelling, she went to Pobé, Fatumbi was delighted to see her, they had got used to each other, he paid homage to Eshu before he cast to see the future, when the discs fell into the wooden bowl his eyes were almost shut in concentration, Mariana asked if there was anything new, he said:

'Your two sons will have difficult times. Be careful with them.'

'Can I do anything?'

You couldn't usually do anything, only take care of the ones near you, who has any power over what happens?,

229

who can change what is to be?, perhaps Ifa, Mariana promised sacrifices to Ifa, the road from Porto Novo to Lagos seemed long to her, she decided to buy a new car, found the town bigger, the notice **omi agua water** was leaning to one side, Mariana went in, embraced her mother, got a chair, went back outside and straightened the notice, then sat down with Bill on her knee, Fat Maria appeared in the doorway, flung her arms wide in joy, they embraced, Mariana thought she had got thinner, or perhaps it was herself who had got fatter, she looked at her mother, her face was almost grey, she looked like old Ainá had on board the *Esperança*, her black skin had changed colour, gone dull, perhaps she wasn't rubbing herself with ori any more, but not Fat Maria, no, she was gleaming, every time she turned her head the light from outside glistened on her face, Mariana asked her mother:

'Who is living in Antônio's house?'

'Nobody. Antônio asked Jerónimo to go and sleep there to keep thieves away.'

Seu Gaspar was bedridden, he didn't go out any more, she went across the street to visit him, his Sinhá! when he saw her was full of happiness, he told her what was the matter with him:

'I have no strength in my legs.'

But his hands were still at work, carving away delicately at a piece of wood, a big egungun mask lay in a corner, Mariana told him about Joseph coming back, she wanted to offer a ram to Shango, the whole of the next week she spent buying things, got a quarter of an ox from the market, Fat Maria, Abigail and one of Dona Zezé's daughters cooked the meat, they boiled big pieces of cassava, the ship would dock in Lagos in the middle of the week, by Sunday everything that could be prepared in advance was ready, Mariana made up her son's bed with sheets and new blankets, when the time came she put on her best dress and with her mother, Jerónimo,

Joseph's grandparents, João the Carpenter, Fat Maria and the twins, who had arrived the day before from Ibadan, she went on board the white and green ship as soon as it had docked, she saw him straight away, he was wearing a dark suit, had grown a moustache, he was tall and smiled, she hugged him close to her, he kissed her hand, all of them crowded round him, a little to one side an Englishman with very fair hair, fine features, pock-marks on his face, seemed to be waiting, Joseph introduced him:

'This is Mr Adolph Twelvetrees, who is coming to live in Lagos.'

He spoke in English, before everyone had been talking in Portuguese and Yoruba, Mariana held out her hand to her son's friend, said:

'Come to our house today. We are going to celebrate Joseph's return.'

He accepted and thanked her, first there was the blessing and thanksgiving in the church, Father O'Toole, who had arrived in Lagos the Christmas before, sprinkled each one with Holy Water, the communion rail was crowded with people, they all joined in the singing led by Fat Maria, a ray of sunlight came through the stained glass of the window and fell on the statue of a saint, Mariana prayed that her son would have a fine career, after the service Joseph stood at the door of the church for a while, people embraced him, congratulated him, he saw people he didn't even remember, before he got back to the sobrado he stopped in the street to talk to a group of young men in long Yoruba robes, the party went on all evening and all night, at one time Mariana took the Englishman who had come with her son by the hand, said:

'Come and try a potato sweetmeat, Adolph.'

Joseph laughed and said to him:

'It's just as well to get used to it. Everybody will call you by your first name. It's the Brazilian style. From now on you're just Adolph. You can forget the Twelve-trees.'

All the girls in Bangboshe Street had put on their best dresses, there was Ana, Abigail's daughter, she was twenty, she had naturally red lips that stood out against the black of her skin, and Julia, Luzia Borges's daughter, who was studying in Lagos, and Severina, daughter of a Brazilian family from Warri, and Joana, and Leticia, and Francisca, and Nair, each of them came up to Joseph for a moment, said something to him, Mariana watched them, it was good to see the young people seeking each other out, attracting each other. Adolph stayed apart, she decided to keep him company, got a glass of whisky for him, someone was playing an accordion, outside the dancing was just beginning, everything seemed to give off heat, the Englishman asked:

'Is it always hot like this?'

'Almost always, but the worst thing is the humidity. We're used to it now, but anyone who has just arrived complains about it, even if they are African.'

He sat down very correctly in a chair, crossed his legs, she went on:

'Have you known my son for long?'

'Goodness, yes. Since the first year he arrived in London.'

'Did you study together?'

'We did, but I didn't finish the course. I didn't find the law very attractive. I left at the end of the third year.'

Laughter came from the other room, Joseph appeared in the doorway, shouted:

'Come and see an African dance.'

Adolph got up, very well-bred, leaned against the doorpost, stood there watching a group of boys and girls dancing separately, moving their arms forward and then back, Mariana wondered what her son would do now that he was qualified, suddenly she looked at Adolph and saw that he was completely withdrawn, his face had no

232

feeling in it, quite lifeless, perhaps it was a sickness, she decided to ask Joseph afterwards what was wrong with his friend, the noise of voices in the street was getting louder, the drummers were quickening their beat, Ana had turned out to be very pretty, just like her mother but with finer features and a gay smile, in the movement of the dance she came near Joseph and then withdrew from him, her blue dress had fallen off one shoulder, sweat was running freely on her skin and she let one breast brush gently against Joseph, who smiled, Mariana was happy watching them moving gracefully together, she turned to Adolph and smiled, he looked at her with empty eyes, she thought that perhaps she had lost the way of getting along with white people, she hadn't had much to do with any for the last ten years, except for Monsieur Casteller, him and Seu Haddad, because you couldn't count the Englishmen and the Frenchmen she saw in the way of business, with them everything was very quick, a few words, a check on prices, an agreement, that didn't count, or it was possible that the young white people these days had a different way of reacting, Mariana felt that she ought to be pleasant to her son's friend, there was suffering in that strange immobility, pain that showed and then hid itself, that showed in his face and had no name, untouched by the sound of the drums and the heat of the night.

Every time she saw him, during the weeks that followed the party, Mariana looked into his eyes, saw him lost in strange surroundings, wanted to help him, talk to him, but it was difficult, as if the English she spoke was not the same language as his, Joseph avoided the subject, the two friends went about a lot together, went to Ikoyi, where the Englishman had rented a nice-looking house, Mariana heard that he had started working in his office, he saw Joseph every day, her son didn't seem in a hurry to do anything, he talked about going to see lawyers in Lagos, getting friendly with them, getting to know what

233

was going on, but he stayed in bed until late, he would get up just before midday, sit in the front parlour, then walk slowly along Bangboshe Street, wait in the shop on the sea-front, soon Adolph would arrive, they had lunch together, Joseph would go back to the shop at about three in the afternoon, lie down on a mat in the back room, sleep until five, as dusk was falling he would go out and sit on the grass beside the sea, pulling stalks and chewing them, watching the people go by, later he and Adolph would drink whisky and stay talking until late, as the days went by Mariana found that she couldn't bring herself to protest against this waste of time, it was as if she too were being wasted away, she found she was old, remembered the time when she had never stopped working, the well was a witness of what she had once been able to do, now all she wanted to do was go with her son to the shop, watch him from a distance, Epifânia didn't seem to notice anything that was happening, she was eating a lot, Mariana couldn't remember having seen her like that in the past, some nights her mother and Jerónimo had long conversations in Yoruba, he told her tales about Abeokuta, Mariana stopped what she was doing from time to time to listen to what they were saying, she decided that she couldn't expect any help from Epifânia, Seu Gaspar never left his bed now, but at least you could talk to him and it was him she asked:

'What can be wrong with Joseph?'

Sheet up to his chin, the old man asked:

'Is he ill?'

'I don't know. It's possible.'

She told him what was happening, Seu Gaspar leaned towards her a little to hear better, when she had finished he promised:

'I'll ask some of my friends to find out what is wrong with him.'

'How can they know if I don't?'

234

'They are everywhere, they hear what other people say.'

The sign **omi agua water** caught Mariana's attention, hot sun fell on everything, that night there was a party at Abigail's house, a son who had come back from London, Abigail had got too fat, she was almost the same size as Fat Maria, she couldn't be bothered to get out of her chair, the front of the house was lit up with strings of fairy lights, the rooms were all crowded with people, Mariana didn't stay long, quietly she watched the young people dancing in the street, she missed Joseph, went back home and stood by the window looking up at the sky, the stars burned as brightly as they had during her voyage on the sailing ship, where would Antônio be at this moment?, she wasn't sleepy, lay on the bed with her hands behind her neck, suddenly remembered that in Brazil this was a bad omen, meant a death in the family, she put her hands on top of the sheet, then got up and took off her clothes, the heat had increased and she began to sweat even though she was naked, a great emptiness swept over everything, she was afraid of what might happen, when Sebastian came back from Paris he too might have changed, everything changed, people, things, the child was no longer present in the grown man, but Sebastian seemed no different in his letters, in them he still seemed that boy who had grown up but was still a child, and Ainá, perhaps with women it was different, always easy to know what a woman wants and hopes for, it's usually men who are restless, wanting adventure, wanting to leave wherever they are for somewhere unknown, she felt the sweat soaking the sheet, a mosquito hummed beside her left ear, she slapped at it, she heard Joseph coming in, it must have been late, suddenly she fell asleep and it was morning, she woke and looked out of the window, fragments of cloud gathering in the sky.

When she got the message from Seu Gaspar she knew

she was going to be told what was happening to Joseph, he went straight to the point:

'Your son's friend likes men.'

'What do you mean, likes men?'

'He likes men as if he were a woman. He is a woman for men. You know what I mean, Sinhá?'

She was quiet for a moment, then said, in a low voice:

'Yes, I know.'

Then she said:

'But what has Joseph to do with this?'

'Adolph is in love with Joseph. They sleep together like man and woman. Joseph is the man, Adolph is the woman.'

She saw her son's friend again in her mind's eye, the fine features, the fair moustache which sometimes was scarcely visible, the suffering in his eyes:

'So that's it?'

'That's it.'

She sat there for a long time, without talking, looking at the wooden carvings in Seu Gaspar's room, she felt an emptiness in her head, as if she had lost the ability to think, images came and went, her body seemed isolated, waiting, when she rose to her feet it was with a great effort, she stopped before the bed, said in a scarcely audible voice:

'Thank you very much, Seu Gaspar. You've helped a lot by telling me the truth.'

She went back across the street, sat down in the rocking-chair, the same chair in which she had spent whole days thinking, just after Sebastian's death, she looked at the statue of Santa Ana that had come with her from Piau, the saint had taught Our Lady to read, she remembered Joseph as a child, he had been born when times were hard, born on a mat, she spent the rest of the day quietly, heard sounds out in the street, cars going past, horns, children shouting, the voice of Abigail raised from time to time as she called to one of her grandchildren, waves of smells came through the air, first the smell of roast meat, it was the time of the midday meal in a lot of houses, and the smell of things burning, smell of the sea when the wind came strongly from the direction of the harbour, at this time Joseph would be in the shop waiting for Adolph, or they might have left already and would be walking along the sea-front towards Ikoyi, Mariana realized the immensity of the problem she had to resolve, passed her right hand over her face, sweat was standing out on her skin, there was nobody who could help her, Epifânia had withdrawn from everyday things, she had found a way of life that pleased her, Emilia was still in Dahomey, and even if she came to Lagos she would be no help, Antônio must be in Bahia, and there had been no news from him, perhaps because of the long voyage letters would take a long time to come, she imagined an envelope coming on a sailing ship and being at sea for six months, in a place where people might be dying while the letter, in a bag or in a drawer, waited for the death to be over so that it could get on its way untroubled and arrive in the hands of the person to whom it had been written, yes, Antônio would be the only person she could talk to about this, the image of Sebastian appeared suddenly before her eyes, not her husband, but the Sebastian of now, the one who was studying in Paris and must be taller now than when he left home, and it was a Sebastian who looked very like his father, he seemed to be the sort of man you could lean on when things were difficult, at one time she found herself listening to some women quarrelling, the Yoruba words hung buzzing in the air, and it was night, Epifânia came into her room:

'What's wrong, Mariana? You didn't want to eat?'

'I don't feel well, it will soon pass.'

Her mother switched on the light, the heat of the night grew greater every moment and Mariana felt stifled, when she heard Joseph coming in she went downstairs, saw him standing on the pavement outside, he was happy, how was she going to say to him the thing she had to say?, she called out to him:

'Will you come and talk to me for a while?'

He turned round, not smiling now, she got a chair, took it out into the yard, put it down beside the well, said:

'Get another chair for yourself.'

He obeyed, mother and son sat facing each other, a light from inside the house lit up a patch of the ground, Mariana rested her arm on the wall round the well and began to speak:

'From the beginning I've felt sorry for your English friend, I thought he looked at people without seeing them. I thought he might be ill.'

She paused for a moment, a stone from the wall was hurting her wrist, she went on:

'I saw that you were very good friends, and I thought that he would be able to help you in your career, he would introduce you to English people and get you legal work.'

When she paused Joseph said:

'That's exactly what he is going to go.'

She said nothing for a few moments, absorbed in herself, in what she had to say:

'Now I have found out that he is man who doesn't like women and who gives himself like a woman to other men.'

The dark was thick around them, Mariana looked straight at her son, she couldn't see his face clearly, but she felt tension coming in the darkness and growing, she decided to go on:

'I don't know exactly what goes on between you.'

Who could know? Seu Gaspar didn't seem to have any doubts, but it was impossible to know, she asked:

'Do you sleep together?'

It was hard for Joseph to speak, he seemed as if he wouldn't but finally, across the darkness, came the words:

'It's not quite like that, mother.'

Mariana waited for him to go on, when the silence had gone on for a long time she spoke again:

'The few cases I've known about of men together here in Lagos have ended badly. And in every case it was the worst kind of people. Perhaps in London it's more common than it is here in Nigeria, but to my mind you should think carefully about what you're doing.'

'I'm not doing anything.'

Joseph got up, walked a few steps, sat down again:

'It's hard to explain to you. At first I was terribly lonely in London, I had no one to talk to, it was Adolph who really helped me through. For the last ten years we've seen each other every single day.'

'That explains the beginning, but it doesn't explain why it went on. Did you not have any women friends in London? Did you never sleep with any of them? Didn't you even have a girl friend?'

Joseph was silent, Mariana said:

'I'm not demanding anything of you, son. I'm only asking you to think seriously about what is happening. The right thing would have been for you to come back, start work, find a girl here and marry her. She needn't have been a local girl, she could have been white, black, mulatto, whatever, but a woman. You don't need money, now, but you have to think of the future and work for your family.'

After these words the silence seemed deeper, the noises of the night intruded, shouts in the night, a child being scolded by its mother not far away, the crying came through the space between the houses, through Mariana and Joseph, eventually he said:

'I am very fond of Adolph, mother. During these last years, even though he's not much older than me, he has been everything to me, father, mother and friend.'

'I see that, I'm very grateful to him for what he has done, but that doesn't mean to say that the two of you

239

should sleep together or that you shouldn't have a girl friend or a woman because of him.'

'I know Adolph, I know he'll suffer badly if I have a woman, it will need time for him to get used to the idea.'

'We're not short of time. We have the whole of time ahead of us.'

Epifânia appeared at the door, said:

'Ah, there you are. I've been looking for you everywhere, I thought you'd gone out.'

Mariana forced her voice to be calm:

'No, mother. Everything's all right. We're talking about things that Joseph has to do.'

Epifânia went back into the house, Mariana lowered her voice:

'The important thing now is for you to start work. Doing nothing like this doesn't help. And it would be a good thing if you didn't see Adolph every day.'

'I can't just do it suddenly like that, mother. He doesn't know anybody here, he came to Lagos because of me.'

'All right. Not all at once then, we have plenty of time.'

She felt tired, there was a word the oldest Brazilians had for this, *consumição* it was *consumição* she felt now, all she wanted to do was go on sitting there and she stayed for a long time after Joseph had gone in, she heard him moving around in the kitchen, going to his room and then going out, Mariana stayed in the same place until late at night, the sounds got less in Bangboshe Street, there were still street-sellers with cola-nuts on boxes, a lamp lit, they would spend the night in the street, talking sometimes until dawn, sleeping in the open air, when she finally got up from her chair she went calmly up the stairs, lay down on her bed and stared up at the dark ceiling, old images came before her as if in a dream, but she knew she was awake, she saw the market place in Bahia, herself lying on her mat beside the stall, the festival of Shango, the glassy eyes of the dead ram, in those

240

days she had no children, no one dependent on her, Father José came again before her eyes, she hadn't thought of him for a long time, he must be dead by now, she was turned forty-six, in Bahia she had only been eleven, Seu Miguel too, she saw him again laughing as he greeted her grandmother, may there always be in your house, Yaya, much palm-oil, much fish, much flour, much yam, fruit in plenty, she saw the mulatto from Pernambuco, who had died on the sailing ship, they said he had died as he was chewing a biscuit, the ship rose and fell, then became still, immobile, shellfish clung to the hull, the stars changed their places and the old people said you couldn't see the Southern Cross any more, she thought of Joseph on the ship, but no, it was Antônio, if Sebastian had been alive he would have been the one who had to solve this problem of her son and Adolph, but she had carried all the responsibility from early days, a man enjoying sleeping with another man was something she found difficult to understand, but anything can happen, anything is possible, perhaps it would be a good thing to go to Pobé and ask Fatumbi, Adolph's eyes appeared in her memory, they were sad and empty, as if they had no thoughts, by the end of the night Mariana could not concentrate on anything, she fell into a half-sleep, but while she slept she was still turning around the problem of what to do, she woke when Epifânia came into her room, to tell her the twins had arrived from Ibadan and wanted to discuss some business with her, she washed her face in the basin, drank some coffee in the kitchen, went to see Cosme and Damião, who were dressed in the Yoruba style, robes down to the ground in gay bright colours.

'We're having some trouble with grandfather's estate. The cocoa plantation is to be divided, but father has disappeared, they say he's preaching in Calabar.'

Mariana listened to them for a while, asked questions, thought about it, the first thing was for the twins to get themselves a lawyer:

'Joseph is here, he's qualified, and he hasn't started work yet. I'll ask him to go with you to Ibadan and see what he can do.'

She asked Epifânia:

'Is Joseph awake yet?'

'He doesn't seem to have slept here last night.'

'Then we'll go to the shop, that's where he'll be.'

He was. When he heard Mariana's suggestion he looked at her unsmiling and asked:

'When will I need to go?'

'Today. Now.'

He bowed his head, thinking, Cosme and Damião went on talking, explaining it all to him, she said:

'You can all go together after we've eaten.'

Joseph agreed, with a rather strange air, said goodbye to the twins, went out and walked away along the sea-front, his dark suit was lost among the brightly-coloured robes that crowded the street, back in the house Mariana waited for them to go off to Ibadan, it was night and Jerónimo had closed the shop when he came and told her:

'The four of them went in a car: Cosme, Damião, Joseph and the Englishman who came with Joseph from London.'

So that was it. She thought of going to Ibadan herself, she would stay with Luzia Borges, visit her friends, but she couldn't bring herself to do it, the weariness had increased, she went across the street and sat for hours with Seu Gaspar, they talked about Shango, he didn't mention the Joseph business, in the end she said:

'Last night I told Joseph that I knew.'

'How did he take it?'

'He says that the Englishman took care of him in London, helped him all he could. They are very close, it's going to be difficult to do anything about it.'

'Nothing is difficult, Sinhá. When you least expect it, things get better.'

Mariana told him about the journey to Ibadan, they

were going to stay there for some time, more than a week, perhaps, she didn't know whether to go there herself or to stay in Lagos, Seu Gaspar said:

'Going to Ibadan isn't going to solve anything, Sinhá, but go if you want to, it can't make things worse either.'

Mariana played with the medal of Bonfim that Father José had given her when they had boarded the ship in Bahia, she asked:

'Is Joseph made this way, will he never change, or is it only a phase?'

'I knew a man who all his life only wanted men. I have known others who looked like women, had gentle voices, swayed their hips as they walked. And I've known some who slept with men for a while just to amuse themselves and gave it up later.'

'Do you think it's only temporary with Joseph?'

'I think it must be, because before he went to London he was always quite normal.'

'Do you remember him here in this room, looking at the carvings, asking questions?'

He nodded, Mariana went out, went along to the shop, decided to change her car and get a new one, two days later there she was with a huge black car, she engaged another chauffeur, an Efik called Silvanus, went across Carter Bridge, visited some Brazilians in Yaba, heard the news from the old ones, who was ill, who wasn't, went to a serenata in Ebutte Metta, the dead woman had been called Nœmia Pereira, she was ninety and had come from Bahia on the *Biáfora*, the whole family was gay, one of her great-grand-daughters said:

'Her mind was clear until the very end. She asked for a big splendid serenata, everybody happy.'

The drums brought back long-forgotten memories to Mariana, there was a whole group of young people she didn't know, but they were all very like the young people years ago, laughing at everything, dancing, the boys and the girls holding hands, she imagined Joseph with one of those girls, one of the dead woman's granddaughters was extremely pretty, she had firm breasts, the tips showed through the light cloth of her dress, O Oshun, queen of beauty and wealth, woman like no other woman, may Joseph find pleasure in women and discover the beauty there is in the breasts, the belly, the sex, the thighs, the feet, the eyes, the mouth, the ears, the hair of a woman.

Four days after Joseph had left for Ibadan a letter came from Antônio. The envelope was thick, there were several sheets of paper inside, her brother's small handwriting covered each side, Mariana looked at the date, it had been written more than two months before:

'Dear sister – read this letter to mother and to all the family because there's a lot of news. It took me a long time to get here. The ship stopped in Luanda for ten days and I used the time to see a bit of Angola and got as far as the Congo to see what it was like there. From Luanda to Bahia didn't take long, when I arrived in the port I remembered a lot of things about it. They told me that the market is in a different place now, not where mother and Granny had their fish stall any more. For the first few days I just walked around and looked at all the streets in the lower part of the city, in the high city there are big buildings now, there's a street called Chile Street, that's always crowded with people. The obis and the orobos stood the voyage well, they arrived in good condition, I started looking for buyers straight away and there were quite a few people interested. Can you imagine, an obi coming from Africa cost fifty times as much here, and sometimes a hundred times. A lot of people speak Yoruba, especially in the market, so that I don't feel strange, it's just like Bangboshe Street or in the market there in Lagos. The people are very friendly, I only needed to say that I was Brazilian and had lived in Africa since I was a child, they asked me to lunch, to dinner, to parties, I went to a dance in the high city, danced until morning, everybody is very gay here, they never seem to pay any attention to sad things, the girls laugh a lot, you'd have to see the way they are, you can't imagine. I've managed to make friends with the people who look after the orishas, they are the people who really need obis, and orobos, and the red parrot feathers that we call ekudidé and they have the same word here, the plants, and it was here — '

Mariana had trouble finding the next bit, the sheets of paper had got out of order, some were upside down, finally she found it:

' — that I did good business selling my things. I have become very friendly with Dona Aninha, Yalorisha of a saint's house, Opô Afonjá, outside the city, I've slept there, spent a whole week up there, it's on the top of a hill and there are houses dedicated to Shango, Yemoja, Oshala, Oshose, Oshun, all very well organized and beautifully kept. Mother Aninha is very well thought of and she has asked me to bring them more obis and orobos, or to send her them from Africa, and everything else they need here for the cult. I've been to a lot of good festivals in her house, one, for Oshose, like I've never seen before, I think I must belong to Oshose. Mother Aninha has a lot of girls dedicated to the saint, out of them all my best friend is Senhorazinha, she has a big long name and it reminds me of Piau where we were born because you always tell me that the Holy Ghost is the patron of Piau and there's a picture of Him there in the form of a dove, well Senhorazinha's full name is Maria Bibiana do Espírito Santo. Mother Aninha has another candomblé house in Rio de Janeiro, I thought of going to see it but life in Bahia is very good and there's no time. Mother Aninha and Senhorazinha ask me all about Lagos and about the feasts of the saints there, how the orishas are worshipped, what our obligations are, what our songs are like, I remembered some that I learnt from Seu Gaspar, they have all heard about Seu Gaspar, a lot of people from Lagos have turned up in Bahia and told them about us all. If it weren't for mother and all the family I would stay over here, but if I stayed I wouldn't earn much money, the best thing is to find a market for our things here, and send them from Lagos, the reason why I want to stay is because I've met a girl called Esmeralda and I would like to marry her. But I've asked her and she's agreed to come to Lagos with me, speaking of marriage how is Bill? I hope he's not being too much of a trouble to you, mother, I think of him a lot, soon it will be time to send him to London to stay with his grandfather for a while, like I promised. Esmeralda's father has a little boat and goes out to sea and catches fish, who knows, perhaps he did business with mother and Granny in the old days? I took Esmeralda to see Mother Aninha and Senhorazinha, they like her very much and think that we would be right to marry, they threw cowries for Shango, so I think everything will be all right. As soon as I decide about the wedding I'll write to you again, love to you and Emilia, I ask a blessing from mother and send my blessing to Bill. Your brother Antônio.'

Mariana sat there with the letter in her hand, she saw again the Holy Ghost of Piau, with its wings spread wide on the high altar, it would be a good thing if Antônio got married again, but perhaps a Brazilian woman used to the life in Bahia wouldn't like Lagos, she remembered her mother in those first months in Lagos, how hard it had been for her to adapt herself, she got up and went to see Bill, he was ten now, she found him lying on the pavement, he must have been playing hard, he was sleeping relaxed and untroubled, she picked him up and carried him into the house, Joseph came back from Ibadan earlier than she had expected him, he came into the house looking ill at ease, and said to Mariana:

'Cosme and Damião's troubles are sorted out. At any rate they can act in their father's name for as long as he doesn't appear, but Emilia will have to send them a document stating that they are authorized to represent her in any decision relating to old Kinoyi's inheritance.

Mariana let a few seconds pass before she asked:
'Did Adolph like Ibadan.'
'Yes, he did.'
'I think I'm going to talk to him.'
'Why?'
She changed the subject:
'I've had a letter from Antônio. He wants to marry a Brazilian girl called Esmeralda.'
'When is he coming back?'
'He didn't say, but I think it won't be till after he's married.'

At dawn Mariana went to see that Joseph was still asleep, put a shawl round her shoulders, went out along Bangboshe Street, said good morning to the women who were selling things to eat, it was getting light when she crossed the bridge on to Ikoyi Island, Adolph's house was painted white, she pressed the bell, waited for a long time before he opened the door, he was wearing a light-coloured dressing-gown over his pyjamas, he looked at her with the same absent air, asked her inside, Mariana sat in a big armchair, he said:

'I'm sorry I took so long to open the door. I got very tired with the journey from Ibadan.'

'It doesn't matter. You must forgive me for coming to see you so early, but it's urgent.'

Did he understand her English? The lack of reaction in his face made her feel that her words weren't reaching him. His voice was impersonal as well:

'Your servant, Mrs Silva.'

'I don't know if Joseph told you that I have been talking to him about the situation you and he find yourselves in.'

'Joseph? No, he didn't tell me anything.'

Mariana looked into his eyes, they were blue and transparent and seemed far away from all this. Again she wondered if her English was getting across what she wanted to say:

247

'I talked to him because I have been told that you and he have been sleeping together since you were in Europe and that you came to Lagos to be able to live near my son. Is it true?'

He didn't reply straight away, seemed to be thinking, then he asked:

'Is what true?'

He paused again, then went on:

'Is it true that we sleep together or is it true that I came to Lagos because of Joseph? These are matters that one doesn't talk about, Mrs Silva, that one doesn't even put into words.'

Mariana insisted:

'I think my son is normal and he only fell into this way of life through your influence. I would like him to be normal again.'

'Your son is free to do whatever he wants.'

For the first time Mariana noticed that he was nervous, there was a slight twitching below his right eye, his face seemed to be afraid of this tremor, he turned his head to one side and hid the twitching nerve, and she was sorry to be doing what she was doing, but what choice had she? Looking at his profile as the early sun fell on it through the window, she said:

'Mr Adolph, I have nothing against you personally and I don't want this business to leak out and get talked about. All I want to do is convince you that this is the wrong way to behave and get you to leave my son alone and go away.'

He turned towards her, looked at her for a long moment, his voice spoke an English she could scarcely understand:

'And don't you think that, if I could, I wouldn't be far away from here, doing other things? If I could, if I had been strong enough, I would have stayed in England. I came to Lagos because I could do nothing else.'

Mariana felt compelled to go on:

248

'I believe you, but a little strength of will might help. Why don't you make an effort?'

He rose, excused himself and went out of the room, after a few minutes a servant came in with a cup of coffee, Mariana remembered that she had had nothing to eat, drank the hot liquid, felt better, Adolph came back fully dressed:

'I have to go to the office. You can rest assured that I will try to make Joseph keep away from me.'

'I am very grateful to you.'

On the way back she kept thinking about his face, most of the time it was still, without emotion, the eyes that impossible blue, but now and then they were filled with suffering, in the house she saw Joseph having his coffee, he had got up early that morning, Mariana changed her clothes and went out to the shop, Epifânia and Jerónimo were attending to customers, Bill was sitting on the door-step, there was noise in the street, happy noise, she looked at the grass along the edge of the sea and thought of her beach at the Water House in Dahomey, she missed it, how would life be getting along in the sobrado?, and the shops in Cotonou and Aduni?, Emilia, Jean da Cruz, Ricardo and Atondá were looking after the business there, she would have to go and see how things were, but not now, she couldn't leave while Joseph was caught up in this situation, an Ewe sent by Emilia arrived with letters and messages, the export of palm-oil had increased during the last weeks, there had been a burglary in the Cotonou shop, nothing big, they all wanted to know when she would be coming back, a letter from Sebastian spoke of his studies, then went on:

'In his recent speeches Hitler has thrown off all pretence, and a lot of people who used to admire him have recognized now that we were right to be afraid of his avenging spirit, but he seems to have bewitched the German nation. How is it possible that the Germans, who individually are such kind people, can permit the

249

persecution of the Jews? Mother, it's very possible that a new world war may break over us and I keep wondering what will become of Africa and all out part or the world that is already so poor. I have talked to other Africans who are studying in Paris and they are all afraid of what is coming.'

Another war, the last one had not long been finished, without knowing why Mariana remembered that she hadn't felt the need of a man recently, it must be old age, she was afraid of becoming weak, unable to walk, one afternoon she felt a pain in her heart, it soon passed, but the fear of falling ill remained with her, and it had to be just now when Joseph was in trouble, when she needed to be strong, once when she was drawing water from the well she almost fell, had to cling on to the wall, when he got in that night Joseph came to find her, he seemed on edge, he said:

'I only found out today that you had been to see Adolph.'

'Yes. We talked for a while.'

'What about?'

'About the two of you.'

He walked away to the other side of the room, his back was turned to Mariana, when he spoke his voice was strained:

'What am I going to do, mother?'

'Have you decided to do something then?'

'Yes, but I'm afraid.'

Mariana lowered her eyes and looked at the floor, when she raised her head again Joseph had left the room, he had gone out and was sitting in the garden where his father was buried, thinking about what his life had been like in London, those first desolate months, he had spent hours in Hyde Park without anyone to talk to, his landlady, a fat ugly woman, was the only person he exchanged any words with, after two days of loneliness he found even her ugliness pleasant, later on in Law School Adolph had come into his life like a miracle, he had seen England through Adolph's eyes, it was from him he had learnt how to eat well, how to recognize a good wine, with him he had wandered through the English countryside, felt the joy that comes from looking at a peaceful rural scene, the sexual side, when it happened, was no surprise, Adolph's white body in contact with his own black one, the important thing had been the human contact that had grown up between them, the few times he went with a woman in London he tried to hide the fact from Adolph, who combined a woman's actions with an attitude of protection, but what had not seemed immoral in London looked different in Lagos, a full year before Joseph's course finished Adolph had decided to find a job in Nigeria, during the voyage Joseph had often wondered how he was going to introduce him to everyone at home, now he couldn't find a way out of it all, he didn't want to hurt his friend, he owed him so much, had grown to love the England that Adolph had shown him, think as he might he could find no solution, unless it were to just let everything go on as it was, he could find himself work, get some cases, go to court, that didn't mean he had to give up Adolph's friendship, he had looked at the girls in Bangboshe Street, one of them in particular he found very attractive, he hadn't ever gone near her, routine had come to dominate his life, he slept late, went to the shop, waited for Adolph to come, had lunch with him, talked for a while, rested after lunch, at night they gathered in groups where there were only men, drank whisky or beer, talked, in the mornings his head was always heavy, at the weekends they went and bathed in Tarqua Bay, they hired a boat on the sea-front, crossed the harbour entrance, the waters of the bay were calm.

In her room, Mariana tried to think of a way to get her son away from Adolph, the next morning she went back to Ikoyi, talked with him again, he didn't seem disposed to help her, at any rate he said very little, she talked nearly the whole time, said everything that was going through her head, the third time she went to see him his servant opened the door and said that Adolph had gone out, Mariana stood for a few minutes in front of the house, not sure whether she believed him or not, one day she thought it might help if she consulted Fatumbi, she called Silvanus, it took four hours in the car from Lagos to Pobé, she saw the countryside going past outside the window, there were stretches of the road that she knew well by now, bridges where she had stopped, sometimes she caught sight of the lagoon she had crossed so many times going to Topo, at the frontier the wait before they could show their papers irritated her, when she found herself face to face with Fatumbi she found him looking a lot older, they were all getting old, she had to find a solution to this before old age conquered her, Fatumbi greeted her:

'May Ifa give a peaceful future to my friend.'

'Your friend is in a bad state.'

Mariana told Fatumbi about her son and the trouble he was in, she wanted to find out from Ifa how he could escape from the situation, they made offerings to Eshu first, then Fatumbi placed a wooden bowl on the ground, it was circular, with figures carved around the edges, he took up a handful of cowries and threw them into the bowl, examined the position of each one, said something in a low voice, once more threw the shells into the bowl, one of them rolled away on the ground, Fatumbi picked it up and gathered together the other shells, in the end he turned his eyes to Mariana and said:

'There's nothing you can do.'

'Nothing?'

'No. It will have to work itself out.'

'And I have to keep quiet?'

'You won't be able to. You can do whatever comes into your head, but when the solution does come it will be quite independent of you.'

She went straight back to Lagos, night had fallen by the time she reached Bangboshe Street, Bill was asleep on Epifânia's knee, Joseph had gone out, she went up to bed exhausted, fell straight into a deep sleep.

She awoke with a strange feeling of discomfort, a pain in her heart, but her right side was hurting as well, a touch of fever, she had never been ill, this would be the first time, Epifânia asked something and Mariana scarcely heard, she found that replying took a big effort, she took up the statue of Santa Ana for a moment, she had to fight back against this weakness, from time to time a Brazilian caught malaria, but never the people who had been born here, they seemed immune, she prayed to the saint that it wouldn't be malaria, made an invocation to the Holy Ghost and one to Shango, remembered that she had to offer sacrifices to Ifa, that night, when she had drunk some coffee, she realized that she had wasted the whole day, she had done nothing, had only seen Joseph in the distance, she went to bed early, slept until late the next day, a certainty that her son's trouble had to be sorted out quickly, the more time went by the worse it would get, the girls must be wondering already why Joseph wasn't coming after them, they might be asking each other who he was sleeping with, she thought of talking about it to one of the priests, but they might not understand how serious it was, for a priest a man sinning with a woman might be just as bad as a man sinning with a man, both sins were an offence against God, but the truth was that when a man sinned with a woman it wasn't really a sin, it was just nature, it came from inside you, but when a man sinned with another man there was no point, it produced no fruit, she felt better as the day went on, decided to go and find Adolph again.

It was their third meeting alone together. She went into the house, waited for a while and he came quietly into the room, he seemed more kind than on her other visits, Mariana said:

'I want to know what you intend to do about my son. I don't ask you to leave Lagos. You can stay here, as long as you leave Joseph.'

He looked at her with something like serenity:

'I can't imagine living any other way than the way I'm living at this moment.'

'But there are other young men, stronger, without families, who are not going to be married. You could choose one of them.'

'Are you thinking of getting Joseph married?'

'I am.'

'I can assure you he hasn't the least intention of marrying.'

Mariana let the silence grow longer, when Adolph said no more she said:

'Again I must insist that you leave Joseph in peace.'

'You can insist as much as you like, it's not in my hands. I repeat that Joseph is free to do whatever he wishes.'

That afternoon she was in the shop, Joseph came and stood beside her, hooked his thumb into the corner of his pocket, seemed about to say something, then walked away and Mariana only saw him again that night, he appeared suddenly at her side, said in a rush:

'Today I spent the whole day without seeing Adolph.'

Straightway she replied:

'You did right.'

And she went on, repeated:

'You did right, but it's not enough. He has to understand that your life is going to be different.'

However the following day she found out that they had had lunch together, Joseph didn't sleep at home for three nights running, Mariana tried not to sleep, lay on the bed, listening all the time, any noise could be Joseph coming into the house, up the stairs, she went to the front window, looked out over Bangboshe, a few feet away from Abigail's house a group of women were talking

254

quietly, sometimes a car threw beams of light into the darkest corners of the street, during the day Mariana did what was necessary, left her room, went to the well, pulled up a bucket of water, washed her face, had some coffee and boiled cassava, went along to the shop, dealt with the day's business, wrote letters to England and to Brazil, talked to Epifânia, saw Jerónimo coming and going, went back to the house, played with Bill, in the evening she undressed in her room and rubbed ori on her body, she felt that Joseph might come back at any moment, but he didn't, she lived in a state of quiet anxiety and forced herself to be calm, and a letter came from Antônio which said:

'Dear Sister – I'm going to marry Esmeralda. I have spoken to her parents, her mother cried because her daughter's going away to Nigeria with me, but in the end we all agreed. I've asked Senhorazinha to be my sponsor, and her son, who's still only a boy, has been telling me stories of weddings in the house of Opô Afonjá. I've learnt other stories here, some are about Shango, some about Eshu. The wedding will be in the church of Pelourinho. The best man is Miguel Santana, a big shipowner in Bahia. I'm a bit worried because Esmeralda isn't thirty yet and I'm already forty, but Senhorazinha doesn't think this is important so in the end I asked her parents and now I've got to marry her. I don't know yet what ship we will come back to Lagos in, but as soon as I do I'll send you word. Tell mother that Esmeralda knows you all already, she's heard me talk about you so much, and she loves Bill and will look after him as if he were her own son. Everything else fine, I'm looking forward to the wedding, your loving brother – Antônio.'

Epifânia didn't look too pleased when she heard all this, why force another Brazilian woman to live in Nigeria? People from outside weren't happy in Lagos, each country has its own way, what happened with

Elizabeth might happen all over again with Esmeralda, Mariana's voice cut in:

'It's a good thing he's getting married, mother. A man without a woman is no good.'

Epifânia looked at her a little oddly, Mariana wondered how much she knew about Joseph, often she got the feeling that her mother knew it all, and wasn't saying anything because she didn't want to make the situation even more complicated, it was a mother's problem, not a grandmother's, Fat Maria seemed as if she was trying to help when she said:

'Ana is very fond of Joseph, but he's not bothering. She's a pretty girl, her mother came on the *Esperança*.'

'He probably just hasn't noticed. Men are slow about these things. I'll see to it that he notices Ana.'

On the fourth day, when she saw Joseph coming in, she talked to him quite normally, he was the one to seem ill at ease, Mariana made a point of going out and leaving him alone, before she went she said:

'Fat Maria tells me that Ana thinks a lot of you.'

'Which one is she?'

'Abigail's daughter.'

'I know the one. Pretty.'

'Very pretty.'

Mariana spent the whole day in the shop, she replied to Antônio's letter and told him to go ahead, everyone approved of his marriage, men needed women, and women needed men, there was no need to hurry back, he could stay there as long as he liked, it was worth taking some time to get firm orders for the shipments of obis and orobos and to arrange for the shipping of dried salt meat from Bahia, once she lifted her eyes, saw a ship coming into the harbour, it looked different now from the way it had looked all those years ago, now the sea-front was well-kept, the buildings were bigger, the ship had white masts, its hull was white and its name was written in green letters, she went back to her letter and asked her brother to give his bride a kiss from her.

The next day she went to see Abigail, who was sitting in a huge armchair, she laughed a lot, sometimes you you could still see the girl on the ship who never stopped dancing, who cried because she had to go ashore in Lagos without her pretty dress, it was strange the way the two of them had spent their lives more or less together, they were always meeting, at parties, in church, she hadn't ever become very rich, her husband had a good job on the railway, he was manager of the district offices, Abigail's Portuguese was like Epifânia's, with the soft consonants that they had in Bahia, Mariana felt thin beside her, when she was leaving she said:

'Ask Ana to come over to our house. She gets prettier every day, God bless her. I want to get to know her better.'

Ana came to see her that same night, the two of them sat in the front parlour, Mariana asked her if she was studying:

'I finish grammar school this year.'

'What are you going to do afterwards?'

'I want to go to the teachers' training college and then teach in Lagos.'

'It's a good thing to be, a teacher. In my time I've given lots of lessons.'

She thought of the rainy days when the classes had dragged on and on, from the minute she had put up the sign **omi agua water** over the door of the house she had never given another lesson, her life had changed, followed other paths, Ana had a pleasant way with her, Mariana said:

'You haven't talked to Joseph much since the party we had here.'

'I've met him in the street, but we didn't say much.'

'He likes you a lot. It mightn't show because he's shy. You ought to go to a party together. Isn't there one this

Saturday at Seu Pereira's house? Why don't you go with him?'

'If he asks me to I will.'

'Listen, Ana: men are more frightened of us than we are of them. Don't wait for him to ask you. Let him know you want to go.'

The girl didn't say anything, she looked down at her hands resting on her lap, rubbed her thumb against her first finger, Mariana added:

'Look, I'll tell Joseph that you want to talk to him. While you're talking tell him about the party.'

After Ana had gone Mariana stayed sitting there, she heard a child crying, someone shouting at it, a smell of sea and fish came in with the heat of the night, she closed her eyes, slept for a while, heard her own voice talking to Joseph and woke up with a start, the room was deserted, only a dog barking in the street and a ship hooting in the distance.

It was midday, Joseph was going out, Mariana called to him from the window:

'Are you going to the shop?'

'Yes.'

'Stop off at Abigail's house, Ana wants to speak to you.'

'Did she say what it was about?'

'No.'

She watched him going into her friend's house, waited for a few minutes at the window, then went downstairs, crossed Bangboshe, walked along past the cathedral, a happy group of women was coming out of church, she heard a piano being played in a house on the corner, arrived at the shop, Epifânia was talking to a customer, her mother was good at keeping the price up, she loved spinning out a sale, was disappointed when someone agreed to the first price she asked, perhaps they ought to change the system, it was all right for African goods, you asked a high price and went down, the customer argued, made jokes, said funny things, went away, came back and

258

started all over again, but it didn't work with goods imported from England, you had to have fixed prices, at any rate the English said you had to, the price of beer, for instance, was the same everywhere, Mariana preferred to sell it wholesale to other shops rather than sell it retail, she sat at the back of the shop and sorted out the letters that needed replying to, suddenly she saw Joseph standing at the door, she went up to him:

'Did you speak to Ana?'

'Yes, I did.'

'What did she want?'

'She asked me to go to a party with her on Saturday. Her mother won't let her go by herself.'

Before Saturday came Mariana went to see Adolph at his office in the import-export company. He was wearing a dark suit, he seemed at ease in the office, frowned when he saw who it was who wanted to speak to him, put a pencil down on his desk, got to his feet, took Mariana into another room, as soon as she sat down she said:

'I've come to say that you mustn't try to see my son any more. Joseph needs to work, make friends with the people he meets, see other lawyers, and with the life he's leading now it's impossible for him to do it.'

Adolph was quite civil, but firm, his voice clear:

'Madam, I beg you to do me the honour of never coming to my office again to see me. If you should wish to speak to me, go to my house, I shall be very happy to receive you there. But not here.'

She rose:

'Thank you very much.'

She went out of the building into the sunlight, the street was crowded, cars moving along amongst the people, beggars asking for money, a cripple blocked her path, she gave him a shilling, went into an Indian shop, beautiful materials were draped in a showcase, she remembered Seu Haddad, her shops in Cotonou and Aduni, she would have to write to Emilia, Ricardo, Atondá and Jean da Cruz about buying new stock, as she was turning into Campos Square she realized that the burrinha hadn't been out for a long time, the feast of Bonfim wasn't for a while yet.

When Joseph and Ana met to go to the party Mariana was sitting in front of the sobrado, they said goodbye to her, a few minutes later Abigail came down the street, asked for a chair, Jerónimo went inside to get one, the two women sat there quietly looking at the night and people until Abigail said:

'They seemed happy enough together.'

'Age is on their side, and there's every reason why they should get on with each other.'

'Are you wanting them to get married?'

'Yes, if that's what they want themselves. And why wouldn't they?'

'You know that I only saw my husband on the day of the wedding. My mother arranged everything.'

'It was different with me. Sebastian courted me for a long time before he asked my mother and we had the betrothal party.'

On Sunday she noticed that Joseph seemed tired, he woke up annoyed because it was so late, he had arranged to go to Mass with Ana, Mariana went into church with a lighter heart, she heard the Latin chants, she had almost forgotten them by now, she sang the Credo in a clear voice, afterwards everyone gathered outside the main door of the church, relatives and friends greeted each other, the children had their best clothes on, all the afternoon Bangboshe Street seemed as if it was celebrating, Mariana was used to the Water House where there weren't so many people, and she enjoyed seeing all the brightly-coloured dresses, an egungun went by, the wooden mask was beautifully painted, many-coloured strips of cloth hung down to the ground.

Seu Gaspar, when she went to see him, was sitting on his bed and looking out of the window, when he saw Mariana he smiled, said:

'I saw Joseph and Abigail's girl going out together. How is it all now?'

'Much better.'

Mariana crouched down in front of an image of Shango with his double-headed axe, touched the ground with her hand, all that day there was music coming from a house nearby, the clear sound of the flute standing out among the other sounds, the week went by quickly, there were letters to write, negotiations with an Englishman who had come selling cheap textiles, news arrived from Dahomey, the shops were doing well, a ship had left for Brazil with a cargo of palm-oil, on Friday afternoon Mariana saw Adolph coming into the shop, she offered him a chair, he said:

'I haven't seen your son for several days, but I think this might not be a good thing for him. You didn't know, but when he first arrived in England he used to drink a lot and it was I who cured him of it.'

'I could do as you did and say that I don't like people coming to see me in the place where I work, but here I'm the owner, not an employee, and you are welcome.'

She paused. Before she could go on, he said:

'I hope you haven't been saying things about me to Joseph. Even if I never see him again, I want him to go on thinking well of me. We've been friends a long time.'

'I'm not directly responsible for Joseph not coming to see you any more. To tell you the truth, I hoped he wouldn't, but he didn't say anything to me, and I wouldn't have known now what was happening if you hadn't come and told me.'

'Is he all right?'

'As far as I can see. At any rate he isn't drinking, if that's what you're afraid of.'

'I have always had a good influence on Joseph. You must have realized that.'

Adolph's blue eyes were full of that sadness that Mariana had seen in them on the very first day, and his lips were half open as if he were on the point of doing something violent, yet an outsider would have thought him quite calm, the silence went on for longer than either of them expected or wanted, he said goodbye in a scarcely audible voice and went out of the door, not walking very fast, but a very slight sway of his hips might have been taken as an almost feminine desire to hurry.

A letter from Sebastian the next day broke into Mariana's obsessive thoughts, he said that things were getting much worse in Europe, in France the government was not stable, and quite incapable of mobilizing the country in the face of danger, Hitler was arming and no-one seemed to be paying any attention, apart from all this Sebastian's studies were going well, he had started to give lessons to his younger friends, that way he got both money and experience, he had met other boys from Zorei in Paris, sometimes they talked about how more schools could be started in Zorei and the people prepared for a future when they might have more independence, but for the most part the young people weren't interested in things like that, Paris had so many other attractions, how was Joseph getting on in his new professions?, was he practising yet?, he had heard about Ainá from other friends, she had been an excellent student it seemed and would make an outstanding doctor, best wishes to everyone and blessing, when she had finished reading Mariana tried to imagine what Sebastian's face would be like now, he must have grown so much during these last years, had he a serious girlfriend?, or did he have a woman?, would she be African or French?, there hadn't been many letters from Ainá lately, all the news they got of her was what they heard from friends.

Two weeks later Mariana was horrified to see Ana

looking as if she had been crying, she was going along the street, Mariana went after her, caught her by the arm, asked what was the matter.

'Nothing, nothing, Dona Mariana.'

'Have you been fighting with Joseph?'

'I haven't seen him for a long time.'

'What went wrong?'

'I don't know. He seemed a bit strange, said he didn't want to see me for a while.'

'It happens. I wouldn't see Sebastian for quite a long time. It was while we were betrothed.'

She paused for a moment then said:

'Or was it before? I don't remember.'

She went and knocked on Adolph's door, it was the sixth time they had been alone together, his face was worried, he asked:

'What is it now, Madam?'

'Has Joseph come back to you?'

'Yes, he has. At this very moment he's asleep in that room. Do you want me to wake him?'

'No. It's not necessary. It's you I want to talk to.'

'Your servant.'

'There is one very big reason why you should keep away from my son.'

'What is that?'

'It is that you can't give my son a child.'

'I beg your pardon?'

'You cannot be mother of a child by my son.'

Silence rose up like a wall between them. Adolph's eyes hardened, Mariana's face remained immobile, after what seemed to her a very long time she said:

'Every mother dreams of her son having children. I want Joseph to marry in a normal way and give me grandchildren.'

The servant came in with a cup of coffee which Mariana drank slowly, Adolph's words came slowly too:

'You may be right in what you say, but I cannot do

263

anything to help you. I still think that it's Joseph's problem rather than mine.'

She hardly saw anyone on the way back, everything had been done that could be done, it might come right of itself, she crossed the bridge and went to Ebute Metta, she had heard that there was a Hausa who had some ground-nuts for sale, she was out the whole day, at night she found a letter waiting for her, it was from Antônio, he was married, Senhorazinha had been his sponsor, the boy they called Didi had sung at the party, Antônio said that there wouldn't be a ship sailing direct to Lagos for some months, he would wait, because there was a lot to be done in Bahia, he was thinking of setting up an office there to deal with the import of goods from Nigeria, some of Esmeralda's relatives could look after it, Esmeralda was the most beautiful girl in the whole world, she was longing to come to Lagos with him, after Mariana had read the letter she asked Jerónimo to go and get Ana, she talked to the girl for more than two hours, but she scarcely mentioned Joseph's name, her brother's letter had made her want to talk about Piau and Bahia, long forgotten things came back to her memory, from the fish they had caught with sticks in the River Piau to Father José saying goodbye, the cachaça he used to drink, the times when he used to climb the church tower drunk and ring the bell, the feast of Bonfim, the voyage in the sailing-ship, the dead bodies thrown into the sea, the first one had floated, they had to tie heavy things to the bodies so that they would sink but the captain said they couldn't use any more weights, he needed them all, their arrival in Lagos, the first days, at one point Ana asked:

'And what about the well? How did you get the idea of the well?'

'I can't remember properly. All I know is that a long time before they had even started to dig I could see the well as clear as could be, as if it was there in front of me asking to be dug.'

After Ana had gone she went on sitting there, only when she realized that Joseph wouldn't be coming in did she decide to go and sleep, sweat streamed off her body.

She spent the next week very cheerfully, went to Antônio's house, engaged men to come and clean it out, went to the market a lot, got some adirés, bought beads to make necklaces, noticed that Ana and Joseph were going out together again, talked for hours to Fat Maria, who wanted to know:

'Do you think this Brazilian girl of Antônio's is going to settle down here?'

'Esmeralda? Why not? We came from there, didn't we?'

'But when she arrives she'll have responsibilities, married already and with her husband's little son to look after.'

Ainá wrote at last, said that she was working in a hospital now as an intern, it was even better than she had imagined it would be, she was going to need more training, one or two years, before she would feel ready to come and work in Lagos, Epifânia listened to Mariana reading the letter and said:

'Just imagine. My granddaughter a doctor of medicine.'

Deep inside her, Mariana let her great worry about Joseph lie in a sort of quiescence, it wouldn't help to disturb it any more, things sort themselves out, without anyone interfering, and solutions come naturally, during all this time she behaved to her son with a mixture of gaiety and restraint, she avoided having any long conversations with him, accepted every invitation that took her away from the house, went over to the other side of the town and spent afternoons and evenings with some of the older Brazilians, Seu Justino and his wife hadn't noticed anything different about Joseph, they accepted him as if he hadn't changed at all and was still the child of long ago, ever since the welcome party they were always asking about him, talking about marriage, they wanted to know which girl he would choose, sometimes Seu Justino came to the sobrado to talk to Mariana, he almost always said exactly the same things, he would begin:

'Here's my daughter-in-law looking better every day.'

One day he asked:

'Who is the boy going to marry?'

'He's going out with Ana.'

'Abigail's daughter? I don't think I've noticed her. What's she like?'

'A very good girl.'

Joseph went to see his grandparents several times a week, Seu Justino liked going out with him, showing him off to his friends, saying:

'He's a lawyer.'

Mariana knew Joseph was unhappy, she saw him sitting in front of the house looking as if he didn't know where he was, when he told her he had started going to the office of an English partnership in Lagos, with the idea of working with them, all she said was:

'Good.'

He explained:

'At first it will only be to get experience, later on I can have my own cases.'

She met Adolph once in the street, he said good-day, she replied, she knew that he and her son were seeing very little of each other now, the one who was drinking was Adolph, one Sunday she heard that he had broken all the furniture in the house where he lived, nobody knew exactly how it had started, it had happened on the Saturday night, when Joseph had gone to a party with Ana.

There seemed to be more beggars in the streets of Lagos now, there were cripples, people dragging themselves along the ground, others showing wounds, blind men, Mariana remembered the beggars in Bahia, there was no difference between those and the ones here, one day Fat Maria came almost running, she said to Mariana:

'Emilia's husband is with a crowd of beggars beside the bridge.'

'Ebenezer?'

'Yes. He's all in rags and preaching to the others.'

Mariana tied a cloth round her head, went along Bangboshe, she recognized Ebenezer from a long way off, he had aged, nothing in him now of the young man who had come all those years ago to ask for Emilia's hand, his hair had grown long and was nearly white, he had an old overcoat on with pieces of paper sticking out of the pocket, when he spoke his voice was still strong:

'It is easier for a camel to pass through the eye of a needle than for a rich man to enter the kingdom of heaven. The poor are the salt of the earth. All of us here are asking alms of you who pass by, but woe unto those who do not see on us the sign of Christ, who was poor like us and has numbered us among his chosen.'

An almost naked beggar shouted:

'Shut your mouth!'

Ebenezer looked at him and said:

'Woe unto those who deny the word of God and repent not of their sins for they will burn in the fires of hell.'

He seemed ill, a little later he fell silent, lay down on the ground and slept, his head pillowed on his right arm, Mariana went back to the house, called Silvanus, sent him in the car to Ibadan to fetch the twins, perhaps their father was going to need looking after, Cosme and Damião arrived the next day, went with Mariana to the place where Ebenezer had been speaking, but the crowd of beggars had gone across the bridge and were now in Yaba, night had fallen by the time they found their father, some of the people told them he had fainted many times during the last few weeks, the twins put him in the car, once when Ebenezer opened his eyes he said:

267

'Who are you?'

But he fell asleep again, or fainted, he was thin and dirty, the twins thought it would be best to take him to Ibadan, Mariana agreed:

'Take the car.'

She thought for a moment then asked:

'Do you think I should send for Emilia?'

'No, let Mother stay in Dahomey. She's happy there and wouldn't be any good looking after a sick man.'

'I'll write to her. She might want to come.'

Joseph talked to his mother that night, he wanted to know about Ebenezer:

'Why did he decide to be a preacher?'

'He'd always wanted to be, but his father wouldn't let him.'

Joseph was silent for a long time, looking out into the middle of the street, then he asked:

'Was that where father died?'

'Yes.'

'Did he suffer much?'

How to know if a man suffers as he dies? Mariana saw her husband surrounded by people, O night of terror and death, how to forget a man fallen suddenly still?

'He can't have suffered much.'

After Joseph went out she closed her eyes, sat there utterly weary, Ebenezer's face wouldn't leave her mind, for the first time in years she saw Sebastian's face again, the way he had looked the day they were married and the things he had done, as if he had wanted her to remember it all, the journey they had made to Ibadan together just before he died, the way he leaned his arms on the windowsill and how he pulled off his shirt, the way he had of opening his lips for a moment just before he spoke, the calm way he did things, again she thought of Ebenezer, old and white-haired, she went to look at herself in the mirror, thought her own face looked different, on the way to being old.

268

Throughout the next few days her body was touched by some indefinable tension, perhaps she had a fever, she talked to Joseph without really noticing what she said or what he replied, but she was conscious that the ways were getting narrower, soon everyday life would become unbearable, she felt as if she wanted to shout, O shout that would not come into the open and stayed imprisoned in the throat, O god of the shout lend your hand to pull from my throat this lump which tries to become sound but remains in silence, if Ana came to see her she can't remember it, she knows that she talked to Bill, spent hours with Epifânia, drew water from the well, she thinks she caught sight of Adolph in Bangboshe Street, sometimes she would stop and ask herself if she had eaten that day, Seu Justino came looking for her and wanted to talk about Joseph's future, she thinks she managed to reply to him sensibly, when she tried to see the date on a calendar she couldn't seem to come to any conclusion about it, one day she slept until one o'clock in the afternoon, she hadn't noticed the morning coming, could scarcely put her legs out of the bed, that night she spent hours sitting beside her son, he seemed about to say something, she became alert, waiting, her sense and concentration suddenly alive again, but Joseph opened his eyes wide and didn't say a word, it was dawn when they came to find him, Mariana went down the stairs, there were Nigerian policemen and an Englishman in charge of them, she asked:

'What's happened?'

'An accident or a suicide. Your son has to come and identify the man, he was a friend of his.'

'Can I come as well?'

'Yes.'

Joseph went on ahead, the darkness seemed thicker in the spaces between the streetlamps, on the other side of Tinubu Square the building where Adolph worked was lit up, they went up the stairs, in an inside hall crowded

with people Adolph was lying with one side of his face
on the ground, a thread of blood trickled down his face
and made a red mark on the white tiles, his fair hair lay
untidily in a little pool of blood, Joseph was bending
down beside the body, an officer held him back, asked
him:

'Do you know who he is?'

'My friend Adolph Twelvetrees.'

'Did he work here?'

'His office is on the fourth floor.'

'He must have fallen from there.'

The soldiers went up to the fourth floor landing, there
was a balustrade and you could see down to the hall
below, the officer went with them, they were up there a
long time, when they came down again the Englishman
said:

'There are marks on the balustrade. It looks as if he
climbed up on to it and threw himself off. When did you
see him last?'

'Last night.'

'What time?'

'Eight o'clock.'

'Here?'

'No, in his house. When I left I thought he was asleep.'

'The porter says he left here at seven and came back
again, alone, at eleven.'

Mariana looked at Adolph's nose, at his arms spread
wide and defenceless on the ground, how to know if a
man suffers as he dies? She thought they ought to lift
the body up from where it lay there, it still seemed to be
suffering, the officer and the soldiers were talking, saying
things, asking questions, but they weren't bothering to
make the body peaceful, lay it down straight, put its
hands together, on the way back Mariana and her son
went through streets awakened by the morning, went into
the house together, she went upstairs with him to his
room, closed the door, sat down on the bed, Joseph was

270

weeping silently, he knelt on the ground, put his head on his mother's lap and began to sob, at the same time he was talking:

'How could I know that this would happen. You don't know what these last days have been like, I couldn't even bear to talk to him, but I was sorry, I loved him as a friend, he helped me so much, he wanted me to go to bed with him and I wouldn't. In London it was different, it all seemed quite normal there, here it started to be ugly and every time I saw Ana I knew I had to change. Last night he asked me to spend the night there, he wanted to talk to me, I wouldn't. Now I feel it was my fault.'

Mariana let him talk on, tell her of his struggle to get away from his friend, but he didn't want to get away completely, he thought he might be able to marry Ana and still be friendly with Adolph, but there was something very wrong even in the way he and Adolph talked together, they understood each other without words, a silence was enough for one of them to know what the other was thinking, couldn't there have been some other way for it to have ended, not this, not death, and perhaps he hadn't known the right way to go about it, but in spite of Adolph being the passive partner sexually he was the one who thought, reasoned, planned, all Joseph did was live, let time go by, not worrying about what would happen later, deep down he had been hoping that in the end Adolph would find some way out of the problem, but not that way, Mariana stroked her son's hair, and after a moment of silence he lifted his head and looked at her:

'Did he suffer?'

That question again, Mariana made Joseph lie down on the bed, she went downstairs, found the officer who was dealing with the case, wanted to know who would be looking after the funeral arrangements.

'I was thinking of asking the people in his office. Perhaps they would see to it.'

271

'If they are agreeable, my son and I will look after everything. He was a close friend of my son, ever since England, they came back to Lagos together.'

'I can't see any objection to that. We've already sent a telegram to his family in London, there will be a post-mortem tomorrow at eleven and after that you can have the body for burial.'

Mariana went here and there, saw people in the import company, hired a hearse, ordered the coffin, decided it would be best if the body left from the house on Ikoyi, when she got back to the sobrado she asked Joseph:

'What religion was he?'

'Anglican.'

She asked Seu Justino to speak to an Anglican minister, the cemetery on Ikoyi wasn't far away from the house, the service didn't last long, Joseph put on dark clothes, heavy wool, he began to sweat in the heat of the afternoon, Mariana bowed her head, prayed that the saints and the orishas would find she had been right in doing what she did, she had only been defending her son, she hadn't wanted anyone to die, had just been fighting for what was right, hadn't often felt anger against Adolph, perhaps she thought of him the same way as she thought of the man who had killed Sebastian, Adolph had deserved to live, his eyes had been blue and they had looked sadly right inside you, he had arrived on the same ship as Joseph, he had come to the welcoming party, he had walked through these streets, above all he had loved Joseph, loved in the wrong way, but loved, O Shango who have the gift of justice look at me and see that I fought for life, not death.

Part IV

THE GREAT LEADER

Mariana, I see her tranquil during those days of harmattan, the wind blew over the town, she felt the need of
silence, the dry air touched her body and filled her with a
sense of well-being. I see her walking along Bangboshe
not noticing anything around her, she threw herself into
work as she had perhaps never done before, wrote letters,
discussed the price of goods, checked accounts, decided
to have the sea-front shop painted, chose a shade of
green, stayed out late watching the painters at work, a
few days after Adolph's suicide she had news of the death
of Ebenezer, the twins had given him a fine serenata, they
thought their father had lived a good life, anyhow that
was what they told Mariana, who sometimes now
realized that she herself was old and would be given a
serenata if she died, she remembered that she had been
going to write to Emilia about her husband's illness, she
hadn't written because she couldn't face concentrating
on a letter, I see her now sitting at the back of the shop,
her pen poised for a moment above the paper before she
begins: 'My dear sister Emilia. Ebenezer is dead, it's
best to tell you straight away what happened. I had come
across him with a group of beggars he was preaching to,
this was near the bridge in Lagos. I sent word to Cosme
and Damião to come at once, they found their father and
took him to Ibadan. Ebenezer was looking a lot older.
We have to be sorry for him, sister, he wanted so much to
be a preacher, in the end he spent years far from his
family and without any comfort. Who can know what he
suffered? I've had some trouble about a friend of
Joseph's. This friend was an Englishman and he com-

mitted suicide here in Lagos a few days before Ebenezer died. It was because of all this that I didn't let you know Ebenezer was ill, but I think it was better that way because you wouldn't have been able to do anything anyway. Cosme and Damião gave him a good big serenata, all our friends in Ibadan were there. We must pray for Ebenezer because he never harmed anyone, only himself. Antônio has got married in Bahia to a Brazilian girl called Esmeralda. Who would have thought that one of us would have gone back to Brazil to marry? He'll soon be back in Lagos with his wife. Mother sends you her love and blessing. From your sister who loves you—Mariana.'

She knew that she ought to be in Dahomey, dreamt about the Water House, she was missing her friends, Atondá, Jean da Cruz, Marie, Pedoké, Adjá, Monsieur Casteller, Seu Haddad, but there were things to do in Lagos, when she got the letter from Antônio telling her that he and Esmeralda would be arriving soon she thought she had better wait and see the couple, she joined in the celebration for the feast of Bonfim that year, Seu Clemente, a Brazilian she hadn't met before, he had just recently come from Ifé, put on a bumba-meu-boi that shook the whole of Bangboshe Street with gaiety, Mariana sat for hours watching the antics of the ox, the ostrich, the giant woman, she felt calmed by these images moving in front of her, the traditional chants filled the air, O ox that makes the children shout and squeal with laughter, the next day she went to the garden where Sebastian was buried, it was years since she had visited his grave, sometimes she caught sight of Joseph and Ana out walking together, she hadn't mentioned Adolph to him again, was just treating him naturally, he seemed to be coming to terms with himself, he had started to work in a lawyer's office, a letter from Adolph's family in England had thanked Mariana for taking care of the funeral, she thought there was a faint tone of irony in the letter, but perhaps it was just her awareness that she hadn't been able to do anything, nobody could have helped the Englishman to solve his problem.

It was May when Antônio and Esmeralda arrived, the ship docked in the afternoon, the whole family was there waiting, and some friends as well, from a distance Mariana saw that Esmeralda was a light mulatto, with a thin face, big eyes, beautiful in a strange way, her face was expressive and intelligent, it changed every moment and spoke her thoughts better than words, from the moment they embraced Mariana decided she was going to like her, whether she was good or bad, the Portuguese her new sister-in-law spoke was smooth, she softened the t's and the d's, Mariana saw herself back in Bahia hearing the language as they spoke it there, the Portuguese spoken in Lagos had some sounds like Yoruba, in the middle of a phrase or between two words they would say hanh, hanh, it sounded like long sighs, at first she had found it very odd, one day she realized that she had begun to use the same way of replying to questions, the same way of expressing surprise and astonishment.

They all went to the cathedral and received the blessing of welcome, the priest sprinkled holy water over everybody, Antônio's sobrado was all ready, Esmeralda had taken Bill by the hand, gone into church with him, Mariana saw all this, saw that the girl was making a point of showing everybody that she was going to be his new mother, perhaps she didn't need to show it quite so plainly, Antônio was delighted to get back to his house, rushed upstairs to see the bedroom, tables and chairs had been put out in the street for the party which began with drums beating alone, no other music, two boys had been practising on the drums for a long time while Esmeralda and Antônio looked out of the upstairs window and laughed with people in the street, Joseph spent the whole night sitting in a chair, drinking beer, when Ana arrived he got up and talked to her for a long time, he didn't dance, his eyes moved slowly from face to face, Seu Justino, who was half drunk, sang:

> He who goes, goes weeping
> He who comes, comes over the sea,
> He who goes, goes sadly,
> He who comes, brings gifts for me.

Everybody laughed, the next morning Mariana helped Esmeralda to unpack, there were beautiful lengths of material, kerchiefs for the head, Antônio had brought hats to give to his friends, what pleased Mariana most was the dried salt meat, it was a long time since she had tasted it, they had some at midday, she chewed each piece slowly, the taste went deep into her tongue and up into the roof of her mouth, she saw herself sitting on the ground in Bahia market, the fish smell everywhere, when she decided to go back to Dahomey and take Fat Maria with her she chose a good big piece of dried meat for Emilia, the road stretched ahead in the morning light, first she went to Pobé, talked to Fatumbi, he was even older now, bent, his movements as he threw down the shells to reveal the future were slow and he spent even longer looking at the position of each disc, the settlement hadn't grown any bigger, it was still exactly the same, Fatumbi asked:

'How is your son Joseph?'

'It worked itself out.'

He straightened his whole body and looked into her eyes, said:

'As it was foretold.'

Mariana said:

'But there was a death.'

'Sometimes it is inevitable.'

At midday he offered rice with peppers to Mariana, Fat Maria and Silvanus, there were wooden platters with newly-fried bean-cakes, they ate slowly with their hands, sometimes looked up at the huts round about, there were

276

children playing on the ground, a goat pulling at a rope that tethered it to a wooden post, at the end of the meal women brought jugs of water, they all washed their hands, Mariana asked where Fagbemi was, they told her he was living in a village called Idigny, she said goodbye, and in the car on the way to Porto Novo she wondered how she would find the sobrado in Ouidah, it was years since she had seen it, she scarcely noticed the villages they passed, before she got there she would see the beach, the stretch of sand and the Water House, they made a familiar group, Mariana opened the car door, embraced Emilia who had just come down the stairs, saw Jean da Cruz standing beside a boy who must be his son, when she went into the parlour she went straight to the window and stood looking out at the sea there in the distance, there was a wind stirring the coco-palms and whipping up the waves, they crashed foaming white on the yellow sand.

They were peaceful days, those. Mariana took possession once more of all her things, opened the chest just for the sake of opening it, rummaged around among the clothes, sat looking for a long time at a blue dress or a yellow blouse, walked around outside, talked to Atondá, the Ewes, Jean da Cruz, Marie, went to the Portuguese fort to visit the Commandant, at night she sat with Emilia and Fat Maria, remembering things, she didn't know how to reply when her sister asked her:

'What was Ebenezer like?'

She tried to remember her brother-in-law's face, didn't speak for a minute or two, Emilia had to repeat her question before Mariana said:

'He was looking a lot older, but to tell the truth the only way I can remember him was the way he looked the day he came to ask for your hand in marriage.'

Fat Maria said:

'He was worn out. I've never seen anyone age so quickly.'

Gradually Mariana became her normal self again, when Joseph turned up at the Water House she was filled with happiness to see that he too looked serene. She listened to what he had come to say:

'I'm going to marry Ana.'

The smell of the sea came into the room, in the kitchen the servants were talking, Mariana looked up at Joseph, said quietly:

'That's good. She's a good girl.'

The two of them were silent, it was a while before she said:

'When is it to be?'

'We're not in a hurry. Perhaps in a year or two.'

He walked around the property, saw the palm-oil being made, looked at the well, held long conversations with Jean da Cruz, the morning he left for Lagos he was very gay, joked with his mother and Emilia, teased Fat Maria. As soon as she had seen him off Mariana's mind turned to the shop in Aduni, she ought to find out how everything was going there, decided to cross the frontier the next day, Seu Haddad gave her a great welcome, she went to see Monsieur Casteller, he was thin, but strong, as they lay together in his bed it was raining over the town, Mariana realized that during all that time in Lagos she had never had a man, it must be old age, the teacher had had a letter from Sebastian, said he thought Sebastian ought to come back as soon as possible, Zorei needed Africans who could teach, Mariana felt that Sebastian should stay in Paris as long as he thought necessary, there was no need to rush, everything happened so quickly, there would be plenty of time to come back and take responsibility in Zorei.

One night when there were stars in every corner of the sky she sat with Seu Haddad in front of the shop, they talked until after midnight, he spoke of the Lebanon:

'Beirut is a beautiful place, Dona Mariana. The air

seems lighter there, even when the drains are smelling there still seems to be a perfume all around you.'

'You haven't been back for a long time?'

'Not for forty years.'

And it was forty years, or nearly that, since she had seen Brazil, she felt African now, liked the feeling of change, the going from one place to another, having one house in Dahomey and another in Nigeria, handling business in different towns, she never managed to think in any other language but Portuguese, but she enjoyed talking in English and in French, in Yoruba and Ewe, even in German which she hadn't spoken now for such a long time, Seu Haddad's French, for example, had a charm all its own, it was different from Monsieur Casteller's French, like the different Yoruba in Ijebu-Ode and Abeokuta, in Ifé and Pobé, sometimes there were sounds in one that didn't exist in another, suddenly she heard herself saying:

'It's a long time since I left Brazil. My brother went there not long ago and he's come back married to a Brazilian. A girl from Bahia. I arrived in Lagos when I was thirteen. We came on a sailing ship called the *Esperança*, we were six months at sea.'

'Can you remember the voyage?'

'As if it were yesterday. I can remember the sky at night, lots of stars, I can remember the people who died, I can remember the smell of the ship.'

'The ship that brought me from Lebanon had a special smell as well, but it wasn't a sailing ship, it was a little steamer that rolled all the time.'

'Do you never want to go back?'

'Sometimes. And sometimes I'm afraid of wanting to.'

Aduni had grown, there were new roads now where before it had all been bush, Mariana walked around the town, saw the robes worn by the people from the Gold Coast, one day she talked to a Gurunsi, she had a feeling

279

they had known some Gurunsis in Bahia, her grandmother had once said something about a Gurunsi family
that had gone back to Africa, as soon as she began to miss
the Water House she took the car and went back there,
she spent whole days in Shango's room, looking at the
carvings, putting the stones before the god, a male
phallus, symbol of Eshu, stood in front of the door of a
cabin up at the top of the beach, the Water House was the
centre of a little village now, Mariana visited all the
homes at least once every month, she had got used to
living in silence with her sister, it was Fat Maria she
talked to most, her old friend from the *Esperança* looked
after the house, organized the cooking, Mariana saw her
fat figure everywhere seeing to things, Emilia talked more
when Cosme and Damião arrived, they told her about
their father's death, said he had seemed to be happy as
his life neared its end, the serenata had been very gay,
the cocoa plantations were doing well again, from time to
time Emilia asked a question, she wanted to know about
the Borges sisters, what had happened to the house she
used to live in, which of Ebenezer's father's wives were
still alive, as they were saying goodbye one of the twins
asked her:
'Don't you want to come back to Ibadan with us?'
'No. Thank you, but I don't want to. I was unhappy
there and I'm all right here.'
The long Yoruba robes of Cosme and Damião disappeared into the distance, Emilia fell back into her way
of not talking much, she stayed close to Mariana and
went for hours without saying a word, when she was
sewing her movements were calm and she was peaceful,
almost an object in the room, Mariana watched her,
thought of the beautiful young girl she had been, saw
herself again playing with her sister in the market in
Bahia, afterwards on the ship the two of them running
around together, today Emilia looked older than she did
herself, bent there over her hemming old age held her

280

fast. It was just about then that a letter came from Sebastian:

'Dear Mother.—I think it's time now for me to come back to Zorei and begin work there. In Europe things are getting worse and worse. Chamberlain went to Munich and everyone is saying that he prevented a war. I'm not so sure. War could come any day, Hitler won't stop now. What will happen to France if there is a war? My friends tell me that the country is ready to face Germany and defeat her in record time. I wonder if it's true. No matter who wins, I still think it would be better if war could be avoided. I'm writing to Monsieur Casteller as well. I intend to return to Zorei within the next three months. There is a school in Aduni that has offered me a post, I'm going to accept it. How are you all? Is Joseph practising now? And what about Ainá? I haven't heard from her recently. As soon as I know what ship I'm coming on I'll send you word. From your son who loves you. Sebastian.'

The day was fixed for Joseph's wedding to Ana, as soon as she got the news Mariana had herself a new dress made, put Emilia and Fat Maria in the car, went to Pobé first, Fatumbi was sitting on the ground, he looked at the women getting out of the car, smiled when he saw who it was, later, inside, when the two of them were alone, Mariana felt an unexpected peace fall on her, as if she had done all that had to be done and was free now to look around her in tranquillity, she watched Fatumbi's movements, the way he untied the cloth that held the cowries and the discs that foretold the future, the way he placed the wooden bowl on the dark ground, she spread her right hand and leaned her palm on the earth, felt a coldness coming in through her skin, Fatumbi's house isolated her from the rest of the world, at the moment when he threw the shells the noise they made in the bowl attracted her eyes, the man's voice filled the room:

'The marriage will be lasting and fruitful.'

All through the celebrations Mariana thought about these words, about the long years that Joseph and Ana would be married, about the children they would have, she thought that the sobrado in Bangboshe needed some alterations, Epifânia was against it, said she wasn't to interfere, the house was fine as it was, the morning of the wedding began with Joseph coming to find his mother in her room:

'I've had some cases already. It's going well.'

'Of course it is.'

And how could it be otherwise? With every turn of her head now Mariana radiated confidence, when she went into Abigail's house she carried this feeling of confidence with her, found her friend crying, remembered that in Brazil the bride's mother always cried on the wedding day, she herself couldn't remember crying at all, she put her arms round Abigail's fat body, rocked her from side to side, comforted her, Abigail said:

'They will be happy, won't they, Mariana?'

'Of course they will.'

Why all this worry? Yes, they would be happy, like young people always are, and even if they weren't completely happy they would look back later on and see their past as something gay and pleasant, these days you had cars at a wedding, not when she was young, no, she had walked to church with Sebastian, the two of them in front and the guests following behind, when she saw Ana she thought she looked beautiful, her long white dress fell to the ground, her head was covered with an embroidered veil, an English lawyer and his wife were Joseph's sponsors, Ana had chosen her oldest brother and his wife for hers, the church was just the same, what had become of Father O'Malley?, they told her that he had gone back to Ireland because he was very old, but he hadn't been happy there, had wanted to come back to Nigeria again, the bishop wouldn't let him, this priest today, much younger, got through the Latin very fast, at the end he gave a little sermon in English, said that the husband and wife must love one another, follow the rules of the Catholic religion, bring up their children in it and be united in one spirit and one flesh, until death.

The party was in Abigail's house, people came and went, a huge cake on the table, as the music started up Mariana remembered Adolph, his blue eyes, his sad face, the body lying in the hall, the funeral cortège, she forced herself to listen to the flute, looked to see if it was the same man, but it wasn't, this man had a young face, somehow it made his flute look longer, Seu Justino came over to talk to her, Mariana hadn't noticed until then how old he had become, his thin hair was a dirty white, yellowish, she listened to what he was saying, Sebastian hadn't been like his father, perhaps he was more on his mother's side, whenever Mariana had seen her she had been silent, she scarcely ever spoke, listened quietly to her husband, laughed at the things he said, Jerónimo was looking very old as well, at one moment a tall young girl, with her hair plaited in the African style, sat down beside Mariana, who asked her:

'Who are you, child?'

'Julia, I'm Ana's sister.'

'I can remember you when you were a little girl.'

'Ainá and I are great friends. I was in London at the same time as her, we spent all the weekends together. I studied accountancy in London.'

'She mentioned you in one of her letters.'

'Ainá's marvellous. Once we had a vote to choose the most intelligent African student of our group. Ainá won. None of the boys we knew were as intelligent as she was. When will she be coming back?'

'She's finished her course now. She's practising in a hospital before coming back here.'

A thin man with a little beard got Julia up to dance, it was a clarinet now that led the music, Mariana sat watching Joseph and Ana, the girl had taken off her wedding dress and was wearing a red dress trimmed with white, Abigail came up looking tired, her fat arms glistened with sweat as the lights shone on them, she sat down beside Mariana, took a handkerchief from between her breasts, began to wipe her arms, smiled happily as she looked around her, it was past midnight when Mariana embraced her old friend, Joseph and Ana had already gone to bed, Abigail said:

'Well then, my dear, all we have to do now is wait for our grandchildren.'

Mariana was going into the sobrado when she saw that Seu Gaspar's window was open, she went up to it and asked:

'Are you still awake?'

From inside the room he replied:

'I was watching the party from my bed here. Very nice.'

She wanted to talk, but he said no, she must be tired, better go and sleep, the wedding of the first son was a great joy, he thought Joseph looked a fine young man, he would make a good husband and increase the number of Silvas, Ana looked the child-bearing type, she would have many children, Mariana said goodnight, when she went in she sat down in the rocking-chair, thinking about her own wedding-night, there had been no well then, on this same spot there had been a little low house, they had only had a mat, and Joseph had been born on a mat as well, it was only starting with Ainá that she had had her children in a bed, suddenly the images ran together and she slept, she didn't waken until morning, with the sun coming in through the window.

She felt full of energy, went walking down Bangboshe Street like she used to when she was young, went to Antônio's house, found Esmeralda talking to Bill, asked:

'Well, what about a baby?'

Esmeralda smiled:

'There's one on the way.'

'Good news.'

The house was looking lovely, the room well furnished, vases of flowers at the windows, Esmeralda sat down with Mariana for a while, they talked about Joseph's wedding, Mariana had been wondering:

'Have you got used to Nigeria yet?'

'Yes, completely. I feel as if I'd been born here.'

'Don't you miss Bahia at all?'

'Only when I remember my parents.'

Mariana went out again and walked along Odunlami Street, into Broad Street, across Balbina Street, stopped for a moment in Tinubu Square, went into an Indian shop, bought some incense, there were new buildings going up everywhere, in this part of the city you didn't see many sobrados in the Brazilian style, she came to a market, began to look at adirés, English cloth, now she said a few words in Yoruba, the woman replied, then she was speaking English, she ended up buying some gold-coloured cloth with blue patterns on it, when she got back she found Emilia eating a plate of cassava, she chewed away and looked at Mariana, Fat Maria had put some water into a frying pan and was cooking pieces of dried salt meat, after a while Emilia said she wanted to go back to Dahomey, she was missing her room and all the things she was used to, Mariana said:

'Just be patient for a while. We'll go back the day after tomorrow.'

That afternoon she checked the accounts in the shop, they were selling bed-clothes and table-linen now as well as furniture, and all sorts of textiles, and soap, and in one corner there were crates of beer being stored until they went out to the retailers in the interior, by the evening the heat had become unbearable, Mariana went to the well, it was a long time since anyone had bought any water, but it was still there, the wall crumbling a bit, the old bucket, it needed a new rope, the next day she took the car and went to Ikoyi Island where the English had built some lovely houses, she thought of buying one of them, the one she liked was in the middle of a plot of land with gardens all around it, but she would feel lonely, it was only in the Brazilian quarter that she felt really happy, she knew who lived in every house, that night she talked to Antônio, who had just heard that Esmeralda's father was intending to come to Lagos and bring a big shipment of dried meat and tobacco, it was early morning when Mariana, Emilia, Fat Maria and Silvanus set out in the car, they crossed the frontier between Nigeria and Dahomey, stopped in Porto Novo to fill up with petrol and arrived at the Water House in time for lunch.

Then there began for Mariana a period of tranquillity, the days interlaced with each other, it seemed there was no work to be done anywhere in the house, Fat Maria wouldn't let her cook, Pedoké did whatever she wanted, Ricardo was managing the shop in Aduni and came to Ouidah once a week, Jean da Cruz and Atondá were looking after the palm-oil, the copra and the Cotonou shop, Emilia spent part of her time in Cotonou and part in Zorei, Mariana found herself surrounded by attentions, when she went near any of the huts scattered around the sobrado everyone came out to talk to her, they waited for her to speak to them first, in his heavy Portuguese the Commandant of Ajudá invited her to coffee, and, when they had finished, escorted her to the gate of the fort, they stopped in front of the cashew-trees, Mariana loved to bite the fruit, she remembered Bahia, the juice running down her chin, even when the news arrived that Ainá was coming back they wouldn't let her rush around, Fat Maria, a huge white apron covering her massive bosom, said:

'There's no hurry. You can go to Lagos the day before. Antônio and Joseph will look after the welcome party.'

Just one day before Ainá was due to arrive the car took the three women to Lagos, Mariana tried to remember what Ainá's face looked like, but she couldn't, when the time came she saw that it was still the face of the little girl of twenty years ago, but now the body was a woman's body, a fine woman. She stood looking at her for what seemed to Ainá a long time, then she held her tight, their two faces together, smelt her perfume, Ainá's voice was clear and happy:

'Well, Mother? What do you think of me?'

'Wonderful.'

They left the ship talking fast, Seu Justino exclaimed:

'If I'd met my granddaughter in the street I wouldn't have recognized her.'

Ainá was laughing all the time, Julia arrived and embraced her, in the church the priest sprinkled them all with holy water, the family and Ainá's friends, the party was in the sobrado, once again it was crowded with people, Ainá looked all around the house, put her things in one of the rooms upstairs, went with her mother to the window, looked out along Bangboshe Street, said:

'The number of times I've pictured every bit of this street! Thank goodness it's still just the same.'

She went down to meet more friends, all her movements were strong and confident, she spoke freely, words came readily to her, she listened when it was time to listen, knew how to inquire without asking too many questions, her way of agreeing encouraged you to say more, she danced at the party, talked to a lot of young men, Epifânia said to Mariana:

'She's my granddaughter and she's a doctor.'

When everyone had left Ainá said to her mother:

'I've been asked to run the pediatrics department in the hospital here. I've accepted and I start in three days' times.'

'You'll end up head of the whole hospital.'

She laughed:

'It's possible. As long as they don't have any prejudices against women.'

287

After a moment, she asked:

'How is Joseph's marriage?'

'It's going well.'

'And Adolph, how did he die?'

'Did you know Adolph?'

'I knew him well.'

'And you knew what he was like?'

'Yes. I even thought of writing to you, but I thought it was best for you to find out for yourself. How did he die?'

'He committed suicide.'

Ainá was silent for a while, then she said:

'Ana seems a nice girl.'

Mariana looked at her, asked:

'And what about you, are you going to get married now?'

'Certainly not. I must work, that's quite clear. Only if somebody very special turns up, but no-one has so far. In England most men were a bit worried by me, they thought I was too clever. None of my affairs came to anything.'

'It's different here. Africans like important women.'

'We'll see. Basically, I want to be a good doctor, and I'm not thinking of getting married.'

Ainá went to the hospital the next morning, at lunch she told Mariana:

'Of course the working conditions are much worse than they were in London, but that's inevitable.'

That first week a great many people from the Brazilian quarter came to see Ainá, one of them brought a child who had a pain, another had a mother who was crippled, some came to her because they had a headache, she listened to all their troubles, went to see Seu Gaspar, felt his legs, Mariana was hoping he could be cured, but Ainá put an end to her hopes:

'In cases like this it's almost impossible, because you can't be sure what the trouble is. It might simply be old age.'

Ainá spoke Portuguese to all the old Brazilians, she had forgotten some words, but she soon got back into the way of using Portuguese exclamations, Epifânia wouldn't speak to her in any other language, Mariana kept switching languages, as she had been doing now for so long, sometimes she spoke Portuguese, then Yoruba, then English, Ainá thought that Yoruba was the most important for Lagos, she began to take note of the way the Yorubas described their illnesses and said what they felt like, within a month the news that there was a doctor who spoke Yoruba had reached Abeokuta, Ibadan and Ife, people came from the interior to see her.

Mariana decided to go back to the Water House, she took Emilia and Fat Maria with her again, all this time while she had been watching the beginning of Ainá's career as a doctor she had been doing almost nothing, receiving visitors, talking to Abigail, to Seu Justino, to João the Carpenter, back in Ouidah she took up again the peaceful life of chief of her territory, some nights she thought she wasn't tired, but sleep soon came, she dreamed a lot, usually about Bahia, or about Sebastian, her husband, in the dream she was on the ship, Sebastian was fishing and not catching anything, Suliman arrived with a basket full of fish, suddenly she was in the market in Bahia, the smell of fish all around her, old Ainá was offering fish to the people passing by, Mariana woke with the salt smell still in her nostrils, a wind off the beach had filled the room with the smell of the sea, one night she dreamt that she was having another child, she held her legs open as wide as she could but it wouldn't come out, suddenly she heard someone speaking German, she was in a hospital, there was a dream about Adolph too and he didn't say anything, just looked at her, his eyes very blue, and a man with an egungun mask on was coming towards her and she couldn't run away, it was a wooden mask and painted all over, she saw her grandmother's face and heard her saying that the flood that year had been worse than ever before, the water was rising in the River Piau, from a long way away Mariana saw the rushing water, it was the sea coming up to Uncle Inhaim's house, one day she thought it was time she counted up all she had, in money and property, for weeks she sorted through papers, nobody knew that she kept a lot of money hidden in her room, the money in the bank was only a small part of it, there was English money, French money, and she had some German money, she couldn't remember what the Brazilian money was like, when Antônio had come back from Bahia he had brought her some four hundred real coins, but she didn't know what the notes looked like, perhaps she ought to include everything that was owing to her, there were sums credited to her in London, in Paris, in Bahia, after four weeks of counting she decided she had enough money to last her for ever, she would decide later on about how to divide it up between herself, Emilia, Antônio and the children, but there was no hurry for that, she noticed that the sobrado needed repainting, hired some men from Cotonou, but Jean da Cruz took care of it all, she only kept an eye on them, she organized festivals in honour of Shango, Yorubas from Cotonou, Porto Novo, Pobé, Queto and even farther off came to dance, Mariana saw them arriving, they sat down on the wide expanse of ground in front of the sobrado, the bright-coloured robes moving to and fro, deep blue, yellow, scarlet, when she went out many of them came up to her, she felt fat among all those slim men, the drums sounded out the first homage to Eshu, the padê which must be beaten at the beginning of every party in case Eshu should cause trouble during it, the spirit of Shango entered into a lot of people, one of Marie's sisters appeared with a pot full of fire on her head, she danced with quick lively movements, took the pot from her head and placed a piece of burning coal in her mouth, Mariana received peace from each moment, at one with everything around her, for hours she sat with her eyes fixed on the dancing shapes, her ears became accustomed to the beat of the drums and the chanting, Fat Maria, sitting beside her, sometimes got up and joined in the dancing, the mistress of the sobrado became lost in the images before her eyes, a sense of well-being came up from her legs, rose through her whole body, touched her shoulders, the music and the rhythm swept over her and filled her with happiness, torches lit up the changing scene, Emilia was going around offering plates full of yellow corn cakes and black bean cakes, the people who had come a long way danced for hours without eating, without seeing anything around them, a young man with a calm face leapt from the ground, stirring up the dust, his eyes closed, as if he were dancing inside himself, in his hands he held a double-headed axe of Shango, the axe was worn, its colour had changed, Mariana followed it with her eyes, saw the symbol of the orisha rising and falling in the air, sometimes a gleam of light from the fires lit up the wood, she saw that everything was bound together, it was all one, she could have died in that moment, a great peace had fallen on everything, the festival in Bahia, when the ram had been killed, was the same as this one today, one festival grew out of another, the Shangos were one, night gathered in the chanting and the drums, when she got back to the sobrado she went full of peace up to her room, her dress was tight, she took it off and lay down on her bed, from far away there came the sound of other drums.

The letter saying that Sebastian was ready to come back reached her one afternoon luminous with sun, she sat down beside the window, opened the envelope, her son's writing had become firmer:

'Dear Mother—I've finished my post-graduate studies and the teacher training course. Now I can come home. This is what I plan to do: I'll leave Paris in a week's time, go and have a look at London, then I'll come back through France to Italy. In two months' time I'll sail from Marseilles, the ship is called the *Nancy* and it's due in Lomé on 10th May. I'm beginning to pack for the journey. I've just put in the wooden carving of the Holy Ghost. It has gone with me everywhere, into hotel rooms and into friends' houses. I think I'm ready to face a new life in Zorei. I'm determined to work hard and become the sort of teacher who will be able to help our bit of Africa to progress. In Europe, the situation is getting worse all the time. No-one believes that peace can last or that it's even worth trying to keep it. There has to be a war. What effect will it have on us, in Africa? No-one can tell what will happen. I only hope it won't hurt us too badly. I heard about Joseph's wedding. What was the party like? Now that I'm going to London, Joseph and Ainá aren't there any more. How is my sister? Africans from London who have come to Paris have been telling me that she is an extraordinary person. And what about Granny? How is she? is Aunt Emilia still living in Ouidah? I'm writing to Monsieur Casteller as well to tell him about my plans. Every good wish to you. From your son who loves you. Sebastian.'

She began to think about the welcome for Sebastian as soon as she had finished reading the letter. He would arrive in Lomé, go first to the Water House, then to Zorei, the party would be in the sobrado, she would have to ask Ainá, Joseph, Seu Justino, her mother, friends from Cotonou, Porto Novo, Aduni, Seu Haddad of course, she wondered whether Fatumbi would come, would he want to leave Pobé? She called out to Emilia and Fat Maria, told them the news:

'Sebastian's coming back.'

She told them the date, talked about the party, her sister had some ideas, they could kill an ox, buy one from the Fulanis, there were people in Cotonou who knew how to kill big animals, no need to go so far, Atondá would be able to do it, they would have tables and chairs in the open air, Fat Maria asked:

'I wonder if he likes sweets?'

Emilia didn't think that Africans were very fond of sweet things, the best would be to have a lot of salty food, and drinks, palm wine for the people who liked it, whisky, French wine, beer, there might be some cachaça to be found in Lagos, a Brazilian ship was due in, perhaps it had a lot of cachaça on board, that night the three women sat in the darkened parlour, the wind came in off the sea, they talked about the party, suggested dishes, how to arrange the furniture, Mariana wondered where Sebastian would decide to live. Fat Maria said:

'In Aduni, of course. That's where he's going to teach.'

'Then we'll have to get the house in Aduni painted.'

The next morning she went across the frontier, took Atondá with her, talked to Seu Haddad, to Monsieur Casteller, Ricardo got some men to do the painting, she spent a whole week visiting people, sometimes she stopped in front of a tree and felt herself filled again with the restlessness of times gone by, O tree in this town of my son, may your shade be generous to everyone, O house that is being painted may your roof shelter good luck and happiness, one night she thought about Sebastian's wedding, it should be soon, perhaps he had chosen a girl already? Or was he going to take his time? Mariana got tired, sweat ran down her face, she rubbed her brow with a handkerchief, in the afternoon she got some ori, the purest quality she could find, rubbed the vegetable oil into her body, stayed quiet for a minute so that it would sink into her skin, and she sat by the window while the bustle outside grew greater, then died down, as the night drew in, Atondá was going to make her dinner, sometimes they ate Lebanese food with Seu Haddad, pumpkin, chick-peas, that bread shaped like a hat, she went out into the streets when the moon was shining, Sebastian had been born in this town, Mariana loved it, she felt happy walking around it at night, listening to the dogs barking, seeing little alleys stretching away up the

293

hillsides, naked children playing on the corners, she got back exhausted, went to bed feeling that the time had got less, each day brought her son's arrival nearer.

In Ouidah again, she visited all the neighbouring houses, the Yorubas joked with her, wanted to know about Sebastian, one of them said:

'They say he is a powerful chief and respected by the French.'

Another said:

'He is a clever man and will teach our children to be clever too.'

They were teasing and affectionate, Mariana was pleased and laughed, she replied:

'I don't know whether he's a chief or how clever he is. But I know he is a serious man and a good man.'

The Ewes, the Fons, the Adjas, the Gurunsis, the Mahis, people from all over Dahomey, from Nigeria, from Zorei and from Togo, talked to Mariana, asked her questions about her son, he was the first person from Ouidah ever to have gone to study in Paris, she said:

'He isn't from Ouidah. He was born in Aduni.'

'But he has always lived here.'

The Commandant of the Ajudá fort came to see her, gave her a big bottle of Portuguese wine as a present:

'It's for your son's welcome party.'

They would have to ask a priest to come and give the blessing, but where would they all go to be blessed? Perhaps it would be best to invite the French priest from Cotonou to come as a guest and then he could bless everyone at the house, during the last few weeks before 10th May Mariana saw things happening before her and felt as if everything was misty, but it was a good feeling, she let herself be carried along as if she were on a cloud, she had heard of flying carpets, perhaps she was on a floating carpet and could sail over houses and people, today there were aeroplanes, men could fly, sometimes people told her about flying machines landing in Lagos, and she felt as if she were floating and flying, João the Carpenter arrived at the Water House, saw to all the tables and chairs, the Yorubas were weaving canopies of branches so that everyone could eat in the open air, Jean da Cruz came and talked to Mariana, he wanted to send his eldest son to study in Paris, she said:

'It's the very best thing you can do, Jean. If you don't, he will grow up tied to all the old ways and will never make a good life for himself.'

In Paris classes started in September, it would be a good thing if he sent his son to talk to Monsieur Casteller, he would see what could be done, the young da Cruz boy could leave in August, Sebastian would be able to suggest something as well, when he arrived he would tell them what to do.

A week before the day, the car went to Lagos to pick up the rest of the family, Epifânia came, and Joseph, Ana, Jerónimo, Seu Justino and his wife, Antônio had a car now, Esmeralda and Bill came with him, and two of Ana's brothers, the twins came from Ibadan with three friends, in a new car, Mariana arranged places for them all to sleep, there were mattresses and mats all over the house, Emilia liked to sleep in Shango's room when there were visitors in the house, the sobrado was full of life, bright colours everywhere, gay voices would rise suddenly, laughter in the front room, Bill loved the beach, Esmeralda was expecting a child, Mariana asked:

'When is it due?'

'In July.'

Ana seemed older, she had matured into a woman now, before she had been a child, pretty, yes, but in a childish way, Ainá visited the house of every person who lived on her mother's land, talked to the children, saw the sick people, went to the Portuguese fort, Esmeralda had learnt English, she spoke it with a Bahian accent, she found the French they spoke in Ouidah very difficult to understand and was happier speaking Portuguese,

295

Epifânia didn't say much, she was a little bent now, but she seemed to find everything very amusing, sometimes she sat with Emilia, the day before Sebastian was due Fatumbi arrived, it had taken him a whole day to walk from Pobé to Ouidah, he had two of his wives with him who helped him along, you could see the long pale robe he was wearing from far away, he sat down on a stone in front of the house before going in, Mariana welcomed him with great joy, gave him her own room, she would sleep in the parlour or with Emilia, on the morning of 10th May they all set off for Lomé, beyond Anécho the road ran along the sea-shore, coco-palms stretched out mile upon mile, the ship had anchored off-shore, the passengers came to land in little boats. It was just like the arrival in Lagos, the sailing-ship lying at anchor in front of the town, but this was a big ship, letting off clouds of smoke, a boat was approaching the shore, the family and all the friends gathered behind Mariana who was standing at the end of the jetty, a little apart from them, the wind blowing on her face and into her eyes, perhaps Sebastian wouldn't be in the first boat, but he was, that tall, slim man, dressed in blue, it must be him, the boat grounded on the stones, the young man jumped out. It was him.

Sebastian was ten metres away from Mariana. He looked at the group, recognized his mother, went towards her, while he was still a little way away from her he threw himself full length on the ground and touched it three times with his head, then got up smiling and took her in his arms, he was much taller than her, Mariana's head rested on his shoulder, she asked:

'What was all that, son?'

'That what?'

'Lying down on the ground.'

'That's the right way for a son to greet his mother. It's an old African custom and it shouldn't be forgotten.'

The others were still standing a little way off, Mariana held her son away from her, looked at him in silence, no, she wasn't crying, she felt brimming with happiness, a strange pleasure was making her arms tingle, she recognized the child Sebastian, serious now, and dignified, but it was still the little boy of long ago, he was looking at her too, they stood there for a few moments, then Mariana turned to the others and said:

'What's this? Come and welcome Sebastian.'

They all ran, the noise of the voices then showed how deep the silence had been before Antônio and Joseph took hold of Sebastian, one on each side, Emilia came up with Epifânia, the new arrival embraced his grandmother and didn't know what to say to anyone, the twins were wearing long Yoruba robes, Sebastian said:

'You two look very impressive.'

Cosme and Damião smiled, Sebastian embraced Ainá and said:

'My scientist sister.'

'No, a healer with a certificate.'

Seu Justino and his wife wept as they held Sebastian's head, the old man, fat now, slapped him on the back:

'The name Sebastian didn't bring luck to my son but it will to my grandson.'

At one moment, when he had seen who was there, Sebastian asked:

'Who's that pretty girl?'

'She's your new aunt, Esmeralda, a Brazilian from Bahia. She married Antônio.'

'Can she speak French?'

'No, she lives in Lagos, she's learning English, but she's far happier with Portuguese.'

The whole group of them set off together through the town, all the luggage followed behind in one car, they took a long time deciding who was going in which car, as they were driving along the sea road Sebastian said:

'I had forgotten how beautiful it is here.'

In Ouidah people were crowding around the sobrado, clothes of every imaginable colour and design, from the kente of the Gold Coast to the white robes of the Hausas, Sebastian stopped in front of the Water House, looked at all the other buildings that surrounded it, Monsieur Casteller and Seu Haddad were waiting for him, he embraced his teacher, thought he was looking a lot older, his face was dried up and wrinkled, they were both of them very moved, Seu Haddad said something in Lebanese, Atondá came up to them and said:

'O chief of the region, may your return be welcomed by the orishas, may your presence in this land which is ours make us more wealthy and powerful, may your wisdom discern the good from the evil and judge with justice what happens amongst us, may your kitchen be always full of the aroma of good food, may your wives be fertile and bear you many sons, may your sons care for you in your old age, may Ifa watch over your destiny and see nothing but good in your future.'

Sebastian gave his thanks in the manner of a Yoruba oriki, he said:

'May your greeting, Atondá, reflect upon yourself, and may all the good things you have wished for me be your own.'

Father Pierre was waiting upstairs, they all knelt down in the parlour, the statue of Santa Ana had been put on the table, the priest put on a surplice, took a flask of holy water out of his case, sprinkled a few drops over Sebastian, Mariana, Epifãnia, Seu Justino and the rest, when he had finished they started to let off fireworks outside, people crowded to the windows, Ricardo took hold of a rocket in his right hand, lit the touch-paper with the other, at the bang people clapped their hands, the small scratch of the rocket stick fell down over the beach far away.

The feast began straight away, dishes and more dishes of meat, rice, cassava dumplings, corn-cakes and bean-cakes were carried to the tables underneath the leaf canopies, each person took a plate, Sebastian, Mariana

298

and the rest of the family sat down in the middle, they opened bottles of wine, toasts were proposed on all sides, the sound of drums and xylophones filled the air with rhythms, Fatumbi was sitting by Mariana, he ate with a will, now and then he said an oriki in praise of the feast, the children were running around among the grown-ups, some of them with plates in their hands, others holding bananas or pieces of cassava, gleams of sun shone through the leaves on to the happy faces of everyone eating, a bottle of cachaça that Seu Justino had managed to get hold of went from hand to hand, Atondá and Pedoké preferred the palm wine, Father Pierre praised the Portuguese wine, the Commandant of the fort, who was sitting not far away, thanked him, some young girls went out on to the bare stretch of ground beyond the canopy and danced to the sound of the drums, one of them danced slowly, the others moved more quickly, now and then someone stuck a coin on the sweating forehead of one of the dancers, she thanked them and went on, the sun seemed hotter now, everybody was sweating and there was a general feeling of well-being, they stayed sitting there until nightfall, and then there came from behind the sobrado the figures of a bumba-meu-boi, they had been brought from Porto Novo in honour of Sebastian, the ox ran after the children, the huge figures moved to and fro against the night sky, Mariana looked at them with a feeling of rediscovery, it was a long time since she had had a burrinha, it was getting dark, Atondá lit torches around the area where they were dancing, when it was really dark and the ox was dancing surrounded by the ostrich, the giant woman and the donkey more food arrived, this time pastries and minced meat, more bottles of wine and beer were opened, a xylophone played alone for a while until the drums once more began to shake the darkness with their beating. Jean da Cruz set off a rocket in the middle of the compound, the blaze of light lit up people's faces, every now and then someone left the group for a while, then came back, at one time when Sebastian was alone for a moment with his mother he said what a wonderful party it was, people had come from Ouidah attracted by the noise and the gaiety, faces were smiling in the light of the flames, Emilia danced for as long as she could, Mariana remembered when her sister had been young, beautiful, before she married Ebenezer, her body wasn't much fatter now, you could still see her young as she danced, but when she stopped Mariana saw how tired she was, smiling still, but her arms hung heavily, she sat down beside the twins, one of them kissed her on the cheek, the other pulled Ana up and began to dance with her, the man stood in front of the woman, they danced to each other, their arms moving, sometimes their feet never left the same spot, still dancing they lowered themselves almost to the ground, then rose up again, everyone clapped, for a while now the wind had been blowing more strongly off the sea, it made the bonfire flare up, shook the leaves, Father Pierre said goodnight, so did the Commandant from the fort, the Yorubas beat the salute for Shango, the drums broke into new rhythms, Sebastian asked:

'Where are the orishas?'

Mariana took him to the room where Emilia was sleeping, the wooden figures were there, Shango and Oloshoshi and Oya, Yemoja and Ogun, the torch that Atondá was holding threw a flickering light on the carved faces, the shadow of the double-headed axe was big on the walls, Mariana bowed down in front of Shango's stones and cloths, Sebastian did the same, when they went out again the yard was almost empty, the wood of the fire was glowing red, she took her son to his room upstairs, the wind was blowing through the house filling it with the smell of the sea.

When he unpacked Sebastian had presents for everybody, Mariana had a white necklace, he told her:

'They are pearls.'

She went to look at herself in the mirror, the necklace had a serene and calm beauty, there were pieces of silk for her too, and perfume, Sebastian had something for everyone, a brooch, a bracelet, a tie, lots of bottles of eau de cologne, Esmeralda wanted a length of taffeta, Emilia chose a French dress, Pedoké smiled happily at the watch he had asked for, Atondá insisted that he wanted a brooch, he pinned it on to his robe, Sebastian said:

'Brooches are for women.'

Atondá laughed:

'I don't care. It's too pretty for a woman. Looks better on a man.'

And he went off happily with it.

Sebastian picked up a carving of a bird, said to his mother:

'Do you remember?'

The next afternoon they set off for Aduni, Sebastian wanted to live in the house there that had been freshly painted, he was going to give some classes in one school in the town and teach for one day each week in another about forty kilometres away, he would have to get a car, he told Mariana that he wanted to buy one with the money he earned teaching, she objected:

'But I'll give you a car today.'

'No, the school will send a car for me on the day I have to go there. In any case, it's you who will really be paying for the car when I buy it—after all, I'm going to be living in this house, having all my meals free, I won't have any of the expenses that teachers usually have, but I think it would be better if I could buy a car with my own money. It's not the money that matters, it's the principle.'

Mariana understood and agreed, but said:

'Son, everything I have is yours.'

'I know: but I must learn what it is like to be an African teacher in his own country, without a rich family behind him.'

301

On the fourth day he got up early and went to give his classes, Mariana watched him as he went out, he walked erect, like someone who knew where he was going, but there was no arrogance in him, perhaps it was his smile that made people feel so easy with him, even when they had just met him it seemed as if they had known each other for years. A week later, when Mariana thought that Sebastian had got into the way of living in Aduni again, she said goodbye:

'I'm going to the sobrado. Whatever you want, you've only to call me. I'll come and see you now and then.'

'I'll be coming to Ouidah whenever I can.'

She was getting into the car, Silvanus was holding the door open for her, when she seemed to remember something and turned to him:

'Are you thinking of getting married, son?'

'Yes, but not yet. The girl is still in Europe.'

Antônio, Esmeralda, Joseph, Ana, Seu Justino, Epifânia and the twins had all gone back to Nigeria, Antônio had told her that Bill's grandfather wanted the boy in London, he was sending him on a ship that would leave in a few days' time, Mariana took up her old life again, but now with a feeling of fulfilment, perhaps she did still need a man, or not a man so much as a companion to talk to, to joke with, say stupid things to, or just be quiet with, on certain days the air was so luminous that she covered her eyes with her hand and let the sun fall freely on her body, people came from a long way off to see her and tell her things, Fatumbi stayed with her for a few more days, she wanted him to choose one of the huts nearby and come there to live, but he refused, his place was Pobé, from there he could see things clearly, even the place where he threw the discs and the shells to foretell the future had been the same for the last fifty years, Mariana took him back in the car, he wanted to stop in Porto Novo, in the market place he said:

'I spent part of my childhood in this market. My mother sold things for the cult in this exact place.'

There were naked children playing on the ground, women with cloths tied round their breasts shouted to each other, the air was full of noise and gaiety, when they got to Pobé Mariana agreed to stay there for a meal, one of Fatumbi's wives cooked chicken with ground-nuts, a boy of about thirteen sat on the ground beside her, he ate with delicate movements, Mariana looked at him, thought he was more beautiful than any child she had ever seen, asked Fatumbi:

'Is he your son?'

'Yes. His name is Fadori.'

'I've never noticed him before.'

Fatumbi laughed:

'Neither had I. I have so many sons. This one I only saw when he got big.'

Fadori smiled at Mariana, suddenly Fatumbi said:

'Would you like to have him?'

'Have him?'

'Bring him up, he's an intelligent boy. You have no children now. It will be something for you to do. When he is grown he will go out into the world by himself, but until then it will be good for him to be cared for and to learn things.'

Mariana looked at Fadori, no-one was smiling now, she said:

'Agreed, I'll have him.'

On the way back Mariana looked at the houses and the people, the road crowded with travellers coming and going, groups of people who had stopped to talk, the boy scarcely spoke during the journey, he looked at everything, he was wearing a simple short robe, he had brought nothing with him, when they arrived at the sobrado Mariana took him upstairs, to the room which had been Sebastian's, said:

'This will be your room.'

He smiled again, he was beautiful when he smiled, his teeth very white, his eyes wide open and clear, that night Mariana pulled a blanket over him, stood looking at him for a few moments, then went to her own room and slept.

Emilia and Fat Maria were none too pleased with the presence of the boy, Emilia thought he was rather old to be brought up by anybody, Fat Maria's objection was short and to the point:

'He's too pretty.'

During the first few weeks Mariana and Fadori got used to each other, they played the fool, he said things to make her laugh, they talked to each other all the time, on the beach they ran after each other, the Yoruba language could be strangely comical, sometimes one sound out of tone, a *ha*, could be funny, or at any rate Mariana found it so, she laughed all the time, in the late afternoon the boy and she would go out together holding hands, would walk along the shore, sit down to see the sun sinking into the horizon, they they would walk back talking, or silent, sometimes they joined the others in the darkening parlour, Emilia, Fat Maria, Atondá, Jean da Cruz, Ricardo, talked for a while, then went and slept peacefully, after a month Mariana put a little bed in her own room for Fadori, she used to go and look at him when he was asleep, they spent the whole of each day together, when she heard that another war had begun in Europe she woke up from her happiness and asked:

'Between France and Germany again?'

'Other countries are fighting as well, but France and Germany are on opposite sides.'

'Just as well there aren't any more Germans here, otherwise we would be having a war as well.'

The war brought changes, sometimes French soldiers went past the Water House, on their way to Togo or to Zorei, or coming back again, Mariana went to Aduni, as soon as Sebastian saw her he threw himself to the ground and touched it three times with his head, afterwards he told her:

'The war could change everything here.'

They talked for a while, Sebastian said:

'The girl I told you about is in Paris now and she will have to come back quickly because of the war.'

'What is she like?'

'She's Ewe, she's studying nursing and she knows all about you already because I've talked about you so much, you and the Water House, and Lagos and the well, everything.'

Sebastian met Fadori, Mariana explained:

'Fatumbi gave him to me, he's going to stay with me.'

Sebastian shook hands with the boy, smiled, said:

'It's a good idea. He'll be company for you, and you'll have something to think about.'

'Have you bought a car yet?'

'I'm going to get one this week. Now there's a war it's possible that the prices of that sort of thing will go up.'

Sebastian went back with Mariana and Fadori, he stayed at the Water House for two days, at the same time as the first news about the war was coming through they heard that Seu Justino had died, there was no time for anyone from Dahomey or Zorei to go to the serenata, Joseph came to see his mother and told her that it had been a good party, Brazilians from all over the city had come and had a good time in honour of Seu Justino's memory, he had been one of the oldest Brazilians in Lagos, there had been drums, food, drink, it had gone on till dawn, apparently the oldest people in the community now were Seu Gaspar and Epifânia, the Association of Brazilian Descendents had asked Epifânia to be their President, Joseph hardly took any notice of Fadori, he went back to Lagos and suddenly it was Christmas, Mariana went to Cotonou with Fadori, bought lots of pretty things, all bright colours, maps, drawing books, at night the two of them would spend hours colouring in

305

the pictures, Fadori used the coloured pencils to draw pictures of the Water House, or of the huts in Pobé, when he went to bed Mariana would hold his hand and sit by his side for hours, she felt young, stronger than she had felt for many years, she walked more quickly, sometimes ran, she remembered that she was over fifty, this business of age was foolishness, when she was a girl she had thought that any woman over thirty was old, now she realized that at fifty you could still be young, full of life, suddenly she realized that she was doing exactly the same as Ricardo's father-in-law, the Ashanti called Yao, with him it had been a young girl, almost a child, who made him happy, played with him, held his hand, with her it was a boy, then she looked at Fadori and said:

'Shall we run to the beach?'

'Yes.'

They both ran, threw themselves down on to the sand, Fadori decided to build a city, he dug streets, made a house, Mariana said:

'I'm going to make a church.'

She began to mould it, pulling together the sand, making it firm, got a piece of driftwood and smoothed down the sides, in the end it did look a bit like a church, afterwards they started to draw, Mariana did Shango's double-headed axe, Fadori drew Ifa's bowl with shapes and lines and heads of people all round it, Mariana asked him:

'Are you going to consecrate yourself to Ifa?'

'That depends on Ifa and on my father.'

'Have you learnt anything yet?'

'Yes. My brothers and I all learnt some things when we were very little.'

It was getting dark when they tired of drawing things in the sand, the tide had risen and a wave came and washed away the drawings, Shango's axe, which had been drawn deeply, stayed visible until the fourth wave, the two of them walked back together, stopped at

Atondá's house, stayed there talking, Fat Maria shouted from the sobrado:

'It's time to eat.'

They went up the stairs, the cassava-flour, the beans, the rice, the fish were all more delicious that night, afterwards they sat outside, people from the huts round about came and joined them, someone brought out a xylophone, the music made everyone happy, Jean da Cruz's young children pulled at Fadori's robe, there were whole weeks and months when the woman and the boy were left alone together, especially on the rainy season, Emilia never left her room, Fat Maria stayed in the kitchen, the two of them covered the table with books and papers, Fadori drew maps, one day he drew the whole of Europe and started to show Mariana:

'This is France, this is Germany, this is England.'

'Where did you learn all that?'

'I studied in Pobé with a priest.'

'Where is London?'

He pointed with his finger:

'Here.'

'And Paris?'

'Here.'

So Sebastian had lived in that dot, Joseph and Ainá in that one higher up, it wasn't far between the two cities, Mariana asked:

'Where are they fighting?'

'It must be here.'

And he pointed on the map to the frontier between France and Germany.

A few days later they heard that the Germans had overrun Belgium and Holland and were advancing on Paris, they looked at it on the map, Mariana said:

'There's Belgium. It's not far from Paris.'

Sebastian seemed depressed, he came to stay for a week-end, told them:

'If Paris falls, anything may happen.'

307

'Are you feeling sad?'

'Yes, Paris is my second home.'

'And what's going to happen here?'

'I don't know. Togo and Zorei used to belong to the Germans, if they win the war the least they will want is to have their old possessions back.'

Sebastian helped Fadori to find all the places on the map, he showed him the road out of Belgium to Paris, pointed out the place Dunkirk that everybody was talking about just then, Mariana and Fadori heard that Paris had fallen just after Sebastian had gone back to Aduni, they had a hard time finding Vichy where the new French government had been set up, one day Mariana gave Europe up and drew Brazil, she showed Fadori where Bahia was, she couldn't find Piau, perhaps because it was such a small place, but she found Juiz de Fora and Rio de Janeiro, she drew the Amazon river in blue, Fadori wanted to know if there were any books about Brazil, Mariana read bits of *The Guarani* to him, he decided to paint the characters, he did Cecilia a sort of blackish brown, Mariana wasn't sure if that was right:

'I don't know. She might have been white. Anyway she was the daughter of a Portuguese.'

'She might have been mulatto.'

'She might.'

Peri came out very black, Mariana thought that Brazilian Indians were black, but they had feathers on their heads, one day she bought a French book full of pictures of Africa, for months on end they pored over it, Fadori drew everything, the lions, the elephants, the lizards, the cobras, the trees, one day he painted a baobab tree, there were some baobabs on the road to Aduni, he became a specialist in baobabs, both of them liked the great wide trunks, they took the car and, with Silvanus driving, went to see a baobab near Togo, Fadori went up to the tree, embraced it, opening his arms wide and hugging the trunk, Mariana stood for a moment watching him from a distance, the boy and the trunk became one, she sat down beside the tree, took things to eat and drink out of a basket, got out a napkin and spread it on the ground, they began the meal in silence, later they slept, it was evening when they went back, the picture Fadori drew of the baobab with all the scenery around it was the best he had ever done, when Sebastian came to the Water House he said:

'Put the drawing up on the wall. It's very good.'

They all three stood back to see the effect, the baobab stood out from the wall, later Sebastian told her:

'Segui has arrived. I'm going to bring her here next Sunday to meet you. We want to get married, but not yet.'

Mariana got ready to receive her future daughter-in-law, had all the towels washed, and the bedcovers and the sheets, asked Atondá to kill a ram, when she saw the girl she liked her, found her very warm, intelligent, whenever Sebastian saw her after being some time away he prostrated himself on the ground in greeting, but Segui didn't, Segui knelt down on her right knee in front of Mariana, who raised her up affectionately, embraced her warmly, introduced her to Fadori, Emilia, Fat Maria, Pedoké, Atondá, Jean da Cruz, Marie, she knew Ricardo already, because he spent most of his time in Aduni, they all had lunch in the parlour, the conversation turned to the war, Sebastian was saying:

'Germany is fighting on more than one front now. It's going to be difficult for her to win.'

Segui stayed in the Water House for a few days, saw all around the property, went to Cotonou and Porto Novo, Sebastian had bought a second-hand French car, took his fiancée to Lomé, the Commandant of the Portuguese fort came to see them, as they were saying goodbye Mariana asked them:

'Why don't you get married straight away? The quicker the better.'

Segui laughed:

'That's what I think, but Sebastian wants to wait.'

'What for?'

'For me to get used to Zorei again, after all those years in France. But I'm used to it already, he just doesn't believe me.'

Once again Mariana and Fadori spent months almost completely alone, the boy's drawing was improving, since he had never seen Lagos she decided to cross the frontier and take him to Nigeria, Fadori thought the city was beautiful, it was the biggest he had ever seen, he liked the sobrado in Bangboshe Street, and the well, straight away he got a piece of paper and drew the well, Mariana was touched when she looked at his drawing, the well, the yard behind it, a tree, they were all there, clear in every detail, the younger girls chatted happily to Fadori, after all this time Ana was expecting a child, her belly was huge, Bill was still in England, his grandfather wrote that he himself would bring the boy back to Lagos as soon as he could, Joaquim, Antônio's young son, was already walking, it was him that Mariana saw now playing naked on the ground, running around in the street, Antônio had built an extension to his sobrado, Esmeralda had turned into a perfect Nigerian, it was she who looked after the shop now, and helped to run Mariana's sobrado, engaged servants for Epifânia, bought things for the house, went there every day, Jerónimo was very old, all he did was sit in the shop, look hard at everyone who came in, his hair was white, Mariana went to see Abigail, Suliman's son, Seu Justino's widow, showed Fadori to them all, everyone was enchanted by the boy, she took him often to visit Seu Gaspar, Fadori loved the carvings, he picked up a Shango, turned it round in his hands, looked at it carefully, from being a child he had been used to seeing his father carve bowls for Ifa, he got a knife and a piece of wood, copied the figure Seu Gaspar had made,

Mariana and the old man stayed quiet watching the boy's hands as he worked, he seemed to hold them quite still but a tiny movement was enough to shape an angle of the carving, there were days when Fadori went into Seu Gaspar's room at eight o'clock in the morning and didn't leave again until eight at night, Mariana brought food for them all, she stayed with them for most of the time, one Sunday she took the boy to Mass, when they got back he became engrossed in a big drawing, he kept looking out of the window and turning back to his paper, when he had finished she saw that it was a part of Bangboshe Street, one house behind another, right along to Campos Square, that night Fadori said:

'I miss the Water House.'

They left the next morning, the car turned off the main road and went to Pobé, Fatumbi was sitting on the ground with his head bowed, when he looked up he saw Mariana and his son, he greeted them:

'May Ifa make our ways pleasant and help my loved ones reach the end of their road.'

They ate together, Fadori ran from one hut to the next, came back with some brothers, Mariana looked at them all, none of them were like her boy, there was one who was terribly ugly, his face seemed all pulled to one side, may Shopona, god of sickness, free us from all ills, at one time Fatumbi said:

'I have been looking at Sebastian's future. He will have great power, but he will go through many difficulties before he achieves it.'

He paused for a moment, then said:

'And afterwards, too.'

In Ouidah, Mariana put up the drawing of Bangboshe Street on the wall, now the room was full of scenes, on the day the Japanese attacked Pearl Harbor Sebastian came to see her, he thought Fadori's work was very good, at one time he talked about the war:

'Now the United States will have to send soldiers into Europe.'

'And will that help to end the war?'

'It will help a lot.'

As he was leaving Sebastian put his arms round Mariana's shoulder and walked with her for a while, he told her:

'Segui and I are going to be married in about four months. It will be in April, on her birthday.'

'Lovely. Where do her parents live?'

'Quite near Aduni. The party will be in an uncle's house in Aduni.'

Mariana received the news that Joseph and Ana had a son, he was to be called Mauricio, where had they got that name from? Just before Christmas Joseph, Ana, Epifânia and the baby arrived at the Water House, Mariana realized that this was her first grandchild and Epifânia's first great-grandchild, she was fifty-four now, she didn't feel in the least old, she had before, during the time of Adolph, but not now, now she ran about with Fadori, played with him, she was young, the boy lifted Mauricio high up in the air, they all laughed, Mariana was curious:

'Where did you get the name Mauricio?'

'Out of a Brazilian book we found in Dona Abigail's house. Apparently it was the name of a Dutch prince who lived in Brazil.'

Ainá arrived in a little car, she came with Antônio, Esmeralda and Joaquim, she said:

'I nearly couldn't come at all. There was so much work at the hospital?'

'When are you going to be running this hospital.'

'I don't know about this one, Mother, but I might be put in charge of a hospital in Ibadan. I've been offered the job and I think I might accept.'

Sebastian arrived in the evening, he brought Segui, none of the relatives from Lagos had met her yet, they went to Midnight Mass in Porto Novo, afterwards they all sat down to supper together, the family and Atondá, Pedoké, Fat Maria, Jean da Cruz, Marie and their children, Ricardo and his wife, Monsieur Casteller, who had arrived just before Mass, Adjá, who was very old now, Father Pierre and Fatumbi hadn't been able to come, the parlour was crowded, Fat Maria had made rabanada, the special dish that is always eaten at Christmas in Brazil, the electric lights lit up Fadori's drawings, Mariana opened bottles of wine, Sebastian raised his glass and said:

'May the war soon be ended.'

Everyone answered Amen, Antônio said:

'May my son come home safe and sound from England.'

Ainá spoke up, she turned towards Sebastian and Segui:

'May the engaged couple soon be married and may they be happy always.'

Atondá shouted:

'May we all be blessed with peace and happiness.'

They were all talking at the same time, you couldn't hear what was being said at the other side of the room, Mariana and Fadori were sitting next to each other, since she had brought him from Pobé they had never been apart for more than a few minutes, he was laughing and eating rabanada, it was almost dawn when Mariana took him by the hand, put him to bed, she saw how tall he was, he was going to be as tall as Sebastian, when they had all left she kept remembering the feel of Mauricio's skin, a tiny person like a little animal, she and Fadori went out and walked along the road, for whole days they were out of doors from morning until night, they went along narrow paths, bushes and trees all around them, they forgot time, when they came back hungry Fat Maria would complain:

'What sort of behaviour is this? staying out all day long?'

313

Fadori would go for weeks without drawing or painting at all, suddenly he would start to work again very fast, Mariana and the boy hand in hand walked all around the district, a young girl with a pitcher of water on her head would stop to talk to them, or perhaps an old man whom nobody knew, Mariana learned to walk along roads and talk to people she had never seen before, there was a freedom and a joyfulness in everything they did, in a lot of places where they stopped people knew who she was:

'Aren't you Dona Mariana, from that big house beside the frontier?'

One day a letter came from Antônio, saying that his father-in-law had managed to book a passage in a ship, he was going to bring Bill to Nigeria, because it was safer there than in London, Antônio said as well that Ainá had accepted the job in the hospital in Ibadan, the ship would be docking in Lagos within a week, Mariana wrote straight back and invited the Englishman to come and stay with her in the Water House, perhaps he would like to see Dahomey, and she thanked God, the Holy Ghost, Shango and all the orishas for bringing Bill safely home again.

Bill's grandfather accepted her invitation, he arrived in Ouidah in Antônio's car, Bill was with them, he was a big boy, his green eyes stood out against his brown skin, he was very well-behaved, looked straight at you, but he didn't talk much, only when he was asked a question, Mr William Hill was a big man, he seemed a nice person, incredible that he should have had a daughter like Elizabeth, so fragile, his first words were:

'I want to thank you for the great kindness you always showed to my daughter. Elizabeth talked so much about you, told us what a great African lady you were, how well you entertained people, what a generous heart you had.'

'It's I who must thank you, Mr Hill.'

During the days he was at the Water House he told

her that he had retired, Elizabeth had been his only child, he didn't know what to do now, with all the trouble in Europe it might be best to stay in Africa, but he had a married sister living in Essex and she might need him, Mariana said:

'Why don't you stay in Lagos? You might even get a job in an English firm there.'

'It's not a bad idea, and that way I would be near Bill.'

He looked around him, saw Fadori's drawings, the luminous sun outside, laughed gently and said:

'I never thought that I would have a grandson called William Santos. Nor that he would be mulatto and beautiful like Bill.'

Mariana smiled, the cloth of life was woven with strange threads, she liked Mr Hill, he was a sincere man, simple, used to working hard every day, saying what he thought, thinking what he liked, when he set off back to Lagos with Bill she watched the car as it went away down the road, he would get on well in Nigeria, he seemed to be a realist, accepted each day as it came and tried to see the good in everything, Mariana became absorbed in getting new clothes for Fadori, he was growing all the time and none of his clothes fitted him any more, she got him to try trousers and shirt and a jacket as well as the long Yoruba robe, he liked them, thought that the trousers were very tight, but that the jacket was a good idea, one Sunday she took him to Pobé wearing them so that Fatumbi could see him, when they arrived all the children crowded around him and shrieked with joy, one of the little ones tugged at his jacket, Fadori laughed, Fatumbi sat down with Mariana, said:

'The boy is getting big.'

'He's getting more and more intelligent.'

'What are you going to do with him?'

'I'm thinking of sending him to study in Europe. What do you think?'

315

Fatumbi looked at his son, replied with another question:

'Do you think he will be happy there?'

'People are happy when they understand things better. I think he could learn a lot in Europe.'

Fatumbi stretched his legs out on the ground, lowered his voice:

'My problem has always been to choose someone to take my place in the cult. Ifa doesn't seem to want any of my sons to do this. And remember I have sixteen wives and I don't know how many sons. It's a nephew I have found who loves the cowries and can read the future and interpret signs. He's over thirty already. I want to introduce him to you.'

He raised his head and shouted:

'Fatondê!'

Out of a nearby hut there came a thin man, almost naked, all he wore was a cloth tied round his waist, his legs were strong, the muscles in his thighs stood out, his jaw was long and finely-drawn, his eyes dark. Fatumbi said:

'Fatondê, this is my friend Yaya Mariana. She is looking after my son Fadori, she is very dear to me, we have been friends for many years. If she should need anything, and I am not here, help her in every way you can.'

The man nodded his head, agreeing, his uncle commanded:

'Sit down there.'

He obeyed. He stayed there looking at the ground while Fatumbi and Mariana were talking, Fadori arrived surrounded by children, he had a baby on each arm, on their way back Mariana and he talked about Fatondê, she asked:

'Where did he come from?'

'He was born in the village. He's the son of one of father's older sisters.'

316

'Do you know him at all?'

'No. Nobody talks to him much. Or rather, he doesn't want to talk to anybody. He goes for days without speaking.'

They were making preparations for Sebastian's marriage to Segui. March was a lovely month, Jean da Cruz checked the number of coconuts they had split, looked after the copra extraction, a week before the day Mariana, Emilia, Fat Maria and Fadori went to Aduni, Seu Haddad promised to make some Lebanese sweets for the party, Segui's parents came to visit the bridegroom's family, her father was Ewe, her mother was half Ewe and half Yoruba, Mariana said:

'Now I understand why she is called Segui, it's a Yoruba name.'

The mother said:

'It was my mother's name.'

The relatives from Lagos arrived in several cars, Cosme and Damião came as well, neither of them had married yet, Aduni seemed more cheerful now, Mariana had the front of her house decorated with streamers of coloured paper, like they did in Brazil, this had an interesting result, a man knocked at the door and inquired who lived there, Mariana asked him why he wanted to know:

'My name is Gil Sousa. My parents were Brazilians and they used to decorate our house like this.'

Mariana made him come inside.

'I'm Brazilian too and it's a long time since I saw this sort of decoration. I just remembered about it today. Where are you from?'

'From Accra, on the Gold Coast. We have a Brazilian community there called the *tabom* community, with a queen and everything.'

'You do?'

'Yes.'

'We don't have queens in Nigeria or in Dahomey, but

317

we do have associations with presidents, vice-presidents, secretaries and treasurers. My mother is President of the association in Lagos. My name is Mariana.'

'Ah, then you must be the woman with the well?'

'That's right, surely they don't know about me on the Gold Coast?'

'I heard that story about the well in Lagos a long time ago. I think it was my father who told it to me to prove how intelligent the Brazilians were.'

Fadori talked to the man, they invited him to the wedding, when the time came Sebastian put on a dark, sober suit, a gold-coloured tie, a handkerchief in his top pocket, they all went to the church and waited for the bride, Segui came in smiling shyly, her father, a huge black man, he must have been more than two metres tall, he was bigger than anyone else in the church, led her up to the altar, gave her to Sebastian, the choir sang, the priest came out and began the ceremony, Mauricio cried in Ana's arms, cried and wriggled about, the priest gave her an angry look, she rocked the baby and he fell quiet, now all that could be heard was the priest's voice, he was French and he didn't seem to know how to smile, when he had married them he hooked his hands in his stole, told them how happy he was to have celebrated yet another marriage between Catholics, warned them never to abandon their religion and to bring up their children in it, the French he spoke sounded hard, it wasn't always easy to understand what he was saying, his hands quite still, on his stole, his eyes were severe, he looked as if he were telling somebody off, when he had finished the sermon he paused for a moment and then said:

'I congratulate the newly-married couple and their families.'

The group broke up, in the sacristy Sebastian and Segui signed the papers, people began to come and congratulate them even before they had finished, the house where the party was to be held was on the other side of town, they set off in Mariana's car, all sorts of people came to embrace them, every now and then Sebastian led a smiling young man up to Mariana:

'This one studied in Paris with me, mother. He was studying medicine.'

Or:

'He and I saw the South of France together.'

There was dancing, all the inhabitants of the quarter seemed to have left their own houses and come to stand in the street and watch, some of them came in and joined the party, others just stood there, looking at the lights and the people going to and fro, Seu Haddad tried to dance, he soon got tired, some Frenchmen from the local government office and from the school where Sebastian was teaching seemed to enjoy all the gaiety, Monsieur Casteller was talking to Antônio and Ainá, Mariana thought it strange that she had never seen him talking to any French people, he only mixed with Africans, Ainá was talking loudly, French with an English accent, she was talking about the hospital, at one point Mariana heard her say:

'I don't think we need African doctors. It would be far better if we could give a year or two's training to a group of medical auxiliaries, men and women, so that they would be able to give injections, diagnose common ailments and, mainly, treat all the obvious illnesses. That is what we need in Africa. It takes a long time for a doctor to qualify and our sick can't wait.'

Casteller seemed to agree with her, everyone began to discuss what she had said and give their opinion, suddenly Sebastian said:

'I think Ainá is right, especially if we get our independence soon.'

Joseph said:

'Get what?'

'Independence. If the Germans were to win the war—

319

and it looked as if they were going to at one time—it might be difficult, but if the allies win then independence will be a possibility at any rate. After all, the allies are saying that they are fighting for the principle of self-determination.'

A great silence fell on the room, some of the guests looked towards the Frenchman, Monsieur Casteller spoke:

'It's obvious that one day, sooner or later, all these areas of Africa will be independent.'

Segui's mother came into the middle of the room and said with a smile:

'The conversation is getting too serious. Let's dance and forget our troubles.'

One of Segui's brothers got Ainá up and started to dance with her, groups broke up and new groups formed, Mariana and Fadori waited until the party was nearly over, then left with Seu Haddad, the car moved slowly through the streets of Aduni, in the main square Seu Haddad pointed to the Governor's Palace and said:

'That's where the German administrator lived. Now the French administrator lives there.'

They stopped for a moment, Mariana looked at the imposing stone steps that rose up and were lost among massive columns, then Silvanus accelerated, by the time they got back Fadori's eyes were closing, they slept until late the next day and then had lunch together, Antônio, Joseph and Ainá had all gone back to Lagos, Fadori got some paper and drew the front of Seu Haddad's shop, Seu Haddad looked at the drawing and exclaimed:

'But it's exactly right.'

His French was funny, he mixed up the consonants, Fadori said:

'Would you like to keep the picture? Please have it.'

Back at the Water House, life took up its gentle happy rhythm once more, Mariana would look for long moments at Fadori, who was turning into a handsome man, she felt he was her son, her brother, her husband, not a husband in the sense that she wanted to go to bed with him, but in the sense that they understood each other without words, they would spend hours together in silence, him drawing, her busy with something or other, or looking at maps, nothing disturbed their peace, one day he asked if Monsieur Casteller had any books, Mariana thought he probably had, but first they looked all over the house, there was a *History of France* that Sebastian had brought back from Paris, Fadori began to read it, now and then he told Mariana what he was reading about, he got very enthusiastic about the French Revolution, discussed it all with her, she had heard of Marie Antoinette, the two of them still went walking along the beach together hand in hand, but the things they talked about were different now, one afternoon Fat Maria was listening to them, she asked:

'Do you think Marie Antoinette was fat like me?'

They all laughed, Fadori said:

'I don't think she was. The French have bad taste, they like thin women. They don't realize that it's fat women who are really beautiful. The fatter the better.'

Fat Maria laughed, slapped him on the back:

'Anyway once a fat woman gets hold of a man she never lets him go again.'

Sebastian and Segui arrived to see them, Fadori had done a lot more drawings, he began asking questions about the French Revolution, Sebastian said to Mariana:

'I think Fadori should go and study painting in Paris. Not now, because of the war, but when the war is over.'

A few days later a messenger came from Sebastian with a parcel, Mariana opened it. It was a book on the French Revolution, and Fadori began to read it that very day, Mariana listened to whole chapters of it, she thought of that strange world that had been forced to change, the court of the king and queen where everything had changed, she looked around her, saw things changing everywhere, yesterday Fadori had only been a child, now he was big, Mariana drank in the pleasure of each moment knowing that it must all change, she walked with the boy hand in hand, she felt as if life were rising up like water in a flood and everything was so beautiful that you had to be careful not to drown in the pleasure of simply being alive, it was a pleasure and it was a sense of waiting that perhaps wasn't pleasurable, but although the anticipation was always there it always seemed to be on the point of disappearing and your breast was filled to bursting with the joy of every second that passed, while Fadori was drawing Mariana got the book and read the story of the guillotine, that was the thing that impressed her most, killing people in great spurts like that, the bottom edge of the guillotine looked like part of Shango's axe, when she heard that Seu Justino's widow had died and that Joseph had held another serenata she saw that the past was unwinding in her hands, escaping, and all she had to do was let it go and she would be free, able to go on capturing each moment as it unfolded, the supreme moment of her marriage with Sebastian came to her memory, the night he penetrated her, so many years ago it had been and it seemed like something happening now, the link that bound her to Fadori was strong because he wasn't her son, if he had been her son it would have been different, it was strong too because he wasn't her husband and didn't sleep with her, if he had slept with her he would have been like the others, but he was a son and he was a husband, he was near and he was far away, soon now he would be able to go away, leave her, live his young animal life, he would have played a decisive part in her life, pulled her back into a stream of movement that carried her onward, made her interested in the smallest things, in a book, a map, a drawing, every walk along the beach took on an extraordinary import- ance, she didn't look forward to the future because she had learnt never to expect anything, but to let events

322

take her along with them, there is a wisdom in things that people sometimes try to go against, but they can't, things are stronger, they impose their own course, push people along a certain path and nothing will turn them aside, the path can never be any other, perhaps Mariana might have preferred it if there had been no change, one afternoon she took Fadori with her into Shango's room, they sat down on the ground, he picked up a bowl dedicated to Ifa, looked at the carvings round the side, took some cowries out of a little bag, threw them into the bowl, she sat there watching what the boy was doing, without saying anything, she knew more or less what it meant when the shells fell with the opening underneath or on top, for a long time he kept gathering up the cowries and throwing them down again, gradually she felt she was losing herself in the movement of the shells, she felt freed from the earth, as if she, Fadori, Shango, Ifa and all the orishas were together in some place where perhaps there would be no change, but where life was vibrant and good like when there was change, Shango's double axe caught a ray of the sun, then the sun moved slowly to one side, soon the axe was in shadow, Mariana looked and saw that Fadori had fallen asleep on the ground, a handful of cowries in his right hand, Ifa's bowl lying in the earth floor.

Ainá arrived without telling anyone she was coming, she had come to ask her mother's permission to get married, Mariana asked:

'Who is the man?'

'A lawyer who lives in Ibadan.'

'Yoruba, Ibo or Hausa?'

'Yoruba. He's called Kayodê. Fagum Kayodê.'

'Are we going to have the wedding in Lagos or here?'

'It would be better in Lagos.'

'It must be in the house of the bride's family. It can be here or there.'

'It would really best if we could have it in Ibadan, I'm

living there and so is Fagum. After all I'm thirty-eight, I'm a bit old to have a big wedding party.'

'No. You must have a party. When are you thinking of getting married?'

'June is a good month. It will have started to rain, but not too much.'

'Then June it is. I'll come to Lagos a month before.'

'Do you have to come so early, Mother? I don't want to take you away from all your responsibilities.'

'Look, my dear, I love Lagos and nothing could make me happier than seeing my little Ainá married. How is the hospital in Ibadan?'

'It's going well. Lots of work, too many ill people, especially children, that's the worst of it, I need people to help me, but there isn't anybody.'

Mariana sent word to Sebastian, and he came the next day to see his sister, Emilia and Fat Maria were very happy to know that Ainá was getting married, they talked it over for hours, Sebastian arranged for them all to go to Lagos together, Mariana wanted to know if he had any news yet about a child, Sebastian replied:

'Not yet, Mother. It's not that Segui and I don't want one. We would dearly love one, but no luck yet. What is new is that I'm getting interested in politics in Zorei, and government administration.'

Ainá told them that Mr Hill had found a job in a bank, he was happy to be living in Lagos, near his grandson, he was at Antônio's house nearly every day, Bill was devoted to him, after Ainá had left the whole household began to look forward to the wedding, Fadori, who had started to draw out of his head, without looking at the things he was drawing, did a bride with a veil and a garland, nobody thought it looked like Ainá, he said:

'But it isn't Ainá. It's any bride.'

He got interested in weddings, what all the different nationalities wore, he asked Sebastian for books and got a note in return:

'Here's a book about a bride and bridegroom. It's called *The Betrothed* and it was written by an Italian who was a great writer, Manzoni. I hope you like it. It's a good translation into French. Love from Sebastian.'

Fadori started to read the book, he wouldn't put it down until after dark, Mariana asked him:

'Is it good?'

'Very sad.'

The next morning Fadori said to her:

'You read it as well so that we can talk about it.'

The French the book was written in seemed different from the French of everyday life, there were pretty scenes, and the love affair was beautiful, but there was sadness in the beauty just as there was something beautiful in the sadness, Mariana didn't feel quite at ease in the world the book portrayed, she preferred things to be more clear-cut, so that you could grasp everything that was going on, but it was certainly beautiful, a betrothal that might have happened in Brazil, when they were talking about it Fadori said:

'It makes you understand other people'.

'Do you think that Ainá and Fagum Kayodê are anything like those two?'

'Yes and no. They are very different, but in some ways all engagements are the same.'

He told her that he had been thinking of drawing the betrothed couple at different times, in the places where they lived, sometimes he imagined something funny happening to them, making it all more lively, the bridegroom appearing at the church with his face hidden by an egungun mask, the priest refusing to perform the marriage ceremony, suddenly he took the mask off and he wasn't the bridegroom at all but another lover of the bride who was determined to stop the wedding, Mariana laughed at his ideas, they stopped talking about the book and talked again about how happy Ainá seemed, he asked thoughtfully:

'Are all brides happy like that?'

Mariana remembered when she was betrothed, she said:

'Yes. The bridegroom makes a woman feel that soon she will have a child. And that is a thing that makes you very happy.'

A few days leter Fadori came to her with a very complicated drawing, of the couple at the altar, there were figures all around them, it was the priest who had the egungun mask on, the statues of the saints all had Shango's axe in their hands, the next time Sebastian came to spend the weekend at the Water House Mariana showed him the drawing, he said:

'It's the best thing he has done so far.'

Mariana and Fadori set out for Ainá's wedding, the road stretched out ahead gay with people thronging it every step of the way, like a city street, groups of women with pitchers on their heads, or huge roots of yam, or calabashes full of palm wine, it was like market day in the middle of the road, from time to time men with flocks of sheep seemed to fill its whole width, the tall trees were wet at night, the humidity in the air made it seem as if the car were going forward through very fine layers of mist, when she saw Lagos in the distance, the bridge, the houses on the island, Mariana realized how much she loved the city, she had chosen to live far away from it because of the peace of the Water House and because of her first instinct after Sebastian's death, today there were even more styles of dress, all Nigerian, there were Ibo robes, Kanuri, Hausa, Calabari, Efik, Itsekiri, Yoruba, there were changes in the way people dressed within the same region, from one village to another even, the sobrados in the Brazilian quarter were looking more handsome now, they had aged and were like the ones in Bahia, as she went into the house she noticed the sign omi agua water, you could still read the words, perhaps they should get it repainted, she found Epifânia sewing a dress, Mariana made a start and began to get people together, she called João the Carpenter, he was very old now, but smiling and full of life as ever, he hadn't got fat like so many Brazilians of the older generation, Mariana wanted a celebration such as Bangboshe Street had never seen before, Ainá was her only daughter, she was going to give people a party they would never forget, she began to buy huge quantities of drink, brightly coloured tables and chairs, there would have to be a canopy of coconut leaves or banana leaves in front of the house, she wanted an extra-special group of musicians, with drums, xylophones, flutes, guitars, clarinets, agogos and any other instrument that could be found in Lagos, she went across the street to talk to Seu Gaspar, who pulled himself up in bed, laughed as she came in:

'Now it's the girl's turn. She's marrying a very good man.'

'Do you know this Fagum Kayodê?'

'I know him well. A very good brain. He's going to be somebody in this country.'

'I'm very happy to hear it, but I would have been satisfied with anyone, as long as Ainá chose him.'

She talked to him about the party, Fadori had caught some of her excitement, he listened and made suggestions:

'We'll draw the symbol of medicine. It's a snake. I'll draw it and you can put it up over the door of the house.'

Seu Gaspar said:

'The snake is a good sign.'

Mariana agreed:

'All right, you can do a snake. And I want some coloured curtains to put up at the doors. And new clothes for me, and my mother, and you, the whole family.'

Ainá heard that her mother was in Lagos, brought Fagum from Ibadan so that the two could meet, he was very black and rather fat, but charming and sensitive, he sat with Mariana for two whole hours, they talked about

327

everything imaginable, he jumped from one subject to another, always had something to say, when Mariana spoke he looked straight at her, gave her his full attention, at one point he said:

'Ainá told me that her brother Sebastian thinks it's possible that all of us in this part of Africa might soon have our independence. I think it's still a long way off, it won't happen in our time, but we need people like him who are brave enough to think that way.'

'You like all those things as well?'

'What things?'

'Governments and wars, improving this and that. Like Sebastian.'

'Yes I do.'

It was hot, Mariana got some bottles of beer, opened one, the liquid rose up the glasses, Fadori served them all, a little fleck of froth stayed on Fagum's top lip as he talked about the wedding, Ainá had said she didn't want a party, but he didn't agree, of course they had to have a party, a wedding without a party wasn't a wedding at all, he was glad that Mariana was taking care of it all, because if it had been left to Ainá nobody would even have known they were getting married, Ainá was smiling as he talked, Fadori sat down beside the two of them, looked from one to the other, Mariana realized that he was looking so that he could draw them afterwards, Fagum and Ainá went back to Ibadan and all that night, the boy sat trying to capture their features, Mariana stood behind him, watching his efforts, at one moment she could see Ainá clearly but then as he drew in another line her face was lost.

There was a meeting of the Association of Brazilian Descendents, Mariana hadn't been to one for a long time, it made her happy to see Epifânia sitting at the top table, but there weren't many people in the room, she counted eighteen women and ten men, in the old days there would have been over three hundred people at one of these meetings, true there weren't many of the old Brazilians left now, and it wasn't coming up to a religious feast, which was when most people came to the meetings, this one was for the President to give a statement of the cost of the celebrations held the previous week in honour of Our Lady of Joy.

Ana was a real woman now, handsome, Mariana spent a lot of time talking to her, Mauricio was beginning to run around naked, Joseph spent the morning in his office or in court, in the afternoon he came home and slept, at night friends came in to drink beer and talk. Antônio's sobrado was a meeting-place now for business-men and importers, Mariana went to see Esmeralda nearly every day, Bill was studying hard, Joaquim cried a lot, one night Mr William Hill came to see Mariana, Bill sat near them, listened to his grandfather talking about England, just before he left the old man said:

'Ainá has always been very kind to Elizabeth and to me. I'm happy that she is getting married.'

'How is your job going?'

'It's just a routine one, but it helps to pass the time. When the war is over, if I'm still alive, I might go back to London and see my sister. I would like Bill to come with me. He could go to university and study whatever he wants.'

Fadori's curiosity embraced everything now, he got hold of Joseph's books, tried to understand the English, he could speak it a bit now, Seu Gaspar looked at the boy one evening, asked him to go and fetch a glass of water then said to Mariana:

'Has he been with a woman yet?'

'No, not yet. Do you think he should?'

'It depends on him. Has he never seemed to wan it?'

'No.'

Fadori came back in, Mariana looked at him, he was fully grown, was he eighteen now, or nineteen? He had grown into a strong man, he could give a woman great pleasure, perhaps it was time to do something about it, but it would be better if he decided it for himself, no-one needs to be taught these things, she felt the time was coming when he would go off in search of his own life, he had spent many years with her, now she couldn't hold him any more, as soon as the war was over she would have to send him to Europe to study, that night Mariana and Fadori went along Bangboshe Street hand in hand, they walked as far as the seashore, the lights on the other side were reflected in the water, there was a smell of flowers coming from some English house, from another came the sound of music, that European music that made you sad, and again Mariana told herself that everything must change, it was along this very same stretch of water that she had gone to the school in Topo, in the days when drinking water was difficult to get, things were changing every moment and now the change was going to leave her an old woman, almost sixty years old.

In the week before the wedding the rhythm of work became faster. Antônio's father-in-law, who hadn't managed to get to Lagos because of the war, had sent them a big consignment of dried salt meat, Mariana bought six sheep, bottles of whisky, beer, calabashes of palm-wine, Joseph asked her to try and find some gin, he said that it was a good drink for that climate if you had it with ice, everybody worked hard, Antônio and Esmeralda, Joseph and Ana, João the Carpenter, Fadori, Abigail's children, Ainá arrived three days before, she said:

'I nearly couldn't get away from the hospital even to get married.'

The curtains at the doors and windows were a great success, a lot of people stopped in the street to admire them, João the Carpenter got some workmen to drive stakes into the ground and put up the canopies, and the tables and chairs were set out underneath them, Mariana talked to a flute player, it was the first time she had seen this one, he was nothing like the one who had played for parties in the old days, this one was short and squat with big eyes and didn't say much, she only managed to get one xylophone, it belonged to a Hausa who was well known for the way he could carry a tune, the clarinet must be in fashion, in Bangboshe Street alone there were three clarinetists, anybody could play an agogo and there were drummers by the hundred.

Sebastian arrived the day before, very elegant, in a smart suit, Segui was smiling at everybody, the two of them made a hit that night, Mr William Hill came to see them, talked to Sebastian about the war in Europe, the opening of the second front, the positions England and France would be in when the war ended, Ainá's wedding dress had been modelled on one worn by a countess who had been married in England before the war, Emilia and Fat Maria, who had come with Sebastian, got hold of the dress, felt the material, looked at the lace, sniffed the smell of the new cloth, on the morning of the wedding Sebastian woke up very early, drank some coffee in the kitchen, went out to the well, lifted up its wooden cover, looked down, got a stone and dropped it, the splash sounded clearly as it hit the water in the bottom, Mariana went out and found him leaning over the wall listening, Segui came out of their room wearing a pale blue dress, Ainá came to the window upstairs, looked out along the street, Fadori talked in Yoruba to Sebastian, Epifânia ate some cassava, soon the sobrado was full, Antônio arrived with Esmeralda and Joaquim, then Abigail, Jerónimo, Luzia Borges and some of her children, they had come from Ibadan, two of Dona Zezé's sons, Cosme and Damião, João the Carpenter, a grandson of Seu Machado, when she put her dress on Ainá found it was too tight, Epifânia and Emilia got hold of the scissors, opened a seam and sewed it up again, the bridegroom

331

was at the church, waiting, Ainá and everyone with her arrived in cars at the main door of the church, three English lawyers, friends of Joseph, and several doctors, friends of Ainá, English and Nigerian, were already sitting up at the front of the church, Mariana went in after Ainá ,who was on Joseph's arm, her elder brother's, Fagum Kayodê began to smile long before the bride reached his side, the priest came out of the sacristy door, he was an Irishman with fair hair going white and glasses with thick lenses, he read the Latin texts very slowly, his slow voice seemed to make the words more solemn, sometimes he paused for a moment between one sentence and the next, at the end he gave a short sermon and embraced Ainá and Fagum.

The wedding party returned to Bangboshe Street, this time accompanied by all the guests, you could hear radios everywhere, it seemed as if every house they passed had the radio switched on, as they were going into the sobrado they heard the sound of a rocket being let off, somebody ran out of a door shouting:

'The second front has opened! The allies have invaded Normandy.'

A lot of people began to shout, suddenly the radios became important, Antônio sent to the shop for one he had there, Ainá got changed, the guests sat down happily at the tables, they were all talking at the same time, about the invasion, Mariana heard Sebastian say:

'The war won't last long now.'

Whisky was served, the English drank a toast to the invasion, one of them, with white hair and heavy eyebrows, said:

'To victory over Hitler.'

Sebastian said:

'To the end of the war.'

The dried salt meat was a success, one of the Englishmen wanted to know what it was, bottles of beer were opened and put on all the tables, the wind fluttered the paper streamers that Mariana and Fadori had been making for weeks, now the war was going to end, it was time to send Fadori to Europe, more rockets exploded in the distance, news kept coming in on the radio.

The young people soon forgot about the invasion of Normandy and began to dance, a lot of parties recently had only had music from the radio or from a gramophone, the presence of real live musicians made a big difference, people Mariana couldn't remember ever having met came up to speak to her, sometimes she thought she recognized a young man, but no, she realized that he must be the son of one of the old Brazilians, the priests from the church were starting a Catholic recreation club and she had heard it said that this could mean the end of the Association of Brazilian Descendents, because it was the people of Brazilian origin who made up the greater part of the congregations for Mass and communion, there were Ibo Catholics as well, but it wasn't for nothing that Yoruba only had one word, *agudá*, for both Catholic and Brazilian, she remembered that someone had told her about a society called Flower of the Day that had organized athletic meetings for Brazilians in Campos Square, with boxing matches and corridas, but it had fallen off over the last twenty years, she fell into a reverie as she thought that it was more than thirty years ago that she had built the Water House in Dahomey, now, with the war ending, Fadori could go to Europe and she would go back to looking after the copra production, the buying for the shops, the sound of the radio filled the air again and the musicians fell quiet as they listened to the news of the landing of allied troops all along the Normandy coast, Mariana looked at the people standing there, their attention fixed on the news, when it had finished there were shouts and cheers, the musicians took up their instruments and began to play with fresh enthusiasm, Ainá and Fagum came to sit beside Mariana, who asked her daughter:

333

'Are you happy?'

'Very.'

After a moment, Ainá went on:

'Would you mind very much if we left for Ibadan today?'

'Not at all. It's a good idea.'

Strangers who were walking along Bangboshe Street came and joined in the party, which became a celebration for the invasion of Normandy, men wearing yellow and white and green agbadas, the long Yoruba robes standing out among the European suits, the turbans of the women coming and going in the movements of the dance, Sebastian was surrounded by Nigerians who were talking politics, for the first time Emilia didn't dance at a party, she stayed in a chair at the door of the house, the snake that Fadori had painted had been put up beside the sign omi agua water, it was getting dark when Mariana said to the boy:

'Why don't you go and dance as well?'

He looked straight at her, replied:

'I'd rather stay here and watch.'

She didn't press him, from time to time she glanced at his face, his profile had changed, it was a man's now, she noticed his hands, lying relaxed on his knees, and the stillness suited them, was a part of them, like the stillness of the statues of the orishas, Shango holding his axe, Yemoja placing her hand on children, Ana and Esmeralda were seeing to the serving of the food, Mariana filled a big plate and took it to Seu Gaspar, the orishas seemed to be staring at her, her friend looking tired as he lay there on his bed, a car full of Europeans stopped to look at the party, Mariana heard Joseph and Antônio asking the people to come and dance and have something to drink, a tall young man with fair hair—for a moment Mariana remembered Adolph—said in a clear voice:

'Why not?'

334

He took a glass of whisky, as she was going back to her chair Mariana caught a phrase:

'Paris will fall within two weeks and Berlin within two months.'

You could see the stars in between the leaves of the canopies, once while the musicians were resting the radio began to play military marches, Abigail was dozing in a chair, Ana shook her, told her it was time to go home, Abigail looked around her, said yes, it was, got to her feet and came and embraced Ainá, a child began to cry inside the house, after a moment Esmeralda appeared holding Joaquim by the hand, Bill was sitting beside Fadori, looking very serious and solemn, nobody noticed when the newly-weds left the party, when it was getting towards dawn Mariana sat talking to Sebastian and Segui, said:

'Shall we all go back together tomorrow?'

In Porto Novo, where they arrived before midday, the market was crowded, Sebastian was recognized and surrounded, he answered questions, he bought a carving of Ibejes, done in a light wood, Mariana laughed:

'Do you want to have twins?'

Fadori got hold of the statues, turned them over and looked at them from every angle, Emilia disappeared into the market for over half an hour, came back with some perfume she had got cheap, Mariana bought a radio in Cotonou, they arrived at the Water House in time for lunch, Sebastian went on to Aduni, Mariana found that Adjá had died, the serenata had been very gay, Fadori put up wires on the roof and got the radio going, the news about the war seemed exactly the same as they had heard the day before, the sound of the radio became familiar in the sobrado, Mariana heard it wherever she went, Fat Maria and Emilia never switched it off, Fadori, after the first few days when he listened all the time, soon went back to his drawing again, the two of them when they walked together now walked in silence,

the months went by, and as they went Mariana felt
calmness growing within her, she lost herself in what each
day brought, happy to have what she had, to see what she
saw, before Christmas she sent word to all the relatives
that the party would be in Ouidah, Sebastian and Segui
arrived with lovely presents for her, the ones that
Antônio and Esmeralda brought were funny, there were
toys for all the children, Joseph and Ana hardly went
anywhere now because she was very tired, she seemed ill,
Bill and Joaquim helped to carry Mauricio, Epifânia
and Jerónimo didn't have much to say, Mr William Hill
and Monsieur Casteller, who had both been invited,
tried to understand each other with one speaking
English and the other French, Cosme, Damião, Ainá and
Fagum arrived at the last minute, all the people who lived
near the Water House came as well, Fadori was in a
very gay mood, sometimes now you could sense a
nervousness in him, as if he were about to say something
unexpected, or make a sudden movement, or open his
arms in an embrace, but the only thing that was different
was his voice when he said:
   'A Happy Christmas to everybody.'
The drums beat out after midnight, no-one went
outside, but the sound of the drums pulsed through the
house, wine was making the party go, Mr Hill and
Monsieur Casteller were arguing about the fall of Paris,
Sebastian was talking about De Gaulle and Leclerc, they
slept in the morning, and woke in the afternoon to find
the countryside transformed by the harmattan, the wind
was shaking the coco-palms and drying up the humidity
in the air, after they had all gone Mariana and Fadori
stood at the upstairs window watching groups of
people talking down below, Atondá, Ricardo, a few
women, from time to time a burst of laughter inter-
rupted their words, in the New Year Mariana felt
like getting the bumba-meu-boi out and invited the
Commandant of Ajudá fort, he stood for a long time

looking at Fadori's drawings that were up on the wall, asked:

'Where did he study art?'

Mariana said:

'He taught himself. When the war is over, he's going to study in Europe.'

Some mornings the air was so luminous that outlines became blurred and shimmering, she used to put a chair near the window, sit looking endlessly at the sea and the sand, sometimes Fadori sat on the ground beside her, with a book in his hands, he would read for hours, the silence around them seemed to transform them both into inanimate things, they would have stayed there all day if Fat Maria or Emilia hadn't come to tell them something or to say that it was time to eat, once Fat Maria said to Mariana:

'You're almost sixty years old. You ought to get out of the house, walk around, take some exercise. You can't just stay still all day long.'

Mariana was amazed at Fadori's capacity for utter stillness, he was different from other young people, his stillness seemed like the stillness before some onslaught, but the repose was never broken, his hands, his arms, his neck, his head, everything was at rest, when they talked there were long silences, they understood each other without words, sometimes without even needing to look at one another, only when Sebastian came did Mariana leave the isolation in which she lived with Fadori, Sebastian prostrated himself before her, touched the ground three times with his head, she watched his face, it was thinner, he smiled but showed signs of worry, on the day they heard that the war in Europe had ended he arrived unexpectedly, he was happier than she had seen him for a long time, from then on Mariana began to prepare for Fadori's journey, I see her looking at newspapers and magazines, finding out about the conditions of life in Paris, the rains began and she looked out, saw

337

the drops falling on the sand, the compound wet and deserted, Sebastian gave his approval to all her plans, once he told her:

'I think I'm going to stand as a candidate to represent Zorei in the French Assembly. If I win I'll be there to help Fadori.'

For a moment Fadori's departure for Europe left her mind, Mariana looked at her son, astonished:

'Represent Zorei in the Assembly?'

He nodded, Mariana thought of her son winning the admiration of unknown people, each time she saw him a great happiness rose up inside her, this son born to her after his father's death, in a strange land, in a hospital filled with German voices, in that town of Aduni which had changed so much, this son moved through life serenely, his face so like his father's, his eyes grave like the eyes of someone with judgement and foresight, so close to her that she never felt the need to prove his closeness, the rains were coming to an end when Mariana thought the time had come for Fadori to leave for France, Emilia and Fat Maria seemed to like him more now that he was about to leave, everything was got ready, new clothes, it was very cold in Paris and Fadori would need heavy overcoats, a week beforehand he and Mariana went to Pobé, they sat on the ground in Fatumbi's hut, he looked at his son and said:

'So you are going abroad?'

'Yes.'

'May you be very happy and may you achieve your desires.'

It was impossible to tell whether he was happy or sad, his face gave nothing away, children and women came up and crowded round Fadori, on the way back Mariana fell to thinking about her departure from Piau, the horse going up and down the hills, that night Emilia and Fat Maria talked about the voyage from Bahia to Lagos, Mariana, remembering, began to sing:

Don't play me false love
Just like the other
Sweetly deceiving
My heart was broken
By someone like you
Loving and leaving.

Silence fell in the room, Fadori had on a new woollen shirt, he was sweating in the heat of the night, as the boat drew out his eyes were fixed on Mariana, he had held her hand fast all the way from Ouidah to Lomé, he boarded the ship and stood there waving goodbye, Mariana watched as the ship drew away, until she could see him no more, then she turned her back on the sea and got into the car, told Silvanus:

'To Ouidah.'

That same night I see Mariana's life taking a new direction, shots fired by some unknown person, a fire in one of the huts near Atondá's, French soldiers arrived to find out what had happened, by the next morning Sebastian was fairly certain that it had been the work of a rival political group, a small, stockily-built Frenchman with black hair and a dark skin came and questioned Mariana:

'Did you see who it was?'

'No, the fire was well alight by the time I left the house.'

The Frenchman said:

'Burning down people's homes is a strange way of conducting politics.'

The Commandant of the Portuguese fort came to visit Mariana, had some bitter things to say about political fanatics, several people came from Cotonou to see her, she offered beer to one, wine to another, it was three days later when she found time to think that Fadori was in mid-ocean, on his way to a foreign country, he was doing what he had to do, Mariana concentrated on Sebastian's work, each time she went to Aduni she found herself

339

surrounded by people she didn't know, supporters of her son, Seu Haddad helped with the campaign, Monsieur Casteller sat talking to young men who came looking for Sebastian, there were meetings and discussions far into the night, Mariana was busy for days on end, people came to see her at the Water House, another incident, this time an explosion on the stretch of ground outside the house, brought another visit from the French, one of them asked her:

'Has your son got any enemies?'

How could one know whether a person had enemies or not?, there is no reason in enmity, O Shango you who hold the double axe of justice don't let my son's enemies prevail against him, but the next day Mariana heard that Sebastian had been imprisoned by the French, straight away she got into the car and went across the frontier, found Segui surrounded by friends, Monsieur Casteller was explaining something, he stopped talking when he saw Mariana, her words fell into a great silence:

'Why is he in prison?'

'Because he talked about independence.'

Mariana sat down and thought, she felt the silence of the house stretching out to cover the whole city, Segui came up to her, kissed her hand, the old woman's voice was strong:

'I want to see my son.'

They went out of the house and through the streets, walking close together, in front of the building where Sebastian was being held prisoner there was an African soldier who, when he saw so many people together, opened a door and seemed to be saying something to someone inside, a white officer came out, he stopped a few metres away from the advancing crowd and waited, as Mariana came forward and said:

'I want to see my son, Sebastian Silva, who is inside there.'

The Frenchman looked at her:

'So you are his mother?'

'Yes.'

'Well, you'll have to ask permission higher up, because no-one here has authority to let you see the prisoner.'

Segui came up to them, took Mariana's arm, pulled her back, saying:

'Don't go on.'

The whole crowd went back to the house, men and women all started to shout at the same time, everybody said what they thought should be done, the best thing would be for a delegation to go to the Governor the next morning, Mariana scarcely spoke, when they had all left she went into the bedroom, waited for everything to become silent, then went out, through the streets of the quiet city, sat down on a bench in a square opposite the prison, folded her hands in her lap and let the time go past, she began to think about what she had heard, independence, many people had thought that Sebastian was going too fast, it wasn't time yet, the younger ones had agreed with her son, the sooner the better, Mariana felt bound to this earth, she had been in Africa long enough to know that it had formed her ideas and imprinted itself on her life, she had become African before all else, she belonged to Lagos and the Water House and Aduni, she couldn't see much difference between all these places, but it was here that her dearest child, her last child, the one who had always made her feel safe, the son who bore her husband's name, who was born after the death of his father, it was here he worked and lived, here he had been imprisoned, this was her land, the same as the Water House or Lagos, she had never thought much about independence, perhaps because she had always felt herself to be independent, because she had come from Brazil which was already independent and she had never felt herself dependent on the English or the Germans or the French. She had hardly ever spoken to them, only once had she felt dependent, when the

341

English had insisted that all the Brazilians in Lagos had to speak English, and during the war between the French in Dahomey and the Germans in Zorei, but her son was right, the time had come for each region to look after its own affairs, she remembered that she was a big landowner in three different places in Africa, her opinion must carry some weight, after an hour the stillness of her body made her forget herself, her arms lost their weight, her whole being became concentrated on waiting, a sort of happiness took possession of her body, her legs, then her stomach, her breasts, her shoulders, her neck, and her head remained turned towards the door of the prison, a dog came up to her, smelled around her feet, lay down beside the bench, the morning light was touching the walls when the white officer came out of his house, saw the woman sitting there, came towards her:

'What are you doing here?'

'Waiting to speak to my son.'

'I've already told you that you must get permission from a higher authority.'

'I'll wait.'

He stood looking at Mariana for a few moments, then turned his back on her and went into the house again, it was daylight when Segui arrived, she sat down beside the old woman:

'Have you been here all night?'

'Yes.'

More and more people kept arriving, Monsieur Casteller took Mariana's hand in his, asked Segui to go and get some bread and milk, soon there was a small crowd around the bench, Mariana chewed the bread slowly, drank some milk, once she got up and went into a house near the prison, asked the owner where she could make water, a huge black woman in a red dress took her and showed her the place, afterwards Mariana came back, just before midday the French officer shouted from a window:

342

'A delegation has been to see the Governor, and he has refused permission for the prisoner to receive visitors. No-one can see him, and it will make no difference if you stay there all day.'

They brought food for Mariana, who ate with her hand, like she had when she was a child, she washed her fingers in a basin of water and again fixed her eyes on the door of the prison, more people were arriving all the time, by dusk the square was full and the sidestreets were becoming impassable, night fell upon the multitude and the silence seemed even greater now because it was the silence of so many, some people lit fires, now and then a dog barked or a child cried, on the third day a peace such as she had never felt before took possession of Mariana's body, the silence was doing her good, the prison was surrounded by armed soldiers, a tall officer with fair hair came through the crowd, spoke in a firm voice:

'Which is the mother?'

'I am.'

'Come with me.'

She got to her feet, realized that her legs were numb, turned round and saw that the multitude was packed more closely, she followed the officer into a room full of tables, then into a smaller room, a big fan hung from the ceiling and made a humming noise in the air, the man asked her to sit down:

'Will you please wait here for a moment.'

A few minutes later she saw Sebastian coming into the room, he was thinner, it suited him, the officer said:

'I must ask you to disperse the crowd when you leave. You are free to talk to each other.'

'Why was my son put into prison?'

'The charge was sedition and it is being investigated.'

Sebastian lay down on the ground before Mariana, touched his head to it three times, when he stood up again he said:

'I did nothing to incite sedition or rebellion. All I did was to say that this part of Africa should become independent within ten years.'

The officer told Sebastian to sit down and said:

'And is that not sedition?'

'Perhaps it is. But it is bound to come. And however difficult it may be we must all, Africans and French, try to work together towards that time.'

He turned to look at Mariana, the noise of the fan seemed to grow louder, she noticed two deep lines round her son's mouth, remembered the time so many years ago when that mouth had received water, salt, honey and oil in the naming ceremony in Lagos.

'How are you, my son?'

'I am well.'

Sebastian's eyes hardened as he asked:

'You sat for three days in front of the prison?'

The officer's voice came between them:

'The investigation of the indictment will take another two days. Then he will be released. In my personal opinion he should never have been imprisoned in the first place. An interrogation would have been enough. But my superiors think differently. I want to ask you to send the crowd away and I give you my word that your son will be freed within three days.'

She looked at Sebastian, he agreed:

'That will be all right, mother. If I'm not released by then you can talk to my friends and think of some other solution.'

She took him in her arms and kissed him, outside the afternoon sun seemed stronger, straight away she was surrounded by Segui, Monsieur Casteller, Ricardo, Atondá and many others, she told all of them what the officer had said about releasing Sebastian, the word went round what had happened, Mariana walked across the square, it was only when she got into the house that she realized how exhausted she was, she sat down in an

344

armchair, saw that there were people all around her, Monsieur Casteller was saying:

'I think you should talk to Sebastian's friends and tell them what has happened.'

She breathed deeply and wiped the sweat from her face and neck:

'Very well, but not yet. In half an hour.'

It was getting dark when the men began to come into the room, some were wearing long African robes, others had on a vest and an African cloth thrown over their shoulder, there were men who seemed to be chiefs, they held bulls' tails in their right hands, each one of them greeted her in his own way, many of them she already knew by sight, the oldest of them spoke:

'We greet our great chief, mother of the great chief. Is it true that he will be free within three days?'

Mariana looked around, saw them all waiting.

'It is true. Sebastian was charged with sedition because he said that Zorei should become independent within ten years. The officer asked me to send away the crowd and promised me that within three days he would be released.'

Another old man, with sunken eyes, asked:

'Can this imprisonment prevent the election of a representative of Zorei to the Constituent Assembly in France?'

'No-one spoke of it. My impression is that once Sebastian is free this affair will have no effect on the election.'

A third took issue with Sebastian:

'He was wrong to speak about independence. What we need now is money from France to finance our growth.'

Mariana looked at the bright-coloured robe of the third speaker:

'Sebastian was right to speak of independence. If there is one thing I have learnt in life it is that you have to ask for too much if you are to get anything at all. And besides it is time someone spoke about independence.'

The old man, who had been looking down at the ground, lifted his head:

'I think that we are already doing very well to be electing a representative to the French Assembly. I am afraid that, after what has happened, the French may abandon the idea of an election in Zorei.'

Monsieur Casteller cut in:

'That would be impossible. It's not only Zorei, it's Dahomey, and Togo, the Ivory Coast, Niger, Senegal, the High Volta, Gabon, the Cameroons, and France has given her word to them all.'

One of the youngest men spoke:

'You are French, you should know what you're talking about.'

Mariana:

'Monsieur Casteller is more African than French. We all know that.'

There were murmurs of agreement in the room.

'I don't know if that's true, but I do believe that an independent Zorei will bring advantages to the French as well as to the Africans. The Africans for the most part are aware of this. It's the French who have still to be convinced.'

'My son told me that if he is not free within three days we must discuss what we ought to do next.'

Segui gave bean-cakes to everyone there, opened bottles of beer, other friends of Sebastian said what they thought, in the end Mariana summed up what had been decided:

'In three days' time we will all go to wait for my son to be released from prison. The election campaign is to go on as if nothing had happened. If he is not released, we come back to this house and have another meeting.'

When they had all gone, Mariana and Segui helped

Ricardo and Atondá to clean the room and put all the chairs back into place, the night was hot and stifling, Mariana sweated a lot before she fell asleep, she awoke at dawn with a refreshing wind blowing in through the window, it was on that morning that she had her first letter from Fadori:

'Paris is still disorganized and you can see the effects of the war everywhere. The war is all anyone can talk about, people I meet in the street tell me what life was like before 1939. I have started to study drawing. There seems to be plenty of artists here. I have made friends with some of them already. I am missing you very much, and the house, and everybody. It's going to be very difficult for me to get used to thinking for myself, painting for myself, studying by myself, living by myself.'

She imagined her boy alone in a great city, much bigger than Lagos or Bahia, she wanted to write a letter to him straight away, but Seu Haddad was waiting for her to talk about Sebastian's imprisonment, two village headmen from the interior had come to offer her their assistance, a soldier arrived and said that he would get her into the prison to speak to Sebastian whenever she wanted to, on condition that she paid him, the soldier, five thousand francs each time, Mariana thanked him, told him that Sebastian would be free in two days' time, the man asked:

'Do you believe that?'

'I do.'

That night there was another gathering, Mariana told the attentive faces around her about the soldier's proposition, the older ones thought that it was a bad sign, the next day passed quickly, something happening every moment, Mariana thought of writing to Fadori but there was no time, on the third day she left the house at ten in the morning, with Segui, Atondá, Ricardo, Monsieur Casteller, Seu Haddad, she sat down on the same bench in the square, people began to gather, the soldiers who

347

were guarding the prison were looking uneasily at the throng, a French officer came up to Mariana:

'I think I asked you not to bring any more people together here in front of the prison?'

'It's just that, as you know, my son is going to be released today. As we don't know what time it will be we have decided to stay here and wait.'

'It will be at two o'clock this afternoon, immediately after lunch.'

'We'll wait.'

At the time when the sun was hottest, when the prison door opened and Sebastian appeared, a sudden movement ran through the square, he came across the street, threw himself down in front of Mariana, touched his head to the ground three times, and all around them people were crying out and cheering.

There was no room in the house for all the people who came that night, Sebastian spoke calmly about what had happened, discussed some aspects of the campaign, said:

'I think we should call our group the Democratic Group of Zorei, DGZ, it will help us work with more discipline and team spirit. The campaign is to be fought now on two levels: here in Zorei, which is the basis of it all, and in Paris, where representatives will go from many parts of Africa to sit in the French Constituent Assembly. I hope to represent Zorei in this Assembly and to work alongside the representatives of the other French colonies in Africa towards the day when we may all of us enjoy greater autonomy.'

Mariana scarcely rested for a moment from then until the the day of the elections, she met an enormous number of people, talked to them all, from time to time Sebastian spent hours with her and Segui, the three of them talked, discussed what was happening, spoke of people who were supporting Sebastian, tried to assess the temperament and the character of the village headmen who were coming to the house now in ever greater numbers, when they learnt that the election had been won and he would have to go to France Sebastian tried to make Mariana go with them, she refused:

'Certainly not, I'm nearly sixty and I'm tired.'

It was a gentle tiredness, it didn't show much, but she couldn't shake it off, it made her stay in bed later in the mornings, when she heard Sebastian's last speech in the main square she felt he was a stranger but at the same time she felt so close to him, he was saying:

'I can promise nothing except to try to be worthy of the mandate you have given me. I am going to fight in Paris for our interests, for the construction of roads through the interior, for better hospitals and for the Africanization of the civil service in Zorei. I will keep you fully informed of all that I do, I will come to Aduni whenever I am needed, and I will tell each one of you and the whole world what I have done, how I did it and why I did it.'

People shouted and applauded, a boy naked to the waist shouted:

'Long live Sebastian Silva!'

The name seemed big, more important, when the time came for farewells Mariana took her son in her arms, watched him leave with Segui, three days later she got into the car and went to Lagos, the city seemed to be in a state of tension, some papers carried news about changes in the administration, Ainá's husband was in conflict with the English in Ibadan, Joseph and Ana had had new furniture made for the house, Mr Hill came to see her.

'It's a good thing you have come. I want to go to London and take Bill with me. It's time he started at university. Antônio agreed at first, but now he thinks we should wait until things improve in England.'

Bill had grown a lot, he had a way of looking at you that was at the same time quiet and ironic, he seemed to get on very well with his grandfather, when Mariana

349

spoke to her brother Antônio didn't reply for a few minutes:

'The academic year started long ago in England, Mr. Hill can wait.'

Antônio was a powerful man, he had taken to wearing a Yoruba filá on his head, Esmeralda didn't say what she thought, she went about holding Joaquim by the hand, Seu Gaspar couldn't move much now, he spoke very slowly, how old would he be?, perhaps nearly ninety, an old woman who never said a word cooked his food, Mariana talked about taking him with her to Ouidah, he said no, Epifânia seemed very lively, insisted on going to the shop every day, walked with a firm step, you could recognize her from a distance by her long dress, when she got back to Ouidah Mariana felt that everything around her was changing more and more quickly, I see her calmly accepting the passing of the days, sitting at the window of the sobrado, she made Jean da Cruz, Atondá, Ricardo and Pedoké discuss every aspect of the businesses with her, the women from the huts round about brought her presents, one day Epifânia arrived, in Antônio's car, she told them:

'Jerónimo is dead. There was nothing more for me to do there. I've come to die here.'

She seemed well and strong, but she knew what she was saying, she died a week later, in her sleep, Fat Maria found her in bed, peaceful, Mariana knelt down in front of her mother, prayed, rose to her feet, went out into the compound, according to the ritual, stopped at each house and said:

'Our mother has gone. Our mother will never return.'

She sent Silvanus to Lagos, to bring the relatives, and began to wash the body, the three women in the sobrado took off Epifânia's clothes, put her on to the big table, began to wash her, rubbing her skin hard with brushes and soap, they called together the young girls from the houses round about to help with the washing, then they

350

dressed the body in the best clothes there were in the house, Mariana opened the chest and took from it the sheets that had lain there for so many years, cars arrived with Antônio, Esmeralda, Joseph, Ana, Bill, Cosme and Damião, Ainá, Fagum, the children, one by one the cars arrived and Epifânia was lying on the table, the drums were beating in the compound, two xylophones welcomed the guests, everyone who came to the serenata was given coins and paper money, Mariana sat up in the parlour and watched the party going on down there below, everyone was drinking freely, now and then she turned to look at the dead woman, she wanted to talk, she fell to thinking about the flood in Piau, her mother holding her on her knee, the journey on horseback, the time in Bahia, she remembered Father José, drinking his cachaça, suddenly she saw the packing-cases and her mother selling the obis and orobos in Campos Square, Mauricio was playing with one of the xylophones, Mariana went to get the statue of Santa Ana and put it beside the body, she was the patron saint of mothers, O patron saint may my mother come back to this earth soon and may she be happier this time, not that she had been unhappy, but she had been through a lot of changes and she was the sort of woman who liked staying in one place, she had belonged in Piau, in Uncle Inhaim's house, in the Church of the Holy Ghost, Fat Maria came into the sobrado and took out trays of bean-cakes, it was the stillness of the body that struck Mariana, from being a child she could only remember her mother moving around, busy, in the house or in the street, now she sat and waited for the serenata to end, the beach was ready to receive the body, at this very moment Atondá would be digging the grave, seven palms below the surface of the sand, the morning broke with strong sunlight, a smell of the sea filled everything, the body was wrapped in a sheet, placed in the coffin and carried outside, as it was being lowered a strong gust of wind swept across the sand

and around the people, Mariana got a man to paint on a cross: Epifânia Santos—Born in Piau, Brazil—1867—Died in Ouidah, Dahomey—1946—R.I.P.

I see Mariana surrounded by death, Fat Maria died a month after Epifânia, only the people from the houses round and about came to her serenata, it had been on the ship that Mariana had seen Fat Maria for the first time, as she was washing the body Mariana noticed that her friend wasn't as fat as she had been, she had got thinner during the last months of her life, but her breasts were still huge, one of the neighbours, as she soaped them, made a joke about breasts that had never given suck to children, Mariana laughed, it was a good thing to laugh at the beginning of a serenata, when the drums began to beat and the sound of a flute rose on the night air Mariana danced alone with slow and subtle movements, the death of Monsieur Casteller came five days after Fat Maria's, Seu Haddad sent word, straight away Mariana left for Aduni, but there was no serenata, it was a white man's death, the Frenchmen who had taken it upon themselves to bury him had long faces, they spoke in whispers, and he deserved music, he had lived well, he had died in peace, during the vigil Mariana wrote to Sebastian:

'You know already about the death of your grandmother Epifânia, and Fat Maria. And now our friend Monsieur Casteller has died today. I have come to Aduni for the ceremonies. He was a good man, he knew how to help people without seeming to help them. I hope that you and Segui are well. From your mother—Mariana.'

The teacher's body left the house in the evening, it was almost dark, the cemetery in Aduni was outside the city, Mariana went with the cortège, afterwards she shook hands with the Frenchmen who carried the coffin, she got back to Ouidah in the middle of the night, the trees that lined the road looked like huge human shapes bending over the car, seeing a baobab made her remember Fadori, she didn't think of him often these days, the boy had to find himself, look inside himself, do things for himself, and even her thinking about him might be enough to disturb him, she took up her life once more, now it was only Emilia who walked through the rooms of the sobrado, Jean da Cruz's wife offered to look after the house in Fat Maria's place, Mariana engaged two more servants to do the cooking and the washing, both young, it was only a few days later that she received one letter from Sebastian and another from Fadori, the first said:

'I owe a lot to Granny Epifânia, to Fat Maria and to Monsieur Casteller. Each one of them taught me something, with Granny it was how to work hard without making a show of it, with Fat Maria it was how to be happy, with Monsieur Casteller it was a sense of responsibility. I am sad to think that I will come back to Ouidah but that I'll never see these three again.'

Fadori's letter, a longer one, told her about Paris:

'I walk through the city as if I own it. I paint a lot, but I go out a lot as well, I spend hours talking in cafés. I go to the Café Flore, meet people from all over the world. I met Sartre the other day. He listens very carefully to what people say to him. In a café in Montparnasse where I've been a few times I've met some Brazilians. They are all amazed that I can speak some Portuguese and that I know the story of *The Guarani*. The one who was most surprised was a writer called Jorge Amado. He's a very gay man and his wife is called Zelia. A Brazilian journalist called Zora interviewed me and asked me questions about African art. What do I know about African art? nothing or almost nothing. I know what my father did and still does in Pobé: carvings for the cult, bowls for Ifa. Can it be that what I do is African art? Sebastian is doing great things in the Assembly. His speeches are very impartial. I heard that Granny Epifânia and Fat Maria have died, and the French teacher too. I can imagine what the serenatas must have been like at the Water House.

353

Sometimes I miss everything and everyone so much, I feel as if I can't bear it any more and I've got to come back, but it passes and before long I'm happy again. Always your—Fadori.'

His face rose up before her, a month later she decided to go and see Fatumbi, he looked thin but vigorous, seemed to have got smaller, Mariana told him about Fadori, I see her sitting on the ground in the village, still as a stone, peaceful, hearing the sounds of life coming from the huts around her where Fatumbi's wives lived, people talking, a child crying, the noise of animals, sheep, hens, a little boy playing with mud, he was shaping little figures of clay, smiling, Mariana slept in Pobé that night, there was no electric light and it reminded her of Piau, and of Lagos at the beginning of her life there, the oil lamp that Epifânia used to put on top of the boxes when she sold obis and orobos, then the convent school in Topo, a great silence filled the hut, she fell into a dreamless sleep, awoke refreshed and ready to start her journey.

There was going to be another election, this time for the French National Assembly, and Sebastian, who had been attending a meeting of African leaders in Bamako, arrived in Ouidah one rainy afternoon, Mariana hugged him to her, asked where Segui was, he said that she had stayed behind in Paris, the two of them talked for hours, the next day they went to Aduni where there were meetings that went on through the night, Mariana had got used to saying what she thought about everything, sometimes she talked about the problems of buying and selling, and men from the interior who also lived by buying and selling listened with interest to what she thought, one night an old man from the North of Zorei asked her how to dig a well, Mariana laughed at the sudden question:

'I'll introduce you to my friend Ricardo, who has already made me two wells. He knows more about it than anyone.'

Ricardo took the old man into another room, time went by quickly, suddenly it was the day of the election and the DGZ won, which didn't please some of the French in Aduni, Sebastian set off for Paris once again, for months afterwards Mariana kept on receiving threats, but couldn't find out who was making them, ill-written letters saying that she was not to invite any more politicians to her house, or that she mustn't think she could speak for the whole region, or that she was not to promote meetings of men who were against the people of Zorei, when he heard what was going on in Aduni Sebastian wrote to her:

'Who are these people of Zorei you are supposed to be plotting against? The French? or the Africans who don't support us? We are a people, yes, we are a nation, in the truest sense of the word. We are not—or at least, not yet —a State, a Government. Only independence can bring us to that stage of development, which we all desire. I'm afraid for your safety, when I'm so far away. Please ask Atondá, Jean da Cruz and Ricardo to organize guards to defend you and your house. I'm writing to them about this as well.'

In Aduni or at the Water House, Mariana began to see men posted some distance away from wherever she was, Atondá wouldn't let her go about alone, when they were out together Jean da Cruz's wife quarrelled with her when she lingered anywhere, Emilia didn't say anything, she was talking less and less, Mariana thought of going to Lagos, perhaps she wouldn't need all this protection in Nigeria, one day she wrote a long letter to Fadori, suddenly she missed him, felt old, two years over sixty now, wanting to fill her day with things that would make her forget the time passing.

She didn't go because she got a letter from Sebastian saying that he would be arriving in Aduni in a few weeks' time, the thought that she would see him was enough to calm her, when Sebastian lay on the ground before her and kissed the earth three times happiness rushed up inside her like a flood, she took hold of his hand, embraced Segui, only when the political discussions started up again did she realize that there were hundreds of people gathered outside in the street, she saw the old men coming in, heard the words they said, during the meeting an African who was Director of one of the administrative services in Aduni asked if there had been any progress towards self-government, Sebastian told him:

'We are not alone now. There are many of us, people from all over Africa, speaking French like us, all working for self-government. The English-speaking Africans are doing the same in London. We need to prove, to ourselves first of all and then to the rest of the world, that there is such a thing as African civilization, and African culture, and that they are in no way inferior to other civilizations and other cultures. In Paris we have a movement called 'Présence Africaine' which is fighting to make the black races more self-aware, in it there are Africans like Senghor and D'Arboussier, and non-Africans like Césaire, who is from the Antilles, and Damas, from Guiana, they campaign unceasingly on behalf of the colonized peoples. This is not enough, because it is only through political activity that we will achieve complete autonomy, but it is preparing the way throughout the world.'

At the end of the meeting he said:

'For any political matter, when I am not here, I ask you all to talk to my mother, here or at the Water House, just beyond the Frontier in Dahomey. She knows what I think and has enough good sense to resolve any unexpected problem.'

Sebastian and Segui left Zorei a few days later, a French official came to see Mariana and told her she must not hold political meetings in her house, she thought it would be best to go back to Dahomey and anyone who

356

wanted to see her could come there, as the car went by a baobab tree she thought that it looked like the body of a woman bending to pick something up from the ground.

I see her now surrounded by births, Ainá arrived at the Water House pregnant, she was smiling happily, her stomach bulging hugely, she spent a week-end with Mariana, opened the chest and took out the petticoats and sheets, visited the children who lived in the compound, saw the ones who were ill, told Mariana about Fagum, who had stopped fighting with the English and was now having disagreements with other groups of Yorubas, there were problems in the Government which he thought should be dealt with by Africans, one rainy day Antônio and Esmeralda arrived by car, Bill had left for London with his grandfather, she said she was going to have another child, Joaquim ran all over the house, up and down the stairs, went into Shango's room, got hold of the statues, put his hand on a phallus of Eshu, Atondá shouted:

'Leave that alone.'

And then there was Joseph and Ana's new son, Alexandre, another grandchild for Mariana to hold on her knee, take out to the beach with her, they would have to see about a new lease for the shop, Joseph wanted to change it all, since the end of the war business had improved and the best thing now would be to pull it down and build a sky-scraper with a shop on the ground floor, the upper storeys could be let off as offices, in Lagos there was a Yoruba word for sky-scraper, Joseph told her:

'It's ilê-gogorô.'

The sonorous Yoruba word made Mariana smile, perhaps it would soon be time for the shops in Cotonou and Aduni to be rebuilt, enlarged, transformed into ilês-gogorôs, one Christmas time the whole family, except for Sebastian and Segui, came to be with her, the twins, who still hadn't married, came from Ibadan, Ainá and Fagum, their son was called Adebayo, Joseph

and Ana with Mauricio and Alexandre, Antônio and
Esmeralda with Joaquim and their new son, whom they
had called Augusto, Mariana didn't have much to do
for that party, the servants had seen to it all, women she
didn't know, some of them married to men who worked
in the palm-oil plant or the copra, they cleaned the room,
swept the yard, an amazing number of children played
and shouted everywhere, young men from the interior
came to her asking for advice and help, once she received
a group of young girls with naked breasts, she kept
looking at one of them, a pretty girl, it reminded her of
when she had arrived in Lagos all those years ago, when
she had first seen women going around with their breasts
showing she had thought it was a good idea, mainly
because of the heat, one day she realized that Emilia
never replied properly when you asked her something,
the next time Cosme and Damião came she talked to
them about it, one of them said:
'But this has been happening for a long time, Auntie.
Ever since Ainá got married Mother has been mixing
things up.'
'I hadn't noticed. But she's younger than me!'
She was much younger, and suddenly Mariana was
afraid that she too would go like that, not knowing who
was with her, not recognizing people, looking at Sebastian
and not knowing that he was Sebastian, she began to
look at Emilia more carefully, her sister spent hours
looking at the sea, she loved water, would fill basins and
put her hands in the water, opening her fingers, she
lingered at the well, drew up pails and pails of water,
took long baths, there was one phrase in Portuguese that
she was always saying, whenever Mariana appeared
Emilia said:
'I like you very much.'
Mariana had news of Sebastian, not only by letter, but
through the newspapers, now and then a friend would
bring her a French paper, with a speech Sebastian had

made in the Assembly, or a statement on African affairs, in one of the papers there was a photograph of him with his arms spread wide, Jean da Cruz and his wife said:

'He looks marvellous.'

The political restlessness in Zorei overflowed into Dahomey, on several occasions unnamed groups of people destroyed outbuildings of the Water House, stole animals, burnt down huts, all it needed was for Sebastian to make a statement that displeased the people in Aduni and Mariana knew she would have a visit from a French official, Atondá decided to strengthen what he called the defence force, he got together labourers from the district, arranged for them to sleep at strategic points on the property, once when Sebastian was in Zorei and came to the Water House Mariana found that she was analysing politically each problem her son dealt with, it was as if she had suddenly acquired a new and deeper under-standing of things, she noticed Segui's brightly-coloured dresses, all in the European style, she thought they looked lovely, Emilia didn't seem to notice that her nephew had arrived, all the time she kept trying to touch water, some-times she put her hands into a basin full of water and held them there as if she were resting, one day Sebastian talked to the men who were defending the Water House, he got them together in the parlour:

'You are doing a very great service to the DGZ and to me. Your wages are paid by the party and by some of my friends. Officially, you don't exist, you don't belong to any government institution. But seeing the DGZ has won more than eighty per cent. of the votes in Zorei in the last four elections I think we are justified in organizing pro-tection for ourselves, in defence of the people's choice.'

As Sebastian was speaking Mariana came across Emilia in the passage outside, her sister said:

'I like you very much.'

Mariana helped her to a rocking-chair, sat down beside her, asked Sebastian:

'Is there no hope of a child?'

'Yes, there is. A doctor in Paris thinks that if Segui has some treatment she may be able to have a child.'

Mariana went with Sebastian to Aduni, there were parties and speeches, an atmosphere of tension surrounded his every step and every word, Seu Haddad, very old, sat in front of his shop, whenever Mariana arrived anywhere everyone stood up, well-dressed ladies whom she had never seen before brought her presents, when Sebastian was leaving for Paris again she asked:

'How is Fadori?'

'In some ways he's all right. He's studying hard, and working for a firm that makes picture frames, but he's a bit mixed up. He's afraid to draw and paint, he thinks everything he does is no good. It must be a phase he's going through. It will probably pass.'

She heard Emilia, standing behind them, saying 'I like you very much,' she looked up at Fadori's pictures on the wall, said:

'Who knows, it might not have been good for him to go to Paris.'

'Who knows? But I still think he will get over it.'

'He used to do such lovely things.'

'He still does. He's the only one who doesn't like them.'

'Tell him to come back. This is still his home.'

'I'll tell him.'

'When will you come to Zorei again?'

'As soon as I can.'

The news got worse, Mariana would listen to the radio for hours on end, the sound of music filled the room, you could hear it outside in the compound, from time to time a great feeling of weakness swept over her, she had the radio on when the news broke that De Gaulle had mentioned the possibility of independence, the Gold Coast was already a country, it was called Ghana, she thought of Ricardo's father-in-law, he must be dead by now, it was a long time since he had stayed at the Water House, with his thirteen-year-old companion, later she and Fadori had re-enacted that companionship, the French words coming from the radio were full of enthusiasm for new epochs, changes, improved trade, opportunities for all, the young people were filled with a new gaiety, all those days seemed brimming with light, it was in the middle of all this happiness that she heard that Fatumbi had died, at once she got into the car, when she arrived in the village beyond Pobé she found the ceremonies had already started, he was going to be buried in his own hut where he had lived all his life, animals were being killed for the feast, the women were gathered together in a corner talking, Mariana's car attracted the attention of the children, she was praying to the saints and the orishas, to know about the future now she would have to ask Fatumbi's successor, his nephew whom he had introduced her to that time, but what did she care about the future now, she thought she saw Fat Maria in one of the groups, it was a fat Yoruba woman who was laughing just like her, there were brothers of Fadori everywhere, a lot of them looked like him, when she got back to the Water House she heard that independence was being talked of in Nigeria as well, a French official from Aduni came to see her, said:

'Sebastian should come back to Zorei immediately. From now on all the important things will be happening here.'

Mariana thought that Sebastian must know what he was doing, it occurred to her to ask Fat Maria what she thought, then she remembered she was dead and got frightened that she was beginning to forget things, getting like Emilia, a Frenchman had told her that it was arteriosclerosis of the brain, there was no cure for it, Mariana remembers sitting for a whole day thinking that she was almost seventy-two, she had never known exactly when her birthday was, but Epifânia had told her once that she had been born in May 1887, when she rubbed herself with ori she noticed that her skin had got dryer, but not on her face, she still had no wrinkles on her face, she realized that she had stopped wanting men years ago, it hadn't worried her, she got undressed one night and found that her body had become misshapen, her stomach was slack, her breasts hung down to her navel, Ainá was at the Water House with her son, Adebayo read a bit of an English book to his grandmother, looked at a French book and said:

'I can't read this language.'

Mariana heard that Fagum had become an important person, he might get a Ministry in the new Government, he had been to London several times, to have talks with the English about Nigeria's future, Bill it seemed was doing a course in economics, the children of Joseph and Antônio were studying in Lagos and belonged to youth movements there, they made inflammatory speeches, one of them had been imprisoned by the police after a disturbance in Tinubu Square, but he had been released the next day, the news that Sebastian was coming back made her so happy that she couldn't sleep at night, he was coming by plane, that was the way people travelled these days, sometimes an aeroplane went across the sky over the Water House, Mariana would look up and see a shape something like Shango's axe, the day Sebastian was due to arrive she went into the room of the orishas, lay full length on the ground, the statues were old, dirty with spiders' webs and oil, stained, they were Shangos that had lived, experienced, innumerable prayers had been offered to them, they were like companions from the old days, people she had known for many years, they seemed ready to sit down and have a chat with you, Mariana looked at the carvings in silence, sat there without thinking of anything, without giving form to any desire, just being what she was, a body sitting on the ground, the earth felt cold to her skin, a lizard came into the room, ran from one end of it to the other, shook its head like lizards do, turned this way and that, seemed as if it was looking at Mariana, and the two of them stayed there, the lizard and the woman, in a silence that must have lasted for hours, Atondá had to come and call her, Sebastian was coming, the car bringing him from the airport was approaching the sobrado, the mother saw her son touch his head to the ground, she held him close to her, noticed that Segui was smiling, as they were going up the stairs she told her the news:

'I'm going to have a child.'

Mariana turned to her quickly:

'Is it true?'

'Yes.'

'How wonderful.'

She looked Segui up and down, saw that her stomach was already bulging a little in the line of her body, remembered an old saying of her mother's:

'Happy as the water in a fountain.'

That was just how she felt, how long was it since she had seen a fountain, and in her memory she saw the big fountain in Rio de Janeiro, water spurting high, that night men from Aduni she hadn't seen before came to the sobrado, she was told they were tribal chiefs, kings from the interior of Zorei, they had come to talk to Sebastian about independence, her son welcomed them with dignity, they talked for hours, there were difficulties, chiefs of ancient kingdoms did not like things to change, one of them said:

'My enemies in the West must not hold any posts in the Government.'

Sebastian listened to them calmly, when the time came to speak he spoke clearly, in short sentences, one thing he said was:

'It is essential for us to be united under one leader.'

One of the chiefs put in:

'Under you.'

'Perhaps under me, but it could be anyone, as long as it is only one man.'

Mariana served whisky and beer, coca-cola and mineral water, the servants carried round trays of biscuits and sweets, as they were leaving a tall fat man, wearing a gold and green tunic, with a staff in his hand, said:

'We will carry on our talks in Aduni, when all the other tribal chiefs have gathered.'

Mariana went to Zorei with Sebastian and Segui, Ricardo was waiting for them in the house, the shop had been freshly painted, meeting after meeting was held, there was always someone who disagreed, the old woman listened carefully to everything that was said, it seemed almost impossible for them to reach any agreement, one night they heard that there had been another fire near the Water House, the arguments became more heated, one man said that was what you got for being too tolerant:

'Violence is the only language they understand.'

Sebastian, looking very serious, replied:

'My mother is used to this sort of thing. Her house in Ouidah had been attacked several times, but that won't stop us from acting as we think right.'

They all looked at Mariana, who nodded, she agreed with Sebastian, he mentioned the fire again in a speech he made the next day, at the end of it everyone applauded him, his mother, Zorei, the approaching independence, the city of Aduni.

While all these discussions were going on Mariana noticed that Segui wasn't well, she could scarcely take in what was happening, seemed cut off from it all, a few weeks later, when Sebastian had to go back to France for important meetings, De Gaulle had invited the leaders of French-speaking Africa to debate the preliminaries to independence, Segui decided to stay behind, she was getting more and more dispirited, Mariana would look after her, Sebastian told them:

'It would be best if you stayed in Aduni, when I come back I'll come to the airport there instead of going to Cotonou.'

The chiefs went on coming to see Mariana, many of them asked her advice about the running of their affairs, I see her listening carefully to them all, telling them what she thought, she had got used to these men, some of them about her own age, all with problems that were familiar to her, how to produce more ground-nuts, how to improve their cattle, how to pipe water, a few days later a letter came from Sebastian:

'I won't be here much longer. I'm writing this to give you news of Fadori and to send you a letter that he gave me for you. I'm meeting President De Gaulle tomorrow. Fadori's letter tells you everything so I needn't say more here. Tell Segui I might be back almost as soon as this letter reaches you.'

What Fadori had to say was that he was flying to Brazil, after all those years in Paris he had made himself a good reputation as a painter but he still felt there was something missing, he had decided to accept an offer made to him by the university in Rio de Janeiro to teach Yoruba there, he went on:

'I'm accepting because of you. Do you remember when we used to look for places on the map? Now I'm going to a city we were always looking at on that map of ours.'

Mariana went to meet her son at the airport, for the first time she saw an aeroplane from close to, when Sebastian prostrated himself in front of her a group of white men who were coming from the plane stopped and looked, a lady raised her camera and took a photograph of the scene, Sebastian was surrounded by the chiefs in their brightly-coloured robes, there were handshakes, questions, gay remarks, when they were alone together in the car he asked:

'How is Segui?'

'Not too well, but she's been feeling better these last few days.'

The arguments started all over again, the chiefs wanted to know every word that De Gaulle had said at the meeting, someone asked:

'What sort of aid will we get from France after independence?'

One of the things Sebastian said that struck Mariana was:

'The first requirement of independence is unity in the face of the colonizing power.'

There was a silence, some of the chiefs lowered their eyes and Sebastian went on:

'Once independence has been won, then we can have opposition, conflict, argument. But not before.'

Mariana looked at the face of each tribal chief, each village headman, there were all sorts of faces, one looked like Father José, another one was a bit like Suliman, there was one old man, unsmiling, who looked like Sebastian's father, tall men and short, fat and thin, now talking, now falling silent as they listened to Sebastian's words, what were they all thinking as they sat there listening to her son?

Segui spent most of the time now in bed, after each meeting Sebastian went to see her, told her what had happened, once she looked at him as if he were a child and spoke to him those Yoruba words which she had learnt long ago and which women can say to their husbands and masters:

'Ogá mi.'

These words my lord, my man, made Sebastian stop talking about independence and look at her, her face was thin, her stomach stood out more now, he looked questioningly at Mariana, she seemed quite calm, later they talked, when they had gone into the parlour:

'The doctor says all is well, but I'm afraid, my son.'

Ainá arrived in Aduni, went into Segui's room, they

366

talked for a long time, Mariana went to see the doctor, she thought of going to Pobé to consult Fatumbi's nephew, but there was so much to do in Zorei, more and more meetings, Ainá came to one of them, she said:

'In Lagos and Ibadan we're having the same sort of thing. Nigeria will be independent before the year is out.'

Mariana thought of the sobrado in Bangboshe Street, the well, all the joys of her life in Lagos, how in her youth she had walked through those streets as if she owned them, how she had grown up, now there were people from all over living in Lagos, the children of the old Brazilians for the most part only spoke English and Yoruba, they were all studying, getting qualified, she thought about Fadori going to Brazil, strange how people's destiny works out, one day Mariana had seen the boy in Fatumbi's village, Fatumbi had said perhaps without meaning it, or simply for something to say:

'Would you like to have him?'

Now Fadori was in Rio de Janeiro, teaching Yoruba, starting a new life, Ainá went back to Ibadan with letters for Antônio and Joseph, Mariana went on feeding the men who argued about politics, Sebastian had engaged a secretary, Michel, a Mahi who treated her with great respect, as time went by she learnt the names of her son's closest companions, a group began to form which supported Sebastian in the meetings, defended him when the others attacked him, one of these men was found dead one night not far from Mariana's house, the French held an inquest, there had been a disagreement between Sebastian's followers and the representatives of a group of northern villages, after that there were armed guards outside all the meetings, she asked if they belonged to the police, was told no, they were friends of her son who had arranged it among themselves.

Segui still seemed very depressed, when the baby was due Mariana went with her to the hospital, it was the same one as Sebastian had been born in, in those days

367

they had spoken German in Aduni, when the pains started Segui lost consciousness, they wouldn't let Mariana stay with her, took her away into another room, Sebastian stayed there for hours without moving, he only raised his head when the door opened, once it was a black-haired French doctor who came in, he sat down beside Mariana and Sebastian, said:

'We did all we could. The baby girl has been born and will live, but the mother is dead.'

Sebastian sat looking at him as if he couldn't believe it, he got up and went with the man, he began to weep when he saw Segui's face on the pillow, thinner than it had been in life, and he wept as no-one had ever seen him weep before, even when he was a child, Mariana held his head as if she were holding a little boy, violent death in a young person was a shattering thing, it broke a circle, broke the natural sequence of events, it had seemed that Segui would live until she was old, would be given time and tranquillity to think about the past and reflect on all that had happened to her, live through it all again, when Mariana took the baby from the arms of a nurse she carried it to Sebastian, he raised his head, looked hard at his mother, touched the baby's face with his hand, then took it from her and went to lay it beside Segui, the doctor wouldn't let him, gave the baby back to its grandmother, and Mariana thought then that someone would have to prepare the body, not for a serenata, death had been unexpected and Segui had been young, but for a ceremony of mourning, Atondá and Jean da Cruz, who had come from Ouidah, took care of it all, a long procession formed in the Catholic church in Aduni, it was the first big funeral Mariana had seen, Sebastian's friends were all wearing their best clothes, flowers and wreaths everywhere, a French priest with a hoarse voice intoned the Latin words, just before the body left the church the chiefs filed past to pay their respects, Segui's family went with the coffin in the hearse, someone counted more than a hundred cars following behind, Sebastian hadn't spoken a word since his storm of weeping in the hospital, he walked about slowly, shook hands with people who came up to him, seemed as if he didn't really notice anyone, as soon as it was all over Mariana went back to the hospital, the doctor let her take the baby, at the Water House there was an Ewe called Nuadjá who had just had a child, she could feed the baby, Sebastian nodded in agreement and spoke his first words since Segui had died:

'I've already decided on her name. It will be Mariana.'

As the car was nearing Ouidah the baby began to cry a little, as soon as they drew up in front of the sobrado Mariana sent for Nuadjá, who gave suck to it there in front of the house, then Mariana took her grand-daughter into Shango's rooms, showed her to the orishas, O gods of all things, wind, water, fire, health, sickness, growing things, let this child grow free and strong, let her enjoy the protection of each one of you, let her be good and learn how to bear suffering, let her love life, let her love life, let her love life, the old Mariana looked at the young Mariana, the small lips were tightly closed, a lizard ran across the middle of the room, outside the women were waiting for Mariana to come out with her grand-daughter, they crowded round her, Ricardo's wife took the baby, then gave her to Jean da Cruz's wife, the ones from the next generation, the girls whom Mariana saw sometimes at parties and who came to the sobrado when she needed help, were all laughing, one of them lifted Sebastian's daughter high up in the air, in the parlour the familiar sight of Fadori's pictures welcomed Mariana, she looked at them with eyes that looked back into her past, was he painting now in Rio de Janeiro?

A few days later Sebastian arrived at the sobrado, a lot of other people came with him in cars, he was never alone now, wherever he went a huge retinue followed him, when he was alone with his mother he asked her if she could go outside with him for a minute, they walked across the sand, stopped in front of the cemetery, he said:

'Segui should have been buried here, not in the city.'

'It's right that she is where she is: near her parents.'

From where they stood the cars parked in the compound, under the trees, all along the sides of the big house, glinted in the sunlight, Mariana said:

'What a lot of people come with you, son.'

'Sometimes I want to rest, be by myself for a while, but I can't allow myself that luxury. We are fighting for independence and we need the strength of every single person. If I were to demand privacy they would think I was deserting.'

He paused for a moment, then went on:

'A politician has no right to a private life.'

He stayed at the Water House for more than two weeks, each day cars came across the frontier, new faces began to appear at the meetings, people were beginning to talk about independence in Dahomey too, men from Abomey, Cotonou, Porto Novo, Ketu and towns farther to the north came in search of Sebastian and the men from Zorei, an idea was being talked about for a union of the three provinces – Zorei, Togo and Dahomey – but no agreement was reached, the system of administration in each of the three had always been different, of the cars that kept arriving some had registration plates from Zorei, some from Togo and a great many from Dahomey, men whom Mariana had never seen before came to pay her their respects, some of them prostrated themselves like Sebastian, others bowed with a hand on their breast, they all wore different kinds of robes, she heard some of them saying that Sebastian ought to wear African dress, but he told them:

'It would be demagogy on my part. I am of Brazilian stock and the Brazilians have always worn trousers and a jacket, it's only the youngest of our people who are getting used to wearing the agbada and other sorts of African dress. If I had ever worn that sort of clothing in the past I would be quite ready to wear it again now. But to wear it simply for the sake of political advantage seems to me to be pure demagogy.'

A chief who was present, one of the oldest, didn't agree with him, the way you dressed was important, it was an external sign of Africanization, but the great majority accepted Sebastian's decision, he had got into the way of talking the meetings over with Mariana, she said:

'I think you could wear Yoruba robes. After all, we are Yoruba, me, your father, your grandparents, and the Yoruba dress is very handsome. But if you really don't want to, then don't, just dress as you always have.'

On the subject of the three provinces uniting Mariana also had something to say:

'I think it would be a good thing. The ordinary people don't speak French, they all speak the African dialects, and the ones who live in the towns all know Yoruba and Fon and Ewe. Even Nigeria could join the union, they speak Yoruba there.'

Sebastian said:

'Perhaps you are right, and if we were to unite we would have a much bigger and more powerful country. But there are political difficulties, and every region where the Europeans have set up an administration that is different from the one next door is bound to end up as a separate country.'

The little Mariana smiled a lot, she spent most of the time tied on her grandmother's back, the people who lived around the Water House got used to the sight of the old woman carrying her grand-daughter everywhere, sometimes on foot, often in the car, one day she went to the Portuguese fort, the Commandant was different, she had lost count of the Commandants there had been there these last forty years, this man was taciturn, or perhaps he was just being politic, they talked about the independence of Dahomey, these days conversations had a habit of turning into passionate arguments, with violent opinions, angry replies, one day Mariana heard Ricardo and Jean da Cruz arguing, one asserting, and the other denying, that Zorei would soon be the most important country in West Africa.

When Antônio arrived, with Esmeralda, Joseph, Ana, Fagum, Ainá and all their children, all three families had decided to come to the Water House together, Mariana sensed an air of happiness in them all, what she had so far only heard in French she now heard in English, that Nigeria would soon be independent, would be developed, the great possibilities that lay ahead, they were all delighted with the child, the little Mariana, who was crawling around the floor, Ainá said:

'Sebastian has beaten me to it. I've only had a son so far, but if I had had a girl I was going to call her Mariana.'

Mariana promised to go to Lagos as soon as possible, Sebastian heard that his brother and sister were in Ouidah, came to see them, found his nephews had grown up, they all had their own political views, Joaquim, who was twenty now, said:

'The Europeans won't leave Africa without a fight. Independence won't come as easily as all that.'

Fagum thought that it was in the Europeans' own interest to leave Africa now, at the worst they would still be able to rule the continent through a network of banks, investments, companies, different types of business all of which would remain after the governments had gone, it would be a sort of neocolonialism, Sebastian said:

'I think that we should fight battles as we come to them. The battle now is for political independence pure and simple. Economic independence comes later and on that depends another important battle, the one for technological independence. We are going to need a great many Africans who can cope with administration, use typewriters, do accounts, deal with hydro-electricity, in

372

short people who know how to make use of the instruments of progress. And when are we going to be equipped to handle nuclear energy?'

After they had all gone there began for Mariana a time of great happiness with the child, I see her playing with her grand-daughter in the parlour of the big house, or sitting with her on the sand, or visiting the shop in Cotonou, where Atondá, his hair white now, would hold the child on his knee and show her all the things on the shelves, the brightly-coloured cloth, the things to eat, one day Mariana got into her car, went to Fatumbi's village, his nephew had grown to look like him, the same body, the same way of looking at you, the same smile, Mariana showed the new Mariana to the new diviner, he paid homage to Eshu and threw the discs to see the future, he predicted good things for the child, she would be an important person some time around the end of the century, she would reach greater heights than any other woman in that part of Africa, about Sebastian he said:

'The great leader will have trouble.'

When she got back she found Sebastian waiting for her, he wanted to talk to her, she looked at her son's face, saw the face of a man who had already left youth behind him, a few white hairs were beginning to appear on his temples, she remembered that she herself had not yet a single white hair, Sebastian sat down and said:

'Everything is more or less settled. I'm to be President of the Republic of Zorei.'

She repeated the words, calmly:

'President of the Republic.'

'Yes. We are going to hold elections for an Assembly. The Assembly will sit, and will elect a President. The President will be me. Then the French will hand over the administration to me and Zorei will be independent.'

'When is all this going to happen?'

'Within the next four months.'

Sebastian played with his daughter's feet, went on:

'There might be some trouble here. They might set fire to another hut or perhaps do something even worse. You have Atondá, Pedoké, Jean da Cruz and a lot of others to take care of you. But I'm still going to send some people from Aduni to organize the defence. When the Assembly sits you and the child will come to live with me in Aduni.'

Just then Emilia came into the room, sat down beside them, she didn't notice Sebastian but looked at Mariana and said:

'I like you very much.'

The child suddenly shouted, out of pure good spirits, Emilia seemed to notice her for the first time, Sebastian took his aunt's hand, kissed it, Emilia's eyes as she looked at him seemed to hold something like recognition, Atondá appeared at the door and cried:

'O powerful chief, may Shango give you the instruments of justice and may all you lay your hand to be successful, may your wisdom always lead you along the right path.'

Sebastian laughed and said:

'What's the matter, Atondá?'

'Everybody knows who's going to be the first President of Zorei.'

Outside all the people from around the Water House were waiting for Sebastian, he came out with Mariana, they all prostrated themselves, women came to kiss the hands of both of them, Mariana and her son passed amongst them, Emilia had come to the window and was standing there looking at the great crowd of people, it was like a party, suddenly a rocket exploded in the air, Atondá, beaming with happiness, was getting ready to let off another, Sebastian said goodbye to Mariana and got into his car.

Then followed a period when nothing seemed real, Mariana saw unknown people arrive, kiss her hand, talk to people in the house, chiefs appeared with great retinues, bringing her presents, the child played with their robes, laughed at the people who walked about in the house, in the moments of silence, when Mariana was alone in the sobrado with the child and Emilia, she thought of that son who had been born in the hospital, born after his father's death, not born in the place she had chosen for her home, she remembered the voyage, the flood in Piau, the things Sebastian had said when he was little, the serious way he did everything, how he had studied, his departure for France, the letters he had written to her, his return, the way he prostrated himself on the ground each time he saw her after a long absence, it was sad that Segui was not here, Segui who had trusted Sebastian so completely, called him ogá mi, my lord, and she had looked at him as if he were her lord, her master, husband and man, now the heaviest part of the rainy season began, the days seemed long, the water fell on the beach, on the huts, the child loved watching the pools of water that formed on the ground, the young men from Zorei who were guarding the sobrado chatted in the compound, Mariana looked for a long time at the only photograph she had of her husband, in it she and the other Sebastian were standing side by side, Joseph and Ainá were very young, you could hardly recognize them, one morning very early she was woken by a noise, shots were fired quite near, a house belonging to a Fon, not on Mariana's land, had been burnt down, the rain went on for weeks, when it came to an end it was time to get ready and leave for Aduni, the elections for the Assembly would take place in a week's time, Sebastian came to fetch his mother and daughter, as they crossed the frontier the guards saluted.

People coming and going, the house full of a life that made nonsense of timetables, sometimes Mariana had lunch at five in the afternoon, delegations from the interior came to see Sebastian, propaganda posters were stuck up on every wall in the street, the women who came with the village headmen sat on the ground in front of the house, Sebastian never stopped, he went to conferences with the representative of the French government, got back late, before going to bed he talked to his mother, told her what he had been doing, whom he had been with, when the polls were nearly over and Sebastian knew he had won in Aduni Mariana said:

'I was worried. Everything had been agreed, but what if you hadn't been elected to the Assembly?'

'Then I couldn't have been President.'

'That's what I thought. I asked Shango to make everything come right. Shango and the Holy Ghost.'

The inaugural meeting of the Assembly was a holiday for the whole city, the streets were crowded with people, men, women and children slept out of doors, people cheered and shouted, groups of boys playing drums marched across the city squares, gathered outside the Government Palace, streamers with the national colours, scarlet and white, Sebastian had fought for this combination of colours, they knew that Nigeria's was going to be green and white, Mariana had helped choose them, scarlet and white were Shango's colours, the flag was to have three vertical stripes, the centre one white and the ones on the outside scarlet, at the session when Sebastian was elected President of the Assembly Mariana wore a red and white dress, sat in the section reserved for guests of honour, sitting near her, in full dress uniform, was the representative of France, the next morning the celebrations began that marked the transference of power, Antônio, Joseph and Ainá arrived with the rest of the family, Fagum was the official representative of Nigeria at Zorei's Independence Day celebrations, everyone was talking about an important speech that had just been made by the President of Togo, Silvanus Olympio, throughout the city people gathered to talk about the new countries that were being born up and down the length of the African continent, that last night

376

before the decisive moment Sebastian scarcely slept, at about four in the morning Mariana went into his room:

'Nervous?'

'A bit. Tired more than anything. So tired I can't get to sleep.'

'Lie down anyway. Lie down even if you don't sleep, your body will be rested.'

He stretched out on the bed, she put her hand on his brow and said:

'It's going to be an exhausting day.'

At six o'clock it was already broad daylight, a band started up in front of the house, all the church bells in the city rang out at the same time, rockets were let off, Sebastian got up, bathed, put on a dark suit, a shirt with silver cufflinks, a scarlet tie, handkerchief in his top pocket, he went into the parlour with Mariana, a group of men headed by Michel were waiting there for him, there were more outside, mother and son got into a car, he sat on the right and she on the left, they drove slowly through the crowd in the main square, in the centre a space was roped off, the car stopped, Sebastian got out, went up on to the platform where the delegate of France was waiting for him, the two of them stood there alone, Mariana and the others with her were some distance behind them, in the middle of the square the soldiers began to march, first a platoon of French soldiers, then Africans, fanfares were sounded in front of Sebastian and the representative of the French government, after the parade a band played the Marseillaise and the national anthem of the new country, there had been a lot of argument about that as well, they had thought of holding a competition, but it would have taken too long, in the end they had decided on a popular song, which had been adapted by a musician and made more rousing, the Assembly would always be able to change it later on and decide on a better one, after the anthems had been played Sebastian and the Frenchman came down from the platform together, walked side by side to the two flagpoles that stood in the middle of the square, one was flying the French flag, the other had no flag, at the same moment as the Frenchman pulled down the French flag Sebastian raised the flag with two red stripes and one white, and a great shout rose up from the huge crowd that was pressing against the barriers, the French representative shook Sebastian by the hand and returned to the platform, the leader of the new state stood there alone in front of the flag, and the soldiers, African and French, marched past the flag of Zorei at the salute, while Mariana looked up at the building in which her son had been imprisoned.

The next thing was the official lunch, to which all the chiefs of the interior had been invited as guests of the President of the Republic, Sebastian left straight away for the Government Palace, Mariana remembered that she had stopped in front of that same building on the night her son had been married, then it had been the seat of the French administration, Michel had had rooms prepared for Sebastian and Mariana, in the main dining room there was a huge table, beautifully laid, with places for almost a hundred people, here and there on the table little flags of Zorei, when it was time for lunch Sebastian and the guests from the interior sat down at the table, Mariana took the women with her into another room, where they all talked happily together, a group of musicians played non-stop, the tunes were almost inaudible over the beat of the drums, sometimes Mariana heard words she couldn't understand, the women must have been from the north or from some tribe that Mariana wasn't acquainted with, the languages she heard most were Ewe and Nago, there were some women who had studied in France as well and spoke beautiful, meticulous French.

It was almost three in the afternoon when Sebastian, followed by six other men, came into the ladies' room, he told Mariana:

378

'These are my Ministers.'

She looked at them one by one, she had seen them already at the meetings, nearly all of them were older than Sebastian, they each greeted her in the fashion of their tribe.

Sebastian, Mariana and the guests went out on to the top of the steps in front of the Palace, everywhere people were dancing, in the middle of the Palace garden girls in bright-coloured dresses leapt high to the beat of drums, stretching their arms out in front of them, men swayed and jumped in frenetic dances, Sebastian went down into the square, immediately he was surrounded by people, all the little boys had flags of Zorei in their hands, at five o'clock Sebastian went to the Sports Stadium where there were gathered together groups of warriors in traditional dress, representatives from every tribe in the country, men with wooden spears, men with their faces painted, some carrying in front of them a man who was sticking a knife right through his own arm, some of them were surrounded by a sort of guard of men on stilts, others wore wooden masks, their eyes flashed behind the masks, and the whole time the drums were beating, Mariana saw a group of geledé masks, they must have come from the Yoruba part of the country, a troupe of dancers appeared all holding the double axe of Shango, at six-thirty Sebastian was back in the Palace again to receive the foreign delegations and the special envoys, there were men with fair hair, tall men, black ones and ones with dark skin, men with oriental features, men with cloths draped over their heads like Arabs, Mariana wondered if Brazil had sent a delegation but she couldn't find out, perhaps Michel would know, but no, he didn't, he went away to look at a list, came back and told her:

'No, Brazil hasn't sent a representative. The only ones from the American continent are the United States and Canada.'

At eight in the evening there was a dinner for the

members of the Assembly and the foreign delegations, Sebastian sat in the middle, Mariana was next to the representative of France, he asked her a lot of questions, all sorts of women leaned to this side and that trying to hear what their neighbour on the left or on the right was saying to them, Mariana looked at them all, the English woman with her pearl necklace, the Swedish woman with her blonde hair, the one from the United States, who hardly spoke but smiled all the time, once she touched her medal of Our Lord of Bonfim, she had put it on that morning, before the end the Frenchman got to his feet and proposed a toast to the new country and its President, they all stood, Mariana took up her glass of champagne, thought that it might make her ill if she drank it, after all she was seventy-three, afterwards when they had all left she noticed that there were soldiers on guard all round the Palace and beyond the garden, outside the gate, there was a sentry box with another soldier in it, Sebastian sat down beside her, took little Mariana on his knee, the knot in his tie was still perfect, but his face was drawn and tired.

'I've called a meeting of Ministers for tomorrow at nine. It will be the first one. Then we must go and lunch with the French delegate.'

'You need some sleep.'

'How will I ever get to sleep after a day like this has been?'

Nevertheless he fell asleep there, in the chair, with the child still on his knee, Mariana took her gently from him, gave her to Nuadjá, made a sign for the woman to go, a few minutes later Sebastian woke up with a start:

'I've been asleep.'

'Yes. Now go to bed.'

They got up, Mariana waited for him to close his door then went into the room that was to be hers, there was a double bed, a handsome one, she remembered the first bed she had ever had, in Lagos, and the day she had asked João the Carpenter to make it for her, it was in that bed that Ainá had been born, the next morning she and Ainá talked about the celebrations, Joseph had been very impressed with it all, he said:

'Now I'm somebody. I have a brother who is President of the Republic.'

Ainá said:

'I never thought I would see a different flag flying from that flagpole. Next month it will be Nigeria's turn.'

'What will Fagum be doing in the Government?'

'He'll be a Minister, he doesn't know yet of what.'

Soon Sebastian arrived, embraced Joseph and Ainá, kissed Antônio's hand:

'Did you like the party, Uncle Antônio?'

He joked with Joaquim and Mauricio, but he was serious, tense, at half-past eight he called Michel:

'Draw up an agenda for today's meeting. First: budget. Second: the armed forces. Third: agriculture.'

Mariana took the rest of the family on a tour of the Palace which she scarcely knew herself yet, they went down into the garden, people who were peering through the railings cheered, the red and white flag fluttered above them.

Sebastian came to find her when it was time to leave for lunch, they went together in the same car, Mariana asked him:

'Are you sure it's a good thing for me to come with you?'

'Of course it is. I'm a widower, the country has no first lady. You're the first lady.'

The lunch party was more lively than the dinner had been the night before, the French representative was very gay and talked a lot, in the afternoon Mariana thought she would go back to the old house, she walked through the streets, people were still dancing everywhere, some of them recognized her. Seu Haddad was waiting for her, looking older than ever, he hardly went out these days, preferred to stay at the back of his shop and chat to customers, more chat than business, Mariana sat down beside him, said:

'Just like old times.'

Seu Haddad said:

'What a day it was yesterday! I heard it all on the radio, Sebastian's speeches and everything.'

Mariana couldn't remember a single word that Sebastian had said on the platform or at the lunch party, all the neighbours came in to see her, afterwards Mariana said:

'Seu Haddad, come to the Palace with me, Sebastian will be very happy to see you.'

They went by car, Mariana looked at Silvanus, the chauffeur, he was getting old, it was a long time since she had really looked at him, he was always so hard-working and full of smiles, but she saw now that his hair was white, they were all getting old, she felt less tired today than she had done in the past, sometimes she had to spend the whole day just sitting in a chair and there were nights when a pain gripped at her heart, then, yes, she was afraid, she breathed more deeply, the red and white flag flying above the Palace pulled her out of her thoughts, Seu Haddad was already getting out of the car.

Sebastian was giving an audience to some cocoa planters, there was a danger of a fall in prices, the biggest producers were Ghana, Brazil, Nigeria and Zorei, along with the Cameroons and the Ivory Coast they produced the greater part of the world's crop, for weeks now Mariana had been listening to people arguing about cocoa, she remembered the cocoa plantations that Cosme and Damião had in Ibadan and the cocoa in Bahia, cocoa had first come to Africa from Brazil, Seu Haddad sat down in the main reception-room, looked round at its vast size and said:

'What a fine big shop you could make out of this.'

Mariana laughed, asked him:

382

'How is your shop doing?'

'I'm not selling much, but it's doing quite well. It keeps me happy. And what about yours?'

'I suppose they are all right. These days it's Antônio, Atondá, Jean da Cruz and Ricardo who see to all the business. They must be all right because I haven't heard any complaints.'

Sebastian came out of the audience, saw Seu Haddad, came towards him smiling, the old man got to his feet, the President shook him by the hand and straight away more visitors arrived, Michel brought them into the reception room, men with drums who had come to greet the President, that night a Te Deum was sung in the Catholic cathedral, Mariana knelt behind her son, the priest's vestments were magnificent, a delight to the eyes, the whole of the church was ablaze with lights, the statues stood there motionless looking at you, at the end some priests and nuns came up to Sebastian, stood talking to him, the night air outside was heavy with the scent of flowers, the noise of the drums had never stopped, now they were dancing in the squares, there were shouts that cut across all other sounds and hung isolated in the air.

The next day Antônio, Joseph and Fagum said goodbye, Sebastian spent more than an hour talking to his brother-in-law, Ainá was calling Adebayo who had wandered away through the rooms of the Palace, as they were leaving Fagum said:

'In a month's time, Nigeria.'

Mariana was holding little Mariana, she embraced her son, her daughter, her brother and her son-in-law, said a word to each of them, thought of her family that was being scattered, they all lived in different places, new families would be growing up, Mauricio would soon be marrying and forming another little group, there would be great-grandchildren, she thought of little Mariana living in the Water House, walking on the beach, beginning a new cycle, but she still felt strong herself, the independence celebrations didn't seem to have tired her much, later on she talked to Michel about the running of the household, she said:

'You'll have to engage a man who can take care of all the domestic arrangements, give the servants their orders, look after the kitchen. It will be his job to see that the whole establishment runs smoothly.'

Later on Sebastian said to her:

'You're going to stay with me.'

'Yes, but I want to be able to go away every now and then, spend a few months at the Water House, go to Lagos. Anyway you're going to need a specialist for this job. Even if you did marry again—and you ought to— you would need someone to take care of the running of the house.'

In the days that followed she was present at many of her son's audiences, listened to what he said to the different groups of people, in his farewell speech to the village headman he said:

'Independence has given us all a feeling of euphoria. And it's quite right that it should. But it's a dangerous thing. We tend to think now that all our problems have been solved automatically. We are independent, and it's as if some heavenly power will see to everything, increase production, balance our budget, make the people happy. But we know that this is not going to happen. On the contrary, independence is going to increase our problems. The colonizers had centuries of experience and technological expertise behind them, but we are only beginning. We have a culture, we have a civilization which are in no way inferior to those of any European power, but often we are lacking in even the most rudimentary technical skills. And that is why we must strive towards a state of self-awareness, we must realize that the date of our independence was only the beginning of our fight for true independence. Independence can only be won gradually. We will have won it in a few years from now, provided we know how to run the country. This struggle for independence must be fought by each one of us. We can't just sit back happily now that we are free. We must work hard, take advantage of every moment of time. We must learn how to spend the nation's money, how to keep the administration free from corruption, no matter how small our part is in public life we will have to make sacrifices. Zorei asks of each one of us this spirit of sacrifice, hard work, integrity. The truth is that we are poor. We are beginning our life as an independent nation in a time of change. The winds of independence that have blown upon us are the fruit of change. We must learn to understand them, to look objectively and realistically at our own situation in the world today and within the African community. You are the leaders of the communities which make up our nation. You are the fathers of the groups which are the basis of our political reality. The conquest of our true independence is in your hands as much as mine. The nation has its roots in the village. And it is there where you all work together often in a communal system, each of you helping the other, it is there that Zorei is truly alive, and everything you do in the villages will be echoed in Aduni, will have its effect on the way the nation develops. I am saying goodbye to you now, but I need your help daily if I am to discharge my duties as I should. You, in your villages, and we, here in this Palace, must work together. And I ask you this. If you have any great problem, come to the capital, come and find me in this Palace which will not be a palace so much as a workshop. I will be here waiting for you, ready to do what you ask. Thank you all for having come to the celebrations with which we began our journey into independence. Your presence added lustre to our festivities and gave me greater strength to face the responsibilities which lie ahead. Many thanks, and until we meet again.'

They applauded noisily, clapping their hands and beating their staffs on the floor, the drums beat out along with the applause, Sebastian began to receive embraces and greetings, but Mariana heard one of the chiefs saying, his face angry:

'He's too pessimistic.'

Another took up Sebastian's defence:

'No. He's quite right.'

Mariana got into the way of going out every morning, she would visit the shop, listen to Ricardo's news, she heard that Emilia was well enough physically, she got back to the palace around lunch-time, that was when she talked to Sebastian who had been receiving people and presiding over meetings from the early hours, when she heard that Seu Gaspar had died she sat for long hours in silence trying to remember things that she and the dead man had said to each other over all the years, Antônio sent a servant to Aduni specially to tell Mariana about his death, scores of egunguns, with huge masks, brightly-coloured robes, had come out into Bangboshe Street in the afternoon before Seu Gaspar's serenata, Mariana thought of the room where he had spent his last years, bedridden, when she went to Lagos next she would miss those talks, with their long silences, that she used to have with him, a letter from Fadori forced her to think of other things:

'I'm living in Brasilia now, the new capital of Brazil. They needed a Yoruba teacher here and I decided to leave Rio de Janeiro. You can't imagine how wonderful it feels to be here in this silent capital, a city without people. It's more than fifteen years since I left Dahomey, I thought I was only going to be away for four years, but Ifa decided otherwise. If I hadn't come to Brazil when I did I don't know what would have become of me. I've started to paint again here, only I don't do figures any more. I only do abstracts and sometimes geometrical figures that are something like the symbols of the orishas. The other day I did a series of axes of Shango in light

brown on a dark background. These things I am doing
are having quite a success and are being talked about
a lot because Shango is even more popular here than in
Dahomey, there are a lot of groups who dance for Shango.
I'm thinking of getting married. I've met a Brazilian girl
called Lucia, who was studying Fine Arts in Rio de
Janeiro and is at the University of Brasilia now. I think
I'll live here until I die. I can speak Portuguese fluently.
I would be ashamed of myself if I couldn't when I learnt
so much in the Water House. The other week I was sad
and happy at the same time, because of the news that
Sebastian was going to be President of Zorei. I was sad
because I couldn't be there, see it all, be with Sebastian
at the celebrations, because I think of him as my brother.
And happy to know that he has become the man we all
knew he had it in him to be. And your face, Mariana,
I remember it always. I can never forget the time we
spent together, all that you taught me simply by being
there, it was the best time of my whole life. My warmest
congratulations to Sebastian and to the people of Zorei
and a big hug from this one who asks your blessing.'

Mariana thought about her boy, perhaps she should
have been more firm with him and made him come back
to Dahomey while he still could, Fadori might have been
waiting for her to do that, but you could never really
learn how to deal with people, you could never really
see what was going to happen, people had motives which
you couldn't understand, now he was going to get
married and live in Brazil, how old would he be?, over
thirty, getting on for forty, Adolph's face rose up in her
memory, with him it had been difficult to find the right
way to act, and who could say whether she had done
right or not?, Mariana looked out from the top floor of
the palace over the roofs of the houses of Zorei, that night
Sebastian talked to her until late, he wanted to know
what papers she held, she told him:

'I've got a paper from Nigeria that they gave me when

I was married. And I've still got that paper from Brazil from when we went aboard in Bahia.'

'You're going to need papers from Zorei now, I'm thinking of sending you to represent our Government in the Nigerian independence celebrations.'

She sat there for a minute or two without speaking, she was afraid she would do the wrong thing, wouldn't know the right way to address people, she felt old, listless, seventy-three years are a big weight to carry, perhaps she wouldn't be able to cope with all the standing, she looked at her son and saw that he wasn't waiting for her to say yes or no, he had simply told her what he had decided, and then she thought how happy Antônio and Joseph and Ainá would be if she were to turn up in Lagos in such grand circumstances, Sebastian went on:

'You won't be alone, of course, Michel will go as your secretary and there will be some members of the Assembly in the delegation.'

Mariana ordered a dress to be made of red and white brocade, some girls who had studied in France chose hats for her, the whole of that week they talked of nothing else at the palace, once when she was talking to Seu Haddad Mariana said:

'I wish it were all over and I was back again.'

Michel wrote down what she was to say when she addressed the new Governor-General of Nigeria, and the Prime Minister, one of the things he wrote Mariana liked very much:

'The people of Zorei send their greetings to you, their Nigerian brothers, on this day of good omen for all the African peoples.'

It was the same sort of language that Atondá used in the orikis, O young nation may you be happy and make your people happy, O leader of this new nation may you have strength, goodness and wisdom enough to carry your people along the true path, the day she tried her dress on she was very pleased with it, she ran her hands

388

over the cloth, her hat was of the same brocade folded and pleated, she got a message from the Water House asking her to stop there on her way to Nigeria so that they could all see her, when she set out, in a big limousine, with Michel sitting on her left, a lot of other cars followed behind, she looked out at the scenery, it was so familiar to her, yet today she seemed to see it for the first time, when they arrived at the Water House she was amazed at the huge number of people gathered there waiting, as she got out of the car they clapped and shouted and the drums began to beat all around her, Atondá knelt down on the ground, kissed her right hand, Mariana embraced Emilia, who looked at her quite unsurprised and smiled in recognition, then said, the Portuguese words slurring together now:

'I like you very much.'

Mariana went round all the houses, embraced Jean da Cruz's wife, saw the sons of the sons of the first people who had come to live there, there was no time for her to go into Shango's room, they had to keep to their schedule, at Dahomey's frontier with Nigeria she was greeted officially by a Nigerian representative, as she entered Lagos her car was preceded by outriders, she was to stay in a new hotel that had just been built, the whole family was there waiting for her, Fagum in front, Ainá was wearing a long dress that trailed on the ground, Joaquim and Mauricio were in Yoruba robes, once she was in her room Mariana embraced them all, one by one, Ainá had put on some weight, Adebayo was tall now, Mauricio and Alexandre were getting to look more and more alike, afterwards there was the assembly of the foreign representatives, Mariana was received by the Governor-General, who was dressed all in white, he was a tall Ibo, with glasses and a kind smile, he was smiling as he turned to her and said:

'You know I used to live in Bangboshe Street when I was a child, right opposite your sobrado? I loved watching you draw water from your well. That well seemed like a miracle to me.'

She laughed:

'I'm honoured and delighted that you should have been my neighbour, at a time when neither of us thought that this part of Africa would ever be independent.'

The English princess who was there to represent the Queen shook hands with Mariana during the celebrations, the bright colours of all the robes and the dresses mingled together, two days later Mariana managed to get to Bangboshe Street, Maria Ojelabi, Romana, all the neighbours were there to see her, Abigail started to cry when she saw her, through her tears she said:

'That *Esperança* that brought us from Bahia brought great blessings with us.'

Mariana embraced her old friend, Joseph told her he was thinking of buying a house on Ikoyi, the sobrado would go to Mauricio when he married, Mariana looked at her grandson, he was old enough to marry at any time now, she stopped below the sign omi agua water, put her hand on the well, looked quickly round the house and then had to hurry back to the hotel for another reception, this time she met the representatives from Brazil, two young diplomats whose Portuguese sounded different from the Portuguese spoken in Lagos, they were amazed to find a representative from one of the African countries speaking their own language, Fagum Kayodê, who had been appointed to a Ministry the day before, came to see Mariana, talked over some administrative problems, Mariana said to him:

'Sebastian says that it's now that independence begins, after the party.'

Before she left she stood at the window of her room, and looked out over the sea, towards the channel where the *Esperança* had lain at anchor, in quarantine, said to Ainá:

'I don't feel as if I've been to Lagos at all this time.

I'll have to come back again soon, but without all this fuss.'

As the car was going along towards Dahomey and Zorei Mariana realized how much she had missed her little grand-daughter, wondered how Nuadjá had been looking after her, she decided not to stop at the Water House, went straight on to Aduni, the car radio was switched on, someone was talking about Sebastian's new policies, and how he had announced his intention of attending at the next Assembly of the United Nations, when they would be discussing matters of interest to the new African countries.

I see Mariana now always with the child on her knee, or tied to her back, the palace became just like any other house, with a child needing all the things that children need, once when they were at the Water House she was woken at night by the sound of bells, she looked at the bed beside her and saw that the little girl had got up and was gazing at her terrified, the two Marianas went out into the darkness, there were people running towards the centre of Ouidah, a voice shouted:

'The Portuguese fort is on fire.'

'Who started it?'

No one seemed to know, Mariana picked the child up, went towards the Ajudá Fort, where she had spent so many happy times, the light of the flames was reflected off the clouds, Atondá appeared at her side and said:

'It seems it was the Portuguese Commandant himself who set fire to it so that he wouldn't be forced to hand it over to the Government of Dahomey.'

The wind was blowing hard, Mariana stood there watching the fire leap up to the sky, she had never thought the fort would end like this, sometimes change was slow and gentle, other times it came with fire and violence, when Sebastian left for New York his mother and his daughter went to the airport, several Ministers were going with him, now and then Mariana heard talk of trouble, in the interior some of the village headmen were fighting with the neighbouring villages, sometimes people were shot and died, representatives from both sides came to ask for Sebastian's support, the cocoa output was falling off, new buildings were going up in Aduni, French firms were building sky-scrapers, it was about this time that Russian visitors began to appear, one day Mariana saw a Chinese delegation going into the palace to be received by Sebastian, Michel and the young men who were closest to the President spent their whole time criticizing each other behind each other's backs, soldiers returning to Zorei from service in Europe were demanding higher pay, one day little Mariana walked by herself, Sebastian brought dolls back from New York, sat down on the ground with his daughter, said funny things to her, helped her to undress the doll and dress it again, Mariana, sitting in a rocking-chair, looked at her son and her grand-daughter, later she heard his tales of New York, of the United Nations, I see Mariana getting older, more than seventy-eight years old, once on a short visit to the Water House she left the flag of Zorei in the big room there, she decided she needed to see Lagos again while she was still strong enough to make the journey, sometimes age plays tricks on you, the child was beginning to read, she was showing signs of being extremely intelligent and seemed to have a great gift for languages, old books from Fadori's time came back into action once more, Mariana read stories aloud to her, one afternoon the child discovered the maps, turned into a question machine and wanted to know everything at once, what is this?, what is that?, what country is this?, what river is that?, the news from Nigeria wasn't good, Fagum had left the Government and was now in the Opposition, Mariana had a letter from Ainá about it all:

'You must have read about it in the papers. Fagum has left the Ministry. He felt he couldn't go on serving the Government when he thinks along entirely different lines

392

from all the other people in the federal administration. He's still practising law, and carrying on with politics. It's getting a bit difficult for members of the Opposition these days, but I think things will improve. Adebayo leaves for England today. He's going to study there. It was Bill who arranged everything for him, he's working in a big engineering firm in Liverpool. How's the President?, and little Mariana? Give them both our love. From your daughter.'

She heard that Joseph's house in Ikoyi was beautiful, Mauricio was going to be married to an Ibo girl, but the wedding was to be in Enugu not in Lagos, the girl's parents had insisted that it should be at their home, Mariana sat down one day and wrote to Mauricio:

'My dear grandson. I am very happy that you are getting married. Unfortunately I won't be able to come to the wedding. Enugu is too far away for an old woman like me. If it had been Lagos nothing would have stopped me. I can remember the time your father and mother first brought you to Ouidah, when you were just a tiny little thing. I thought your name was very strange and they told me you had been called after some prince. What is your fiancée like? I like the Ibos very much. I had a friend at school who was Ibo, even now I think of her very often, we got on very well together. I am very happy that you and your wife are going to live in the sobrado in Bangboshe Street. That house has played a big part in my life. When I first went to live in the house that was there before that one was built I was only thirteen years old. I had just arrived from Brazil in a sailing-ship. Afterwards I built the sobrado, it took a lot of effort and a lot of sacrifices. Can I ask you one thing, not to take down the bit of wood with the word water on it. And will you look after the well? Don't ever let it dry up. The President will be sending you a gift. I promise to come and see you and your wife as soon as I can. Give her my love, and to you I send my blessing.'

I see her in the month of her seventy-eighth birthday, visiting the Water House with the child, she sat down in a chair and stayed there without moving, listening to the noises of the day, the servants in the kitchen, the children out in the compound, Jean da Cruz's son giving orders to the labourers, the sea breaking on the shore, I see her leaning out of the window and watching a car drive up, a man got out, he was short, wearing glasses, carrying a book in his hand, he shouted in Portuguese:

'Ô de casa!'

In Piau, someone coming to a house would call out to the people inside just like that, Mariana saw the woman beside him, who was smiling as she looked up at the window, Mariana said:

'Please come up.'

They were both white, the man spoke Portuguese just like the diplomats she had met in Lagos, the woman was wearing a red and white dress, Mariana took to her for that, they shook hands, the man followed her up the stairs, he was smiling even more broadly, his glasses had thick lenses, Mariana asked them to sit down, he said:

'Please forgive us, but we've come a very long way especially to see you.'

He stopped as if coming up the stairs had tired him, she waited, then he went on:

'My wife and I have heard a lot about you. The whole world knows about President Sebastian Silva, but we particularly wanted to meet you.'

She smiled:

'You are from Bahia?'

'No, Minas Gerais.'

'So am I.'

'Yes, I know. My wife comes from Ouro Prêto. I'm from Ubá, which is very near Piau. My mother was from Piau, like you.'

'Then you knew I was born in Piau?'

'Once a long time ago I read a story about you in a

394

newspaper, how you had been born in Piau and went to school in Bahia.'

The little Mariana came into the room, her grandmother called to her:

'Come here. Say hello to your granny's friends. They are Brazilians.'

The child gave her hand to each of them, said some words in French, the woman from Ouro Prêto said:

'You can't imagine how happy it made us to see your house, just like the sobrados in Brazil, we might have been in Bahia or Ouro Prêto.'

Mariana looked at her, her hair was cut short, she looked you straight in the eyes, she must be a sincere person, Mariana said:

'You're wearing Zorei's colours.'

'They are pretty colours. They are Shango's colours too.'

Mariana laughed and said:

'Yes, they are.'

Then she asked them:

'Would you like some coffee?'

She called the servant, they asked her some questions about the sobrado, she replied:

'I can scarcely remember. I built this one fifty years ago. Or more. Before that I built another one, in Lagos, in Bangboshe Street. This house here is more like the ones in Piau because there was more space. When I arrived here this place was a desert. There wasn't even a hut. Everything stopped at Ouidah, up to the frontiers with Togo and Zorei there was nothing at all.'

The coffee arrived, Mariana filled the cups, gave them to the couple.

'Who built the sobrado? It was Ricardo, a Brazilian from Lagos who came here with me. He and some bricklayers. Ricardo lives in Aduni now, he looks after my shop.'

'And you've never been back to Brazil?'

'Never.'

'Is it true you have a son in Brasilia?'

'A son? Ah, yes . . . I have.'

Finally Mariana asked:

'How is Piau?'

'It must be exactly as you left it.'

'And Bahia?'

'Bahia has changed a lot. It's a great city now.'

'It was big in my time.'

Before they left the man gave Mariana the book he had brought with him:

'This is for you. It's called *Gabriela, Clove and Cinnamon*. It's a story of the cocoa belt, about what Brazil was like in the days after you sailed from Bahia. The author lives in Bahia, his name is Jorge Amado.'

Mariana made a movement of recognition:

'I've heard the name somewhere.'

The woman in red and white got to her feet, embraced Mariana, the man kissed her hand, after they had gone she stood looking after the car as it disappeared round the curve of the shore road, she remembered the day when she had been woken up by the flood, the store on the corner in ruins, so Piau hadn't changed, she got to her feet, took the child by the hand, went down the stairs with her, one of Jean da Cruz's grandchildren, a lot older than little Mariana, came running from the other side of the compound, she let the two of them play there, they were making a pretend road with some bits of stone, the next day Mariana began to read the book, it was a long time since she had last opened one, ever since Fadori had gone she hadn't read much, where was *The Guarani* now?, perhaps in the palace in Aduni, she remembered that she had taken a few books there with her, the story of Gabriela was different, it brought Brazil back to her after all these years, she tried to imagine what the girl in the book would look like, perhaps mulatto like Esmeralda, when she arrived from Bahia Esmeralda had been beautiful, with the sort of colouring that you never saw in Lagos, that light brown colour that made you think of happy things, she thought of the Indian Peri in that other book, Gabriela was a child and at the same time a woman, she liked going to bed with men, knew the pleasure that was to be found in food, and Mariana felt in the book the heat of that land that she had never seen again, when she got back to Aduni she found Sebastian thinner, he must have been working very hard, she asked Michel and he told her:

'He stays up until three or four in the morning studying papers, signing things, writing.'

She heard that her first great-grandson had been born, Mauricio had called him Sebastian after his uncle, Mariana had a letter from Joseph telling her how happy he was to be a grandfather, she thought of Ana being a grandmother, Abigail and herself great-grandmothers, time was going by, in Lagos there had been two changes of government and Fagum was back in the Cabinet again, Mariana felt euphoric one week when the harmattan was blowing, she decided to go to Nigeria and take the child with her, she was eight years old now, the chauffeur drove them through Dahomey, Mariana had had a letter from Mauricio:

'The fighting in Biafra is very bitter. My wife Maud never stops crying. Nobody knows where her parents are, nor any of her other relatives. They used to live in Enugu, but now that there is fighting all around the town nobody knows what has happened to them. And all of us here, in this January of 1968, are fearing the worst because if everything had been all right we would surely have heard of it somehow.'

Mariana thought of her Ibo schoolfriend, of the Catholic Ibos she had known all her life, now suddenly people were talking about Biafra and there was war, man seemed to spend his whole life fighting, she remembered the Catholic church in Lagos, always full of Brazilians

397

and Ibos, when she arrived in Lagos she found the city had spread enormously, sky-scrapers everywhere, new hotels, Victoria Island covered in big new houses, she insisted on staying with her grandson, in the sobrado on Bangboshe Street, Maud was a pretty, slim young girl, when she greeted Mariana she kissed both her hands, little Sebastian was playing beside the well, Mariana noticed that the sign **omi agua water** was still in the same place, Mauricio took her to Ikoyi, Joseph's house was huge, they all went together to look at the sky-scraper that was being built where the shop had been, she thought it was just as well they had pulled down the shop when she wasn't there, she was thrilled at the height of the new building, the twins arrived in Lagos to see her, a lot older-looking now, neither of them had ever married, it was said they had children scattered all around the cocoa settlements on the outskirts of Ibadan, but they had neither of them wanted to marry, Fagum and Ainá spent a lot of time talking to Mariana, they showed her some photographs of Adebayo in London, in one of them he was wearing a dark heavy overcoat and was standing beside a snowman, Mariana spoke of Biafra with sadness, asked Fagum if he couldn't do anything to help find Maud's parents, he told her:

'We've already done everything possible. I spoke to the commander-in-chief of the operations in that area, he made investigations, questioned several prisoners who said they were friends of Maud's family, but nothing came of it. It's possible they fled even further into the interior and now they have no way of sending letters or perhaps they don't want to write.'

Sometimes she took up a newspaper, read the news of the war, once Joseph showed her a report:

'Mrs Mariana Silva, mother of President Sebastian Silva of Zorei, and mother-in-law of Cabinet Minister Fagum Kayodê, is at present in Lagos on a visit to her family. Mrs Silva lived for many years in our city, it was here that she first set up in business (her shop on the sea-front was a familiar sight to the inhabitants of Lagos for more than half a century) and she was a leading figure in our local Brazilian community. She has lived in Dahomey now for many years, and, since President Silva is a widower, she accompanies him on his social engagements, being in fact the First Lady of Zorei. We wish Mrs Silva a happy stay among us.'

The same day a representative of the Nigerian Head of State came to see her, and placed himself at her disposal, in case she needed anything, she said no, thank you, the only thing she would have liked them to do for her would have been to try and get in touch with Maud's parents, but Mr Kayodê had already done all he could, her visitor told her that he knew all about it, the Minister had spoken to the Head of State about it, and he had given his personal attention to the problem of locating the girl's parents, no one wished more than the Head of State himself that the dreadful happenings in Biafra would soon be at an end and that both sides could live amicably together once more, as the feast of Bonfim drew near the Brazilians began to gather round Mariana, they got the figures of the bumba-meu-boi out of the ware-house, put on a show such as hadn't been seen in the neighbourhood for years, she and Abigail watched the procession together, it was all more serious now than it had been in the old days, then the whole charade had been a great joke, the dolls had danced and rushed about merrily, the children had shouted, now it was as if every-one were remembering the past, and their memories made them look gravely at the antics of the ox, the ostrich, the donkey, the giant woman, at one point there was a lot of shouting, but there were far more people just standing and looking than there were actually taking part, Mariana recognized the dolls that she herself had helped to make, the paint had worn off here and there, but what struck her most was the solemnity of their movements, and later, in her bedroom, as she lay looking up at the ceiling which reflected the light coming in from the street, she thought of Mauricio asleep in Maud's arms in the other room, of her great-grandson who was called Sebastian, of little Mariana who lay asleep beside her, clasping a doll, of Adebayo, Ainá's son, in London now, with snow all around him, of Joaquim and Alexandre, Antônio's sons studying and working at the same time, of Fadori teaching Yoruba in Brazil, she thought of her grandmother Ainá who had uprooted the whole family from Piau and brought it to Lagos, of Epifânia who was buried on the beach in front of the Water House, of this country which, in those days, hadn't been called Nigeria but the Protectorate of Lagos, of the war in Biafra that was causing them all such anguish, of Sebastian who had been her husband, such a man and so easy in his manhood, in the morning she felt she had to get back to the Water House and to Aduni, little Mariana ran up and down Bangboshe Street like all the children had over all the years, she made her farewell visits that day, saw Antônio, who had the 'flu and was at home, talked to Ana, João the Carpenter, went out with Ainá, had a run round Ikoyi with Joseph, before the February dawn broke she set out along a road that was still wet with dew, the child was bouncing around on the car seat, Porto Novo came and went quickly, they arrived in Ouidah and she saw the Water House while it was still morning.

Mariana got out of the car, went up the stairs, embraced Emilia, who simply looked at her, drank a glass of water and sat down, the radio was switched on, playing a waltz, the voice of an announcer broke into the music and said:

'We interrupt this programme to tell you that news has just come in of a coup d'état which took place this morning in Aduni, capital of Zorei. The army garrison and the soldiers of the presidential guard mutinied at dawn, attacked the post office and the radio station, and seized the government ministers. Nothing is known of the whereabouts of President Sebastian Silva. Another news broadcast will follow shortly.'

Mariana sat there motionless, the radio had gone back to playing music, she began to doubt whether she really had heard the voice, but then Atondá came into the room, his eyes open wide, Jean da Cruz came in after him, Nuadjá ran up from the kitchen, all the servants crowded round the door, Mariana looked at the radio as if it were alive, after a few moments a different announcer came on, his voice was harsh like metal:

'Information which has just reached us suggests that the military uprising which took place this morning in Aduni has been successful. There are rumours, as yet unsubstantiated, that President Sebastian Silva was killed by the soldiers of the palace guard during the first minutes of the revolt. We repeat that this item has not yet been confirmed. Stay tuned for further information.'

Mariana closed her eyes, felt her heart beating heavily, her blood was running faster and a vein pulsed in her forehead, she heard steps in the room but didn't open her eyes, the radio seemed to be playing martial music now, she became unaware of whether she was sitting, or standing, or lying down, it felt as if they were carrying her through the air, there was no contact with the earth, she felt someone touching her right arm, opened her eyes, it was Atondá, she saw that there were women everywhere, leaning against the wall, beside the table, in front of the window, a wail, the wail of a woman came from the top of the stairs, Mariana shouted:

'No tears!'

Silence fell for a few moments, the music on the wireless had stopped as if someone had switched it off, but no, the announcer spoke again, very tense:

'We have just received confirmation of the death of President Sebastian Silva, one of the liberators of the new

401

Africa. No one knows who fired the shot that killed him, it appears that the members of the government barricaded themselves in the palace and attempted to put up resistance, but the palace guard sided with the rebels against them. We confirm the report of the death of President Sebastian Silva.'

Jean da Cruz brought Mariana a glass of water, she didn't notice it, just went on gazing at the radio, now wails rose up from the compound, as Mariana went to the window the wailing grew louder, she looked outside, men and women were crowding together in the open space in front of the sobrado, she turned back, saw the glass that Jean da Cruz was holding out to her, took it and swallowed a mouthful, called for the chauffeur, went downstairs with the child, got into the car, Atondá and Jean da Cruz sat together in the front seat, the car moved slowly through the mass of people which was growing all the time, set out for the frontier with Zorei, the trees were motionless, there was no wind, there was a baobab you could see from a long way off, long before the car came near it, Mariana fixed her eyes and her attention on the tree, it was like a human figure with its arms stretched high, the huge trunk of it drew nearer, passed on one side and fell back into the distance, the frontier was closed, Mariana didn't leave her seat, Atondá and Jean da Cruz went to talk to the soldiers, as they came back towards the car the metal rod of the frontier gate was being raised, the car went on, in Zorei the countryside still looked the same, baobabs and smaller trees, here and there an ox grazing, Aduni was silent, nobody in the streets, the square was deserted where they had held the military parade and raised the red and white flag at Independence, the car drew up at the main gate of the palace and Mariana got out.

She walked round the walls until she found four soldiers. One of them asked her:

'What do you want?'

She replied in French:
'I am the mother.'
The soldier looked at her with surprise, left her there and went to the sentry box, spoke down the telephone, then came back, opened the gate, she went inside.

Mariana climbed up the steps to the palace, an officer was waiting for her, she repeated:
'I am the mother.'
'I know. This way, madame.'
He led her though the main reception room, where they had held the independence dinner, and on the other side of it, in a little room, where the woman Nuadjá had slept, was Sebastian's body. The officer said:
'It wasn't this we wanted. We wanted to get rid of the Ministers but keep the President. It all turned out wrong.'

Mariana placed her hand on the head of her son, the wound was in his right temple, the bullet had gone in on the side and hadn't come out again, the blood had stopped flowing, they had wrapped Sebastian's head in a white cloth but now it was scarlet, the officer asked:
'What do you want to do?'
'I will take him to my house in Ouidah.'
'Do you need any help?'
'Only as far as the car. I'll take him with me in my car.'
The officer called four soldiers, they took up Sebastian's body, lifted it off the bed, carried it out, Mariana walked behind them, they went down the steps, across the garden, the gate was opened once more, Atondá and Jean da Cruz came up, Mariana got into the car first, said:
'Atondá will come at the back with me.'
And, pointing to her son:
'Put his head on my knees, Atondá will hold the rest of his body.'
Then:
'The little girl and Jean sit in front.'
They had brought a sheet with the body, Mariana

wrapped it round the head and shoulders of her son, the car moved along slowly, in Aduni people were standing at the doors of their houses, the road seemed longer now, Mariana touched the man's hair with her hand, his face was cold, his mouth had fallen open with the movement of the car, she shut it with her hands, her son's body didn't weigh much, he had got thin, sometimes the child looked round, Jean da Cruz forced her to look ahead again, this time the car wasn't held up at the frontier, once again the baobab tree appeared in the distance, Mariana kept her eyes fixed on the hands of the dead man, O dead one who died when I was not there, who died from violence like your father died, O dead one who was not meant to die, the car arrived at the Water House at nightfall, the crowd was waiting in the compound, they opened the door and began to lift the body out, Mariana saw Antônio, Joseph, Ainá and Fagum, then she found Mauricio standing by her side, she led the way, took the body of her son into the big room, they laid Sebastian on the table, Atondá stood before the dead man and said:

'O powerful chief, who has abandoned us, who has left us in solitude, you who were master of all the virtues, who were faithful to women and to children, to men and to the gods, may you return to this world with greater power and greater strength so that the deeds of your enemies may not prevail against you.'

Mariana went into her bedroom, opened the chest, stood for a moment looking at the patterns on the lid, she saw again her grandmother buying the chest in Bahia, ran her hands over the sheets inside, took them out one by one, chose a sheet that had never been used, that had come from Bahia almost sixty-eight years ago, its whiteness was marked with pale yellow, she carried it into the room, asked Antônio, Joseph and Ainá to help her lift her son's body, put the sheet beneath it, then covered Sebastian with it, the coffin arrived very late, then Mariana

404

insisted that the body should be lifted and placed in the coffin with the sheet around it, she sent Atondá to get the flag of Zorei that was at the end of the room, the red and white stuff came floating in his hands and they spread it over the dead man, in the compound they had lit a bonfire, there was a general murmur of conversation and lament which seemed to grow greater as the night wore on, Jean da Cruz's wife managed to find food for most of the people, Mariana sat at her son's side, holding his hand in hers, the wind from the sea swept across the room, someone from the Dahomean Government wanted to speak to her, offered her any help she might need, she thanked him, said she didn't need anything, when dawn broke she decided it was time to take the body out, it was less than twenty-four hours since she had arrived from Lagos, ready to take up her life again at the palace, she had thought then how her age was weighing on her more and more, and she looked at her son who had died before he had reached sixty, the priest came from Cotonou, he had on a surplice and a stole, he prayed aloud over the body, then shook hands with each of the family, Mariana, who had been kneeling, got to her feet and said to Atondá:

'It's time. But carry the coffin out open.'

They lifted it up, Mariana went out in front of it, down the stairs, a great wail rose up from the crowd in the compound, Mariana walked through the middle of the people, some of them flung themselves down at her feet, in the distance there sounded the slow beat of a drum, Mariana came to the beach, the grave was open, they put the coffin down, then lowered it deep into the earth, she looked at the faces all around her, a silence fell on everything, she felt the wind from the sea blowing up a little sand round her legs, felt there were too many people, shouted:

'Go away all of you.'

Antônio and Joseph held her arms, she repeated:

'Go away from the beach, all of you. Leave me alone with the girl.'

Atondá, Jean da Cruz, Ricardo, Antônio, Joseph, Fagum and the men who lived around the Water House began to move the people away from the grave, made them all go outside the fence, in the empty cemetery now there was only the coffin, and Mariana, and the girl who by the end of the century would be the most powerful woman in West Africa and who now, motionless with horror, looked at the dark face of her father and the tall figure of her grandmother.

Mariana took hold of the girl, held her tightly, picked up a handful of sand, threw it on the flag that covered the dead man, and suddenly she gave a cry, it was not weeping, for she never wept, but a cry, O cry that came across the sand to the Water House, that made the people who heard it shiver, O cry that held that moment in one single sound, O cry that came from Piau, from Bahia, from the windless sea, from the dead on the high sea, from the blood of the child who was turning into a woman, from the well dragged out of the earth, O cry that came from the navel, from the belly, from the bowels, and rose through her whole body before it came from her mouth, O cry, old woman's cry and child's cry, O cry that was cry, only cry, cry.

Rio de Janeiro, from the 15th of June to the 15th of September, 1968.

Some Brazilian and Yoruba words used in this novel:

Adiré—Yoruba cloth or material, usually in dark blue print
Adupé or *Modupé*—Thank you or I thank you
Agbada—The long suit Yoruba men wear
Agô—Yoruba word meaning 'with your permission'
Agogo—Metal instrument to match the drums and voices
Alafia—Yoruba word for health
Asheshe or Axexê—Ceremonial for the dead
Beru—Yoruba word for fear
Bumba-meu-boi—Brazilian dance in which a big puppet figure ox
    plays the important part with a woman giant, an ostrich and a
    donkey playing other parts
Burrinha—Another Brazilian name for the above dance
Cachaça—Brazilian drink made out of sugar cane
Calunga—The dolls or dummies of the *bumba-meu-boi*
Conquém—Brazilian word for an African chicken usually killed in
    sacrifice to the orishas
Egun or *Egungun*—The Yoruba spirit of the ancestors; name of the
    ceremony to pay homage to the ancestors; name of the
    societies that take care of such homages
Ekudidé—Red feather of an African parrot used in some religious
    ceremonies of the Yoruba
Fado—Portuguese typical music and dance
Celedé—Name of a society of women; the mask used in the dance
    of this society
Ifa or *Ifah* or *Fa*—The god of divination
Ibejes—Yoruba word for twins
Kauô or *Kauô-Kabieci*—Salutation for Shango
Kente—Hand-embroidered material of Ghana
Obatala or *Orisha-inla* or *Oshala* or *Oxalá*—God of peace, father of
    gods, synchretized in Brazil with Our Lord of Bonfim
Obi—Cola-nut that West Africans and some Brazilians chew
Olorum—Heaven: a higher god
Oloshossi or *Oshossi* or *Oxosse*—God of hunting; synchretizes with
    Saint George
Ori—Grease that West African and some Brazilian women spread
    on their skin
Orisha—Afro-Brazilian god or goddess
Orobô—Bitter cola-nut

Oshun—Goddess of the fountains, of love and of wealth; a kind of Venus in the Afro-Brazilian mythology; synchretizes in Brazil with Our Lady of Conception

Oshumare—God of the rainbow

Ossu—When a girl is consecrated to the orishas or gods her scalp is cut and a seed is put under her skin; when she dies this has to be taken out

Oyá or *Iansan*—Goddess of the River Niger; synchretizes in Brazil with Saint Barbara

Piau or *piau-fish*—Brazilian Indian word designating a fish found in Brazilian rivers

Rabanada—Sweet made out of bread, used during the Brazilian Christmas

Serenata—Brazilian word for serenade: it is the name of the party given when someone who has had a fully lived life dies

Seu—Short for *Senhor* (Mister) used by common people before the names of important persons

Shango—God of lightning and justice: in Brazil synchretizes with Saint Jerome

Shopona—The god of diseases: synchretizes with Saint Lazarus

Sinhá—Substitute for *Senhora* (Lady) used by Africans in Brazil to designate an important lady

Sobrado—Two-storey house in the Luso-Brazilian style

Yalorisha—Priestess of the orishas

Yayá—It means mother in Yoruba: it was used in Brazil originally for young ladies and now for any woman

Yemanjá or *Yemojah* or *Yemoja*—Goddess of the sea: synchretizes with Our Lady of Glory

CHRONOLOGY

Catarina leaves Piau with her family	21.3.1898
They arrive in Juiz de Fora	22.3.1898
They leave from Juiz de Fora and arrive in Rio de Janeiro	11.5.1898
They board the ship for Bahia	15.9.1898
They arrive in Bahia	20.9.1898
They leave Bahia for Lagos	3.3.1900
They arrive in Lagos	7.9.1900
Mariana goes to school in Topo Island	20.10.1900
She leaves school	10.6.1901
Catarina (Ainá) dies	3.11.1901
Mariana is betrothed	27.1.1904
Mariana is married	10.5.1904
Joseph is born	29.3.1905
Ainá is born	15.1.1906
Sebastian leaves for Fernando Poo	16.3.1906
The digging of the well begins	27.12.1906
The sign Omi Agua Water is put up and the well begins to work	3.4.1907
Work starts on the building of the sobrado in Bangboshe Street	10.8.1908
The sobrado is finished	28.7.1908
Emilia is married	1.10.1908
Sebastian comes back	20.1.1909
Cosme and Damião, Emilia's sons, are born	20.3.1910
Sebastian dies	25.3.1910
Sebastian is born	10.10.1910
The Water House is completed	7.12.1910
Joseph leaves for England	21.9.1922
Antônio, who had gone with Joseph, comes back from London married to Elizabeth	11.12.1923
Ainá leaves for England	10.6.1924
Bill is born, son of Antonio and Elizabeth	8.7.1924
Sebastian leaves for France	5.9.1925
Elizabeth dies	18.8.1929
Yao comes to stay at the Water House	12.11.1931
Antônio returns from London with Bill	23.7.1932
Antonio goes to Bahia	25.1.1933
Joseph arrived back from London with Adolph	24.6.1933
Adolph dies	21.11.1935

Ebenezer dies	29.11.1935
Antonio returns from Bahia married to Esmeralda	17.5.1936
Joseph is married	10.12.1938
Aina returns from London	3.1.1939
Sebastian returns from Paris	10.5.1939
Mariana meets Fadori	28.5.1939
Joaquim, son of Esmeralda and Antônio, is born	14.7.1939
Mauricio, son of Joseph and Ana, is born	7.12.1941
Sebastian is married	4.4.1942
Ainá is married	6.6.1944
Fadori leaves for Europe	9.9.1945
Sebastian goes to France	22.12.1945
Epifânia dies	1.5.1946
Fat Maria dies	2.6.1946
Monsieur Armand Casteller dies	7.6.1946
Adebayo, son of Ainá and Fagum, is born	20.4.1950
Alexandre, son of Joseph and Ana, is born	27.6.1950
Augusto, son of Antônio and Esmeralda, is born	19.8.1950
Fatumbi dies	17.12.1958
Mariana, daughter of Sebastian and Segui, is born, and Segui dies	10.12.1959
Independence of Zorei	5.10.1960
Sebastian, son of Mauricio and Maud, is born	7.12.1967
Sebastian dies	14.2.1968